CHARLES DICKENS

COMPLETE
WORKS

CENTENNIAL EDITION

Charles Dickens

CHARLES DICKENS

SKETCHES BY BOZ

ILLUSTRATIVE OF EVERY-DAY LIFE
AND EVERY-DAY PEOPLE

II

Illustrations by
George Cruikshank and Phiz

Edito-Service S.A., Geneva, Publishers

CONTENTS

TALES—*continued*

CONTENTS

LIST OF ILLUSTRATIONS

SKETCHES BY BOZ

SKETCHES OF YOUNG GENTLEMEN

SKETCHES OF YOUNG COUPLES

LIST OF ILLUSTRATIONS

THE MUDFOG AND OTHER SKETCHES

TALES—*continued*

CHAPTER IV

THE TUGGSES AT RAMSGATE

Once upon a time there dwelt, in a narrow street on the Surrey side of the water, within three minutes' walk of old London Bridge, Mr. Joseph Tuggs—a little dark-faced man, with shiny hair, twinkling eyes, short legs, and a body of very considerable thickness, measuring from the centre button of his waistcoat in front, to the ornamental buttons of his coat behind. The figure of the amiable Mrs. Tuggs, if not perfectly symmetrical, was decidedly comfortable; and the form of her only daughter, the accomplished Miss Charlotte Tuggs, was fast ripening into that state of luxuriant plumpness which had enchanted the eyes, and captivated the heart, of Mr. Joseph Tuggs in his earlier days. Mr. Simon Tuggs, his only son, and Miss Charlotte Tuggs's only brother, was as differently formed in body, as he was differently constituted in mind, from the remainder of his family. There was that elongation in his thoughtful face, and that tendency to weakness in his interesting legs, which tell so forcibly of a great mind and romantic disposition. The slightest traits

1

of character in such a being, possess no mean interest to speculative minds. He usually appeared in public, in capacious shoes with black cotton stockings; and was observed to be particularly attached to a black glazed stock, without tie or ornament of any description.

There is perhaps no profession, however useful; no pursuit, however meritorious; which can escape the petty attacks of vulgar minds. Mr. Joseph Tuggs was a grocer. It might be supposed that a grocer was beyond the breath of calumny; but no—the neighbours stigmatised him as a chandler; and the poisonous voice of envy distinctly asserted that he dispensed tea and coffee by the quartern, retailed sugar by the ounce, cheese by the slice, tobacco by the screw, and butter by the pat. These taunts, however, were lost upon the Tuggses. Mr. Tuggs attended to the grocery department; Mrs. Tuggs to the cheesemongery; and Miss Tuggs to her education. Mr. Simon Tuggs kept his father's books, and his own counsel.

One fine spring afternoon, the latter gentleman was seated on a tub of weekly Dorset, behind the little red desk with a wooden rail, which ornamented a corner of the counter; when a stranger dismounted from a cab, and hastily entered the shop. He was habited in black cloth, and bore with him, a green umbrella, and a blue bag.

"Mr. Tuggs?" said the stranger, inquiringly.

"*My* name is Tuggs," replied Mr. Simon.

"It's the other Mr. Tuggs," said the stranger, looking towards the glass door which led into the parlour behind the shop, and on the inside of which, the round face of Mr. Tuggs, senior, was distinctly visible, peeping over the curtain.

Mr. Simon gracefully waved his pen, as if in intimation of his wish that his father would advance. Mr. Joseph Tuggs, with considerable celerity, removed his face from the curtain and placed it before the stranger.

"I come from the Temple," said the man with the bag.

"From the Temple!" said Mrs. Tuggs, flinging open the

2

door of the little parlour and disclosing Miss Tuggs in perspective.

"From the Temple!" said Miss Tuggs and Mr. Simon Tuggs at the same moment.

"From the Temple!" said Mr. Joseph Tuggs, turning as pale as a Dutch cheese.

"From the Temple," repeated the man with the bag; "from Mr. Cower's, the solicitor's. Mr. Tuggs, I congratulate you, sir. Ladies, I wish you joy of your prosperity! We have been successful." And the man with the bag leisurely divested himself of his umbrella and glove, as a preliminary to shaking hands with Mr. Joseph Tuggs.

Now the words "we have been successful," had no sooner issued from the mouth of the man with the bag, than Mr. Simon Tuggs rose from the tub of weekly Dorset, opened his eyes very wide, gasped for breath, made figures of eight in the air with his pen, and finally fell into the arms of his anxious mother, and fainted away without the slightest ostensible cause or pretence.

"Water!" screamed Mrs. Tuggs.

"Look up, my son," exclaimed Mr. Tuggs.

"Simon! dear Simon!" shrieked Miss Tuggs.

"I'm better now," said Mr. Simon Tuggs. "What! successful!" And then, as corroborative evidence of his being better, he fainted away again, and was borne into the little parlour by the united efforts of the remainder of the family, and the man with the bag.

To a casual spectator, or to any one unacquainted with the position of the family, this fainting would have been unaccountable. To those who understood the mission of the man with the bag, and were moreover acquainted with the excitability of the nerves of Mr. Simon Tuggs, it was quite comprehensible. A long-pending law-suit respecting the validity of a will, had been unexpectedly decided; and Mr. Joseph Tuggs was the possessor of twenty thousand pounds.

3

A prolonged consultation took place, that night, in the little parlour—a consultation that was to settle the future destinies of the Tuggses. The shop was shut up, at an unusually early hour; and many were the unavailing kicks bestowed upon the closed door by applicants for quarterns of sugar, or half-quarterns of bread, or penn'orths of pepper, which were to have been "left till Saturday," but which fortune had decreed were to be left alone altogether.

"We must certainly give up business," said Miss Tuggs.

"Oh, decidedly," said Mrs. Tuggs.

"Simon shall go to the bar," said Mr. Joseph Tuggs.

"And I shall always sign myself 'Cymon' in future," said his son.

"And I shall call myself Charlotta," said Miss Tuggs.

"And you must always call *me* 'Ma,' and father 'Pa,'" said Mrs. Tuggs.

"Yes, and Pa must leave off all his vulgar habits," interposed Miss Tuggs.

"I'll take care of all that," responded Mr. Joseph Tuggs, complacently. He was, at that very moment, eating pickled salmon with a pocket-knife.

"We must leave town immediately," said Mr. Cymon Tuggs.

Everybody concurred that this was an indispensable preliminary to being genteel. The question then arose, Where should they go?

"Gravesend?" mildly suggested Mr. Joseph Tuggs. The idea was unanimously scouted. Gravesend was *low*.

"Margate?" insinuated Mrs. Tuggs. Worse and worse—nobody there, but tradespeople.

"Brighton?" Mr. Cymon Tuggs opposed an insurmountable objection. All the coaches had been upset, in turn, within the last three weeks; each coach had averaged two passengers killed, and six wounded; and, in every case, the newspapers had distinctly understood that "no blame whatever was attributable to the coachman."

4

ON BOARD THE RAMSGATE STEAMER

"Ramsgate?" ejaculated Mr. Cymon, thoughtfully. To be sure; how stupid they must have been, not to have thought of that before! Ramsgate was just the place of all others.

Two months after this conversation, the City of London Ramsgate steamer was running gaily down the river. Her flag was flying, her band was playing, her passengers were conversing; everything about her seemed gay and lively.—No wonder—the Tuggses were on board.

"Charming, ain't it?" said Mr. Joseph Tuggs, in a bottle-green great-coat, with a velvet collar of the same, and a blue travelling-cap with a gold band.

"Soul-inspiring," replied Mr. Cymon Tuggs—he was entered at the bar. "Soul-inspiring!"

"Delightful morning, sir!" said a stoutish, military-looking gentleman in a blue surtout buttoned up to his chin, and white trousers chained down to the soles of his boots.

Mr. Cymon Tuggs took upon himself the responsibility of answering the observation. "Heavenly!" he replied.

"You are an enthusiastic admirer of the beauties of Nature, sir?" said the military gentleman.

"I am, sir," replied Mr. Cymon Tuggs.

"Travelled much, sir?" inquired the military gentleman

"Not much," replied Mr. Cymon Tuggs.

"You've been on the continent, of course?" inquired the military gentleman.

"Not exactly," replied Mr. Cymon Tuggs—in a qualified tone, as if he wished it to be implied that he had gone half-way and come back again.

"You of course intend your son to make the grand tour, sir?" said the military gentleman, addressing Mr. Joseph Tuggs.

As Mr. Joseph Tuggs did not precisely understand what the grand tour was, or how such an article was manufactured, he replied, "Of course." Just as he said the word, there came tripping up, from her seat at the stern of the vessel,

5

a young lady in a puce-coloured silk cloak, and boots of the same; with long black ringlets, large black eyes, brief petticoats, and unexceptionable ankles.

"Walter, my dear," said the young lady to the military gentleman.

"Yes, Belinda, my love," responded the military gentleman to the black-eyed young lady.

"What have you left me alone so long for?" said the young lady. "I have been stared out of countenance by those rude young men."

"What! stared at?" exclaimed the military gentleman, with an emphasis which made Mr. Cymon Tuggs withdraw his eyes from the young lady's face with inconceivable rapidity. "Which young men—where?" and the military gentleman clenched his fist, and glared fearfully on the cigar-smokers around.

"Be calm, Walter, I entreat," said the young lady.

"I won't," said the military gentleman.

"Do, sir," interposed Mr. Cymon Tuggs. "They ain't worth your notice."

"No—no—they are not, indeed," urged the young lady.

"I *will* be calm," said the military gentleman. "You speak truly, sir. I thank you for a timely remonstrance, which may have spared me the guilt of manslaughter." Calming his wrath, the military gentleman wrung Mr. Cymon Tuggs by the hand.

"My sister, sir!" said Mr. Cymon Tuggs; seeing that the military gentleman was casting an admiring look towards Miss Charlotta.

"My wife, ma'am—Mrs. Captain Waters," said the military gentleman, presenting the black-eyed young lady.

"My mother, ma'am—Mrs. Tuggs," said Mr. Cymon. The military gentleman and his wife murmured enchanting courtesies; and the Tuggses looked as unembarrassed as they could.

"Walter, my dear," said the black-eyed young lady,

after they had sat chatting with the Tuggses some half-hour.

" Yes, my love," said the military gentleman.

" Don't you think this gentleman (with an inclination of the head towards Mr. Cymon Tuggs) is very much like the Marquis Carriwini ? "

" Lord bless me, very ! " said the military gentleman.

" It struck me, the moment I saw him," said the young lady, gazing intently, and with a melancholy air, on the scarlet countenance of Mr. Cymon Tuggs. Mr. Cymon Tuggs looked at everybody; and finding that everybody was looking at him, appeared to feel some temporary difficulty in disposing of his eyesight.

" So exactly the air of the marquis," said the military gentleman.

" Quite extraordinary ! " sighed the military gentleman's lady.

" You don't know the marquis, sir ? " inquired the military gentleman.

Mr. Cymon Tuggs stammered a negative.

" If you did," continued Captain Walter Waters, " you would feel how much reason you have to be proud of the resemblance—a most elegant man, with a most prepossessing appearance."

" He is—he is indeed ! " exclaimed Belinda Waters energetically. As her eye caught that of Mr. Cymon Tuggs, she withdrew it from his features in bashful confusion.

All this was highly gratifying to the feelings of the Tuggses; and when, in the course of farther conversation, it was discovered that Miss Charlotta Tuggs was the *fac simile* of a titled relative of Mrs. Belinda Waters, and that Mrs. Tuggs herself was the very picture of the Dowager Duchess of Dobbleton, their delight in the acquisition of so genteel and friendly an acquaintance, knew no bounds. Even the dignity of Captain Walter Waters relaxed, to that degree, that he suffered himself to be prevailed upon by Mr. Joseph

Tuggs, to partake of cold pigeon-pie and sherry, on deck; and a most delightful conversation, aided by these agreeable stimulants, was prolonged, until they ran alongside Ramsgate Pier.

"Good bye, dear!" said Mrs. Captain Waters to Miss Charlotta Tuggs, just before the bustle of landing commenced; "we shall see you on the sands in the morning; and, as we are sure to have found lodgings before then, I hope we shall be inseparables for many weeks to come."

"Oh! I hope so," said Miss Charlotta Tuggs, emphatically.

"Tickets, ladies and gen'lm'n," said the man on the paddle-box.

"Want a porter, sir?" inquired a dozen men in smock-frocks.

"Now, my dear!" said Captain Waters.

"Good bye!" said Mrs. Captain Waters—"good bye, Mr. Cymon!" and with a pressure of the hand which threw the amiable young man's nerves into a state of considerable derangement, Mrs. Captain Waters disappeared among the crowd. A pair of puce-coloured boots were seen ascending the steps, a white handkerchief fluttered, a black eye gleamed. The Waterses were gone, and Mr. Cymon Tuggs was alone in a heartless world.

Silently and abstractedly, did that too sensitive youth follow his revered parents, and a train of smock-frocks and wheelbarrows, along the pier, until the bustle of the scene around, recalled him to himself. The sun was shining brightly; the sea, dancing to its own music, rolled merrily in; crowds of people promenaded to and fro; young ladies tittered; old ladies talked; nursemaids displayed their charms to the greatest possible advantage; and their little charges ran up and down, and to and fro, and in and out, under the feet, and between the legs, of the assembled concourse, in the most playful and exhilarating manner. There were old gentlemen, trying to make out objects through long telescopes; and young ones, making objects of themselves in open shirt-

8

collars; ladies, carrying about portable chairs, and portable chairs carrying about invalids; parties, waiting on the pier for parties who had come by the steam-boat; and nothing was to be heard but talking, laughing, welcoming, and. merriment.

" Fly, sir?" exclaimed a chorus of fourteen men and six boys, the moment Mr. Joseph Tuggs, at the head of his little party, set foot in the street.

" Here's the gen'lm'n at last!" said one, touching his hat with mock politeness. " Werry glad to see you, sir,—been a-waitin' for you these six weeks. Jump in, if you please, sir!"

" Nice light fly and a fast trotter, sir," said another: " fourteen mile a hour, and surroundin' objects rendered inwisible by ex-treme welocity!"

" Large fly for your luggage, sir," cried a third. " Werry large fly here, sir—reg'lar bluebottle!"

" Here's *your* fly, sir!" shouted another aspiring charioteer, mounting the box, and inducing an old grey horse to indulge in some imperfect reminiscences of a canter. " Look at him, sir!—temper of a lamb and haction of a steam-ingein!"

Resisting even the temptation of securing the services of so valuable a quadruped as the last named, Mr. Joseph Tuggs beckoned to the proprietor of a dingy conveyance of a greenish hue, lined with faded striped calico; and, the luggage and the family having been deposited therein, the animal in the shafts, after describing circles in the road for a quarter of an hour, at last consented to depart in quest of lodgings.

" How many beds have you got?" screamed Mrs. Tuggs out of the fly, to the woman who opened the door of the first house which displayed a bill intimating that apartments were to be let within.

" How many did you want, ma'am?" was, of course, the reply.

" Three."

" Will you step in, ma'am?" Down got Mrs. Tuggs.

The family were delighted. Splendid view of the sea from the front windows—charming! A short pause. Back came Mrs. Tuggs again.—One parlour and a mattress.

"Why the devil didn't they say so at first?" inquired Mr. Joseph Tuggs, rather pettishly.

"Don't know," said Mrs. Tuggs.

"Wretches!" exclaimed the nervous Cymon. Another bill —another stoppage. Same question—same answer—similar result.

"What do they mean by this?" inquired Mr. Joseph Tuggs, thoroughly out of temper.

"Don't know," said the placid Mrs. Tuggs.

"Orvis the vay here, sir," said the driver, by way of accounting for the circumstance in a satisfactory manner; and off they went again, to make fresh inquiries, and encounter fresh disappointments.

It had grown dusk when the "fly"—the rate of whose progress greatly belied its name—after climbing up four or five perpendicular hills, stopped before the door of a dusty house, with a bay window, from which you could obtain a beautiful glimpse of the sea—if you thrust half of your body out of it, at the imminent peril of falling into the area. Mrs. Tuggs alighted. One ground-floor sitting-room, and three cells with beds in them up-stairs. A double house. Family on the opposite side. Five children milk-and-watering in the parlour, and one little boy, expelled for bad behaviour, screaming on his back in the passage.

"What's the terms?" said Mrs. Tuggs. The mistress of the house was considering the expediency of putting on an extra guinea; so, she coughed slightly, and affected not to hear the question.

"What's the terms?" said Mrs. Tuggs, in a louder key.

"Five guineas a week, ma'am, *with* attendance," replied the lodging-house keeper. (Attendance means the privilege of ringing the bell as often as you like, for your own amusement.)

"Rather dear," said Mrs. Tuggs.

"Oh dear, no, ma'am!" replied the mistress of the house, with a benign smile of pity at the ignorance of manners and customs, which the observation betrayed. "Very cheap!"

Such an authority was indisputable. Mrs. Tuggs paid a week's rent in advance, and took the lodgings for a month. In an hour's time, the family were seated at tea in their new abode.

"Capital srimps!" said Mr. Joseph Tuggs.

Mr. Cymon eyed his father with a rebellious scowl, as he emphatically said "*Shrimps.*"

"Well then, shrimps," said Mr. Joseph Tuggs. "Srimps or shrimps, don't much matter."

There was pity, blended with malignity, in Mr. Cymon's eye, as he replied, "Don't matter, father! What would Captain Waters say, if he heard such vulgarity?"

"Or what would dear Mrs. Captain Waters say," added Charlotta, "if she saw mother—ma, I mean—eating them whole, heads and all!"

"It won't bear thinking of!" ejaculated Mr. Cymon, with a shudder. "How different," he thought, "from the Dowager Duchess of Dobbleton!"

"Very pretty woman, Mrs. Captain Waters, is she not, Cymon?" inquired Miss Charlotta.

A glow of nervous excitement passed over the countenance of Mr. Cymon Tuggs, as he replied, "An angel of beauty!"

"Hallo!" said Mr. Joseph Tuggs. "Hallo, Cymon, my boy, take care. Married lady, you know;" and he winked one of his twinkling eyes knowingly.

"Why," exclaimed Cymon, starting up with an ebullition of fury, as unexpected as alarming, "why am I to be reminded of that blight of my happiness, and ruin of my hopes? Why am I to be taunted with the miseries which are heaped upon my head? Is it not enough to—to—to—" and the

11

orator paused; but whether for want of words, or lack of breath, was never distinctly ascertained.

There was an impressive solemnity in the tone of this address, and in the air with which the romantic Cymon, at its conclusion, rang the bell, and demanded a flat candlestick, which effectually forbade a reply. He stalked dramatically to bed, and the Tuggses went to bed too, half an hour afterwards, in a state of considerable mystification and perplexity.

If the pier had presented a scene of life and bustle to the Tuggses on their first landing at Ramsgate, it was far surpassed by the appearance of the sands on the morning after their arrival. It was a fine, bright, clear day, with a light breeze from the sea. There were the same ladies and gentlemen, the same children, the same nursemaids, the same telescopes, the same portable chairs. The ladies were employed in needlework, or watch-guard making, or knitting, or reading novels; the gentlemen were reading newspapers and magazines; the children were digging holes in the sand with wooden spades, and collecting water therein; the nursemaids, with their youngest charges in their arms, were running in after the waves, and then running back with the waves after them; and, now and then, a little sailing-boat either departed with a gay and talkative cargo of passengers, or returned with a very silent and particularly uncomfortable-looking one.

"Well, I never!" exclaimed Mrs. Tuggs, as she and Mr. Joseph Tuggs, and Miss Charlotta Tuggs, and Mr. Cymon Tuggs, with their eight feet in a corresponding number of yellow shoes, seated themselves on four rush-bottomed chairs, which, being placed in a soft part of the sand, forthwith sunk down some two feet and a half—"Well, I never!"

Mr. Cymon, by an exertion of great personal strength, uprooted the chairs, and removed them further back.

"Why, I'm blessed if there ain't some ladies a-going in!" exclaimed Mr. Joseph Tuggs, with intense astonishment.

12

"Lor, pa!" exclaimed Miss Charlotta.

"There *is*, my dear," said Mr. Joseph Tuggs. And, sure enough, four young ladies, each furnished with a towel, tripped up the steps of a bathing-machine. In went the horse, floundering about in the water; round turned the machine; down sat the driver; and presently out burst the young ladies aforesaid, with four distinct splashes.

"Well, that's sing'ler, too!" ejaculated Mr. Joseph Tuggs, after an awkward pause. Mr. Cymon coughed slightly.

"Why, here's some gentlemen a-going in on this side!" exclaimed Mrs. Tuggs, in a tone of horror.

Three machines—three horses—three flounderings—three turnings round—three splashes—three gentlemen, disporting themselves in the water like so many dolphins.

"Well, *that's* sing'ler!" said Mr. Joseph Tuggs again. Miss Charlotta coughed this time, and another pause ensued. It was agreeably broken.

"How d'ye do, dear? We have been looking for you, all the morning," said a voice to Miss Charlotta Tuggs. Mrs. Captain Waters was the owner of it.

"How d'ye do?" said Captain Walter Waters, all suavity; and a most cordial interchange of greetings ensued.

"Belinda, my love," said Captain Walter Waters, applying his glass to his eye, and looking in the direction of the sea.

"Yes, my dear," replied Mrs. Captain Waters.

"There's Harry Thompson!"

"Where?" said Belinda, applying her glass to her eye.

"Bathing."

"Lor, so it is! He don't see us, does he?"

"No, I don't think he does," replied the captain. "Bless my soul, how very singular!"

"What?" inquired Belinda.

"There's Mary Golding, too."

"Lor!—where?" (Up went the glass again.)

"There!" said the captain, pointing to one of the young

ladies before noticed, who, in her bathing costume, looked as if she was enveloped in a patent Mackintosh, of scanty dimensions.

" So it is, I declare ! " exclaimed Mrs. Captain Waters. " How very curious we should see them both ! "

" Very," said the captain, with perfect coolness.

" It's the reg'lar thing here, you see," whispered Mr. Cymon Tuggs to his father.

" I see it is," whispered Mr. Joseph Tuggs in reply. " Queer, though—ain't it ? " Mr. Cymon Tuggs nodded assent.

" What do you think of doing with yourself this morning ? " inquired the captain. " Shall we lunch at Pegwell ? "

" I should like that very much indeed," interposed Mrs. Tuggs. She had never heard of Pegwell ; but the word " lunch " had reached her ears, and it sounded very agreeably.

" How shall we go ? " inquired the captain; " it's too warm to walk."

" A shay ? " suggested Mr. Joseph Tuggs.

" Chaise," whispered Mr. Cymon.

" I should think one would be enough," said Mr. Joseph Tuggs aloud, quite unconscious of the meaning of the correction. " However, two shays if you like."

" I should like a donkey *so* much," said Belinda.

" Oh, so should I ! " echoed Charlotta Tuggs.

" Well, we can have a fly," suggested the captain, " and you can have a couple of donkeys."

A fresh difficulty arose. Mrs. Captain Waters declared it would be decidedly improper for two ladies to ride alone. The remedy was obvious. Perhaps young Mr. Tuggs would be gallant enough to accompany them.

Mr. Cymon Tuggs blushed, smiled, looked vacant, and faintly protested that he was no horseman. The objection was at once overruled. A fly was speedily found ; and three donkeys—which the proprietor declared on his solemn

14

asseveration to be "three parts blood, and the other corn"
—were engaged in the service.

"Kim up!" shouted one of the two boys who followed
behind, to propel the donkeys, when Belinda Waters and
Charlotta Tuggs had been hoisted, and pushed, and pulled,
into their respective saddles.

"Hi—hi—hi!" groaned the other boy behind Mr. Cymon
Tuggs. Away went the donkey, with the stirrups jingling
against the heels of Cymon's boots, and Cymon's boots nearly
scraping the ground.

"Way—way! Wo—o—o—o—!" cried Mr. Cymon Tuggs
as well as he could, in the midst of the jolting.

"Don't make it gallop!" screamed Mrs. Captain Waters,
behind.

"My donkey *will* go into the public-house!" shrieked
Miss Tuggs in the rear.

"Hi—hi—hi!" groaned both the boys together; and on
went the donkeys as if nothing would ever stop them.

Everything has an end, however; even the galloping of
donkeys will cease in time. The animal which Mr. Cymon
Tuggs bestrode, feeling sundry uncomfortable tugs at the bit,
the intent of which he could by no means divine, abruptly
sidled against a brick wall, and expressed his uneasiness by
grinding Mr. Cymon Tuggs's leg on the rough surface. Mrs.
Captain Waters's donkey, apparently under the influence of
some playfulness of spirit, rushed suddenly, head first, into a
hedge, and declined to come out again : and the quadruped
on which Miss Tuggs was mounted, expressed his delight at
this humorous proceeding by firmly planting his fore-feet
against the ground, and kicking up his hind-legs in a very
agile, but somewhat alarming manner.

This abrupt termination to the rapidity of the ride,
naturally occasioned some confusion. Both the ladies indulged in vehement screaming for several minutes; and Mr.
Cymon Tuggs, besides sustaining intense bodily pain, had the
additional mental anguish of witnessing their distressing

situation, without having the power to rescue them, by reason of his leg being firmly screwed in between the animal and the wall. The efforts of the boys, however, assisted by the ingenious expedient of twisting the tail of the most rebellious donkey, restored order in a much shorter time than could have reasonably been expected, and the little party jogged slowly on together.

"Now let 'em walk," said Mr. Cymon Tuggs. "It's cruel to overdrive 'em."

"Werry well, sir," replied the boy, with a grin at his companion, as if he understood Mr. Cymon to mean that the cruelty applied less to the animals than to their riders.

"What a lovely day, dear!" said Charlotta.

"Charming; enchanting, dear!" responded Mrs. Captain Waters. "What a beautiful prospect, Mr. Tuggs!"

Cymon looked full in Belinda's face, as he responded—"Beautiful, indeed!" The lady cast down her eyes, and suffered the animal she was riding to fall a little back. Cymon Tuggs instinctively did the same.

There was a brief silence, broken only by a sigh from Mr. Cymon Tuggs.

"Mr. Cymon," said the lady suddenly, in a low tone, "Mr. Cymon—I am another's."

Mr. Cymon expressed his perfect concurrence in a statement which it was impossible to controvert.

"If I had not been—— " resumed Belinda; and there she stopped.

"What—what?" said Mr. Cymon earnestly. "Do not torture me. What would you say?"

"If I had not been"—continued Mrs. Captain Waters—"if, in earlier life, it had been my fate to have known, and been beloved by, a noble youth—a kindred soul—a congenial spirit—one capable of feeling and appreciating the sentiments which—— "

"Heavens! what do I hear?" exclaimed Mr. Cymon Tuggs. "Is it possible! can I believe my—Come up!" (This last

16

unsentimental parenthesis was addressed to the donkey, who, with his head between his fore-legs, appeared to be examining the state of his shoes with great anxiety).

"Hi—hi—hi," said the boys behind. "Come up," expostulated Cymon Tuggs again. "Hi—hi—hi," repeated the boys. And whether it was that the animal felt indignant at the tone of Mr. Tuggs's command, or felt alarmed by the noise of the deputy proprietor's boots running behind him; or whether he burned with a noble emulation to outstrip the other donkeys; certain it is that he no sooner heard the second series of "hi—hi's," than he started away, with a celerity of pace which jerked Mr. Cymon's hat off, instantaneously, and carried him to the Pegwell Bay hotel in no time, where he deposited his rider without giving him the trouble of dismounting, by sagaciously pitching him over his head, into the very doorway of the tavern.

Great was the confusion of Mr. Cymon Tuggs, when he was put, right end uppermost, by two waiters; considerable was the alarm of Mrs. Tuggs in behalf of her son; agonizing were the apprehensions of Mrs. Captain Waters on his account. It was speedily discovered, however, that he had not sustained much more injury than the donkey—he was grazed, and the animal was grazing—and then it *was* a delightful party to be sure! Mr. and Mrs. Tuggs, and the captain, had ordered lunch in the little garden behind :— small saucers of large shrimps, dabs of butter, crusty loaves, and bottled ale. The sky was without a cloud; there were flower-pots and turf before them; the sea, from the foot of the cliff, stretching away as far as the eye could discern anything at all; vessels in the distance with sails as white, and as small, as nicely-got-up cambric handkerchiefs. The shrimps were delightful, the ale better, and the captain even more pleasant than either. Mrs. Captain Waters was in *such* spirits after lunch !—chasing, first the captain across the turf, and among the flower-pots; and then Mr. Cymon Tuggs; and then Miss Tuggs; and laughing, too, quite boisterously. But as the captain said, it didn't matter; who knew what they were, there? For all the people of the house knew, they might be common people. To which Mr. Joseph Tuggs responded, "To be sure." And then they went down the steep wooden steps a little further on, which led to the bottom of the cliff; and looked at the crabs, and the seaweed, and the eels, till it was more than fully time to go back to Ramsgate again. Finally, Mr. Cymon Tuggs ascended the steps last, and Mrs. Captain Waters last but one; and Mr. Cymon Tuggs discovered that the foot and ankle of Mrs. Captain Waters, were even more unexceptionable than he had at first supposed.

Taking a donkey towards his ordinary place of residence, is a very different thing, and a feat much more easily to be accomplished, than taking him from it. It requires a great deal of foresight and presence of mind in the one case, to anticipate the numerous flights of his discursive imagination; whereas, in the other, all you have to do, is, to hold on, and place a blind confidence in the animal. Mr. Cymon Tuggs adopted the latter expedient on his return; and his nerves were so little discomposed by the journey, that he distinctly understood they were all to meet again at the library in the evening.

The library was crowded. There were the same ladies, and the same gentlemen, who had been on the sands in the morning, and on the pier the day before. There were young ladies, in maroon-coloured gowns and black velvet bracelets, dispensing fancy articles in the shop, and presiding over games of chance in the concert-room. There were marriageable daughters, and marriage-making mammas, gaming and promenading, and turning over music, and flirting. There were some male beaux doing the sentimental in whispers, and others doing the ferocious in moustache. There were Mrs. Tuggs in amber, Miss Tuggs in sky-blue, Mrs. Captain Waters in pink. There was Captain Waters in a braided surtout; there was Mr. Cymon Tuggs in pumps and a gilt waistcoat; there was Mr. Joseph Tuggs in a blue coat and a shirt-frill.

"Numbers three, eight, and eleven!" cried one of the young ladies in the maroon-coloured gowns.

"Numbers three, eight, and eleven!" echoed another young lady in the same uniform.

"Number three's gone," said the first young lady. "Numbers eight and eleven!"

"Numbers eight and eleven!" echoed the second young lady.

"Number eight's gone, Mary Ann," said the first young lady.

"Number eleven!" screamed the second.

"The numbers are all taken now, ladies, if you please," said the first. The representatives of numbers three, eight, and eleven, and the rest of the numbers, crowded round the table.

"Will you throw, ma'am?" said the presiding goddess, handing the dice-box to the eldest daughter of a stout lady, with four girls.

There was a profound silence among the lookers-on.

"Throw, Jane, my dear," said the stout lady. An interesting display of bashfulness—a little blushing in a cambric handkerchief—a whispering to a younger sister.

"Amelia, my dear, throw for your sister," said the stout lady; and then she turned to a walking advertisement of Rowlands' Macassar Oil, who stood next her, and said, "Jane is so *very* modest and retiring; but I can't be angry with her for it. An artless and unsophisticated girl is *so* truly amiable, that I often wish Amelia was more like her sister!"

The gentleman with the whiskers whispered his admiring approval.

"Now, my dear!" said the stout lady. Miss Amelia threw —eight for her sister, ten for herself.

"Nice figure, Amelia," whispered the stout lady to a thin youth beside her.

"Beautiful!"

"And *such* a spirit! I am like you in that respect. I can *not* help admiring that life and vivacity. Ah! (a sigh) I wish I could make poor Jane a little more like my dear Amelia!"

The young gentleman cordially acquiesced in the sentiment; both he, and the individual first addressed, were perfectly contented.

"Who's this?" inquired Mr. Cymon Tuggs of Mrs. Captain Waters, as a short female, in a blue velvet hat and feathers, was led into the orchestra, by a fat man in black tights and cloudy Berlins.

"Mrs. Tippin, of the London theatres," replied Belinda, referring to the programme of the concert.

The talented Tippin having condescendingly acknowledged the clapping of hands, and shouts of "bravo!" which greeted her appearance, proceeded to sing the popular cavatina of "Bid me discourse," accompanied on the piano by Mr. Tippin; after which, Mr. Tippin sang a comic song, accompanied on the piano by Mrs. Tippin: the applause consequent upon which, was only to be exceeded by the enthusiastic approbation bestowed upon an air with variations on the guitar, by Miss Tippin, accompanied on the chin by Master Tippin.

Thus passed the evening; thus passed the days and evenings of the Tuggses, and the Waterses, for six weeks. Sands in the morning—donkeys at noon—pier in the afternoon—library at night—and the same people everywhere.

On that very night six weeks, the moon was shining brightly over the calm sea, which dashed against the feet of the tall gaunt cliffs, with just enough noise to lull the old fish to sleep, without disturbing the young ones, when two figures were discernible—or would have been, if anybody had looked for them—seated on one of the wooden benches which are stationed near the verge of the western cliff. The moon had climbed higher into the heavens, by two hours' journeying, since those figures first sat down—and yet they had moved not. The crowd of loungers had thinned and dispersed; the noise of itinerant musicians had died away; light after light had appeared in the windows of the different houses in the distance; blockade-man after blockade-man had passed the spot, wending his way towards his solitary post; and yet those figures had remained stationary. Some portions of the two forms were in deep shadow, but the light of the moon fell strongly on a puce-coloured boot and a glazed stock. Mr. Cymon Tuggs and Mrs. Captain Waters were seated on that bench. They spoke not, but were silently gazing on the sea.

"Walter will return to-morrow," said Mrs. Captain Waters, mournfully breaking silence.

Mr. Cymon Tuggs sighed like a gust of wind through a forest of gooseberry bushes, as he replied, "Alas! he will."

"Oh, Cymon!" resumed Belinda, "the chaste delight, the calm happiness, of this one week of Platonic love, is too much for me!"

Cymon was about to suggest that it was too little for him, but he stopped himself, and murmured unintelligibly.

"And to think that even this gleam of happiness, innocent as it is," exclaimed Belinda, "is now to be lost for ever!"

"Oh, do not say for ever, Belinda," exclaimed the excitable Cymon, as two strongly-defined tears chased each other down his pale face—it was so long that there was plenty of room for a chase. "Do not say for ever!"

"I must," replied Belinda.

"Why?" urged Cymon, "oh why? Such Platonic acquaintance as ours is so harmless, that even your husband can never object to it."

"My husband!" exclaimed Belinda. "You little know him. Jealous and revengeful; ferocious in his revenge—a maniac in his jealousy! Would you be assassinated before my eyes?" Mr. Cymon Tuggs, in a voice broken by emotion, expressed his disinclination to undergo the process of assassination before the eyes of anybody.

21

"Then leave me," said Mrs. Captain Waters. "Leave me, this night, for ever. It is late: let us return."

Mr. Cymon Tuggs sadly offered the lady his arm, and escorted her to her lodgings. He paused at the door—he felt a Platonic pressure of his hand. "Good night," he said, hesitating.

"Good night," sobbed the lady. Mr. Cymon Tuggs paused again.

"Won't you walk in, sir?" said the servant. Mr. Tuggs hesitated. Oh, that hesitation! He *did* walk in.

"Good night!" said Mr. Cymon Tuggs again, when he reached the drawing-room.

"Good night!" replied Belinda; "and, if at any period of my life, I—Hush!" The lady paused and stared with a steady gaze of horror, on the ashy countenance of Mr. Cymon Tuggs. There was a double knock at the street-door.

"It is my husband!" said Belinda, as the captain's voice was heard below.

"And my family!" added Cymon Tuggs, as the voices of his relatives floated up the staircase.

"The curtain! The curtain!" gasped Mrs. Captain Waters, pointing to the window, before which some chintz hangings were closely drawn.

"But I have done nothing wrong," said the hesitating Cymon.

"The curtain!" reiterated the frantic lady: "you will be murdered." This last appeal to his feelings was irresistible. The dismayed Cymon concealed himself behind the curtain with pantomimic suddenness.

Enter the captain, Joseph Tuggs, Mrs. Tuggs, and Charlotta.

"My dear," said the captain, "Lieutenant Slaughter." Two iron-shod boots and one gruff voice were heard by Mr. Cymon to advance, and acknowledge the honour of the introduction. The sabre of the lieutenant rattled heavily upon the floor, as he seated himself at the table. Mr. Cymon's fears almost overcame his reason.

"The brandy, my dear!" said the captain. Here was a situation! They were going to make a night of it! And Mr. Cymon Tuggs was pent up behind the curtain and afraid to breathe!

"Slaughter," said the captain, "a cigar?"

Now, Mr. Cymon Tuggs never could smoke without feeling it indispensably necessary to retire, immediately, and never could smell smoke without a strong disposition to cough. The cigars were introduced; the captain was a professed smoker; so was the lieutenant; so was Joseph Tuggs. The apartment was small, the door was closed, the smoke powerful: it hung in heavy wreaths over the room, and at length found its way behind the curtain. Cymon Tuggs held his nose, his mouth, his breath. It was all of no use—out came the cough.

"Bless my soul!" said the captain, "I beg your pardon, Miss Tuggs. You dislike smoking?"

"Oh, no; I don't indeed," said Charlotta.

"It makes you cough."

"Oh dear no."

"You coughed just now."

"Me, Captain Waters! Lor! how can you say so?"

"Somebody coughed," said the captain.

"I certainly thought so," said Slaughter. No; everybody denied it.

"Fancy," said the captain.

"Must be," echoed Slaughter.

Cigars resumed—more smoke—another cough—smothered, but violent.

"Damned odd!" said the captain, staring about him.

"Sing'ler!" ejaculated the unconscious Mr. Joseph Tuggs.

Lieutenant Slaughter looked first at one person mysteriously, then at another: then, laid down his cigar, then approached the window on tiptoe, and pointed with his right thumb over his shoulder, in the direction of the curtain.

"Slaughter!" ejaculated the captain, rising from table, "what do you mean?"

The lieutenant, in reply, drew back the curtain and discovered Mr. Cymon Tuggs behind it: pallid with apprehension, and blue with wanting to cough.

"Aha!" exclaimed the captain, furiously. "What do I see? Slaughter, your sabre!"

"Cymon!" screamed the Tuggses.

"Mercy!" said Belinda.

"Platonic!" gasped Cymon.

"Your sabre!" roared the captain: "Slaughter—unhand me—the villain's life!"

"Murder!" screamed the Tuggses.

"Hold him fast, sir!" faintly articulated Cymon.

"Water!" exclaimed Joseph Tuggs—and Mr. Cymon Tuggs and all the ladies forthwith fainted away, and formed a tableau.

Most willingly would we conceal the disastrous termination of the six weeks' acquaintance. A troublesome form, and an arbitrary custom, however, prescribe that a story should have a conclusion, in addition to a commencement; we have therefore no alternative. Lieutenant Slaughter brought a message —the captain brought an action. Mr. Joseph Tuggs interposed—the lieutenant negotiated. When Mr. Cymon Tuggs recovered from the nervous disorder into which misplaced affection, and exciting circumstances, had plunged him, he found that his family had lost their pleasant acquaintance; that his father was minus fifteen hundred pounds; and the captain plus the precise sum. The money was paid to hush the matter up, but it got abroad notwithstanding; and there are not wanting some who affirm that three designing impostors never found more easy dupes, than did Captain Waters, Mrs. Waters, and Lieutenant Slaughter, in the Tuggses at Ramsgate.

CHAPTER V

"Indeed, my love, he paid Teresa very great attention on the last assembly night," said Mrs. Malderton, addressing her spouse, who, after the fatigues of the day in the City, was sitting with a silk handkerchief over his head, and his feet on the fender, drinking his port;—" very great attention; and I say again, every possible encouragement ought to be given him. He positively must be asked down here to dine."

" Who must?" inquired Mr. Malderton.

" Why, you know whom I mean, my dear—the young man with the black whiskers and the white cravat, who has just come out at our assembly, and whom all the girls are talking about. Young——dear me! what's his name?—Marianne, what *is* his name?" continued Mrs. Malderton, addressing her youngest daughter, who was engaged in netting a purse, and looking sentimental.

"Mr. Horatio Sparkins, ma," replied Miss Marianne, with a sigh.

" Oh! yes, to be sure—Horatio Sparkins," said Mrs. Malderton. " Decidedly the most gentleman-like young man I ever saw. I am sure in the beautifully-made coat he wore the other night, he looked like—like—— "

"Like Prince Leopold, ma—so noble, so full of sentiment!" suggested Marianne, in a tone of enthusiastic admiration.

"You should recollect, my dear," resumed Mrs. Malderton,

25

"that Teresa is now eight-and-twenty; and that it really is very important that something should be done."

Miss Teresa Malderton was a very little girl, rather fat, with vermilion cheeks, but good-humoured, and still disengaged, although, to do her justice, the misfortune arose from no lack of perseverance on her part. In vain had she flirted for ten years; in vain had Mr. and Mrs. Malderton assiduously kept up an extensive acquaintance among the young eligible bachelors of Camberwell, and even of Wandsworth and Brixton; to say nothing of those who "dropped in" from town. Miss Malderton was as well known as the lion on the top of Northumberland House, and had an equal chance of "going off."

"I am quite sure you'd like him," continued Mrs. Malderton, "he is so gentlemanly!"

"So clever!" said Miss Marianne.

"And has such a flow of language!" added Miss Teresa.

"He has a great respect for you, my dear," said Mrs. Malderton to her husband. Mr. Malderton coughed, and looked at the fire.

"Yes, I'm sure he's very much attached to pa's society," said Miss Marianne.

"No doubt of it," echoed Miss Teresa.

"Indeed, he said as much to me in confidence," observed Mrs. Malderton.

"Well, well," returned Mr. Malderton, somewhat flattered; "if I see him at the assembly to-morrow, perhaps I'll ask him down. I hope he knows we live at Oak Lodge, Camberwell, my dear?"

"Of course—and that you keep a one-horse carriage."

"I'll see about it," said Mr. Malderton, composing himself for a nap; "I'll see about it."

Mr. Malderton was a man whose whole scope of ideas was limited to Lloyd's, the Exchange, the India House, and the Bank. A few successful speculations had raised him from a situation of obscurity and comparative poverty, to a state of

Horatio Sparkins

affluence. As frequently happens in such cases, the ideas of himself and his family became elevated to an extraordinary pitch as their means increased; they affected fashion, taste, and many other fooleries, in imitation of their betters, and had a very decided and becoming horror of anything which could, by possibility, be considered *low*. He was hospitable from ostentation, illiberal from ignorance, and prejudiced from conceit. Egotism and the love of display induced him to keep an excellent table: convenience, and a love of good things of this life, ensured him plenty of guests. He liked to have clever men, or what he considered such, at his table, because it was a great thing to talk about; but he never could endure what he called "sharp fellows." Probably, he cherished this feeling out of compliment to his two sons, who gave their respected parent no uneasiness in that particular. The family were ambitious of forming acquaintances and connexions in some sphere of society superior to that in which they themselves moved; and one of the necessary consequences of this desire, added to their utter ignorance of the world beyond their own small circle, was, that any one who could lay claim to an acquaintance with people of rank and title, had a sure passport to the table at Oak Lodge, Camberwell.

The appearance of Mr. Horatio Sparkins at the assembly, had excited no small degree of surprise and curiosity among its regular frequenters. Who could he be? He was evidently reserved, and apparently melancholy. Was he a clergyman? —He danced too well. A barrister?—He said he was not called. He used very fine words, and talked a great deal. Could he be a distinguished foreigner, come to England for the purpose of describing the country, its manners and customs; and frequenting public balls and public dinners, with the view of becoming acquainted with high life, polished etiquette, and English refinement?—No, he had not a foreign accent. Was he a surgeon, a contributor to the magazines, a writer of fashionable novels, or an artist?—No; to each

and all of these surmises, there existed some valid objection.
—"Then," said everybody, "he must be *somebody*."—"I should think he must be," reasoned Mr. Malderton, within himself, "because he perceives our superiority, and pays us so much attention."

The night succeeding the conversation we have just recorded, was "assembly night." The double-fly was ordered to be at the door of Oak Lodge at nine o'clock precisely. The Miss Maldertons were dressed in sky-blue satin trimmed with artificial flowers; and Mrs. M. (who was a little fat woman), in ditto ditto, looked like her eldest daughter multiplied by two. Mr. Frederick Malderton, the eldest son, in full-dress costume, was the very *beau idéal* of a smart waiter; and Mr. Thomas Malderton, the youngest, with his white dress-stock, blue coat, bright buttons, and red watch-ribbon, strongly resembled the portrait of that interesting, but rash young gentleman, George Barnwell. Every member of the party had made up his or her mind to cultivate the acquaintance of Mr. Horatio Sparkins. Miss Teresa, of course, was to be as amiable and interesting as ladies of eight-and-twenty on the look-out for a husband, usually are. Mrs. Malderton would be all smiles and graces. Miss Marianne would request the favour of some verses for her album. Mr. Malderton would patronise the great unknown by asking him to dinner. Tom intended to ascertain the extent of his information on the interesting topics of snuff and cigars. Even Mr. Frederick Malderton himself, the family authority on all points of taste, dress, and fashionable arrangement; who had lodgings of his own in town; who had a free admission to Covent-garden theatre; who always dressed according to the fashions of the months; who went up the water twice a-week in the season; and who actually had an intimate friend who once knew a gentleman who formerly lived in the Albany,—even he had determined that Mr. Horatio Sparkins must be a devilish good fellow, and that he would do him the honour of challenging him to a game at billiards.

The first object that met the anxious eyes of the expectant family on their entrance into the ball-room, was the interesting Horatio, with his hair brushed off his forehead, and his eyes fixed on the ceiling, reclining in a contemplative attitude on one of the seats.

"There he is, my dear," whispered Mrs. Malderton to Mr. Malderton.

"How like Lord Byron!" murmured Miss Teresa.

"Or Montgomery!" whispered Miss Marianne.

"Or the portraits of Captain Cook!" suggested Tom.

"Tom—don't be an ass!" said his father, who checked him on all occasions, probably with a view to prevent his becoming "sharp"—which was very unnecessary.

The elegant Sparkins attitudinised with admirable effect, until the family had crossed the room. He then started up, with the most natural appearance of surprise and delight; accosted Mrs. Malderton with the utmost cordiality; saluted the young ladies in the most enchanting manner; bowed to, and shook hands with, Mr. Malderton, with a degree of respect amounting almost to veneration; and returned the greetings of the two young men in a half-gratified, half-patronising manner, which fully convinced them that he must be an important, and, at the same time, condescending personage.

"Miss Malderton," said Horatio, after the ordinary salutations, and bowing very low, "may I be permitted to presume to hope that you will allow me to have the pleasure——"

"I don't *think* I am engaged," said Miss Teresa, with a dreadful affectation of indifference—"but, really—so many—— "

Horatio looked handsomely miserable.

"I shall be most happy," simpered the interesting Teresa, at last. Horatio's countenance brightened up, like an old hat in a shower of rain.

"A very genteel young man, certainly!" said the gratified Mr. Malderton, as the obsequious Sparkins and his partner joined the quadrille which was just forming.

"He has a remarkably good address," said Mr. Frederick.

"Yes, he is a prime fellow," interposed Tom, who always managed to put his foot in it—"he talks just like an auctioneer."

"Tom!" said his father solemnly, "I think I desired you, before, not to be a fool." Tom looked as happy as a cock on a drizzly morning.

"How delightful!" said the interesting Horatio to his partner, as they promenaded the room at the conclusion of the set—"how delightful, how refreshing it is, to retire from the cloudy storms, the vicissitudes, and the troubles, of life, even if it be but for a few short fleeting moments: and to spend those moments, fading and evanescent though they be, in the delightful, the blessed society of one individual—whose frowns would be death, whose coldness would be madness, whose falsehood would be ruin, whose constancy would be bliss; the possession of whose affection would be the brightest and best reward that Heaven could bestow on man?"

"What feeling! what sentiment!" thought Miss Teresa, as she leaned more heavily on her companion's arm.

"But enough—enough!" resumed the elegant Sparkins, with a theatrical air. "What have I said? what have I—I —to do with sentiments like these! Miss Malderton"—here he stopped short—"may I hope to be permitted to offer the humble tribute of—— "

"Really, Mr. Sparkins," returned the enraptured Teresa, blushing in the sweetest confusion, "I must refer you to papa. I never can, without his consent, venture to—— "

"Surely he cannot object—— "

"Oh, yes. Indeed, indeed, you know him not!" interrupted Miss Teresa, well knowing there was nothing to fear, but wishing to make the interview resemble a scene in some romantic novel.

"He cannot object to my offering you a glass of negus," returned the adorable Sparkins, with some surprise.

AN INVITATION TO OAK LODGE

"Is that all?" thought the disappointed Teresa. "What a fuss about nothing!"

"It will give me the greatest pleasure, sir, to see you to dinner at Oak Lodge, Camberwell, on Sunday next at five o'clock, if you have no better engagement," said Mr. Malderton, at the conclusion of the evening, as he and his sons were standing in conversation with Mr. Horatio Sparkins.

Horatio bowed his acknowledgments, and accepted the flattering invitation.

"I must confess," continued the father, offering his snuff-box to his new acquaintance, "that I don't enjoy these assemblies half so much as the comfort—I had almost said the luxury—of Oak Lodge. They have no great charms for an elderly man."

"And after all, sir, what is man?" said the metaphysical Sparkins. "I say, what is man?"

"Ah! very true," said Mr. Malderton; "very true."

"We know that we live and breathe," continued Horatio; "that we have wants and wishes, desires and appetites——"

"Certainly," said Mr. Frederick Malderton, looking profound.

"I say, we know that we exist," repeated Horatio, raising his voice, "but there we stop; there, is an end to our knowledge; there, is the summit of our attainments; there, is the termination of our ends. What more do we know?"

"Nothing," replied Mr. Frederick—than whom no one was more capable of answering for himself in that particular. Tom was about to hazard something, but, fortunately for his reputation, he caught his father's angry eye, and slunk off like a puppy convicted of petty larceny.

"Upon my word," said Mr. Malderton the elder, as they were returning home in the fly, "that Mr. Sparkins is a wonderful young man. Such surprising knowledge! such extraordinary information! and such a splendid mode of expressing himself!"

31

"I think he must be somebody in disguise," said Miss Marianne. "How charmingly romantic!"

"He talks very loud and nicely," timidly observed Tom, "but I don't exactly understand what he means."

"I almost begin to despair of *your* understanding anything, Tom," said his father, who, of course, had been much enlightened by Mr. Horatio Sparkins's conversation.

"It strikes me, Tom," said Miss Teresa, "that you have made yourself very ridiculous this evening."

"No doubt of it," cried everybody—and the unfortunate Tom reduced himself into the least possible space. That night, Mr. and Mrs. Malderton had a long conversation respecting their daughter's prospects and future arrangements. Miss Teresa went to bed, considering whether, in the event of her marrying a title, she could conscientiously encourage the visits of her present associates; and dreamed, all night, of disguised noblemen, large routs, ostrich plumes, bridal favours, and Horatio Sparkins.

Various surmises were hazarded on the Sunday morning, as to the mode of conveyance which the anxiously-expected Horatio would adopt. Did he keep a gig?—was it possible he could come on horseback?—or would he patronize the stage? These, and other various conjectures of equal importance, engrossed the attention of Mrs. Malderton and her daughters during the whole morning after church.

"Upon my word, my dear, it's a most annoying thing that that vulgar brother of yours should have invited himself to dine here to-day," said Mr. Malderton to his wife. "On account of Mr. Sparkins's coming down, I purposely abstained from asking any one but Flamwell. And then to think of your brother—a tradesman—it's insufferable! I declare I wouldn't have him mention his shop, before our new guest— no, not for a thousand pounds! I wouldn't care if he had the good sense to conceal the disgrace he is to the family; but he's so fond of his horrible business, that he *will* let people know what he is."

MR. BARTON NOT ABOVE HIS BUSINESS

Mr. Jacob Barton, the individual alluded to, was a large grocer; so vulgar, and so lost to all sense of feeling, that he actually never scrupled to avow that he wasn't above his business: "he'd made his money by it, and he didn't care who know'd it."

"Ah! Flamwell, my dear fellow, how d'ye do?" said Mr. Malderton, as a little spoffish man, with green spectacles, entered the room. "You got my note?"

"Yes, I did; and here I am in consequence."

"You don't happen to know this Mr. Sparkins by name? You know everybody?"

Mr. Flamwell was one of those gentlemen of remarkably extensive information whom one occasionally meets in society, who pretend to know everybody, but in reality know nobody. At Malderton's, where any stories about great people were received with a greedy ear, he was an especial favourite; and, knowing the kind of people he had to deal with, he carried his passion of claiming acquaintance with everybody, to the most immoderate length. He had rather a singular way of telling his greatest lies in a parenthesis, and with an air of self-denial, as if he feared being thought egotistical.

"Why, no, I don't know him by that name," returned Flamwell, in a low tone, and with an air of immense importance. "I have no doubt I know him, though. Is he tall?"

"Middle-sized," said Miss Teresa.

"With black hair?" inquired Flamwell, hazarding a bold guess.

"Yes," returned Miss Teresa, eagerly.

"Rather a snub nose?"

"No," said the disappointed Teresa, "he has a Roman nose."

"I said a Roman nose, didn't I?" inquired Flamwell. "He's an elegant young man?"

"Oh, certainly."

33

"With remarkably prepossessing manners?"

"Oh, yes!" said all the family together. "You must know him."

"Yes, I thought you knew him, if he was anybody," triumphantly exclaimed Mr. Malderton. "Who d'ye think he is?"

"Why, from your description," said Flamwell, ruminating, and sinking his voice, almost to a whisper, "he bears a strong resemblance to the Honourable Augustus Fitz-Edward Fitz-John Fitz-Osborne. He's a very talented young man, and rather eccentric. It's extremely probable he may have changed his name for some temporary purpose."

Teresa's heart beat high. Could he be the Honourable Augustus Fitz-Edward Fitz-John Fitz-Osborne! What a name to be elegantly engraved upon two glazed cards, tied together with a piece of white satin ribbon! "The Honourable Mrs. Augustus Fitz-Edward Fitz-John Fitz-Osborne!" The thought was transport.

"It's five minutes to five," said Mr. Malderton, looking at his watch: "I hope he's not going to disappoint us."

"There he is!" exclaimed Miss Teresa, as a loud double-knock was heard at the door. Everybody endeavoured to look—as people when they particularly expect a visitor always do—as if they were perfectly unsuspicious of the approach of anybody.

The room-door opened—"Mr. Barton!" said the servant.

"Confound the man!" murmured Malderton. "Ah! my dear sir, how d'ye do! Any news?"

"Why no," returned the grocer, in his usual bluff manner. "No, none partickler. None that I am much aware of. How d'ye do, gals and boys? Mr. Flamwell, sir—glad to see you."

"Here's Mr. Sparkins!" said Tom, who had been looking out at the window, "on *such* a black horse!" There was Horatio, sure enough, on a large black horse, curvetting and prancing along, like an Astley's supernumerary. After a great deal of reining in, and pulling up, with the accompaniments of snorting, rearing, and kicking, the animal consented to stop at about a hundred yards from the gate, where Mr. Sparkins dismounted, and confided him to the care of Mr. Malderton's groom. The ceremony of introduction was gone through, in all due form. Mr. Flamwell looked from behind his green spectacles at Horatio with an air of mysterious importance; and the gallant Horatio looked unutterable things at Teresa.

"Is he the Honourable Mr. Augustus What's-his-name?" whispered Mrs. Malderton to Flamwell, as he was escorting her to the dining-room.

"Why, no—at least not exactly," returned that great authority—"not exactly."

"Who *is* he then?"

"Hush!" said Flamwell, nodding his head with a grave air, importing that he knew very well; but was prevented, by some grave reasons of state, from disclosing the important secret. It might be one of the ministers making himself acquainted with the views of the people.

"Mr. Sparkins," said the delighted Mrs. Malderton, "pray divide the ladies. John, put a chair for the gentleman between Miss Teresa and Miss Marianne." This was addressed to a man who, on ordinary occasions, acted as half-groom, half-gardener; but who, as it was important to make an impression on Mr. Sparkins, had been forced into a white neckerchief and shoes, and touched up, and brushed, to look like a second footman.

The dinner was excellent; Horatio was most attentive to Miss Teresa, and every one felt in high spirits, except Mr. Malderton, who, knowing the propensity of his brother-in-law, Mr. Barton, endured that sort of agony which the newspapers inform us is experienced by the surrounding neighbourhood when a pot-boy hangs himself in a hay-loft, and which is "much easier to be imagined than described."

"Have you seen your friend, Sir Thomas Noland, lately,

Flamwell?" inquired Mr. Malderton, casting a sidelong look at Horatio, to see what effect the mention of so great a man had upon him.

"Why, no—not very lately. I saw Lord Gubbleton the day before yesterday."

"Ah! I hope his lordship is very well?" said Malderton, in a tone of the greatest interest. It is scarcely necessary to say that, until that moment, he had been quite innocent of the existence of such a person.

"Why, yes; he was very well—very well indeed. He's a devilish good fellow. I met him in the City, and had a long chat with him. Indeed, I'm rather intimate with him. I couldn't stop to talk to him as long as I could wish, though, because I was on my way to a banker's, a very rich man, and a member of Parliament, with whom I am also rather, indeed I may say very, intimate."

"I know whom you mean, returned the host, consequentially —in reality knowing as much about the matter as Flamwell himself. "He has a capital business."

This was touching on a dangerous topic.

"Talking of business," interposed Mr. Barton, from the centre of the table. "A gentleman whom you knew very well, Malderton, before you made that first lucky spec of yours, called at our shop the other day, and——"

"Barton, may I trouble you for a potato?" interrupted the wretched master of the house, hoping to nip the story in the bud.

"Certainly," returned the grocer, quite insensible of his brother-in-law's object — "and he said in a very plain manner——"

"*Floury*, if you please," interrupted Malderton again; dreading the termination of the anecdote, and fearing a repetition of the word "shop."

"He said, says he," continued the culprit, after despatching the potato; "says he, how goes on your business? So I said, jokingly—you know my way—says I, I'm never above my business, and I hope my business will never be above me. Ha, ha!"

"Mr. Sparkins," said the host, vainly endeavouring to conceal his dismay, "a glass of wine?"

"With the utmost pleasure, sir."

"Happy to see you."

"Thank you."

"We were talking the other evening," resumed the host, addressing Horatio, partly with the view of displaying the conversational powers of his new acquaintance, and partly in the hope of drowning the grocer's stories—"we were talking the other night about the nature of man. Your argument struck me very forcibly."

"And me," said Mr. Frederick. Horatio made a graceful inclination of the head.

"Pray, what is your opinion of woman, Mr. Sparkins?" inquired Mrs. Malderton. The young ladies simpered.

"Man," replied Horatio, "man, whether he ranged the bright, gay, flowery plains of a second Eden, or the more sterile, barren, and I may say, commonplace regions, to which we are compelled to accustom ourselves, in times such as these; man, under any circumstances, or in any place—whether he were bending beneath the withering blasts of the frigid zone, or scorching under the rays of a vertical sun—man, without woman, would be—alone."

"I am very happy to find you entertain such honourable opinions, Mr. Sparkins," said Mrs. Malderton.

"And I," added Miss Teresa. Horatio looked his delight, and the young lady blushed.

"Now, it's my opinion—— " said Mr. Barton.

"I know what you're going to say," interposed Malderton, determined not to give his relation another opportunity, "and I don't agree with you."

"What!" inquired the astonished grocer.

"I am sorry to differ from you, Barton," said the host, in as positive a manner as if he really were contradicting a position which the other had laid down, "but I cannot give my assent to what I consider a very monstrous proposition."

"But I meant to say——"

"You never can convince me," said Malderton, with an air of obstinate determination. "Never."

"And I," said Mr. Frederick, following up his father's attack, "cannot entirely agree in Mr. Sparkins's argument."

"What!" said Horatio, who became more metaphysical, and more argumentative, as he saw the female part of the family listening in wondering delight—"what! Is effect the consequence of cause? Is cause the precursor of effect?"

"That's the point," said Flamwell.

"To be sure," said Mr. Malderton.

"Because, if effect is the consequence of cause, and if cause does precede effect, I apprehend you are wrong," added Horatio.

"Decidedly," said the toad-eating Flamwell.

"At least, I apprehend that to be the just and logical deduction?" said Sparkins, in a tone of interrogation.

"No doubt of it," chimed in Flamwell again. "It settles the point."

"Well, perhaps it does," said Mr. Frederick; "I didn't see it before."

"I don't exactly see it now," thought the grocer; "but I suppose it's all right."

"How wonderfully clever he is!" whispered Mrs. Malderton to her daughters, as they retired to the drawing-room.

"Oh, he's quite a love!" said both the young ladies together; "he talks like an oracle. He must have seen a great deal of life."

The gentlemen being left to themselves, a pause ensued, during which everybody looked very grave, as if they were quite overcome by the profound nature of the previous discussion. Flamwell, who had made up his mind to find out who and what Mr. Horatio Sparkins really was, first broke silence.

"Excuse me, sir," said that distinguished personage, "I

presume you have studied for the bar? I thought of entering once, myself—indeed, I'm rather intimate with some of the highest ornaments of that distinguished profession."

"N—no!" said Horatio, with a little hesitation; "not exactly."

"But you have been much among the silk gowns, or I mistake?" inquired Flamwell, deferentially.

"Nearly all my life," returned Sparkins.

The question was thus pretty well settled in the mind of Mr. Flamwell. He was a young gentleman "about to be called."

"I shouldn't like to be a barrister," said Tom, speaking for the first time, and looking round the table to find somebody who would notice the remark.

No one made any reply.

"I shouldn't like to wear a wig," said Tom, hazarding another observation.

"Tom, I beg you will not make yourself ridiculous," said his father. "Pray listen, and improve yourself by the conversation you hear, and don't be constantly making these absurd remarks."

"Very well, father," replied the unfortunate Tom, who had not spoken a word since he had asked for another slice of beef at a quarter-past five o'clock, p.m., and it was then eight.

"Well, Tom," observed his good-natured uncle, "never mind! I think with you. I shouldn't like to wear a wig. I'd rather wear an apron."

Mr. Malderton coughed violently. Mr. Barton resumed—"For if a man's above his business——"

The cough returned with tenfold violence, and did not cease until the unfortunate cause of it, in his alarm, had quite forgotten what he intended to say.

"Mr. Sparkins," said Flamwell, returning to the charge, "do you happen to know Mr. Delafontaine, of Bedford-square?"

"I have exchanged cards with him; since which, indeed, I have had an opportunity of serving him considerably," replied

Horatio, slightly colouring; no doubt, at having been betrayed into making the acknowledgment.

"You are very lucky, if you have had an opportunity of obliging that great man," observed Flamwell, with an air of profound respect.

"I don't know who he is," he whispered to Mr. Malderton, confidentially, as they followed Horatio up to the drawing-room. "It's quite clear, however, that he belongs to the law, and that he is somebody of great importance, and very highly connected."

"No doubt, no doubt," returned his companion.

The remainder of the evening passed away most delightfully. Mr. Malderton, relieved from his apprehensions by the circumstance of Mr. Barton's falling into a profound sleep, was as affable and gracious as possible. Miss Teresa played the "Fall of Paris," as Mr. Sparkins declared, in a most masterly manner, and both of them, assisted by Mr. Frederick, tried over glees and trios without number; they having made the pleasing discovery that their voices harmonised beautifully. To be sure, they all sang the first part; and Horatio, in addition to the slight drawback of having no ear, was perfectly innocent of knowing a note of music; still, they passed the time very agreeably, and it was past twelve o'clock before Mr. Sparkins ordered the mourning-coach-looking steed to be brought out—an order which was only complied with, on the distinct understanding that he was to repeat his visit on the following Sunday.

"But, perhaps, Mr. Sparkins will form one of our party to-morrow evening?" suggested Mrs. M. "Mr. Malderton intends taking the girls to see the pantomime." Mr. Sparkins bowed, and promised to join the party in box 48, in the course of the evening.

"We will not tax you for the morning," said Miss Teresa, bewitchingly; "for ma is going to take us to all sorts of places, shopping. I know that gentlemen have a great horror of that employment." Mr. Sparkins bowed again, and declared that he should be delighted, but business of importance occupied him in the morning. Flamwell looked at Malderton significantly.—"It's term time!" he whispered.

At twelve o'clock on the following morning, the "fly" was at the door of Oak Lodge, to convey Mrs. Malderton and her daughters on their expedition for the day. They were to dine and dress for the play at a friend's house. First, driving thither with their band-boxes, they departed on their first errand to make some purchases at Messrs. Jones, Spruggins, and Smith's, of Tottenham-court-road; after which, they were to go to Redmayne's in Bond-street; thence, to innumerable places that no one ever heard of. The young ladies beguiled the tediousness of the ride by eulogising Mr. Horatio Sparkins, scolding their mamma for taking them so far to save a shilling, and wondering whether they should ever reach their destination. At length, the vehicle stopped before a dirty-looking ticketed linen-draper's shop, with goods of all kinds, and labels of all sorts and sizes, in the window. There were dropsical figures of seven with a little three-farthings in the corner; "perfectly invisible to the naked eye;" three hundred and fifty thousand ladies' boas, *from* one shilling and a penny halfpenny; real French kid shoes, at two and ninepence per pair; green parasols, at an equally cheap rate; and "every description of goods," as the proprietors said—and they must know best—"fifty per cent. under cost price."

"Lor! ma, what a place you have brought us to!" said Miss Teresa; "what *would* Mr. Sparkins say if he could see us!"

"Ah! what, indeed!" said Miss Marianne, horrified at the idea.

"Pray be seated, ladies. What is the first article?" inquired the obsequious master of the ceremonies of the establishment, who, in his large white neckcloth and formal tie, looked like a bad "portrait of a gentleman" in the Somerset-house exhibition.

"I want to see some silks," answered Mrs. Malderton.

41

"Directly, ma'am.—Mr. Smith! Where *is* Mr. Smith?"

"Here, sir," cried a voice at the back of the shop.

"Pray make haste, Mr. Smith," said the M.C. "You never are to be found when you're wanted, sir."

Mr. Smith, thus enjoined to use all possible despatch, leaped over the counter with great agility, and placed himself before the newly-arrived customers. Mrs. Malderton uttered a faint scream; Miss Teresa, who had been stooping down to talk to her sister, raised her head, and beheld—Horatio Sparkins!

"We will draw a veil," as novel-writers say, over the scene that ensued. The mysterious, philosophical, romantic, meta-physical Sparkins—he who, to the interesting Teresa, seemed like the embodied idea of the young dukes and poetical exquisites in blue silk dressing-gowns, and ditto ditto slippers, of whom she had read and dreamed, but had never expected to behold, was suddenly converted into Mr. Samuel Smith, the assistant at a "cheap shop;" the junior partner in a slippery firm of some three weeks' existence. The dignified evanishment of the hero of Oak Lodge, on this unexpected recognition, could only be equalled by that of a furtive dog with a considerable kettle at his tail. All the hopes of the Maldertons were destined at once to melt away, like the lemon ices at a Company's dinner; Almack's was still to them as distant as the North Pole; and Miss Teresa had as much chance of a husband as Captain Ross had of the north-west passage.

Years have elapsed since the occurrence of this dreadful morning. The daisies have thrice bloomed on Camberwell-green; the sparrows have thrice repeated their vernal chirps in Camberwell-grove; but the Miss Maldertons are still un-mated. Miss Teresa's case is more desperate than ever; but Flamwell is yet in the zenith of his reputation; and the family have the same predilection for aristocratic personages, with an increased aversion to anything *low*.

CHAPTER VI

ONE winter's evening, towards the close of the year 1800, or within a year or two of that time, a young medical practitioner, recently established in business, was seated by a cheerful fire in his little parlour, listening to the wind which was beating the rain in pattering drops against the window, or rumbling dismally in the chimney. The night was wet and cold; he had been walking through mud and water the whole day, and was now comfortably reposing in his dressing-gown and slippers, more than half asleep and less than half awake, revolving a thousand matters in his wandering imagination. First, he thought how hard the wind was blowing, and how the cold, sharp rain would be at that moment beating in his face, if he were not comfortably housed at home. Then, his mind reverted to his annual Christmas visit to his native place and dearest friends; he thought how glad they would all be to see him, and how happy it would make Rose if he could only tell her that he had found a patient at last, and hoped to have more, and to come down again, in a few months' time, and marry her, and take her home to gladden his lonely fireside, and stimulate him to fresh exertions. Then, he began to wonder when his first patient would appear, or whether he was destined, by a special dispensation of Providence, never to have any patients at all; and then, he thought about Rose again, and dropped to sleep and dreamed about her, till the tones of her sweet merry voice sounded in his ears, and her soft tiny hand rested on his shoulder.

There *was* a hand upon his shoulder, but it was neither soft nor tiny; its owner being a corpulent round-headed boy, who, in consideration of the sum of one shilling per week and his food, was let out by the parish to carry medicine and messages. As there was no demand for the medicine, however, and no necessity for the messages, he usually occupied his unemployed hours—averaging fourteen a day—in abstracting peppermint drops, taking animal nourishment, and going to sleep.

"A lady, sir—a lady!" whispered the boy, rousing his master with a shake.

"What lady?" cried our friend, starting up, not quite certain that his dream was an illusion, and half expecting that it might be Rose herself.—"What lady? Where?"

"*There*, sir!" replied the boy, pointing to the glass door leading into the surgery, with an expression of alarm which the very unusual apparition of a customer might have tended to excite.

The surgeon looked towards the door, and started himself, for an instant, on beholding the appearance of his unlooked-for visitor.

It was a singularly tall woman, dressed in deep mourning, and standing so close to the door that her face almost touched the glass. The upper part of her figure was carefully muffled in a black shawl, as if for the purpose of concealment; and her face was shrouded by a thick black veil. She stood perfectly erect, her figure was drawn up to its full height, and though the surgeon *felt* that the eyes beneath the veil were fixed on him, she stood perfectly motionless, and evinced, by no gesture whatever, the slightest consciousness of his having turned towards her.

"Do you wish to consult me?" he inquired, with some hesitation, holding open the door. It opened inwards, and

44

therefore the action did not alter the position of the figure, which still remained motionless on the same spot.

She slightly inclined her head, in token of acquiescence.

"Pray walk in," said the surgeon.

The figure moved a step forward; and then, turning its head in the direction of the boy—to his infinite horror—appeared to hesitate.

"Leave the room, Tom," said the young man, addressing the boy, whose large round eyes had been extended to their utmost width during this brief interview. "Draw the curtain, and shut the door."

The boy drew a green curtain across the glass part of the door, retired into the surgery, closed the door after him, and immediately applied one of his large eyes to the keyhole on the other side.

The surgeon drew a chair to the fire, and motioned the visitor to a seat. The mysterious figure slowly moved towards it. As the blaze shone upon the black dress, the surgeon observed that the bottom of it was saturated with mud and rain.

"You are very wet," he said.

"I am," said the stranger, in a low deep voice.

"And you are ill?" added the surgeon, compassionately, for the tone was that of a person in pain.

"I am," was the reply—"very ill; not bodily, but mentally. It is not for myself, or on my own behalf," continued the stranger, "that I come to you. If I laboured under bodily disease, I should not be out, alone, at such an hour, or on such a night as this; and if I were afflicted with it, twenty-four hours hence, God knows how gladly I would lie down and pray to die. It is for another that I beseech your aid, sir. I may be mad to ask it for him—I think I am; but, night after night, through the long dreary hours of watching and weeping, the thought has been ever present to my mind; and though even *I* see the hopelessness of human assistance availing him, the bare thought of laying him in his grave without it makes my blood run cold!" And a shudder, such as the surgeon well knew art could not produce, trembled through the speaker's frame.

There was a desperate earnestness in this woman's manner, that went to the young man's heart. He was young in his profession, and had not yet witnessed enough of the miseries which are daily presented before the eyes of its members, to have grown comparatively callous to human suffering.

"If," he said, rising hastily, "the person of whom you speak, be in so hopeless a condition as you describe, not a moment is to be lost. I will go with you instantly. Why did you not obtain medical advice before?"

"Because it would have been useless before—because it is useless even now," replied the woman, clasping her hands passionately.

The surgeon gazed, for a moment, on the black veil, as if to ascertain the expression of the features beneath it; its thickness, however, rendered such a result impossible.

"You *are* ill," he said, gently, "although you do not know it. The fever which has enabled you to bear, without feeling it, the fatigue you have evidently undergone, is burning within you now. Put that to your lips," he continued, pouring out a glass of water—"compose yourself for a few moments, and then tell me, as calmly as you can, what the disease of the patient is, and how long he has been ill. When I know what it is necessary I should know, to render my visit serviceable to him, I am ready to accompany you."

The stranger lifted the glass of water to her mouth, without raising the veil; put it down again untasted; and burst into tears.

"I know," she said, sobbing aloud, "that what I say to you now, seems like the ravings of fever. I have been told so before, less kindly than by you. I am not a young woman; and they do say, that as life steals on towards its final close, the last short remnant, worthless as it may seem to all beside, is dearer to its possessor than all the years that have gone before, connected though they be with the recollection of old friends long since dead, and young ones—children perhaps— who have fallen off from, and forgotten one as completely as if they had died too. My natural term of life cannot be many years longer, and should be dear on that account; but I would lay it down without a sigh—with cheerfulness—with joy—if what I tell you now, were only false, or imaginary. To-morrow morning he of whom I speak will be, I *know*, though I would fain think otherwise, beyond the reach of human aid; and yet, to-night, though he is in deadly peril, you must not see, and could not serve, him."

" I am unwilling to increase your distress," said the surgeon, after a short pause, " by making any comment on what you have just said, or appearing desirous to investigate a subject you are so anxious to conceal; but there is an inconsistency in your statement which I cannot reconcile with probability. This person is dying to-night, and I cannot see him when my assistance might possibly avail ; you apprehend it will be useless to-morrow, and yet you would have me see him then ! If he be, indeed, as dear to you, as your words and manner would imply, why not try to save his life before delay and the progress of his disease render it impracticable ? "

" God help me ! " exclaimed the woman, weeping bitterly, " how can I hope strangers will believe what appears incredible, even to myself ? You will *not* see him then, sir ? " she added, rising suddenly.

" I did not say that I declined to see him," replied the surgeon ; " but I warn you, that if you persist in this extra-ordinary procrastination, and the individual dies, a fearful responsibility rests with you."

" The responsibility will rest heavily somewhere," replied the stranger bitterly. " Whatever responsibility rests with me, I am content to bear, and ready to answer."

" As I incur none," continued the surgeon, " by acceding to your request, I will see him in the morning, if you leave me the address. At what hour can he be seen ? "

" *Nine*," replied the stranger.

" You must excuse my pressing these inquiries," said the surgeon. " But is he in your charge now ? "

" He is not," was the rejoinder.

" Then, if I gave you instructions for his treatment through the night, you could not assist him ? "

The woman wept bitterly, as she replied, " I could not."

Finding that there was but little prospect of obtaining more information by prolonging the interview ; and anxious to spare the woman's feelings, which, subdued at first by a violent effort, were now irrepressible and most painful to witness ; the surgeon repeated his promise of calling in the morning at the appointed hour. His visitor, after giving him a direction to an obscure part of Walworth, left the house in the same mysterious manner in which she had entered it.

It will be readily believed ·that so extraordinary a visit produced a considerable impression on the mind of the young surgeon ; and that he speculated a great deal and to very little purpose on the possible circumstances of the case. In common with the generality of people, he had often heard and read of singular instances, in which a presentiment of death, at a particular day, or even minute, had been entertained and realised. At one moment he was inclined to think that the present might be such a case ; but, then, it occurred to him that all the anecdotes of the kind he had ever heard, were of persons who had been troubled with a foreboding of their own death. This woman, however, spoke of another person— a man ; and it was impossible to suppose that a mere dream or delusion of fancy would induce her to speak of his approaching dissolution with such terrible certainty as she had spoken. It could not be that the man was to be murdered in the morning, and that the woman, originally a consenting party, and bound to secrecy by an oath, had relented, and, though unable to prevent the commission of some outrage on the victim, had determined to prevent his death if possible, by the timely interposition of medical aid ? The idea of such things happening within two miles of the metropolis appeared too wild and preposterous to be entertained beyond the instant. Then, his original impression that the woman's intellects were disordered, recurred; and, as it was the only mode of solving the difficulty with any degree of satisfaction, he obstinately made up his mind to believe that she was mad. Certain misgivings upon this point, however, stole upon his thoughts at the time, and presented themselves again and again through the long dull course of a sleepless night; during which, in spite of all his efforts to the contrary, he was unable to banish the black veil from his disturbed imagination.

The back part of Walworth, at its greatest distance from town, is a straggling miserable place enough, even in these days; but, five-and-thirty years ago, the greater portion of it was little better than a dreary waste, inhabited by a few scattered people of questionable character, whose poverty prevented their living in any better neighbourhood, or whose pursuits and mode of life rendered its solitude desirable. Very many of the houses which have since sprung up on all sides, were not built until some years afterwards; and the great majority even of those which were sprinkled about, at irregular intervals, were of the rudest and most miserable description.

The appearance of the place through which he walked in the morning, was not calculated to raise the spirits of the young surgeon, or to dispel any feeling of anxiety or depression which the singular kind of visit he was about to make, had awakened. Striking off from the high road, his way lay across a marshy common, through irregular lanes, with here and there a ruinous and dismantled cottage fast falling to pieces with decay and neglect. A stunted tree, or pool of stagnant water, roused into a sluggish action by the heavy rain of the preceding night, skirted the path occasionally; and, now and then, a miserable patch of garden-ground, with a few old boards knocked together for a summer-house, and old palings imperfectly mended with stakes pilfered from the neighbouring hedges, bore testimony, at once to the poverty of the inhabitants, and the little scruple they entertained in appropriating the property of other people to their own use. Occasionally, a filthy-looking woman would make her appearance from the door of a dirty house, to empty the contents of some cooking utensil into the gutter in front, or to scream after a little slip-shod girl, who had contrived to stagger a few yards from the door under the weight of a sallow infant almost as big as herself; but, scarcely anything was stirring around: and so much of the prospect as could be faintly traced through the cold damp mist which hung heavily over it, presented a lonely and dreary appearance perfectly in keeping with the objects we have described.

After plodding wearily through the mud and mire; making many inquiries for the place to which he had been directed; and receiving as many contradictory and unsatisfactory replies in return; the young man at length arrived before the house which had been pointed out to him as the object of his destination. It was a small low building, one story above the ground, with even a more desolate and unpromising exterior than any he had yet passed. An old yellow curtain was closely drawn across the window up-stairs, and the parlour shutters were closed, but not fastened. The house was detached from any other, and, as it stood at an angle of a narrow lane, there was no other habitation in sight.

When we say that the surgeon hesitated, and walked a few paces beyond the house, before he could prevail upon himself to lift the knocker, we say nothing that need raise a smile upon the face of the boldest reader. The police of London were a very different body in that day; the isolated position of the suburbs, when the rage for building and the progress of improvement had not yet begun to connect them with the main body of the city and its environs, rendered many of them (and this in particular) a place of resort for the worst and most depraved characters. Even the streets in the gayest parts of London were imperfectly lighted, at that time; and such places as these, were left entirely to the mercy of the moon and stars. The chances of detecting desperate characters, or of tracing them to their haunts, were thus rendered very few, and their offences naturally increased in boldness, as the consciousness of comparative security became the more impressed upon them by daily experience. Added to these considerations, it must be remembered that the young man had spent some time in the public hospitals of the metropolis; and, although neither Burke nor Bishop had then gained a horrible notoriety, his own observation might have suggested to him how easily the atrocities to which the former has since given his name, might be committed. Be this as it may, whatever reflection made him hesitate, he *did* hesitate: but, being a young man of strong mind and great personal courage, it was only for an instant;—he stepped briskly back and knocked gently at the door.

A low whispering was audible, immediately afterwards, as if some person at the end of the passage were conversing stealthily with another on the landing above. It was succeeded by the noise of a pair of heavy boots upon the bare floor. The door-chain was softly unfastened; the door opened; and a tall, ill-favoured man, with black hair, and a face, as the surgeon often declared afterwards, as pale and haggard, as the countenance of any dead man he ever saw, presented himself.

" Walk in, sir," he said in a low tone.

The surgeon did so, and the man having secured the door again, by the chain, led the way to a small back parlour at the extremity of the passage.

" Am I in time?"

" Too soon!" replied the man. The surgeon turned hastily round, with a gesture of astonishment not unmixed with alarm, which he found it impossible to repress.

" If you'll step in here, sir," said the man, who had evidently noticed the action—" if you'll step in here, sir, you won't be detained five minutes, I assure you."

The surgeon at once walked into the room. The man closed the door, and left him alone.

It was a little cold room, with no other furniture than two deal chairs, and a table of the same material. A handful of fire, unguarded by any fender, was burning in the grate, which brought out the damp if it served no more comfortable purpose, for the unwholesome moisture was stealing down the walls, in long slug-like tracks. The window, which was broken and patched in many places, looked into a small enclosed piece of ground, almost covered with water. Not a sound was to be heard, either within the house, or without. The young surgeon sat down by the fireplace, to await the result of his first professional visit.

He had not remained in this position many minutes, when the noise of some approaching vehicle struck his ear. It stopped; the street-door was opened; a low talking succeeded, accompanied with a shuffling noise of footsteps, along the passage and on the stairs, as if two or three men were engaged in carrying some heavy body to the room above. The creaking of the stairs, a few seconds afterwards, announced that the new-comers having completed their task, whatever it was, were leaving the house. The door was again closed, and the former silence was restored.

Another five minutes had elapsed, and the surgeon had resolved to explore the house, in search of some one to whom he might make his errand known, when the room-door opened, and his last night's visitor, dressed in exactly the same manner, with the veil lowered as before, motioned him to advance. The singular height of her form, coupled with the circumstance of her not speaking, caused the idea to pass across his brain for an instant, that it might be a man disguised in woman's attire. The hysteric sobs which issued from beneath the veil, and the convulsive attitude of grief of the whole figure, however, at once exposed the absurdity of the suspicion; and he hastily followed.

The woman led the way up-stairs to the front room, and

paused at the door, to let him enter first. It was scantily furnished with an old deal box, a few chairs, and a tent bedstead, without hangings or cross-rails, which was covered with a patchwork counterpane. The dim light admitted through the curtain which he had noticed from the outside, rendered the objects in the room so indistinct, and communicated to all of them so uniform a hue, that he did not, at first, perceive the object on which his eye at once rested when the woman rushed frantically past him, and flung herself on her knees by the bedside.

Stretched upon the bed, closely enveloped in a linen wrapper, and covered with blankets, lay a human form, stiff and motionless. The head and face, which were those of a man, were uncovered, save by a bandage which passed over the head and under the chin. The eyes were closed. The left arm lay heavily across the bed, and the woman held the passive hand.

The surgeon gently pushed the woman aside, and took the hand in his.

"My God!" he exclaimed, letting it fall involuntarily— "the man is dead!"

The woman started to her feet and beat her hands together. "Oh! don't say so, sir," she exclaimed, with a burst of passion, amounting almost to frenzy. "Oh! don't say so, sir! I can't bear it! Men have been brought to life, before, when unskilful people have given them up for lost; and men have died, who might have been restored, if proper means had been resorted to. Don't let him lie here, sir, without one effort to save him! This very moment life may be passing away. Do try, sir,—do, for Heaven's sake!"—And while speaking, she hurriedly chafed, first the forehead, and then the breast, of the senseless form before her; and then, wildly beat the cold hands, which, when she ceased to hold them, fell listlessly and heavily back on the coverlet.

"It is of no use, my good woman," said the surgeon, soothingly, as he withdrew his hand from the man's breast. "Stay—undraw that curtain!"

" Why ? " said the woman, starting up.

" Undraw that curtain ! " repeated the surgeon in an agitated tone.

" *I* darkened the room on purpose," said the woman, throwing herself before him as he rose to undraw it.—" Oh ! sir, have pity on me ! If it can be of no use, and he is really dead, do not expose that form to other eyes than mine ! "

" This man died no natural or easy death," said the surgeon. " I *must* see the body ! " With a motion so sudden, that the woman hardly knew that he had slipped from beside her, he tore open the curtain, admitted the full light of day, and returned to the bedside.

" There has been violence here," he said, pointing towards the body, and gazing intently on the face, from which the black veil was now, for the first time, removed. In the excitement of a minute before, the female had thrown off the bonnet and veil, and now stood with her eyes fixed upon him. Her features were those of a woman about fifty, who had once been handsome. Sorrow and weeping had left traces upon them which not time itself would ever have produced without their aid ; her face was deadly pale ; and there was a nervous contortion of the lip, and an unnatural fire in her eye, which showed too plainly that her bodily and mental powers had nearly sunk, beneath an accumulation of misery.

" There has been violence here," said the surgeon, preserving his searching glance.

" There has ! " replied the woman.

" This man has been murdered."

" That I call God to witness he has," said the woman, passionately ; " pitilessly, inhumanly murdered ! "

" By whom ? " said the surgeon, seizing the woman by the arm.

" Look at the butchers' marks, and then ask me ! " she replied.

The surgeon turned his face towards the bed, and bent over the body which now lay full in the light of the window. The throat was swollen, and a livid mark encircled it. The truth flashed suddenly upon him.

A GRATIFYING REMINISCENCE

"This is one of the men who were hanged this morning!" he exclaimed, turning away with a shudder.

"It is," replied the woman, with a cold, unmeaning stare.

"Who was he?" inquired the surgeon.

"*My son,*" rejoined the woman; and fell senseless at his feet.

It was true. A companion, equally guilty with himself, had been acquitted for want of evidence; and this man had been left for death, and executed. To recount the circumstances of the case, at this distant period, must be unnecessary, and might give pain to some persons still alive. The history was an every-day one. The mother was a widow without friends or money, and had denied herself necessaries to bestow them on her orphan boy. That boy, unmindful of her prayers, and forgetful of the sufferings she had endured for him—incessant anxiety of mind, and voluntary starvation of body—had plunged into a career of dissipation and crime. And this was the result; his own death by the hangman's hands, and his mother's shame, and incurable insanity.

For many years after this occurrence, and when profitable and arduous avocations would have led many men to forget that such a miserable being existed, the young surgeon was a daily visitor at the side of the harmless mad woman; not only soothing her by his presence and kindness, but alleviating the rigour of her condition by pecuniary donations for her comfort and support, bestowed with no sparing hand. In the transient gleam of recollection and consciousness which preceded her death, a prayer for his welfare and protection, as fervent as mortal ever breathed, rose from the lips of this poor friendless creature. That prayer flew to Heaven, and was heard. The blessings he was instrumental in conferring, have been repaid to him a thousand-fold; but, amid all the honours of rank and station which have since been heaped upon him, and which he has so well earned, he can have no reminiscence more gratifying to his heart than that connected with The Black Veil.

CHAPTER VII

Mr. Percy Noakes was a law student, inhabiting a set of chambers on the fourth floor, in one of those houses in Gray's-inn-square which command an extensive view of the gardens, and their usual adjuncts—flaunting nursery-maids, and town-made children, with parenthetical legs. Mr. Percy Noakes was what is generally termed—"a devilish good fellow." He had a large circle of acquaintance, and seldom dined at his own expense. He used to talk politics to papas, flatter the vanity of mammas, do the amiable to their daughters, make pleasure engagements with their sons, and romp with the younger branches. Like those paragons of perfection, advertising footmen out of place, he was always "willing to make himself generally useful." If any old lady, whose son was in India, gave a ball, Mr. Percy Noakes was master of the ceremonies; if any young lady made a stolen match, Mr. Percy Noakes gave her away; if a juvenile wife presented her husband with a blooming cherub, Mr. Percy Noakes was either godfather, or deputy-godfather; and if any member of a friend's family died, Mr. Percy Noakes was invariably to be seen in the second mourning coach, with a white hand-kerchief to his eyes, sobbing—to use his own appropriate and expressive description—"like winkin'!"

It may readily be imagined that these numerous avocations were rather calculated to interfere with Mr. Percy Noakes's professional studies. Mr. Percy Noakes was perfectly aware of the fact, and had, therefore, after mature reflection, made up his mind not to study at all—a laudable determination, to which he adhered in the most praiseworthy manner. His sitting-room presented a strange chaos of dress-gloves, boxing-gloves, caricatures, albums, invitation-cards, foils, cricket-bats, cardboard drawings, paste, gum, and fifty other miscellaneous articles, heaped together in the strangest confusion. He was always making something for somebody, or planning some party of pleasure, which was his great *forte*. He invariably spoke with astonishing rapidity; was smart, spoffish, and eight-and-twenty.

"Splendid idea, 'pon my life!" soliloquised Mr. Percy Noakes, over his morning's coffee, as his mind reverted to a suggestion which had been thrown out on the previous night, by a lady at whose house he had spent the evening. "Glorious idea!—Mrs. Stubbs."

"Yes, sir," replied a dirty old woman with an inflamed countenance, emerging from the bedroom, with a barrel of dirt and cinders.—This was the laundress. "Did you call, sir?"

"Oh! Mrs. Stubbs, I'm going out. If that tailor should call again, you'd better say—you'd better say I'm out of town, and shan't be back for a fortnight; and if that boot-maker should come, tell him I've lost his address, or I'd have sent him that little amount. Mind he writes it down; and if Mr. Hardy should call—you know Mr. Hardy?"

"The funny gentleman, sir?"

"Ah! the funny gentleman. If Mr. Hardy should call, say I've gone to Mrs. Taunton's about that water-party."

"Yes, sir."

"And if any fellow calls, and says he's come about a steamer, tell him to be here at five o'clock this afternoon, Mrs. Stubbs."

"Very well, sir."

Mr. Percy Noakes brushed his hat, whisked the crumbs off

his inexplicables with a silk handkerchief, gave the ends of his hair a persuasive roll round his forefinger, and sallied forth for Mrs. Taunton's domicile in Great Marlborough-street, where she and her daughters occupied the upper part of a house. She was a good-looking widow of fifty, with the form of a giantess and the mind of a child. The pursuit of pleasure, and some means of killing time, were the sole end of her existence. She doted on her daughters, who were as frivolous as herself.

A general exclamation of satisfaction hailed the arrival of Mr. Percy Noakes, who went through the ordinary salutations, and threw himself into an easy chair near the ladies' work-table, with the ease of a regularly established friend of the family. Mrs. Taunton was busily engaged in planting immense bright bows on every part of a smart cap on which it was possible to stick one; Miss Emily Taunton was making a watch-guard; Miss Sophia was at the piano, practising a new song—poetry by the young officer, or the police-officer, or the custom-house officer, or some other interesting amateur.

" You good creature ! " said Mrs. Taunton, addressing the gallant Percy. " You really are a good soul ! You've come about the water-party, I know."

" I should rather suspect I had," replied Mr. Noakes, triumphantly. " Now, come here, girls, and I'll tell you all about it." Miss Emily and Miss Sophia advanced to the table.

" Now," continued Mr. Percy Noakes, " it seems to me that the best way will be, to have a committee of ten, to make all the arrangements, and manage the whole set-out. Then, I propose that the expenses shall be paid by these ten fellows jointly."

" Excellent, indeed ! " said Mrs. Taunton, who highly approved of this part of the arrangements.

" Then, my plan is, that each of these ten fellows shall have the power of asking five people. There must be a meeting of the committee, at my chambers, to make all the arrangements, and these people shall be then named; every member of the committee shall have the power of black-balling any one who is proposed; and one black ball shall exclude that person. This will ensure our having a pleasant party, you know."

"What a manager you are!" interrupted Mrs. Taunton again.

"Charming!" said the lovely Emily.

"I never did!" ejaculated Sophia.

"Yes, I think it'll do," replied Mr. Percy Noakes, who was now quite in his element. "I think it'll do. Then you know we shall go down to the Nore, and back, and have a regular capital cold dinner laid out in the cabin before we start, so that everything may be ready without any confusion; and we shall have the lunch laid out, on deck, in those little tea-garden-looking concerns by the paddle-boxes—I don't know what you call 'em. Then, we shall hire a steamer expressly for our party, and a band, and have the deck chalked, and we shall be able to dance quadrilles all day; and then, whoever we know that's musical, you know, why they'll make themselves useful and agreeable; and—and— upon the whole, I really hope we shall have a glorious day, you know!"

The announcement of these arrangements was received with the utmost enthusiasm. Mrs. Taunton, Emily, and Sophia, were loud in their praises.

"Well, but tell me, Percy," said Mrs. Taunton, "who are the ten gentlemen to be?"

"Oh! I know plenty of fellows who'll be delighted with the scheme," replied Mr. Percy Noakes; "of course we shall have—— "

"Mr. Hardy!" interrupted the servant, announcing a visitor. Miss Sophia and Miss Emily hastily assumed the most interesting attitudes that could be adopted on so short a notice.

"How are you?" said a stout gentleman of about forty, pausing at the door in the attitude of an awkward harlequin. This was Mr. Hardy, whom we have before described, on the authority of Mrs. Stubbs, as "the funny gentleman." He was an Astley-Cooperish Joe Miller—a practical joker, immensely popular with married ladies, and a general favourite with young men. He was always engaged in some pleasure excursion or other, and delighted in getting somebody into a scrape on such occasions. He could sing comic songs, imitate hackney-coachmen and fowls, play airs on his chin, and execute concertos on the Jews'-harp. He always eat and drank most immoderately, and was the bosom friend of Mr. Percy Noakes. He had a red face, a somewhat husky voice, and a tremendous laugh.

"How *are* you?" said this worthy, laughing, as if it were the finest joke in the world to make a morning call, and shaking hands with the ladies with as much vehemence as if their arms had been so many pump-handles.

"You're just the very man I wanted," said Mr. Percy Noakes, who proceeded to explain the cause of his being in requisition.

"Ha! ha! ha!" shouted Hardy, after hearing the statement, and receiving a detailed account of the proposed excursion. "Oh, capital! glorious! What a day it will be! what fun!—But, I say, when are you going to begin making the arrangements?"

"No time like the present—at once, if you please."

"Oh, charming!" cried the ladies. "Pray, do!"

Writing materials were laid before Mr. Percy Noakes, and the names of the different members of the committee were agreed on, after as much discussion between him and Mr. Hardy as if the fate of nations had depended on their appointment. It was then agreed that a meeting should take place at Mr. Percy Noakes's chambers on the ensuing Wednesday evening at eight o'clock, and the visitors departed.

Wednesday evening arrived; eight o'clock came, and eight

members of the committee were punctual in their attendance. Mr. Loggins, the solicitor, of Boswell-court, sent an excuse, and Mr. Samuel Briggs, the ditto of Furnival's Inn, sent his brother: much to his (the brother's) satisfaction, and greatly to the discomfiture of Mr. Percy Noakes. Between the Briggses and the Tauntons there existed a degree of implacable hatred, quite unprecedented. The animosity between the Montagues and Capulets, was nothing to that which prevailed between these two illustrious houses. Mrs. Briggs was a widow, with three daughters and two sons; Mr. Samuel, the eldest, was an attorney, and Mr. Alexander, the youngest, was under articles to his brother. They resided in Portland-street, Oxford-street, and moved in the same orbit as the Tauntons—hence their mutual dislike. If the Miss Briggses appeared in smart bonnets, the Miss Tauntons eclipsed them with smarter. If Mrs. Taunton appeared in a cap of all the hues of the rainbow, Mrs. Briggs forthwith mounted a toque, with all the patterns of the kaleidoscope. If Miss Sophia Taunton learnt a new song, two of the Miss Briggses came out with a new duet. The Tauntons had once gained a temporary triumph with the assistance of a harp, but the Briggses brought three guitars into the field, and effectually routed the enemy. There was no end to the rivalry between them.

Now, as Mr. Samuel Briggs was a mere machine, a sort of self-acting legal walking-stick; and as the party was known to have originated, however remotely, with Mrs. Taunton, the female branches of the Briggs family had arranged that Mr. Alexander should attend, instead of his brother; and as the said Mr. Alexander was deservedly celebrated for possessing all the pertinacity of a bankruptcy-court attorney, combined with the obstinacy of that useful animal which browses on the thistle, he required but little tuition. He was especially enjoined to make himself as disagreeable as possible; and, above all, to black-ball the Tauntons at every hazard.

The proceedings of the evening were opened by Mr. Percy Noakes. After successfully urging on the gentlemen present the propriety of their mixing some brandy-and-water, he briefly stated the object of the meeting, and concluded by observing that the first step must be the selection of a chairman, necessarily possessing some arbitrary—he trusted not unconstitutional—powers, to whom the personal direction of the whole of the arrangements (subject to the approval of the committee) should be confided. A pale young gentleman, in a green stock and spectacles of the same, a member of the honourable society of the Inner Temple, immediately rose for the purpose of proposing Mr. Percy Noakes. He had known him long, and this he would say, that a more honourable, a more excellent, or a better-hearted fellow, never existed.—(Hear, hear!) The young gentleman, who was a member of a debating society, took this opportunity of entering into an examination of the state of the English law, from the days of William the Conqueror down to the present period; he briefly adverted to the code established by the ancient Druids; slightly glanced at the principles laid down by the Athenian law-givers; and concluded with a most glowing eulogium on pic-nics and constitutional rights.

Mr. Alexander Briggs opposed the motion. He had the highest esteem for Mr. Percy Noakes as an individual, but he did consider that he ought not to be intrusted with these immense powers—(oh, oh!)—He believed that in the proposed capacity Mr. Percy Noakes would not act fairly, impartially, or honourably; but he begged it to be distinctly understood, that he said this, without the slightest personal disrespect. Mr. Hardy defended his honourable friend, in a voice rendered partially unintelligible by emotion and brandy-and-water. The proposition was put to the vote, and there appearing to be only one dissentient voice, Mr. Percy Noakes was declared duly elected, and took the chair accordingly.

The business of the meeting now proceeded with rapidity.

The chairman delivered in his estimate of the probable expense of the excursion, and every one present subscribed his portion thereof. The question was put that " The Endeavour " be hired for the occasion ; Mr. Alexander Briggs moved as an amendment, that the word " Fly " be substituted for the word " Endeavour ; " but after some debate consented to withdraw his opposition. The important ceremony of balloting then commenced. A tea-caddy was placed on a table in a dark corner of the apartment, and every one was provided with two backgammon men, one black and one white.

The chairman with great solemnity then read the following list of the guests whom he proposed to introduce :—Mrs. Taunton and two daughters, Mr. Wizzle, Mr. Simson. The names were respectively balloted for, and Mrs. Taunton and her daughters were declared to be black-balled. Mr. Percy Noakes and Mr. Hardy exchanged glances.

" Is your list prepared, Mr. Briggs ? " inquired the chairman.

" It is," replied Alexander, delivering in the following :— " Mrs. Briggs and three daughters, Mr. Samuel Briggs. The previous ceremony was repeated, and Mrs. Briggs and three daughters were declared to be black-balled. Mr. Alexander Briggs looked rather foolish, and the remainder of the company appeared somewhat overawed by the mysterious nature of the proceedings.

The balloting proceeded ; but, one little circumstance which Mr. Percy Noakes had not originally foreseen, prevented the system from working quite as well as he had anticipated. Everybody was black-balled. Mr. Alexander Briggs, by way of retaliation, exercised his power of exclusion in every instance, and the result was, that after three hours had been consumed in hard balloting, the names of only three gentlemen were found to have been agreed to. In this dilemma what was to be done ? either the whole plan must fall to the ground, or a compromise must be effected. The latter alternative was preferable; and Mr. Percy Noakes therefore proposed that the form of balloting should be dispensed with, and that every gentleman should merely be required to state whom he intended to bring. The proposal was acceded to; the Tauntons and the Briggses were reinstated; and the party was formed.

The next Wednesday was fixed for the eventful day, and it was unanimously resolved that every member of the committee should wear a piece of blue sarsenet ribbon round his left arm. It appeared from the statement of Mr. Percy Noakes, that the boat belonged to the General Steam Navigation Company, and was then lying off the Custom-house; and, as he proposed that the dinner and wines should be provided by an eminent city purveyor, it was arranged that Mr. Percy Noakes should be on board by seven o'clock to superintend the arrangements, and that the remaining members of the committee, together with the company generally, should be expected to join her by nine o'clock. More brandy-and-water was despatched; several speeches were made by the different law students present; thanks were voted to the chairman; and the meeting separated.

The weather had been beautiful up to this period, and beautiful it continued to be. Sunday passed over, and Mr. Percy Noakes became unusually fidgety—rushing, constantly, to and from the Steam Packet Wharf, to the astonishment of the clerks, and the great emolument of the Holborn cabmen. Tuesday arrived, and the anxiety of Mr. Percy Noakes knew no bounds. He was every instant running to the window, to look out for clouds; and Mr. Hardy astonished the whole square by practising a new comic song for the occasion, in the chairman's chambers.

Uneasy were the slumbers of Mr. Percy Noakes that night; he tossed and tumbled about, and had confused dreams of steamers starting off, and gigantic clocks with the hands pointing to a quarter-past nine, and the ugly face of Mr. Alexander Briggs looking over the boat's side, and grinning, as if in derision of his fruitless attempts to move. He made a violent effort to get on board, and awoke. The bright sun was shining cheerfully into the bedroom, and Mr. Percy Noakes started up for his watch, in the dreadful expectation of finding his worst dreams realised.

It was just five o'clock. He calculated the time—he should be a good half-hour dressing himself; and as it was a lovely morning, and the tide would be then running down, he would walk leisurely to Strand-lane, and have a boat to the Custom-house.

He dressed himself, took a hasty apology for a breakfast, and sallied forth. The streets looked as lonely and deserted as if they had been crowded, overnight, for the last time. Here and there, an early apprentice, with quenched-looking sleepy eyes, was taking down the shutters of a shop; and a policeman or milkwoman might occasionally be seen pacing slowly along; but the servants had not yet begun to clean the doors, or light the kitchen fires, and London looked the picture of desolation. At the corner of a by-street, near Temple-bar, was stationed a "street-breakfast." The coffee was boiling over a charcoal fire, and large slices of bread and butter were piled one upon the other, like deals in a timber-yard. The company were seated on a form, which, with a view both to security and comfort, was placed against a neighbouring wall. Two young men, whose uproarious mirth and disordered dress bespoke the conviviality of the preceding evening, were treating three "ladies" and an Irish labourer. A little sweep was standing at a short distance, casting a longing eye at the tempting delicacies; and a policeman was watching the group from the opposite side of the street. The wan looks and gaudy finery of the thinly-clad women contrasted as strangely with the gay sunlight, as did their forced merriment with the boisterous hilarity of the two young men, who, now and then, varied their amusements by "bonneting" the proprietor of this itinerant coffee-house.

Mr. Percy Noakes walked briskly by, and when he turned down Strand-lane, and caught a glimpse of the glistening water, he thought he had never felt so important or so happy in his life.

"Boat, sir?" cried one of the three watermen who were mopping out their boats, and all whistling. "Boat, sir?"

"No," replied Mr. Percy Noakes, rather sharply; for the inquiry was not made in a manner at all suitable to his dignity.

"Would you prefer a wessel, sir?" inquired another, to the infinite delight of the "Jack-in-the-water."

Mr. Percy Noakes replied with a look of supreme contempt.

"Did you want to be put on board a steamer, sir?" inquired an old fireman-waterman, very confidentially. He was dressed in a faded red suit, just the colour of the cover of a very old Court-guide.

"Yes, make haste—the Endeavour—off the Custom-house."

"Endeavour!" cried the man who had convulsed the "Jack" before. "Vy, I see the Endeavour go up half an hour ago."

"So did I," said another; "and I should think she'd gone down by this time, for she's a precious sight too full of ladies and gen'lemen."

Mr. Percy Noakes affected to disregard these representations, and stepped into the boat, which the old man, by dint of scrambling, and shoving, and grating, had brought up to the causeway. "Shove her off!" cried Mr. Percy Noakes, and away the boat glided down the river; Mr. Percy Noakes seated on the recently mopped seat, and the watermen at the stairs offering to bet him any reasonable sum that he'd never reach the "Custum-us."

"Here she is, by Jove!" said the delighted Percy, as they ran alongside the Endeavour.

"Hold hard!" cried the steward over the side, and Mr. Percy Noakes jumped on board.

"Hope you will find everything as you wished, sir. She looks uncommon well this morning."

"She does, indeed," replied the manager, in a state of ecstasy which it is impossible to describe. The deck was scrubbed, and the seats were scrubbed, and there was a bench for the band, and a place for dancing, and a pile of camp-stools, and an awning; and then, Mr. Percy Noakes bustled down below, and there were the pastrycook's men, and the steward's wife, laying out the dinner on two tables the whole length of the cabin; and then Mr. Percy Noakes took off his coat and rushed backwards and forwards, doing nothing, but quite convinced he was assisting everybody; and the steward's wife laughed till she cried, and Mr. Percy Noakes panted with the violence of his exertions. And then the bell at London-bridge wharf rang; and a Margate boat was just starting; and a Gravesend boat was just starting, and people shouted, and porters ran down the steps with luggage that would crush any men but porters; and sloping boards, with bits of wood nailed on them, were placed between the outside boat and the inside boat; and the passengers ran along them, and looked like so many fowls coming out of an area; and then, the bell ceased, and the boards were taken away, and the boats started, and the whole scene was one of the most delightful bustle and confusion.

The time wore on; half-past eight o'clock arrived; the pastrycook's men went ashore; the dinner was completely laid out; and Mr. Percy Noakes locked the principal cabin, and put the key in his pocket, in order that it might be suddenly disclosed, in all its magnificence, to the eyes of the astonished company. The band came on board, and so did the wine.

Ten minutes to nine, and the committee embarked in a body. There was Mr. Hardy, in a blue jacket and waistcoat, white trousers, silk stockings, and pumps—in full aquatic costume, with a straw hat on his head, and an immense telescope under his arm; and there was the young gentleman with the green spectacles, in nankeen inexplicables, with a ditto waistcoat and bright buttons, like the pictures of Paul —not the saint, but he of Virginia notoriety. The remainder of the committee, dressed in white hats, light jackets, waistcoats, and trousers, looked something between waiters and West India planters.

Nine o'clock struck, and the company arrived in shoals. Mr. Samuel Briggs, Mrs. Briggs, and the Misses Briggs, made their appearance in a smart private wherry. The three guitars, in their respective dark green cases, were carefully stowed away in the bottom of the boat, accompanied by two immense portfolios of music, which it would take at least a week's incessant playing to get through. The Tauntons arrived at the same moment with more music, and a lion—a gentleman with a bass voice and an incipient red moustache. The colours of the Taunton party were pink; those of the Briggses a light blue. The Tauntons had artificial flowers in their bonnets; here the Briggses gained a decided advantage—they wore feathers.

"How d'ye do, dear?" said the Misses Briggs to the Misses Taunton. (The word "dear" among girls is frequently synonymous with "wretch.")

"Quite well, thank you, dear," replied the Misses Taunton to the Misses Briggs; and then, there was such a kissing, and congratulating, and shaking of hands, as might have induced one to suppose that the two families were the best friends in the world, instead of each wishing the other overboard, as they most sincerely did.

Mr. Percy Noakes received the visitors, and bowed to the strange gentleman, as if he should like to know who he was. This was just what Mrs. Taunton wanted. Here was an opportunity to astonish the Briggses.

"Oh! I beg your pardon," said the general of the Taunton party, with a careless air.—"Captain Helves—Mr. Percy Noakes—Mrs. Briggs—Captain Helves."

Mr. Percy Noakes bowed very low; the gallant captain did

the same with all due ferocity, and the Briggses were clearly overcome.

"Our friend, Mr. Wizzle, being unfortunately prevented from coming," resumed Mrs. Taunton, "I did myself the pleasure of bringing the captain, whose musical talents I knew would be a great acquisition."

"In the name of the committee I have to thank you for doing so, and to offer you welcome, sir," replied Percy. (Here the scraping was renewed.) "But pray be seated—won't you walk aft ? Captain, will you conduct Miss Taunton ?—Miss Briggs, will you allow me ? "

"Where could they have picked up that military man ? " inquired Mrs. Briggs of Miss Kate Briggs, as they followed the little party.

"I can't imagine," replied Miss Kate, bursting with vexation ; for the very fierce air with which the gallant captain regarded the company, had impressed her with a high sense of his importance.

Boat after boat came alongside, and guest after guest arrived. The invites had been excellently arranged : Mr. Percy Noakes having considered it as important that the number of young men should exactly tally with that of the young ladies, as that the quantity of knives on board should be in precise proportion to the forks.

"Now, is every one on board ? " inquired Mr. Percy Noakes. The committee (who, with their bits of blue ribbon, looked as if they were all going to be bled) bustled about to ascertain the fact, and reported that they might safely start.

"Go on ! " cried the master of the boat from the top of one of the paddle-boxes.

"Go on ! " echoed the boy, who was stationed over the hatchway to pass the directions down to the engineer ; and away went the vessel with that agreeable noise which is peculiar to steamers, and which is composed of a mixture of creaking, gushing, clanging, and snorting.

"Hoi—oi—-oi—oi—oi—oi—o—i—i—i!" shouted half-a-dozen voices from a boat, a quarter of a mile astern.

"Ease her!" cried the captain: "do these people belong to us, sir?"

"Noakes," exclaimed Hardy, who had been looking at every object, far and near, through the large telescope, "it's the Fleetwoods and the Wakefields—and two children with them, by Jove!"

"What a shame to bring children!" said everybody; "how very inconsiderate!"

"I say, it would be a good joke to pretend not to see 'em, wouldn't it?" suggested Hardy, to the immense delight of the company generally. A council of war was hastily held, and it was resolved that the new-comers should be taken on board, on Mr. Hardy solemnly pledging himself to tease the children during the whole of the day.

"Stop her!" cried the captain.

"Stop her!" repeated the boy; whizz went the steam, and all the young ladies, as in duty bound, screamed in concert. They were only appeased by the assurance of the martial Helves, that the escape of steam consequent on stopping a vessel was seldom attended with any great loss of human life.

Two men ran to the side; and after some shouting, and swearing, and angling for the wherry with a boat-hook, Mr. Fleetwood, and Mrs. Fleetwood, and Master Fleetwood, and Mr. Wakefield, and Mrs. Wakefield, and Miss Wakefield, were safely deposited on the deck. The girl was about six years old, the boy about four; the former was dressed in a white frock with a pink sash and dog's-eared-looking little spencer: a straw bonnet and green veil, six inches by three and a half; the latter, was attired for the occasion in a nankeen frock, between the bottom of which, and the top of his plaid socks, a considerable portion of two small mottled legs was discernible. He had a light blue cap with a gold band and tassel on his head, and a damp piece of gingerbread in his hand, with which he had slightly embossed his countenance.

The boat once more started off; the band played "Off she goes:" the major part of the company conversed cheerfully in groups; and the old gentlemen walked up and down the deck in pairs, as perseveringly and gravely as if they were doing a match against time for an immense stake. They ran briskly down the Pool; the gentlemen pointed out the Docks, the Thames Police-office, and other elegant public edifices; and the young ladies exhibited a proper display of horror at the appearance of the coal-whippers and ballast-heavers. Mr. Hardy told stories to the married ladies, at which they laughed very much in their pocket-handkerchiefs, and hit him on the knuckles with their fans, declaring him to be "a naughty man—a shocking creature"—and so forth; and Captain Helves gave slight descriptions of battles and duels, with a most bloodthirsty air, which made him the admiration of the women, and the envy of the men. Quadrilling commenced; Captain Helves danced one set with Miss Emily Taunton, and another set with Miss Sophia Taunton. Mrs. Taunton was in ecstasies. The victory appeared to be complete; but alas! the inconstancy of man! Having performed this necessary duty, he attached himself solely to Miss Julia Briggs, with whom he danced no less than three sets consecutively, and from whose side he evinced no intention of stirring for the remainder of the day.

Mr. Hardy, having played one or two very brilliant fantasias on the Jews'-harp, and having frequently repeated the exquisitely amusing joke of slily chalking a large cross on the back of some member of the committee, Mr. Percy Noakes expressed his hope that some of their musical friends would oblige the company by a display of their abilities.

"Perhaps," he said in a very insinuating manner, "Captain Helves will oblige us?" Mrs. Taunton's countenance lighted up, for the captain only sang duets, and couldn't sing them with anybody but one of her daughters.

"Really," said that warlike individual, "I should be very happy, but——"

"Oh! pray do," cried all the young ladies.

"Miss Emily, have you any objection to join in a duet?"

"Oh! not the slightest," returned the young lady, in a tone which clearly showed she had the greatest possible objection.

"Shall I accompany you, dear?" inquired one of the Miss Briggses, with the bland intention of spoiling the effect.

"Very much obliged to you, Miss Briggs," sharply retorted Mrs. Taunton, who saw through the manœuvre; "my daughters always sing without accompaniments."

"And without voices," tittered Mrs. Briggs, in a low tone.

"Perhaps," said Mrs. Taunton, reddening, for she guessed the tenor of the observation, though she had not heard it clearly—"Perhaps it would be as well for some people, if their voices were not quite so audible as they are to other people."

"And, perhaps, if gentlemen who are kidnapped to pay attention to some persons' daughters, had not sufficient discernment to pay attention to other persons' daughters," returned Mrs. Briggs, "some persons would not be so ready to display that ill-temper which, thank God, distinguishes them from other persons."

"Persons!" ejaculated Mrs. Taunton.

"Persons," replied Mrs. Briggs.

"Insolence!"

"Creature!"

"Hush! hush!" interrupted Mr. Percy Noakes, who was one of the very few by whom this dialogue had been over-heard. "Hush!—pray, silence for the duet."

After a great deal of preparatory crowing and humming, the captain began the following duet from the opera of "Paul and Virginia," in that grunting tone in which a man gets down, Heaven knows where, without the remotest chance of ever getting up again. This, in private circles, is frequently designated "a bass voice."

> " See (sung the captain) from o—ce—an ri—sing
> Bright flames the or—b of d—ay.
> From yon gro—ove, the varied so—ongs— "

Here, the singer was interrupted by varied cries of the most dreadful description, proceeding from some grove in the immediate vicinity of the starboard paddle-box.

" My child !" screamed Mrs. Fleetwood. "My child ! it is his voice—I know it."

Mr. Fleetwood, accompanied by several gentlemen, here rushed to the quarter from whence the noise proceeded, and an exclamation of horror burst from the company ; the general impression being, that the little innocent had either got his head in the water, or his legs in the machinery.

" What is the matter ? " shouted the agonised father, as he returned with the child in his arms.

" Oh ! oh ! oh ! " screamed the small sufferer again.

" What is the matter, dear ? " inquired the father once more—hastily stripping off the nankeen frock, for the purpose of ascertaining whether the child had one bone which was not smashed to pieces.

" Oh ! oh !—I'm so frightened ! "

" What at, dear ?—what at ? " said the mother, soothing the sweet infant.

" Oh ! he's been making such dreadful faces at me," cried the boy, relapsing into convulsions at the bare recollection.

" He !—who ? " cried everybody, crowding round him.

" Oh !—him ! " replied the child, pointing at Hardy, who affected to be the most concerned of the whole group.

The real state of the case at once flashed upon the minds of all present, with the exception of the Fleetwoods and the Wakefields. The facetious Hardy, in fulfilment of his promise, had watched the child to a remote part of the vessel, and, suddenly appearing before him with the most awful contortions of visage, had produced his paroxysm of terror. Of course, he now observed that it was hardly necessary for him to deny the accusation; and the unfortunate little victim was accordingly led below, after receiving sundry thumps on the head from both his parents, for having the wickedness to tell a story.

This little interruption having been adjusted, the captain resumed, and Miss Emily chimed in, in due course. The duet was loudly applauded, and, certainly, the perfect independence of the parties deserved great commendation. Miss Emily sung her part, without the slightest reference to the captain; and the captain sang so loud, that he had not the slightest idea what was being done by his partner. After having gone through the last few eighteen or nineteen bars by himself, therefore, he acknowledged the plaudits of the circle with that air of self-denial which men usually assume when they think they have done something to astonish the company.

"Now," said Mr. Percy Noakes, who had just ascended from the fore-cabin, where he had been busily engaged in decanting the wine, "if the Misses Briggs will oblige us with something before dinner, I am sure we shall be very much delighted."

One of those hums of admiration followed the suggestion, which one frequently hears in society, when nobody has the most distant notion what he is expressing his approval of. The three Misses Briggs looked modestly at their mamma, and the mamma looked approvingly at her daughters, and Mrs. Taunton looked scornfully at all of them. The Misses Briggs asked for their guitars, and several gentlemen seriously damaged the cases in their anxiety to present them. Then, there was a very interesting production of three little keys for the aforesaid cases, and a melodramatic expression of horror at finding a string broken; and a vast deal of screwing and tightening, and winding, and tuning, during which Mrs. Briggs expatiated to those near her on the immense difficulty of playing a guitar, and hinted at the wondrous proficiency of her daughters in that mystic art. Mrs. Taunton whispered to a neighbour that it was "quite sickening!" and the Misses Taunton looked as if they knew how to play, but disdained to do it.

At length, the Misses Briggs began in real earnest. It was a new Spanish composition, for three voices and three guitars. The effect was electrical. All eyes were turned upon the captain, who was reported to have once passed through Spain with his regiment, and who must be well acquainted with the national music. He was in raptures. This was sufficient; the trio was encored; the applause was universal; and never had the Tauntons suffered such a complete defeat.

"Bravo! bravo!" ejaculated the captain;—"bravo!"

"Pretty! isn't it, sir?" inquired Mr. Samuel Briggs, with the air of a self-satisfied showman. By-the-bye, these were the first words he had been heard to utter since he left Boswell-court the evening before.

"De—lightful!" returned the captain, with a flourish, and a military cough;—"de—lightful!"

"Sweet instrument!" said an old gentleman with a bald head, who had been trying all the morning to look through a telescope, inside the glass of which Mr. Hardy had fixed a large black wafer.

"Did you ever hear a Portuguese tambourine?" inquired that jocular individual.

"Did *you* ever hear a tom-tom, sir?" sternly inquired the captain, who lost no opportunity of showing off his travels, real or pretended.

"A what?" asked Hardy, rather taken aback.

"A tom-tom."

"Never!"

"Nor a gum-gum?"

"Never!"

"What *is* a gum-gum?" eagerly inquired several young ladies.

"When I was in the East Indies," replied the captain—(here was a discovery—he had been in the East Indies !)—"when I was in the East Indies, I was once stopping a few thousand miles up the country, on a visit at the house of a very particular friend of mine, Ram Chowdar Doss Azuph Al Bowlar—a devilish pleasant fellow. As we were enjoying our hookahs, one evening, in the cool verandah in front of his villa, we were rather surprised by the sudden appearance of thirty-four of his Kit-ma-gars (for he had rather a large establishment there), accompanied by an equal number of Con-su-mars, approaching the house with a threatening aspect, and beating a tom-tom. The Ram started up——"

"Who?" inquired the bald gentleman, intensely interested.

"The Ram—Ram Chowdar——"

"Oh!" said the old gentleman, "I beg your pardon; pray go on."

" —Started up and drew a pistol. 'Helves,' said he, 'my boy,'—he always called me, my boy—'Helves,' said he, 'do you hear that tom-tom?' 'I do,' said I. His countenance, which before was pale, assumed a most frightful appearance; his whole visage was distorted, and his frame shaken by violent emotions. 'Do you see that gum-gum?' said he. 'No,' said I, staring about me. 'You don't?' said he. 'No, I'll be damned if I do,' said I; 'and what's more, I don't know what a gum-gum is,' said I. I really thought the Ram would have dropped. He drew me aside, and with an expression of agony I shall never forget, said in a low whisper——"

"Dinner's on the table, ladies," interrupted the steward's wife.

"Will you allow me?" said the captain, immediately suiting the action to the word, and escorting Miss Julia Briggs to the cabin, with as much ease as if he had finished the story.

"What an extraordinary circumstance!" ejaculated the same old gentleman, preserving his listening attitude.

" What a traveller! " said the young ladies.

" What a singular name! " exclaimed the gentlemen, rather confused by the coolness of the whole affair.

" I wish he had finished the story," said an old lady. " I wonder what a gum-gum really is ? "

" By Jove ! " exclaimed Hardy, who until now had been lost in utter amazement, " I don't know what it may be in India, but in England I think a gum-gum has very much the same meaning as a hum-bug."

" How illiberal ! how envious ! " cried everybody, as they made for the cabin, fully impressed with a belief in the captain's amazing adventures. Helves was the sole lion for the remainder of the day—impudence and the marvellous are pretty sure passports to any society.

The party had by this time reached their destination, and put about on their return home. The wind, which had been with them the whole day, was now directly in their teeth ; the weather had become gradually more and more overcast ; and the sky, water, and shore, were all of that dull, heavy, uniform lead-colour, which house-painters daub in the first instance over a street-door which is gradually approaching a state of convalescence. It had been " spitting " with rain for the last half-hour, and now began to pour in good earnest. The wind was freshening very fast, and the waterman at the wheel had unequivocally expressed his opinion that there would shortly be a squall. A slight emotion on the part of the vessel, now and then, seemed to suggest the possibility of its pitching to a very uncomfortable extent in the event of its blowing harder ; and every timber began to creak, as if the boat were an overladen clothes-basket. Sea-sickness, however, is like a belief in ghosts—every one entertains some misgivings on the subject, but few will acknowledge any. The majority of the company, therefore, endeavoured to look peculiarly happy, feeling all the while especially miserable.

" Don't it rain ? " inquired the old gentleman before

noticed, when, by dint of squeezing and jamming, they were all seated at table.

"I think it does—a little," replied Mr. Percy Noakes, who could hardly hear himself speak, in consequence of the pattering on the deck.

"Don't it blow?" inquired some one else.

"No, I don't think it does," responded Hardy, sincerely wishing that he could persuade himself that it did not; for he sat near the door, and was almost blown off his seat.

"It'll soon clear up," said Mr. Percy Noakes, in a cheerful tone.

"Oh, certainly!" ejaculated the committee generally.

"No doubt of it!" said the remainder of the company, whose attention was now pretty well engrossed by the serious business of eating, carving, taking wine, and so forth.

The throbbing motion of the engine was but too perceptible. There was a large, substantial, cold boiled leg of mutton, at the bottom of the table, shaking like blanc-mange; a previously hearty sirloin of beef looked as if it had been suddenly seized with the palsy; and some tongues, which were placed on dishes rather too large for them, went through the most surprising evolutions; darting from side to side, and from end to end, like a fly in an inverted wine-glass. Then, the sweets shook and trembled, till it was quite impossible to help them, and people gave up the attempt in despair; and the pigeon-pies looked as if the birds, whose legs were stuck outside, were trying to get them in. The table vibrated and started like a feverish pulse, and the very legs were convulsed —everything was shaking and jarring. The beams in the roof of the cabin seemed as if they were put there for the sole purpose of giving people headaches, and several elderly gentlemen became ill-tempered in consequence. As fast as the steward put the fire-irons up, they *would* fall down again; and the more the ladies and gentlemen tried to sit comfortably on their seats, the more the seats seemed to slide away from the ladies and gentlemen. Several ominous demands were made for small glasses of brandy; the countenances of the company gradually underwent most extraordinary changes; one gentleman was observed suddenly to rush from table without the slightest ostensible reason, and dart up the steps with incredible swiftness: thereby greatly damaging both himself and the steward, who happened to be coming down at the same moment.

The cloth was removed; the dessert was laid on the table; and the glasses were filled. The motion of the boat increased; several members of the party began to feel rather vague and misty, and looked as if they had only just got up. The young gentleman with the spectacles, who had been in a fluctuating state for some time—at one moment bright, and at another dismal, like a revolving light on the sea-coast —rashly announced his wish to propose a toast. After several ineffectual attempts to preserve his perpendicular, the young gentleman, having managed to hook himself to the centre leg of the table with his left hand, proceeded as follows:

"Ladies and gentlemen. A gentleman is among us—I may say a stranger—(here some painful thought seemed to strike the orator; he paused, and looked extremely odd)— whose talents, whose travels, whose cheerfulness—— "

"I beg your pardon, Edkins," hastily interrupted Mr. Percy Noakes,—"Hardy, what's the matter?"

"Nothing," replied the "funny gentleman," who had just life enough left to utter two consecutive syllables.

"Will you have some brandy?"

"No!" replied Hardy in a tone of great indignation, and looking as comfortable as Temple-bar in a Scotch mist; "what should I want brandy for?"

"Will you go on deck?"

"No, I will *not*." This was said with a most determined air, and in a voice which might have been taken for an imitation of anything; it was quite as much like a guinea-pig as a bassoon.

"I beg your pardon, Edkins," said the courteous Percy; "I thought our friend was ill. Pray go on."

A pause.

"Pray go on."

"Mr. Edkins *is* gone," cried somebody.

"I beg your pardon, sir," said the steward, running up to Mr. Percy Noakes, "I beg your pardon, sir, but the gentleman as just went on deck—him with the green spectacles—is uncommon bad, to be sure; and the young man as played the wiolin says, that unless he has some brandy he can't answer for the consequences. He says he has a wife and two children, whose werry subsistence depends on his breaking a wessel, and he expects to do so every moment. The flageolet's been werry ill, but he's better, only he's in a dreadful prusperation."

All disguise was now useless; the company staggered on deck; the gentlemen tried to see nothing but the clouds; and the ladies, muffled up in such shawls and cloaks as they had brought with them, lay about on the seats, and under the seats, in the most wretched condition. Never was such a blowing, and raining, and pitching, and tossing, endured by any pleasure party before. Several remonstrances were sent down below, on the subject of Master Fleetwood, but they were totally unheeded in consequence of the indisposition of his natural protectors. That interesting child screamed at the top of his voice, until he had no voice left to scream with; and then, Miss Wakefield began, and screamed for the remainder of the passage.

Mr. Hardy was observed, some hours afterwards, in an attitude which induced his friends to suppose that he was busily engaged in contemplating the beauties of the deep; they only regretted that his taste for the picturesque should lead him to remain so long in a position, very injurious at all times, but especially so, to an individual labouring under a tendency of blood to the head.

The party arrived off the Custom-house at about two

o'clock on the Thursday morning dispirited and worn out. The Tauntons were too ill to quarrel with the Briggses, and the Briggses were too wretched to annoy the Tauntons. One of the guitar-cases was lost on its passage to a hackney-coach, and Mrs. Briggs has not scrupled to state that the Tauntons bribed a porter to throw it down an area. Mr. Alexander Briggs opposes vote by ballot—he says from personal experience of its inefficacy; and Mr. Samuel Briggs, whenever he is asked to express his sentiments on the point, says he has no opinion on that or any other subject.

Mr. Edkins—the young gentleman in the green spectacles —makes a speech on every occasion on which a speech can possibly be made: the eloquence of which can only be equalled by its length. In the event of his not being previously appointed to a judgeship, it is probable that he will practise as a barrister in the New Central Criminal Court.

Captain Helves continued his attention to Miss Julia Briggs, whom he might possibly have espoused, if it had not unfortunately happened that Mr. Samuel arrested him, in the way of business, pursuant to instructions received from Messrs. Scroggins and Payne, whose town-debts the gallant captain had condescended to collect, but whose accounts, with the indiscretion sometimes peculiar to military minds, he had omitted to keep with that dull accuracy which custom has rendered necessary. Mrs. Taunton complains that she has been much deceived in him. He introduced himself to the family on board a Gravesend steam-packet, and certainly, therefore, ought to have proved respectable.

Mr. Percy Noakes is as light-hearted and careless as ever.

CHAPTER VIII

THE GREAT WINGLEBURY DUEL

THE little town of Great Winglebury is exactly forty-two miles and three-quarters from Hyde Park corner. It has a long, straggling, quiet High-street, with a great black and white clock at a small red Town-hall, half-way up—a market-place—a cage—an assembly-room—a church—a bridge—a chapel—a theatre—a library—an inn—a pump—and a Post-office. Tradition tells of a "Little Winglebury," down some cross-road about two miles off; and, as a square mass of dirty paper, supposed to have been originally intended for a letter, with certain tremulous characters inscribed thereon, in which a lively imagination might trace a remote resemblance to the word "Little," was once stuck up to be owned in the sunny window of the Great Winglebury Post-office, from which it only disappeared when it fell to pieces with dust and extreme old age, there would appear to be some foundation for the legend. Common belief is inclined to bestow the name upon a little hole at the end of a muddy lane about a couple of miles long, colonised by one wheelwright, four paupers, and a beer-shop; but, even this authority, slight as it is, must be regarded with extreme suspicion, inasmuch as the inhabitants of the hole aforesaid, concur in opining that it never had any name at all, from the earliest ages down to the present day.

The Winglebury Arms, in the centre of the High-street,

The Winglebury Duel

opposite the small building with the big clock, is the principal inn of Great Winglebury;—the commercial-inn, posting-house, and excise-office; the "Blue" house at every election, and the Judges' house at every assizes. It is the head-quarters of the Gentlemen's Whist Club of Winglebury Blues (so called in opposition to the Gentlemen's Whist Club of Wingle-bury Buffs, held at the other house, a little further down): and whenever a juggler, or wax-work man, or concert-giver, takes Great Winglebury in his circuit, it is immediately placarded all over the town that Mr. So-and-so, "trusting to that liberal support which the inhabitants of Great Winglebury have long been so liberal in bestowing, has at a great expense engaged the elegant and commodious assembly-rooms, attached to the Winglebury Arms." The house is a large one, with a red brick and stone front; a pretty spacious hall, ornamented with evergreen plants, terminates in a perspective view of the bar, and a glass case, in which are displayed a choice variety of delicacies ready for dressing, to catch the eye of a new-comer the moment he enters, and excite his appetite to the highest possible pitch. Opposite doors lead to the "coffee" and "commercial" rooms; and a great wide, rambling staircase,—three stairs and a landing—four stairs and another landing—one step and another landing—half-a-dozen stairs and another landing—and so on—conducts to galleries of bedrooms, and labyrinths of sitting-rooms, denominated "private," where you may enjoy yourself, as privately as you can in any place where some bewildered being walks into your room every five minutes, by mistake, and then walks out again, to open all the doors along the gallery until he finds his own.

Such is the Winglebury Arms, at this day, and such was the Winglebury Arms some time since—no matter when—two or three minutes before the arrival of the London stage. Four horses with cloths on—change for a coach—were standing quietly at the corner of the yard surrounded by a listless group of post-boys in shiny hats and smock-frocks, engaged in discussing the merits of the cattle; half a dozen ragged boys were standing a little apart, listening with evident interest to the conversation of these worthies; and a few loungers were collected round the horse-trough, awaiting the arrival of the coach.

The day was hot and sunny, the town in the zenith of its dulness, and with the exception of these few idlers, not a living creature was to be seen. Suddenly, the loud notes of a key-bugle broke the monotonous stillness of the street; in came the coach, rattling over the uneven paving with a noise startling enough to stop even the large-faced clock itself. Down got the outsides, up went the windows in all directions, out came the waiters, up started the ostlers, and the loungers, and the post-boys, and the ragged boys, as if they were electrified—unstrapping, and unchaining, and unbuckling, and dragging willing horses out, and forcing reluctant horses in, and making a most exhilarating bustle. "Lady inside, here!" said the guard. "Please to alight, ma'am," said the waiter. "Private sitting-room?" interrogated the lady. "Certainly, ma'am," responded the chamber-maid. "Nothing but these 'ere trunks, ma'am?" inquired the guard. "Nothing more," replied the lady. Up got the outsides again, and the guard, and the coachman; off came the cloths, with a jerk; "All right," was the cry; and away they went. The loungers lingered a minute or two in the road, watching the coach until it turned the corner, and then loitered away one by one. The street was clear again, and the town, by contrast, quieter than ever.

"Lady in number twenty-five," screamed the landlady.— "Thomas!"

"Yes, ma'am."

"Letter just been left for the gentleman in number nineteen. Boots at the Lion left it. No answer."

"Letter for you, sir," said Thomas, depositing the letter on number nineteen's table.

"For me?" said number nineteen, turning from the

84

window, out of which he had been surveying the scene just described.

" Yes, sir,"—(waiters always speak in hints, and never utter complete sentences,)—"yes, sir,—Boots at the Lion, sir,—Bar, sir,—Missis said number nineteen, sir—Alexander Trott, Esq., sir ?—Your card at the bar, sir, I think, sir ? "

" My name *is* Trott," replied number nineteen, breaking the seal. " You may go, waiter." The waiter pulled down the window-blind, and then pulled it up again—for a regular waiter must do something before he leaves the room—adjusted the glasses on the sideboard, brushed a place that was *not* dusty, rubbed his hands very hard, walked stealthily to the door, and evaporated.

There was, evidently, something in the contents of the letter, of a nature, if not wholly unexpected, certainly extremely disagreeable. Mr. Alexander Trott laid it down, and took it up again, and walked about the room on particular squares of the carpet, and even attempted, though unsuccessfully, to whistle an air. It wouldn't do. He threw himself into a chair, and read the following epistle aloud :—

> " Blue Lion and Stomach-warmer,
> Great Winglebury.
> *Wednesday Morning.*

" Sir. Immediately on discovering your intentions, I left our counting-house, and followed you. I know the purport of your journey ;—that journey shall never be completed.

" I have no friend here, just now, on whose secrecy I can rely. This shall be no obstacle to my revenge. Neither shall Emily Brown be exposed to the mercenary solicitations of a scoundrel, odious in her eyes, and contemptible in everybody else's : nor will I tamely submit to the clandestine attacks of a base umbrella-maker.

" Sir. From Great Winglebury church, a footpath leads through four meadows to a retired spot known to the townspeople as Stiffun's Acre." [Mr. Trott shuddered.] " I shall be waiting there alone, at twenty minutes before six o'clock to-morrow morning. Should I be disappointed in seeing you there, I will do myself the pleasure of calling with a horsewhip.

"HORACE HUNTER.

"PS. There is a gunsmith's in the High-street; and they won't sell gunpowder after dark—you understand me.

"PPS. You had better not order your breakfast in the morning until you have met me. It may be an unnecessary expense."

"Desperate-minded villain! I knew how it would be!" ejaculated the terrified Trott. "I always told father, that once start me on this expedition, and Hunter would pursue me like the Wandering Jew. It's bad enough as it is, to marry with the old people's commands, and without the girl's consent; but what will Emily think of me, if I go down there breathless with running away from this infernal salamander? What *shall* I do? What *can* I do? If I go back to the city, I'm disgraced for ever—lose the girl—and, what's more, lose the money too. Even if I did go on to the Browns' by the coach, Hunter would be after me in a post-chaise; and if I go to this place, this Stiffun's Acre (another shudder), I'm as good as dead. I've seen him hit the man at the Pall-mall shooting-gallery, in the second button-hole of the waistcoat, five times out of every six, and when he didn't hit him there, he hit him in the head." With this consolatory reminiscence Mr. Alexander Trott again ejaculated, "What shall I do?"

Long and weary were his reflections, as, burying his face in his hand, he sat, ruminating on the best course to be pursued. His mental direction-post pointed to London. He thought of the "governor's" anger, and the loss of the fortune which the paternal Brown had promised the paternal Trott his daughter should contribute to the coffers of his son. Then the words "To Brown's" were legibly inscribed on the said direction-post, but Horace Hunter's denunciation rung in his ears;—last of all it bore, in red letters, the words, "To Stiffun's Acre;" and then Mr. Alexander Trott decided on adopting a plan which he presently matured.

First and foremost, he despatched the under-boots to the Blue Lion and Stomach-warmer, with a gentlemanly note to Mr. Horace Hunter, intimating that he thirsted for his destruction and would do himself the pleasure of slaughtering him next morning, without fail. He then wrote another letter, and requested the attendance of the other boots—for they kept a pair. A modest knock at the room door was heard. "Come in," said Mr. Trott. A man thrust in a red head with one eye in it, and being again desired to "come in," brought in the body and the legs to which the head belonged, and a fur cap which belonged to the head.

"You are the upper-boots, I think?" inquired Mr. Trott.

"Yes, I am the upper-boots," replied a voice from inside a velveteen case, with mother-of-pearl buttons—"that is, I'm the boots as b'longs to the house; the other man's my man, as goes errands and does odd jobs. Top-boots and half-boots, I calls us."

"You're from London?" inquired Mr. Trott.

"Driv a cab once," was the laconic reply.

"Why don't you drive it now?" asked Mr. Trott.

"Over-driv the cab, and driv over a 'ooman," replied the top-boots, with brevity.

"Do you know the mayor's house?" inquired Mr. Trott.

"Rather," replied the boots, significantly, as if he had some good reason to remember it.

"Do you think you could manage to leave a letter there?" interrogated Trott.

"Shouldn't wonder," responded boots.

"But this letter," said Trott, holding a deformed note with a paralytic direction in one hand, and five shillings in the other—"this letter is anonymous."

"A—what?" interrupted the boots.

"Anonymous—he's not to know who it comes from."

"Oh! I see," responded the reg'lar, with a knowing wink, but without evincing the slightest disinclination to undertake the charge—"I see—bit o' Sving, eh?" and his one eye wandered round the room, as if in quest of a dark lantern and phosphorus-box. "But, I say!" he continued, recalling the eye from its search, and bringing it to bear on Mr. Trott. "I say, he's a lawyer, our mayor, and insured in the County. If you've a spite agen him, you'd better not burn his house down—blessed if I don't think it would be the greatest favour you could do him." And he chuckled inwardly.

If Mr. Alexander Trott had been in any other situation, his first act would have been to kick the man down-stairs by deputy; or, in other words, to ring the bell, and desire the landlord to take his boots off. He contented himself, however, with doubling the fee and explaining that the letter merely related to a breach of the peace. The top-boots retired, solemnly pledged to secrecy; and Mr. Alexander Trott sat down to a fried sole, maintenon cutlet, Madeira, and sundries, with greater composure than he had experienced since the receipt of Horace Hunter's letter of defiance.

The lady who alighted from the London coach had no sooner been installed in number twenty-five, and made some alteration in her travelling-dress, than she indited a note to Joseph Overton, esquire, solicitor, and mayor of Great Winglebury, requesting his immediate attendance on private business of paramount importance—a summons which that worthy functionary lost no time in obeying; for after sundry openings of his eyes, divers ejaculations of "Bless me!" and other manifestations of surprise, he took his broad-brimmed hat from its accustomed peg in his little front office, and walked briskly down the High-street to the Winglebury Arms; through the hall and up the staircase of which establishment he was ushered by the landlady, and a crowd of officious waiters, to the door of number twenty-five.

"Show the gentleman in," said the stranger lady, in reply

to the foremost waiter's announcement. The gentleman was shown in accordingly.

The lady rose from the sofa; the mayor advanced a step from the door; and there they both paused, for a minute or two, looking at one another as if by mutual consent. The mayor saw before him a buxom, richly-dressed female of about forty; the lady looked upon a sleek man, about ten years older, in drab shorts and continuations, black coat, neckcloth, and gloves.

"Miss Julia Manners!" exclaimed the mayor at length, "you astonish me."

"That's very unfair of you, Overton," replied Miss Julia, "for I have known you, long enough, not to be surprised at anything you do, and you might extend equal courtesy to me."

"But to run away—actually run away—with a young man!" remonstrated the mayor.

"You wouldn't have me actually run away with an old one, I presume?" was the cool rejoinder.

"And then to ask me—me—of all people in the world—a man of my age and appearance—mayor of the town—to promote such a scheme!" pettishly ejaculated Joseph Overton; throwing himself into an arm-chair, and producing Miss Julia's letter from his pocket, as if to corroborate the assertion that he *had* been asked.

"Now, Overton," replied the lady, "I want your assistance in this matter, and I must have it. In the lifetime of that poor old dear, Mr. Cornberry, who—who——"

"Who was to have married you, and didn't, because he died first; and who left you his property unencumbered with the addition of himself," suggested the mayor.

"Well," replied Miss Julia, reddening slightly, "in the lifetime of the poor old dear, the property had the incumbrance of your management; and all I will say of that, is, that I only wonder *it* didn't die of consumption instead of its master. You helped yourself then:—help me now."

Mr. Joseph Overton was a man of the world, and an

attorney; and as certain indistinct recollections of an odd thousand pounds or two, appropriated by mistake, passed across his mind, he hemmed deprecatingly, smiled blandly, remained silent for a few seconds; and finally inquired, "What do you wish me to do?"

"I'll tell you," replied Miss Julia—"I'll tell you in three words. Dear Lord Peter——"

"That's the young man, I suppose——" interrupted the mayor.

"That's the young Nobleman," replied the lady, with a great stress on the last word. "Dear Lord Peter is considerably afraid of the resentment of his family; and we have therefore thought it better to make the match a stolen one. He left town, to avoid suspicion, on a visit to his friend, the Honourable Augustus Flair, whose seat, as you know, is about thirty miles from this, accompanied only by his favourite tiger. We arranged that I should come here alone in the London coach; and that he, leaving his tiger and cab behind him, should come on, and arrive here as soon as possible this afternoon."

"Very well," observed Joseph Overton, "and then he can order the chaise, and you can go on to Gretna Green together, without requiring the presence or interference of a third party, can't you?"

"No," replied Miss Julia. "We have every reason to believe—dear Lord Peter not being considered very prudent or sagacious by his friends, and they having discovered his attachment to me—that, immediately on his absence being observed, pursuit will be made in this direction:—to elude which, and to prevent our being traced, I wish it to be understood in this house, that dear Lord Peter is slightly deranged, though perfectly harmless; and that I am, unknown to him, awaiting his arrival to convey him in a post-chaise to a private asylum—at Berwick, say. If I don't show myself much, I dare say I can manage to pass for his mother."

The thought occurred to the mayor's mind that the

lady might show herself a good deal without fear of detection; seeing that she was about double the age of her intended husband. He said nothing, however, and the lady proceeded.

"With the whole of this arrangement dear Lord Peter is acquainted; and all I want you to do, is, to make the delusion more complete by giving it the sanction of your influence in this place, and assigning this as a reason to the people of the house for my taking the young gentleman away. As it would not be consistent with the story that I should see him until after he has entered the chaise, I also wish you to communicate with him, and inform him that it is all going on well."

"Has he arrived?" inquired Overton.

"I don't know," replied the lady.

"Then how am I to know!" inquired the mayor. "Of course he will not give his own name at the bar."

"I begged him, immediately on his arrival, to write you a note," replied Miss Manners; "and to prevent the possibility of our project being discovered through its means, I desired him to write anonymously, and in mysterious terms, to acquaint you with the number of his room."

"Bless me!" exclaimed the mayor, rising from his seat, and searching his pockets—"most extraordinary circumstance —he *has* arrived—mysterious note left at my house in a most mysterious manner, just before yours—didn't know what to make of it before, and certainly shouldn't have attended to it.—Oh! here it is." And Joseph Overton pulled out of an inner coat-pocket the identical letter penned by Alexander Trott. "Is this his lordship's hand?"

"Oh yes," replied Julia; "good, punctual creature! I have not seen it more than once or twice, but I know he writes very badly and very large. These dear, wild young noblemen, you know, Overton—— "

"Ay, ay, I see," replied the mayor.—"Horses and dogs, play and wine—grooms, actresses, and cigars—the stable, the green-room, the saloon, and the tavern; and the legislative assembly at last."

"Here's what he says," pursued the mayor; "'Sir,—A young gentleman in number nineteen at the Winglebury Arms, is bent on committing a rash act to-morrow morning at an early hour.' (That's good—he means marrying.) 'If you have any regard for the peace of this town, or the preservation of one—it may be two—human lives'—What the deuce does he mean by that?"

"'That he's so anxious for the ceremony, he will expire if it's put off, and that I may possibly do the same," replied the lady with great complacency.

"Oh! I see—not much fear of that;—well—'two human lives, you will cause him to be removed to-night.' (He wants to start at once.) 'Fear not to do this on your responsibility: for to-morrow the absolute necessity of the proceeding will be but too apparent. Remember: number nineteen. The name is Trott. No delay; for life and death depend upon your promptitude.' Passionate language, certainly. Shall I see him?"

"Do," replied Miss Julia; "and entreat him to act his part well. I am half afraid of him. Tell him to be cautious."

"I will," said the mayor.

"Settle all the arrangements."

"I will," said the mayor again.

"And say I think the chaise had better be ordered for one o'clock."

"Very well," said the mayor once more; and, ruminating on the absurdity of the situation in which fate and old acquaintance had placed him, he desired a waiter to herald his approach to the temporary representative of number nineteen.

The announcement, "Gentleman to speak with you, sir," induced Mr. Trott to pause half-way in the glass of port, the contents of which he was in the act of imbibing at the moment; to rise from his chair; and retreat a few paces towards the window, as if to secure a retreat, in the event of the visitor assuming the form and appearance of Horace Hunter. One glance at Joseph Overton, however, quieted his apprehensions. He courteously motioned the stranger to a seat. The waiter, after a little jingling with the decanter and glasses, consented to leave the room; and Joseph Overton, placing the broad-brimmed hat on the chair next him, and bending his body gently forward, opened the business by saying in a very low and cautious tone,

"My lord——"

"Eh?" said Mr. Alexander Trott, in a loud key, with the vacant and mystified stare of a chilly somnambulist.

"Hush—hush!" said the cautious attorney: "to be sure—quite right—no titles here—my name is Overton, sir."

"Overton?"

"Yes: the mayor of this place—you sent me a letter with anonymous information, this afternoon."

"I, sir?" exclaimed Trott with ill-dissembled surprise; for, coward as he was, he would willingly have repudiated the authorship of the letter in question. "I, sir?"

"Yes, you, sir; did you not?" responded Overton, annoyed with what he supposed to be an extreme degree of unnecessary suspicion. "Either this letter is yours, or it is not. If it be, we can converse securely upon the subject at once. If it be not, of course I have no more to say."

"Stay, stay," said Trott, "it *is* mine; I *did* write it. What could I do, sir? I had no friend here."

"To be sure, to be sure," said the mayor, encouragingly, "you could not have managed it better. Well, sir; it will be necessary for you to leave here to-night in a post-chaise and four. And the harder the boys drive, the better. You are not safe from pursuit."

"Bless me!" exclaimed Trott, in an agony of apprehension, "can such things happen in a country like this? Such unrelenting and cold-blooded hostility!" He wiped off the concentrated essence of cowardice that was oozing fast down his forehead, and looked aghast at Joseph Overton.

"It certainly is a very hard case," replied the mayor with a smile, "that, in a free country, people can't marry whom they like, without being hunted down as if they were criminals. However, in the present instance the lady is willing, you know, and that's the main point, after all."

"Lady willing," repeated Trott, mechanically. "How do you know the lady's willing?"

"Come, that's a good one," said the mayor, benevolently tapping Mr. Trott on the arm with his broad-brimmed hat; "I have known her, well, for a long time; and if anybody could entertain the remotest doubt on the subject, I assure you I have none, nor need you have."

"Dear me!" said Mr. Trott, ruminating. "This is *very* extraordinary!"

"Well, Lord Peter," said the mayor, rising.

"Lord Peter?" repeated Mr. Trott.

"Oh—ah, I forgot. Mr. Trott, then—Trott—very good, ha! ha!—Well, sir, the chaise shall be ready at half-past twelve."

"And what is to become of me until then?" inquired Mr. Trott, anxiously. "Wouldn't it save appearances, if I were placed under some restraint?"

"Ah!" replied Overton, "very good thought—capital idea indeed. I'll send somebody up directly. And if you make a little resistance when we put you in the chaise it wouldn't be amiss—look as if you didn't want to be taken away, you know."

"To be sure," said Trott—"to be sure."

"Well, my lord," said Overton, in a low tone, "until then, I wish your lordship a good evening."

"Lord—lordship?" ejaculated Trott again, falling back a step or two, and gazing, in unutterable wonder, on the countenance of the mayor.

"Ha-ha! I see, my lord—practising the madman?—very good indeed—very vacant look—capital, my lord, capital—good evening, Mr.—Trott—ha! ha! ha!"

" That mayor's decidedly drunk," soliloquised Mr. Trott, throwing himself back in his chair, in an attitude of reflection.

" He is a much cleverer fellow than I thought him, that young nobleman—he carries it off uncommonly well," thought Overton, as he went his way to the bar, there to complete his arrangements. This was soon done. Every word of the story was implicitly believed, and the one-eyed boots was immediately instructed to repair to number nineteen, to act as custodian of the person of the supposed lunatic until half-past twelve o'clock. In pursuance of this direction, that somewhat eccentric gentleman armed himself with a walking-stick of gigantic dimensions, and repaired, with his usual equanimity of manner, to Mr. Trott's apartment, which he entered without any ceremony, and mounted guard in, by quietly depositing himself on a chair near the door, where he proceeded to beguile the time by whistling a popular air with great apparent satisfaction.

" What do you want here, you scoundrel ? " exclaimed Mr. Alexander Trott, with a proper appearance of indignation at his detention.

The boots beat time with his head, as he looked gently round at Mr. Trott with a smile of pity, and whistled an *adagio* movement.

" Do you attend in this room by Mr. Overton's desire ? " inquired Trott, rather astonished at the man's demeanour.

" Keep yourself to yourself, young feller," calmly responded the boots, " and don't say nothin' to nobody." And he whistled again.

" Now, mind ! " ejaculated Mr. Trott, anxious to keep up the farce of wishing with great earnestness to fight a duel if they'd let him. " I protest against being kept here. I deny that I have any intention of fighting with anybody. But as it's useless contending with superior numbers, I shall sit quietly down."

" You'd better," observed the placid boots, shaking the large stick expressively.

"Under protest, however," added Alexander Trott, seating himself with indignation in his face, but great content in his heart. "Under protest."

"Oh, certainly!" responded the boots; "anything you please. If you're happy, I'm transported; only don't talk too much—it'll make you worse."

"Make me worse?" exclaimed Trott, in unfeigned astonishment: "the man's drunk!"

"You'd better be quiet, young feller," remarked the boots, going through a threatening piece of pantomime with the stick.

"Or mad!" said Mr. Trott, rather alarmed. "Leave the room, sir, and tell them to send somebody else."

"Won't do!" replied the boots.

"Leave the room!" shouted Trott, ringing the bell violently: for he began to be alarmed on a new score.

"Leave that 'ere bell alone, you wretched loo-nattic!" said the boots, suddenly forcing the unfortunate Trott back into his chair, and brandishing the stick aloft. "Be quiet, you miserable object, and don't let everybody know there's a madman in the house."

"He *is* a madman! He *is* a madman!" exclaimed the terrified Mr. Trott, gazing on the one eye of the red-headed boots with a look of abject horror.

"Madman!" replied the boots, "dam'me, I think he *is* a madman with a vengeance! Listen to me, you unfort'nate. Ah! would you?" [a slight tap on the head with the large stick, as Mr. Trott made another move towards the bell-handle] "I caught you there! did I?"

"Spare my life!" exclaimed Trott, raising his hands imploringly.

"I don't want your life," replied the boots, disdainfully, "though I think it 'ud be a charity if somebody took it."

"No, no, it wouldn't," interrupted poor Mr. Trott, hurriedly; "no, no, it wouldn't! I—I—'d rather keep it!"

"O werry well," said the boots: "that's a mere matter of

taste—ev'ry one to his liking. Hows'ever, all I've got to say is this here: You sit quietly down in that chair, and I'll sit hoppersite you here, and if you keep quiet and don't stir, I won't damage you; but, if you move hand or foot till half-past twelve o'clock, I shall alter the expression of your countenance so completely, that the next time you look in the glass you'll ask vether you're gone out of town, and ven you're likely to come back again. So sit down."

"I will—I will," responded the victim of mistakes; and down sat Mr. Trott and down sat the boots too, exactly opposite him, with the stick ready for immediate action in case of emergency.

Long and dreary were the hours that followed. The bell of Great Winglebury church had just struck ten, and two hours and a half would probably elapse before succour arrived.

For half an hour, the noise occasioned by shutting up the shops in the street beneath, betokened something like life in the town, and rendered Mr. Trott's situation a little less insupportable; but, when even these ceased, and nothing was heard beyond the occasional rattling of a post-chaise as it drove up the yard to change horses, and then drove away again, or the clattering of horses' hoofs in the stables behind, it became almost unbearable. The boots occasionally moved an inch or two, to knock superfluous bits of wax off the candles, which were burning low, but instantaneously resumed his former position ; and as he remembered to have heard, somewhere or other, that the human eye had an unfailing effect in controlling mad people, he kept his solitary organ of vision constantly fixed on Mr. Alexander Trott. That unfortunate individual stared at his companion in his turn, until his features grew more and more indistinct—his hair gradually less red—and the room more misty and obscure. Mr. Alexander Trott fell into a sound sleep, from which he was awakened by a rumbling in the street, and a cry of " Chaise-and-four for number twenty-five!" A bustle on the stairs succeeded; the room door was hastily thrown open; and Mr. Joseph Overton entered, followed by four stout waiters, and Mrs. Williamson, the stout landlady of the Winglebury Arms.

"Mr. Overton!" exclaimed Mr. Alexander Trott, jumping up in a frenzy. "Look at this man, sir; consider the situation in which I have been placed for three hours past—the person you sent to guard me, sir, was a madman—a madman—a raging, ravaging, furious madman."

"Bravo!" whispered Overton.

"Poor dear!" said the compassionate Mrs. Williamson, "mad people always thinks other people's mad."

"Poor dear!" ejaculated Mr. Alexander Trott. "What the devil do you mean by poor dear! Are you the landlady of this house?"

"Yes, yes," replied the stout old lady, "don't exert yourself, there's a dear! Consider your health, now; do."

"Exert myself!" shouted Mr. Alexander Trott; "it's a mercy, ma'am, that I have any breath to exert myself with! I might have been assassinated three hours ago by that one-eyed monster with the oakum head. How dare you have a madman, ma'am—how dare you have a madman, to assault and terrify the visitors to your house?"

"I'll never have another," said Mrs. Williamson, casting a look of reproach at the mayor.

"Capital, capital," whispered Overton again, as he enveloped Mr. Alexander Trott in a thick travelling-cloak.

"Capital, sir!" exclaimed Trott, aloud; "it's horrible. The very recollection makes me shudder. I'd rather fight four duels in three hours, if I survived the first three, than I'd sit for that time face to face with a madman."

"Keep it up, my lord, as you go down-stairs," whispered Overton, "your bill is paid, and your portmanteau in the chaise." And then he added aloud, "Now, waiters, the gentleman's ready."

At this signal, the waiters crowded round Mr. Alexander

Trott. One took one arm; another, the other; a third, walked before with a candle; the fourth, behind with another candle; the boots and Mrs. Williamson brought up the rear; and down-stairs they went: Mr. Alexander Trott expressing alternately at the very top of his voice either his feigned reluctance to go, or his unfeigned indignation at being shut up with a madman.

Mr. Overton was waiting at the chaise-door, the boys were ready mounted, and a few ostlers and stable nondescripts were standing round to witness the departure of "the mad gentleman." Mr. Alexander Trott's foot was on the step, when he observed (which the dim light had prevented his doing before) a figure seated in the chaise, closely muffled up in a cloak like his own.

"Who's that?" he inquired of Overton, in a whisper.

"Hush, hush," replied the mayor: "the other party of course."

"The other party!" exclaimed Trott, with an effort to retreat.

"Yes, yes; you'll soon find that out, before you go far, I should think—but make a noise, you'll excite suspicion if you whisper to me so much."

"I won't go in this chaise!" shouted Mr. Alexander Trott, all his original fears recurring with tenfold violence. "I shall be assassinated—I shall be——"

"Bravo, bravo," whispered Overton. "I'll push you in."

"But I won't go," exclaimed Mr. Trott. "Help here, help! They're carrying me away against my will. This is a plot to murder me."

"Poor dear!" said Mrs. Williamson again.

"Now, boys, put 'em along," cried the mayor, pushing Trott in and slamming the door. "Off with you, as quick as you can, and stop for nothing till you come to the next stage—all right!"

"Horses are paid, Tom," screamed Mrs. Williamson; and away went the chaise, at the rate of fourteen miles an hour, with Mr. Alexander Trott and Miss Julia Manners carefully shut up in the inside.

Mr. Alexander Trott remained coiled up in one corner of the chaise, and his mysterious companion in the other, for the first two or three miles; Mr. Trott edging more and more into his corner, as he felt his companion gradually edging more and more from hers; and vainly endeavouring in the darkness to catch a glimpse of the furious face of the supposed Horace Hunter.

" We may speak now," said his fellow-traveller, at length; "the post-boys can neither see nor hear us."

" That's not Hunter's voice !"—thought Alexander, astonished.

" Dear Lord Peter ! " said Miss Julia, most winningly: putting her arm on Mr. Trott's shoulder. " Dear Lord Peter. Not a word ? "

" Why, it's a woman ! " exclaimed Mr. Trott, in a low tone of excessive wonder.

" Ah ! Whose voice is that ? " said Julia; " 'tis not Lord Peter's."

" No,—it's mine," replied Mr. Trott.

" Yours ! " ejaculated Miss Julia Manners; " a strange man ! Gracious heaven ! How came you here ! "

" Whoever you are, you might have known that I came against my will, ma'am," replied Alexander, " for I made noise enough when I got in."

" Do you come from Lord Peter ? " inquired Miss Manners.

" Confound Lord Peter," replied Trott pettishly. " I don't know any Lord Peter. I never heard of him before to-night, when I've been Lord Peter'd by one and Lord Peter'd by another, till I verily believe I'm mad, or dreaming—— "

" Whither are we going ? " inquired the lady tragically.

" How should *I* know, ma'am ? " replied Trott with singular coolness; for the events of the evening had completely hardened him.

100

"Stop! stop!" cried the lady, letting down the front glasses of the chaise.

"Stay, my dear ma'am!" said Mr. Trott, pulling the glasses up again with one hand, and gently squeezing Miss Julia's waist with the other. "There is some mistake here; give me till the end of this stage to explain my share of it. We must go so far; you cannot be set down here alone, at this hour of the night."

The lady consented; the mistake was mutually explained. Mr. Trott was a young man, had highly promising whiskers, an undeniable tailor, and an insinuating address—he wanted nothing but valour, and who wants that with three thousand a-year? The lady had this, and more; she wanted a young husband, and the only course open to Mr. Trott to retrieve his disgrace was a rich wife. So, they came to the conclusion that it would be a pity to have all this trouble and expense for nothing; and that as they were so far on the road already, they had better go to Gretna Green, and marry each other; and they did so. And the very next preceding entry in the Blacksmith's book, was an entry of the marriage of Emily Brown with Horace Hunter. Mr. Hunter took his wife home, and begged pardon, and *was* pardoned; and Mr. Trott took *his* wife home, begged pardon too, and was pardoned also. And Lord Peter, who had been detained beyond his time by drinking champagne and riding a steeple-chase, went back to the Honourable Augustus Flair's, and drank more champagne, and rode another steeple-chase, and was thrown and killed. And Horace Hunter took great credit to himself for practising on the cowardice of Alexander Trott; and all these circumstances were discovered in time, and carefully noted down; and if you ever stop a week at the Winglebury Arms, they will give you just this account of The Great Winglebury Duel.

CHAPTER IX

MOST extensive were the preparations at Rose Villa, Clapham Rise, in the occupation of Mr. Gattleton (a stock-broker in especially comfortable circumstances), and great was the anxiety of Mr. Gattleton's interesting family, as the day fixed for the representation of the Private Play which had been "many months in preparation," approached. The whole family was infected with the mania for Private Theatricals; the house, usually so clean and tidy, was, to use Mr. Gattleton's expressive description, "regularly turned out o' windows;" the large dining-room, dismantled of its furniture and ornaments, presented a strange jumble of flats, flies, wings, lamps, bridges, clouds, thunder and lightning, festoons and flowers, daggers and foil, and various other messes in theatrical slang included under the comprehensive name of "properties." The bedrooms were crowded with scenery, the kitchen was occupied by carpenters. Rehearsals took place every other night in the drawing-room, and every sofa in the house was more or less damaged by the perseverance and spirit with which Mr. Sempronius Gattleton, and Miss Lucina, rehearsed the smothering scene in " Othello "—it having been determined that that tragedy should form the first portion of the evening's entertainments.

"When we're a *leetle* more perfect, I think it will go admirably," said Mr. Sempronius, addressing his *corps dramatique*, at the conclusion of the hundred and fiftieth rehearsal.

In consideration of his sustaining the trifling inconvenience of bearing all the expenses of the play, Mr. Sempronius had been, in the most handsome manner, unanimously elected stage-manager. " Evans," continued Mr. Gattleton, the younger, addressing a tall, thin, pale young gentleman, with extensive whiskers—" Evans, you play *Roderigo* beautifully."

" Beautifully," echoed the three Miss Gattletons ; for Mr. Evans was pronounced by all his lady friends to be "quite a dear." He looked so interesting, and had such lovely whiskers : to say nothing of his talent for writing verses in albums and playing the flute ! *Roderigo* simpered and bowed.

" But I think," added the manager, "you are hardly perfect in the—fall—in the fencing-scene, where you are—you understand ? "

" It's very difficult," said Mr. Evans, thoughtfully ; " I've fallen about, a good deal, in our counting-house lately, for practice, only I find it hurts one so. Being obliged to fall backward you see, it bruises one's head a good deal."

" But you must take care you don't knock a wing down," said Mr. Gattleton, the elder, who had been appointed prompter, and who took as much interest in the play as the youngest of the company. "The stage is very narrow, you know."

" Oh ! don't be afraid," said Mr. Evans, with a very self-satisfied air : " I shall fall with my head ' off,' and then I can't do any harm."

" But, egad," said the manager, rubbing his hands, " we shall make a decided hit in ' Masaniello.' Harleigh sings that music admirably."

Everybody echoed the sentiment. Mr. Harleigh smiled, and looked foolish—not an unusual thing with him—hummed " Behold how brightly breaks the morning," and blushed as red as the fisherman's nightcap he was trying on.

" Let's see," resumed the manager, telling the number on his fingers, " we shall have three dancing female peasants, besides *Fenella*, and four fishermen. Then, there's our man

103

Tom; he can have a pair of ducks of mine, and a check shirt of Bob's, and a red nightcap, and he'll do for another—that's five. In the choruses, of course, we can sing at the sides; and in the market-scene we can walk about in cloaks and things. When the revolt takes place, Tom must keep rushing in on one side and out on the other, with a pickaxe, as fast as he can. The effect will be electrical; it will look exactly as if there were an immense number of 'em. And in the eruption-scene we must burn the red fire, and upset the tea-trays, and make all sorts of noises—and it's sure to do."

"Sure! sure!" cried all the performers *unâ voce*—and away hurried Mr. Sempronius Gattleton to wash the burnt cork off his face, and superintend the "setting up" of some of the amateur-painted, but never-sufficiently-to-be-admired, scenery.

Mrs. Gattleton was a kind, good-tempered, vulgar soul, exceedingly fond of her husband and children, and entertaining only three dislikes. In the first place, she had a natural antipathy to anybody else's unmarried daughters; in the second, she was in bodily fear of anything in the shape of ridicule; lastly—almost a necessary consequence of this feeling—she regarded, with feelings of the utmost horror, one Mrs. Joseph Porter over the way. However, the good folks of Clapham and its vicinity stood very much in awe of scandal and sarcasm; and thus Mrs. Joseph Porter was courted, and flattered, and caressed, and invited, for much the same reason that induces a poor author, without a farthing in his pocket, to behave with extraordinary civility to a two-penny postman.

"Never mind, ma," said Miss Emma Porter, in colloquy with her respected relative, and trying to look unconcerned; "if they had invited me, you know that neither you nor pa would have allowed me to take part in such an exhibition."

"Just what I should have thought from your high sense of propriety," returned the mother. "I am glad to see, Emma, you know how to designate the proceeding." Miss P., by-the-bye, had only the week before made "an exhibition" of herself for four days, behind a counter at a fancy fair, to all and every of her Majesty's liege subjects who were disposed to pay a shilling each for the privilege of seeing some four dozen girls flirting with strangers, and playing at shop.

"There!" said Mrs. Porter, looking out of window; "there are two rounds of beef and a ham going in—clearly for sandwiches; and Thomas, the pastry-cook, says, there have been twelve dozen tarts ordered, besides blanc-mange and jellies. Upon my word! think of the Miss Gattletons in fancy dresses, too!"

"Oh, it's too ridiculous!" said Miss Porter, hysterically.

"I'll manage to put them a little out of conceit with the business, however," said Mrs. Porter; and out she went on her charitable errand.

"Well, my dear Mrs. Gattleton," said Mrs. Joseph Porter, after they had been closeted for some time, and when, by dint of indefatigable pumping, she had managed to extract all the news about the play, "well, my dear, people may say what they please; indeed we know they will, for some folks are *so* ill-natured. Ah, my dear Miss Lucina, how d'ye do? I was just telling your mamma that I have heard it said, that——"

"What?"

"Mrs. Porter is alluding to the play, my dear," said Mrs. Gattleton; "she was, I am sorry to say, just informing me that——"

"Oh, now pray don't mention it," interrupted Mrs. Porter; "it's most absurd—quite as absurd as young What's-his-name saying he wondered how Miss Caroline, with such a foot and ankle, could have the vanity to play *Fenella*."

"Highly impertinent, whoever said it," said Mrs. Gattleton, bridling up.

"Certainly, my dear," chimed in the delighted Mrs. Porter; "most undoubtedly! Because, as I said, if Miss Caroline *does* play *Fenella*, it doesn't follow, as a matter of

105

course, that she should think she has a pretty foot;—and then—such puppies as these young men are—he had the impudence to say, that——"

How far the amiable Mrs. Porter might have succeeded in her pleasant purpose, it is impossible to say, had not the entrance of Mr. Thomas Balderstone, Mrs. Gattleton's brother, familiarly called in the family "Uncle Tom," changed the course of conversation, and suggested to her mind an excellent plan of operation on the evening of the play.

Uncle Tom was very rich, and exceedingly fond of his nephews and nieces: as a matter of course, therefore, he was an object of great importance in his own family. He was one of the best-hearted men in existence: always in a good temper, and always talking. It was his boast that he wore top-boots on all occasions, and had never worn a black silk neckerchief; and it was his pride that he remembered all the principal plays of Shakspeare from beginning to end—and so he did. The result of this parrot-like accomplishment was, that he was not only perpetually quoting himself, but that he could never sit by, and hear a misquotation from the "Swan of Avon" without setting the unfortunate delinquent right. He was also something of a wag; never missed an opportunity of saying what he considered a good thing, and invariably laughed until he cried at anything that appeared to him mirth-moving or ridiculous.

"Well, girls!" said Uncle Tom, after the preparatory ceremony of kissing and how-d'ye-do-ing had been gone through —"how d'ye get on? Know your parts, eh?—Lucina, my dear, act ii., scene 1—place, left—cue—'Unknown fate,'— What's next, eh?—Go on—'The Heavens——'"

"Oh, yes," said Miss Lucina, "I recollect—

'The heavens forbid
But that our loves and comforts should increase
Even as our days do grow!'"

"Make a pause here and there," said the old gentleman, who was a great critic. "'But that our loves and comforts should increase'—emphasis on the last syllable, 'crease,'—loud 'even,'—one, two, three, four; then loud again, 'as our days do grow;' emphasis on *days*. That's the way, my dear; trust to your uncle for emphasis. Ah! Sem, my boy, how are you?"

"Very well, thankee, uncle," returned Mr. Sempronius, who had just appeared, looking something like a ringdove, with a small circle round each eye: the result of his constant corking. "Of course we see you on Thursday."

"Of course, of course, my dear boy."

"What a pity it is your nephew didn't think of making you prompter, Mr. Balderstone!" whispered Mrs. Joseph Porter; "you would have been invaluable."

"Well, I flatter myself, I *should* have been tolerably up to the thing," responded Uncle Tom.

"I must bespeak sitting next you on the night," resumed Mrs. Porter; "and then, if our dear young friends here, should be at all wrong, you will be able to enlighten me. I shall be so interested."

"I am sure I shall be most happy to give you any assistance in my power."

"Mind, it's a bargain."

"Certainly."

"I don't know how it is," said Mrs. Gattleton to her daughters, as they were sitting round the fire in the evening, looking over their parts, "but I really very much wish Mrs. Joseph Porter wasn't coming on Thursday. I am sure she's scheming something."

"She can't make *us* ridiculous, however," observed Mr. Sempronius Gattleton, haughtily.

The long-looked-for Thursday arrived in due course, and brought with it, as Mr. Gattleton, senior, philosophically observed, "no disappointments, to speak of." True, it was yet a matter of doubt whether *Cassio* would be enabled to get into the dress which had been sent for him from the masquerade warehouse. It was equally uncertain whether the principal female singer would be sufficiently recovered from the influenza to make her appearance; Mr. Harleigh, the *Masaniello* of the night, was hoarse, and rather unwell, in consequence of the great quantity of lemon and sugar-candy he had eaten to improve his voice; and two flutes and a violoncello had pleaded severe colds. What of that? the audience were all coming. Everybody knew his part: the dresses were covered with tinsel and spangles; the white plumes looked beautiful; Mr. Evans had practised falling until he was bruised from head to foot and quite perfect; *Iago* was sure that, in the stabbing-scene, he should make " a decided hit." A self-taught deaf gentleman, who had kindly offered to bring his flute, would be a most valuable addition to the orchestra; Miss Jenkins's talent for the piano was too well known to be doubted for an instant; Mr. Cape had practised the violin accompaniment with her frequently; and Mr. Brown, who had kindly undertaken, at a few hours' notice, to bring his violoncello, would, no doubt, manage extremely well.

Seven o'clock came, and so did the audience; all the rank and fashion of Clapham and its vicinity was fast filling the theatre. There were the Smiths, the Gubbinses, the Nixons, the Dixons, the Hicksons, people with all sorts of names, two aldermen, a sheriff in perspective, Sir Thomas Glumper (who had been knighted in the last reign for carrying up an address on somebody's escaping from nothing); and last, not least, there were Mrs. Joseph Porter and Uncle Tom, seated in the centre of the third row from the stage; Mrs. P. amusing Uncle Tom with all sorts of stories, and Uncle Tom amusing every one else by laughing most immoderately.

Ting, ting, ting! went the prompter's bell at eight o'clock precisely, and dash went the orchestra into the overture to "The Men of Prometheus." The pianoforte player hammered away with laudable perseverance; and the violoncello, which struck in at intervals, " sounded very well, considering." The unfortunate individual, however, who had undertaken to play the flute accompaniment "at sight," found, from fatal experience, the perfect truth of the old adage, " out of sight, out of mind;" for being very near-sighted, and being placed at a considerable distance from his music-book, all he had an opportunity of doing was to play a bar now and then in the wrong place, and put the other performers out. It is, however, but justice to Mr. Brown to say that he did this to admiration. The overture, in fact, was not unlike a race between the different instruments; the piano came in first by several bars, and the violoncello next, quite distancing the poor flute; for the deaf gentleman *too-too'd* away, quite unconscious that he was at all wrong, until apprised, by the applause of the audience, that the overture was concluded. A considerable bustle and shuffling of feet was then heard upon the stage, accompanied by whispers of " Here's a pretty go!—what's to be done?" &c. The audience applauded again, by way of raising the spirits of the performers; and then Mr. Sempronius desired the prompter, in a very audible voice, to " clear the stage, and ring up."

Ting, ting, ting! went the bell again. Everybody sat down; the curtain shook; rose sufficiently high to display several pair of yellow boots paddling about; and there remained.

Ting, ting, ting! went the bell again. The curtain was violently convulsed, but rose no higher; the audience tittered; Mrs. Porter looked at Uncle Tom; Uncle Tom looked at everybody, rubbing his hands, and laughing with perfect rapture. After as much ringing with the little bell as a muffin-boy would make in going down a tolerably long street, and a vast deal of whispering, hammering, and calling for nails and cord, the curtain at length rose, and discovered Mr. Sempronius Gattleton *solus*, and decked for *Othello*. After three distinct rounds of applause, during which Mr. Sempronius applied his right hand to his left breast, and bowed in the most approved manner, the manager advanced and said :

"Ladies and Gentlemen—I assure you it is with sincere regret, that I regret to be compelled to inform you, that *Iago* who was to have played Mr. Wilson—I beg your pardon, Ladies and Gentlemen, but I am naturally somewhat agitated (applause)—I mean, Mr. Wilson, who was to have played *Iago*, is—that is, has been—or, in other words, Ladies and Gentlemen, the fact is, that I have just received a note, in which I am informed that *Iago* is unavoidably detained at the Post-office this evening. Under these circumstances, I trust—a—a—amateur performance—a—another gentleman undertaken to read the part—request indulgence for a short time—courtesy and kindness of a British audience." Overwhelming applause. Exit Mr. Sempronius Gattleton, and curtain falls.

The audience were, of course, exceedingly good-humoured; the whole business was a joke; and accordingly they waited for an hour with the utmost patience, being enlivened by an interlude of rout-cakes and lemonade. It appeared by Mr. Sempronius's subsequent explanation, that the delay would not have been so great, had it not so happened that when the substitute *Iago* had finished dressing, and just as the play was on the point of commencing, the original *Iago* unexpectedly arrived. The former was therefore compelled to undress, and the latter to dress for his part; which, as he found some difficulty in getting into his clothes, occupied no inconsiderable time. At last, the tragedy began in real earnest. It went off well enough, until the third scene of the first act, in which *Othello* addresses the Senate: the only remarkable circumstance being, that as *Iago* could not get on any of the stage boots, in consequence of his feet being violently swelled with the heat and excitement, he was under the necessity of playing the part in a pair of Wellingtons, which contrasted rather oddly with his richly embroidered pantaloons. When *Othello* started with his address to the Senate (whose dignity was represented by, the *Duke*, a carpenter, two men engaged on the recommendation of the gardener, and a boy), Mrs. Porter found the opportunity she so anxiously sought.

Mr. Sempronius proceeded:

> "'Most potent, grave, and reverend signiors,
> My very noble and approv'd good masters,
> That I have ta'en away this old man's daughter,
> It is most true;—rude am I in my speech——'"

"Is that right?" whispered Mrs. Porter to Uncle Tom.

"No."

"Tell him so, then."

"I will. Sem!" called out Uncle Tom, "that's wrong, my boy."

"What's wrong, uncle?" demanded *Othello*, quite forgetting the dignity of his situation.

"You've left out something. 'True I have married——'"

"Oh, ah!" said Mr. Sempronius, endeavouring to hide his confusion as much and as ineffectually as the audience attempted to conceal their half-suppressed tittering, by coughing with extraordinary violence—

> ——"'true I have married her;—
> The very head and front of my offending
> Hath this extent; no more.'

(*Aside*) Why don't you prompt, father?"

"Because I've mislaid my spectacles," said poor Mr. Gattleton, almost dead with the heat and bustle.

"There, now it's 'rude am I,'" said Uncle Tom.

"Yes, I know it is," returned the unfortunate manager, proceeding with his part.

It would be useless and tiresome to quote the number of instances in which Uncle Tom, now completely in his element, and instigated by the mischievous Mrs. Porter, corrected the mistakes of the performers; suffice it to say, that having mounted his hobby, nothing could induce him to dismount; so, during the whole remainder of the play, he performed a kind of running accompaniment, by muttering everybody's part as it was being delivered, in an under-tone. The audience were highly amused, Mrs. Porter delighted, the performers embarrassed; Uncle Tom never was better pleased in all his life; and Uncle Tom's nephews and nieces had never, although the declared heirs to his large property, so heartily wished him gathered to his fathers as on that memorable occasion.

Several other minor causes, too, united to damp the ardour of the *dramatis personæ*. None of the performers could walk in their tights, or move their arms in their jackets; the pantaloons were too small, the boots too large, and the swords of all shapes and sizes. Mr. Evans, naturally too tall for the scenery, wore a black velvet hat with immense white plumes, the glory of which was lost in " the flies ; " and the only other inconvenience of which was, that when it was off his head he could not put it on, and when it was on he could not take it off. Notwithstanding all his practice, too, he fell with his head and shoulders as neatly through one of the side scenes, as a harlequin would jump through a panel in a Christmas pantomime. The pianoforte player, overpowered by the extreme heat of the room, fainted away at the commencement of the entertainments, leaving the music of " Masaniello " to the flute and violoncello. The orchestra complained that Mr. Harleigh put them out, and Mr. Harleigh declared that the orchestra prevented his singing a note. The fishermen, who were hired for the occasion, revolted to the very life, positively refusing to play without an increased allowance of spirits; and, their demand being complied with, getting drunk in the eruption-scene as naturally as possible. The red fire, which was burnt at the conclusion of the second act, not only nearly suffocated the audience, but nearly set the house on fire into the bargain; and, as it was, the remainder of the piece was acted in a thick fog.

In short, the whole affair was, as Mrs. Joseph Porter triumphantly told everybody, " a complete failure." The audience went home at four o'clock in the morning, exhausted with laughter, suffering from severe headaches, and smelling terribly of brimstone and gunpowder. The Messrs. Gattleton, senior and junior, retired to rest, with the vague idea of emigrating to Swan River early in the ensuing week.

Rose Villa has once again resumed its wonted appearance; the dining-room furniture has been replaced; the tables are as nicely polished as formerly; the horsehair chairs are ranged against the wall, as regularly as ever; Venetian blinds have been fitted to every window in the house to intercept the prying gaze of Mrs. Joseph Porter. The subject of theatricals is never mentioned in the Gattleton family, unless, indeed, by Uncle Tom, who cannot refrain from sometimes expressing his surprise and regret at finding that his nephews and nieces appear to have lost the relish they once possessed for the beauties of Shakspeare, and quotations from the works of that immortal bard.

CHAPTER X

CHAPTER THE FIRST

MATRIMONY is proverbially a serious undertaking. Like an overweening predilection for brandy-and-water, it is a misfortune into which a man easily falls, and from which he finds it remarkably difficult to extricate himself. It is of no use telling a man who is timorous on these points, that it is but one plunge, and all is over. They say the same thing at the Old Bailey, and the unfortunate victims derive as much comfort from the assurance in the one case as in the other.

Mr. Watkins Tottle was a rather uncommon compound of strong uxorious inclinations, and an unparalleled degree of anti-connubial timidity. He was about fifty years of age; stood four feet six inches and three-quarters in his socks—for he never stood in stockings at all—plump, clean, and rosy. He looked something like a vignette to one of Richardson's novels, and had a clean-cravatish formality of manner, and kitchen-pokerness of carriage, which Sir Charles Grandison himself might have envied. He lived on an annuity, which was well adapted to the individual who received it, in one respect—it was rather small. He received it in periodical payments on every alternate Monday; but he ran himself out, about a day after the expiration of the first week, as regularly as an eight-day clock; and then, to make the comparison

114

George Cruikshank —

Watkins Tottle

complete, his landlady wound him up, and he went on with a regular tick.

Mr. Watkins Tottle had long lived in a state of single blessedness, as bachelors say, or single cursedness, as spinsters think; but the idea of matrimony had never ceased to haunt him. Wrapt in profound reveries on this never-failing theme, fancy transformed his small parlour in Cecil-street, Strand, into a neat house in the suburbs; the half-hundredweight of coals under the kitchen-stairs suddenly sprang up into three tons of the best Walls-end; his small French bedstead was converted into a regular matrimonial four-poster; and in the empty chair on the opposite side of the fireplace, imagination seated a beautiful young lady, with a very little independence or will of her own, and a very large independence under a will of her father's.

" Who's there ? " inquired Mr. Watkins Tottle, as a gentle tap at his room-door disturbed these meditations one evening.

" Tottle, my dear fellow, how *do* you do ? " said a short elderly gentleman with a gruffish voice, bursting into the room, and replying to the question by asking another.

" Told you I should drop in some evening," said the short gentleman, as he delivered his hat into Tottle's hand, after a little struggling and dodging.

" Delighted to see you, I'm sure," said Mr. Watkins Tottle, wishing internally that his visitor had " dropped in " to the Thames at the bottom of the street, instead of dropping into his parlour. The fortnight was nearly up, and Watkins was hard up.

" How is Mrs. Gabriel Parsons ? " inquired Tottle.

" Quite well, thank you," replied Mr. Gabriel Parsons, for that was the name the short gentleman revelled in. Here there was a pause; the short gentleman looked at the left hob of the fireplace; Mr. Watkins Tottle stared vacancy out of countenance.

" Quite well," repeated the short gentleman, when five

minutes had expired. "I may say remarkably well." And he rubbed the palms of his hands as hard as if he were going to strike a light by friction.

"What will you take?" inquired Tottle, with the desperate suddenness of a man who knew that unless the visitor took his leave, he stood very little chance of taking anything else.

"Oh, I don't know—have you any whiskey?"

"Why," replied Tottle, very slowly, for all this was gaining time, "I *had* some capital, and remarkably strong whiskey last week; but it's all gone—and therefore its strength——"

"Is much beyond proof; or, in other words, impossible to be proved," said the short gentleman; and he laughed very heartily, and seemed quite glad the whiskey had been drunk. Mr. Tottle smiled—but it was the smile of despair. When Mr. Gabriel Parsons had done laughing, he delicately insinuated that, in the absence of whiskey, he would not be averse to brandy. And Mr. Watkins Tottle, lighting a flat candle very ostentatiously; and displaying an immense key, which belonged to the street-door, but which, for the sake of appearances, occasionally did duty in an imaginary wine-cellar; left the room to entreat his landlady to charge their glasses, and charge them in the bill. The application was successful; the spirits were speedily called—not from the vasty deep, but the adjacent wine-vaults. The two short gentlemen mixed their grog; and then sat cosily down before the fire—a pair of shorts, airing themselves.

"Tottle," said Mr. Gabriel Parsons, "you know my way—off-hand, open, say what I mean, mean what I say, hate reserve, and can't bear affectation. One, is a bad domino which only hides what good people have about 'em, without making the bad look better; and the other is much about the same thing as pinking a white cotton stocking to make it look like a silk one. Now listen to what I'm going to say."

Here, the little gentleman paused, and took a long pull at his brandy-and-water. Mr. Watkins Tottle took a sip of his, stirred the fire, and assumed an air of profound attention.

"It's of no use humming and ha'ing about the matter," resumed the short gentleman.—"You want to get married."

"Why," replied Mr. Watkins Tottle evasively; for he trembled violently, and felt a sudden tingling throughout his whole frame; "why—I should certainly—at least, I *think* I should like——"

"Won't do," said the short gentleman.—"Plain and free—or there's an end of the matter. Do you want money?"

"You know I do."

"You admire the sex?"

"I do."

"And you'd like to be married?"

"Certainly."

"Then you shall be. There's an end of that." Thus saying, Mr. Gabriel Parsons took a pinch of snuff, and mixed another glass.

"Let me entreat you to be more explanatory," said Tottle. "Really, as the party principally interested, I cannot consent to be disposed of, in this way."

"I'll tell you," replied Mr. Gabriel Parsons, warming with the subject, and the brandy-and-water—"I know a lady—she's stopping with my wife now—who is just the thing for you. Well educated; talks French; plays the piano; knows a good deal about flowers, and shells, and all that sort of thing; and has five hundred a year, with an uncontrolled power of disposing of it, by her last will and testament."

"I'll pay my addresses to her," said Mr. Watkins Tottle. "She isn't *very* young—is she?"

"Not very; just the thing for you. I've said that already."

"What coloured hair has the lady?" inquired Mr. Watkins Tottle.

"Egad, I hardly recollect," replied Gabriel, with coolness. "Perhaps I ought to have observed, at first, she wears a front."

"A what?" ejaculated Tottle.

"One of those things with curls, along here," said Parsons, drawing a straight line across his forehead, just over his eyes, in illustration of his meaning. "I know the front's black; I can't speak quite positively about her own hair; because, unless one walks behind her, and catches a glimpse of it under her bonnet, one seldom sees it; but I should say that it was *rather* lighter than the front—a shade of a greyish tinge, perhaps."

Mr. Watkins Tottle looked as if he had certain misgivings of mind. Mr. Gabriel Parsons perceived it, and thought it would be safe to begin the next attack without delay.

"Now, were you ever in love, Tottle?" he inquired.

Mr. Watkins Tottle blushed up to the eyes, and down to the chin, and exhibited a most extensive combination of colours as he confessed the soft impeachment.

"I suppose you popped the question, more than once, when you were a young—I beg your pardon—a younger—man," said Parsons.

"Never in my life!" replied his friend, apparently indignant at being suspected of such an act. "Never! The fact is, that I entertain, as you know, peculiar opinions on these subjects. I am not afraid of ladies, young or old—far from it; but, I think, that in compliance with the custom of the present day, they allow too much freedom of speech and manner to marriageable men. Now, the fact is, that anything like this easy freedom I never could acquire; and as I am always afraid of going too far, I am generally, I dare say, considered formal and cold."

"I shouldn't wonder if you were," replied Parsons, gravely; "I shouldn't wonder. However, you'll be all right in this case; for the strictness and delicacy of this lady's ideas greatly exceed your own. Lord bless you, why, when she came to our house, there was an old portrait of some man or other, with two large, black, staring eyes, hanging up in her bedroom; she positively refused to go to bed there, till it was taken down, considering it decidedly wrong."

"I think so, too," said Mr. Watkins Tottle; "certainly."

"And then, the other night—I never laughed so much in

my life "—resumed Mr. Gabriel Parsons ; " I had driven home in an easterly wind, and caught a devil of a face-ache. Well ; as Fanny—that's Mrs. Parsons, you know—and this friend of hers, and I, and Frank Ross, were playing a rubber, I said, jokingly, that when I went to bed I should wrap my head in Fanny's flannel petticoat. She instantly threw up her cards, and left the room."

"Quite right ! " said Mr. Watkins Tottle ; " she could not possibly have behaved in a more dignified manner. What did you do ? "

" Do ?—Frank took dummy ; and I won sixpence."

" But, didn't you apologise for hurting her feelings ? "

" Devil a bit. Next morning at breakfast, we talked it over. She contended that any reference to a flannel petticoat was improper ;—men ought not to be supposed to know that such things were. I pleaded my coverture ; being a married man."

" And what did the lady say to that ? " inquired Tottle, deeply interested.

" Changed her ground, and said that Frank being a single man, its impropriety was obvious."

" Noble-minded creature ! " exclaimed the enraptured Tottle.

" Oh ! both Fanny and I said, at once, that she was regularly cut out for you."

A gleam of placid satisfaction shone on the circular face of Mr. Watkins Tottle, as he heard the prophecy.

"There's one thing I can't understand," said Mr. Gabriel Parsons, as he rose to depart; " I cannot, for the life and soul of me, imagine how the deuce you'll ever contrive to come together. The lady would certainly go into convulsions if the subject were mentioned." Mr. Gabriel Parsons sat down again, and laughed until he was weak. Tottle owed him money, so he had a perfect right to laugh at Tottle's expense.

Mr. Watkins Tottle feared, in his own mind, that this was another characteristic which he had in common with this modern Lucretia. He, however, accepted the invitation to dine with the Parsonses on the next day but one, with great firmness: and looked forward to the introduction, when again left alone, with tolerable composure.

The sun that rose on the next day but one, had never beheld a sprucer personage on the outside of the Norwood stage, than Mr. Watkins Tottle; and when the coach drew up before a cardboard-looking house with disguised chimneys, and a lawn like a large sheet of green letter-paper, he certainly had never lighted to his place of destination a gentleman who felt more uncomfortable.

The coach stopped, and Mr. Watkins Tottle jumped—we beg his pardon—alighted, with great dignity. "All right!" said he, and away went the coach up the hill with that beautiful equanimity of pace for which "short" stages are generally remarkable.

Mr. Watkins Tottle gave a faltering jerk to the handle of the garden-gate bell. He essayed a more energetic tug, and his previous nervousness was not at all diminished by hearing the bell ringing like a fire alarum.

"Is Mr. Parsons at home?" inquired Tottle of the man who opened the gate. He could hardly hear himself speak, for the bell had not yet done tolling.

"Here I am," shouted a voice on the lawn,—and there was Mr. Gabriel Parsons in a flannel jacket, running backwards and forwards, from a wicket to two hats piled on each other, and from the two hats to the wicket, in the most violent manner, while another gentleman with his coat off was getting down the area of the house, after a ball. When the gentleman without the coat had found it—which he did in less than ten minutes—he ran back to the hats, and Gabriel Parsons pulled up. Then, the gentleman without the coat called out "play," very loudly, and bowled. Then Mr. Gabriel Parsons knocked the ball several yards, and took another run. Then, the other gentleman aimed at the wicket, and didn't hit it; and Mr. Gabriel Parsons, having finished running on his own

120

account, laid down the bat and ran after the ball, which went into a neighbouring field. They called this cricket.

"Tottle, will you 'go in?'" inquired Mr. Gabriel Parsons, as he approached him, wiping the perspiration off his face.

Mr. Watkins Tottle declined the offer, the bare idea of accepting which made him even warmer than his friend.

"Then we'll go into the house, as it's past four, and I shall have to wash my hands before dinner," said Mr. Gabriel Parsons. "Here, I hate ceremony, you know! Timson, that's Tottle—Tottle, that's Timson; bred for the church, which I fear will never be bread for him;" and he chuckled at the old joke. Mr. Timson bowed carelessly. Mr. Watkins Tottle bowed stiffly. Mr. Gabriel Parsons led the way to the house. He was a rich sugar-baker, who mistook rudeness for honesty, and abrupt bluntness for an open and candid manner; many besides Gabriel mistake bluntness for sincerity.

Mrs. Gabriel Parsons received the visitors most graciously on the steps, and preceded them to the drawing-room. On the sofa, was seated a lady of very prim appearance, and remarkably inanimate. She was one of those persons at whose age it is impossible to make any reasonable guess; her features might have been remarkably pretty when she was younger, and they might always have presented the same appearance. Her complexion—with a slight trace of powder here and there—was as clear as that of a well-made wax doll, and her face as expressive. She was handsomely dressed, and was winding up a gold watch.

"Miss Lillerton, my dear, this is our friend Mr. Watkins Tottle; a very old acquaintance I assure you," said Mrs. Parsons, presenting the Strephon of Cecil-street, Strand. The lady rose, and made a deep courtesy; Mr. Watkins Tottle made a bow.

"Splendid, majestic creature!" thought Tottle.

Mr. Timson advanced, and Mr. Watkins Tottle began to hate him. Men generally discover a rival, instinctively, and Mr. Watkins Tottle felt that his hate was deserved.

"May I beg," said the reverend gentleman,—"May I beg to call upon you, Miss Lillerton, for some trifling donation to my soup, coals, and blanket distribution society?"

"Put my name down, for two sovereigns, if you please," responded Miss Lillerton.

"You are truly charitable, madam," said the Reverend Mr. Timson, "and we know that charity will cover a multitude of sins. Let me beg you to understand that I do not say this from the supposition that you have many sins which require palliation; believe me when I say that I never yet met any one who had fewer to atone for, than Miss Lillerton."

Something like a bad imitation of animation lighted up the lady's face, as she acknowledged the compliment. Watkins Tottle incurred the sin of wishing that the ashes of the Reverend Charles Timson were quietly deposited in the churchyard of his curacy, wherever it might be.

"I'll tell you what," interrupted Parsons, who had just appeared with clean hands, and a black coat, "it's my private opinion, Timson, that your 'distribution society' is rather a humbug."

"You are so severe," replied Timson, with a Christian smile: he disliked Parsons, but liked his dinners.

"So positively unjust!" said Miss Lillerton.

"Certainly," observed Tottle. The lady looked up; her eyes met those of Mr. Watkins Tottle. She withdrew them in a sweet confusion, and Watkins Tottle did the same—the confusion was mutual.

"Why," urged Mr. Parsons, pursuing his objections, "what on earth is the use of giving a man coals who has nothing to cook, or giving him blankets when he hasn't a bed, or giving him soup when he requires substantial food?—'like sending them ruffles when wanting a shirt.' Why not give 'em a trifle of money, as I do, when I think they deserve it, and let them purchase what they think best? Why?—because your subscribers wouldn't see their names flourishing in print on the church-door—that's the reason."

"Really, Mr. Parsons, I hope you don't mean to insinuate that I wish to see *my* name in print, on the church-door," interrupted Miss Lillerton.

"I hope not," said Mr. Watkins Tottle, putting in another word, and getting another glance.

"Certainly not," replied Parsons. "I dare say you wouldn't mind seeing it in writing, though, in the church register—eh?"

"Register! What register?" inquired the lady, gravely.

"Why, the register of marriages, to be sure," replied Parsons, chuckling at the sally, and glancing at Tottle. Mr. Watkins Tottle thought he should have fainted for shame, and it is quite impossible to imagine what effect the joke would have had upon the lady, if dinner had not been, at that moment, announced. Mr. Watkins Tottle, with an unprecedented effort of gallantry, offered the tip of his little finger; Miss Lillerton accepted it gracefully, with maiden modesty; and they proceeded in due state to the dinner-table, where they were soon deposited side by side. The room was very snug, the dinner very good, and the little party in spirits. The conversation became pretty general, and when Mr. Watkins Tottle had extracted one or two cold observations from his neighbour, and had taken wine with her, he began to acquire confidence rapidly. The cloth was removed; Mrs. Gabriel Parsons drank four glasses of port on the plea of being a nurse just then; and Miss Lillerton took about the same number of sips, on the plea of not wanting any at all. At length, the ladies retired, to the great gratification of Mr. Gabriel Parsons, who had been coughing and frowning at his wife, for half-an-hour previously—signals which Mrs. Parsons never happened to observe, until she had been pressed to take her ordinary quantum, which, to avoid giving trouble, she generally did at once.

"What do you think of her?" inquired Mr. Gabriel Parsons of Mr. Watkins Tottle, in an under-tone.

"I dote on her with enthusiasm already!" replied Mr. Watkins Tottle.

"Gentlemen, pray let us drink 'the ladies,'" said the Reverend Mr. Timson.

"The ladies!" said Mr. Watkins Tottle, emptying his glass. In the fulness of his confidence, he felt as if he could make love to a dozen ladies, off-hand.

"Ah!" said Mr. Gabriel Parsons, "I remember when I was a young man—fill your glass, Timson."

"I have this moment emptied it."

"Then fill again."

"I will," said Timson, suiting the action to the word.

"I remember," resumed Mr. Gabriel Parsons, "when I was a younger man, with what a strange compound of feelings I used to drink that toast, and how I used to think every woman was an angel."

"Was that before you were married?" mildly inquired Mr. Watkins Tottle.

"Oh! certainly," replied Mr. Gabriel Parsons. "I have never thought so since; and a precious milksop I must have been, ever to have thought so at all. But, you know, I married Fanny under the oddest, and most ridiculous circumstances possible."

"What were they, if one may inquire?" asked Timson, who had heard the story, on an average, twice a week for the last six months. Mr. Watkins Tottle listened attentively, in the hope of picking up some suggestion that might be useful to him in his new undertaking.

"I spent my wedding-night in a back-kitchen chimney," said Parsons, by way of a beginning.

"In a back-kitchen chimney!" ejaculated Watkins Tottle. "How dreadful!"

"Yes, it wasn't very pleasant," replied the small host. "The fact is, Fanny's father and mother liked me well enough as an individual, but had a decided objection to my becoming a husband. You see, I hadn't any money in those days, and they had; and so they wanted Fanny to pick up somebody else. However, we managed to discover the state of each other's affections somehow. I used to meet her, at some mutual friends' parties; at first we danced together, and talked, and flirted, and all that sort of thing; then, I used to like nothing so well as sitting by her side—we didn't talk so much then, but I remember I used to have a great notion of looking at her out of the extreme corner of my left eye— and then I got very miserable and sentimental, and began to write verses, and use Macassar oil. At last I couldn't bear it any longer, and after I had walked up and down the sunny side of Oxford-street in tight boots for a week—and a devilish hot summer it was too—in the hope of meeting her, I sat down and wrote a letter, and begged her to manage to see me clandestinely, for I wanted to hear her decision from her own mouth. I said I had discovered, to my perfect satisfaction, that I couldn't live without her, and that if she didn't have me, I had made up my mind to take prussic acid, or take to drinking, or emigrate, so as to take myself off in some way or other. Well, I borrowed a pound, and bribed the housemaid to give her the note, which she did."

"And what was the reply?" inquired Timson, who had found, before, that to encourage the repetition of old stories is to get a general invitation.

"Oh, the usual one! Fanny expressed herself very miserable; hinted at the possibility of an early grave; said that nothing should induce her to swerve from the duty she owed her parents; implored me to forget her, and find out somebody more deserving, and all that sort of thing. She said she could, on no account, think of meeting me unknown to her pa and ma; and entreated me, as she should be in a particular part of Kensington Gardens at eleven o'clock next morning, not to attempt to meet her there."

"You didn't go, of course?" said Watkins Tottle.

"Didn't I?—Of course I did. There she was, with the identical housemaid in perspective, in order that there might be no interruption. We walked about, for a couple of hours; made ourselves delightfully miserable; and were regularly engaged. Then, we began to 'correspond'—that is to say, we used to exchange about four letters a day; what we used to say in 'em I can't imagine. And I used to have an interview, in the kitchen, or the cellar, or some such place, every evening. Well, things went on in this way for some time; and we got fonder of each other every day. At last, as our love was raised to such a pitch, and as my salary had been raised too, shortly before, we determined on a secret marriage. Fanny arranged to sleep at a friend's, on the previous night; we were to be married early in the morning; and then we were to return to her home and be pathetic. She was to fall at the old gentleman's feet, and bathe his boots with her tears; and I was to hug the old lady and call her 'mother,' and use my pocket-handkerchief as much as possible. Married we were, the next morning; two girls—friends of Fanny's—acting as bridesmaids; and a man, who was hired for five shillings and a pint of porter, officiating as father. Now, the old lady unfortunately put off her return from Ramsgate, where she had been paying a visit, until the next morning; and as we placed great reliance on her, we agreed to postpone our confession for four-and-twenty hours. My newly-made wife returned home, and I spent my wedding-day in strolling about Hampstead-heath, and execrating my father-in-law. Of course, I went to comfort my dear little wife at night, as much as I could, with the assurance that our troubles would soon be over. I opened the garden-gate, of which I had a key, and was shown by the servant to our old place of meeting —a back kitchen, with a stone-floor and a dresser: upon which, in the absence of chairs, we used to sit and make love."

"Make love upon a kitchen-dresser!" interrupted Mr. Watkins Tottle, whose ideas of decorum were greatly outraged.

"Ah! On a kitchen-dresser!" replied Parsons. "And let me tell you, old fellow, that, if you were really over head-and-ears in love, and had no other place to make love in, you'd be devilish glad to avail yourself of such an opportunity. However, let me see;—where was I?"

"On the dresser," suggested Timson.

"Oh—ah! Well, here I found poor Fanny, quite disconsolate and uncomfortable. The old boy had been very cross all day, which made her feel still more lonely; and she was quite out of spirits. So, I put a good face on the matter, and laughed it off, and said we should enjoy the pleasures of a matrimonial life more by contrast; and, at length, poor Fanny brightened up a little. I stopped there, till about eleven o'clock, and, just as I was taking my leave for the fourteenth time, the girl came running down the stairs, without her shoes, in a great fright, to tell us that the old villain—Heaven forgive me for calling him so, for he is dead and gone now!—prompted I suppose by the prince of darkness, was coming down, to draw his own beer for supper—a thing he had not done before, for six months, to my certain knowledge; for the cask stood in that very back kitchen. If he discovered me there, explanation would have been out of the question; for he was so outrageously violent, when at all excited, that he never would have listened to me. There was only one thing to be done. The chimney was a very wide one; it had been originally built for an oven; went up perpendicularly for a few feet, and then shot backward and formed a sort of small cavern. My hopes and fortune—the means of our joint existence almost—were at stake. I scrambled in like a squirrel; coiled myself up in this recess; and, as Fanny and the girl replaced the deal chimney-board, I could see the light of the candle which my unconscious father-in-law carried in his hand. I heard him draw the beer; and I never heard beer run so slowly. He was just leaving the kitchen, and I was preparing to descend, when down came the infernal chimney-board with a tremendous crash. He stopped and put down the candle and the jug of beer on the dresser; he was a nervous old fellow, and any unexpected noise annoyed him. He coolly observed that the fireplace was never used, and sending the frightened servant into the next kitchen for a hammer and nails, actually nailed up the board, and locked the door on the outside. So, there was I, on my wedding-night, in the light kerseymere trousers, fancy waist-coat, and blue coat, that I had been married in in the morning, in a back-kitchen chimney, the bottom of which was nailed up, and the top of which had been formerly raised some fifteen feet, to prevent the smoke from annoying the neighbours. And there," added Mr. Gabriel Parsons, as he passed the bottle, " there I remained till half-past seven the next morning, when the housemaid's sweetheart, who was a carpenter, unshelled me. The old dog had nailed me up so securely, that, to this very hour, I firmly believe that no one but a carpenter could ever have got me out."

"And what did Mrs. Parsons's father say, when he found you were married?" inquired Watkins Tottle, who, although he never saw a joke, was not satisfied until he heard a story to the very end.

"Why, the affair of the chimney so tickled his fancy, that he pardoned us off-hand, and allowed us something to live on till he went the way of all flesh. I spent the next night in his second-floor front, much more comfortably than I had spent the preceding one; for, as you will probably guess——"

"Please, sir, missis has made tea," said a middle-aged female servant, bobbing into the room.

"That's the very housemaid that figures in my story," said Mr. Gabriel Parsons. "She went into Fanny's service when we were first married, and has been with us ever since; but I don't think she has felt one atom of respect for me since the morning she saw me released, when she went into violent hysterics, to which she has been subject ever since. Now, shall we join the ladies?"

"If you please," said Mr. Watkins Tottle.

"By all means," added the obsequious Mr. Timson; and the trio made for the drawing-room accordingly.

Tea being concluded, and the toast and cups having been duly handed, and occasionally upset, by Mr. Watkins Tottle, a rubber was proposed. They cut for partners—Mr. and

Mrs. Parsons; and Mr. Watkins Tottle and Miss Lillerton. Mr. Timson having conscientious scruples on the subject of card-playing, drank brandy-and-water, and kept up a running spar with Mr. Watkins Tottle. The evening went off well; Mr. Watkins Tottle was in high spirits, having some reason to be gratified with his reception by Miss Lillerton; and before he left, a small party was made up to visit the Beulah Spa on the following Saturday.

"It's all right, I think," said Mr. Gabriel Parsons to Mr. Watkins Tottle as he opened the garden gate for him.

"I hope so," he replied, squeezing his friend's hand.

"You'll be down by the first coach on Saturday," said Mr. Gabriel Parsons.

"Certainly," replied Mr. Watkins Tottle. "Undoubtedly."

But fortune had decreed that Mr. Watkins Tottle should not be down by the first coach on Saturday. His adventures on that day, however, and the success of his wooing, are subjects for another chapter.

CHAPTER ·THE SECOND.

"The first coach has not come in yet, has it, Tom?" inquired Mr. Gabriel Parsons, as he very complacently paced up and down the fourteen feet of gravel which bordered the "lawn," on the Saturday morning which had been fixed upon for the Beulah Spa jaunt.

"No, sir; I haven't seen it," replied a gardener in a blue apron, who let himself out to do the ornamental for half-a-crown a day and his "keep."

"Time Tottle was down,' said Mr. Gabriel Parsons, ruminating—"Oh, here he is, no doubt," added Gabriel, as a cab drove rapidly up the hill; and he buttoned his dressing-gown, and opened the gate to receive the expected visitor. The cab stopped, and out jumped a man in a coarse Petersham great-coat, whity-brown neckerchief, faded black suit, gamboge-coloured top-boots, and one of those large-crowned hats, formerly seldom met with, but now very generally patronised by gentlemen and costermongers.

" Mr. Parsons ? " said the man, looking at the superscription of a note he held in his hand, and addressing Gabriel with an inquiring air.

" *My* name is Parsons," responded the sugar-baker.

" I've brought this here note," replied the individual in the painted tops, in a hoarse whisper: " I've brought this here note from a gen'lm'n as come to our house this mornin'."

" I expected the gentleman at my house," said Parsons, as he broke the seal, which bore the impression of her Majesty's profile as it is seen on a sixpence.

" I've no doubt the gen'lm'n would ha' been here," replied the stranger, " if he hadn't happened to call at our house first ; but we never trusts no gen'lm'n furder nor we can see him—no mistake about that there "—added the unknown, with a facetious grin ; " beg your pardon, sir, no offence meant, only—once in, and I wish you may—catch the idea, sir ? "

Mr. Gabriel Parsons was not remarkable for catching any-thing suddenly, but a cold. He therefore only bestowed a glance of profound astonishment on his mysterious companion, and proceeded to unfold the note of which he had been the bearer. Once opened and the idea was caught with very little difficulty. Mr. Watkins Tottle had been suddenly arrested for 33*l*. 10*s*. 4*d*., and dated his communication from a lock-up house in the vicinity of Chancery-lane.

" Unfortunate affair this ! " said Parsons, refolding the note.

" Oh ! nothin' ven you're used to it," coolly observed the man in the Petersham.

" Tom ! " exclaimed Parsons, after a few minutes' considera-tion, " just put the horse in, will you ?—Tell the gentleman that I shall be there almost as soon as you are," he continued, addressing the sheriff-officer's Mercury.

" Werry well," replied that important functionary ; adding, in a confidential manner, " I'd adwise the gen'lm'n's friends to settle. You see it's a mere trifle ; and, unless the gen'lm'n means to go up afore the court, it's hardly worth while waiting for detainers, you know. Our governor's wide awake, he is. I'll never say nothin' agin him, nor no man; but he knows what's o'clock, he does, uncommon." Having delivered this eloquent, and, to Parsons, particularly intelligible harangue, the meaning of which was eked out by divers nods and winks, the gentleman in the boots reseated himself in the cab, which went rapidly off, and was soon out of sight. Mr. Gabriel Parsons continued to pace up and down the pathway for some minutes, apparently absorbed in deep meditation. The result of his cogitations seemed to be perfectly satisfactory to himself, for he ran briskly into the house; said that business had suddenly summoned him to town; that he had desired the messenger to inform Mr. Watkins Tottle of the fact; and that they would return together to dinner. He then hastily equipped himself for a drive, and mounting his gig, was soon on his way to the establishment of Mr. Solomon Jacobs, situate (as Mr. Watkins Tottle had informed him) in Cursitor-street, Chancery-lane.

When a man is in a violent hurry to get on, and has a specific object in view, the attainment of which depends on the completion of his journey, the difficulties which interpose themselves in his way appear not only to be innumerable, but to have been called into existence especially for the occasion. The remark is by no means a new one, and Mr. Gabriel Parsons had practical and painful experience of its justice in the course of his drive. There are three classes of animated objects which prevent your driving with any degree of comfort or celerity through streets which are but little frequented—they are pigs, children, and old women. On the occasion we are describing, the pigs were luxuriating on cabbage-stalks, and the shuttlecocks fluttered from the little deal battledores, and the children played in the road; and women, with a basket in one hand, and the street-door key in the other, *would* cross just before the horse's head, until Mr. Gabriel Parsons was perfectly savage with vexation, and quite hoarse with hoi-ing and imprecating. Then, when he got into Fleet-street, there was "a stoppage," in which people in vehicles have the satisfaction of remaining stationary for half an hour, and envying the slowest pedestrians; and where policemen rush about, and seize hold of horses' bridles, and back them into shop-windows, by way of clearing the road and preventing confusion. At length Mr. Gabriel Parsons turned into Chancery-lane, and having inquired for, and been directed to Cursitor-street (for it was a locality of which he was quite ignorant), he soon found himself opposite the house of Mr. Solomon Jacobs. Confiding his horse and gig to the care of one of the fourteen boys who had followed him from the other side of Blackfriars-bridge on the chance of his requiring their services, Mr. Gabriel Parsons crossed the road and knocked at an inner door, the upper part of which was of glass, grated like the windows of this inviting mansion with iron bars—painted white to look comfortable.

The knock was answered by a sallow-faced, red-haired, sulky boy, who, after surveying Mr. Gabriel Parsons through the glass, applied a large key to an immense wooden excrescence, which was in reality a lock, but which, taken in conjunction with the iron nails with which the panels were studded, gave the door the appearance of being subject to warts.

"I want to see Mr. Watkins Tottle," said Parsons.

"It's the gentleman that come in this morning, Jem," screamed a voice from the top of the kitchen-stairs, which belonged to a dirty woman who had just brought her chin to a level with the passage-floor. "The gentleman's in the coffee-room."

"Up-stairs, sir," said the boy, just opening the door wide enough to let Parsons in without squeezing him, and double-locking it the moment he had made his way through the aperture—"First floor—door on the left."

Mr. Gabriel Parsons thus instructed, ascended the uncarpeted and ill-lighted staircase, and after giving several subdued taps at the before-mentioned "door on the left," which were

132

The Lock-up House

rendered inaudible by the hum of voices within the room, and the hissing noise attendant on some frying operations which were carrying on below stairs, turned the handle, and entered the apartment. Being informed that the unfortunate object of his visit had just gone up-stairs to write a letter, he had leisure to sit down and observe the scene before him.

The room—which was a small, confined den—was partitioned off into boxes, like the common-room of some inferior eating-house. The dirty floor had evidently been as long a stranger to the scrubbing-brush as to carpet or floor-cloth : and the ceiling was completely blackened by the flare of the oil-lamp by which the room was lighted at night. The gray ashes on the edges of the tables, and the cigar ends which were plentifully scattered about the dusty grate, fully accounted for the intolerable smell of tobacco which pervaded the place ; and the empty glasses and half-saturated slices of lemon on the tables, together with the porter pots beneath them, bore testimony to the frequent libations in which the individuals who honoured Mr. Solomon Jacobs by a temporary residence in his house indulged. Over the mantel-shelf was a paltry looking-glass, extending about half the width of the chimney-piece ; but by way of counterpoise, the ashes were confined by a rusty fender about twice as long as the hearth.

From this cheerful room itself, the attention of Mr. Gabriel Parsons was naturally directed to its inmates. In one of the boxes two men were playing at cribbage with a very dirty pack of cards, some with blue, some with green, and some with red backs—selections from decayed packs. The cribbage board had been long ago formed on the table by some ingenious visitor with the assistance of a pocket-knife and a two-pronged fork, with which the necessary number of holes had been made in the table at proper distances for the reception of the wooden pegs. In another box a stout, hearty-looking man, of about forty, was eating some dinner which his wife—an equally comfortable-looking personage—had brought him in a basket : and in a third, a genteel-looking

133

young man was talking earnestly, and in a low tone, to a young female, whose face was concealed by a thick veil, but whom Mr. Gabriel Parsons immediately set down in his own mind as the debtor's wife. A young fellow of vulgar manners, dressed in the very extreme of the prevailing fashion, was pacing up and down the room, with a lighted cigar in his mouth and his hands in his pockets, ever and anon puffing forth volumes of smoke, and occasionally applying, with much apparent relish, to a pint pot, the contents of which were " chilling " on the hob.

" Fourpence more, by gum ! " exclaimed one of the cribbage-players, lighting a pipe, and addressing his adversary at the close of the game ; " one 'ud think you'd got luck in a pepper-cruet, and shook it out when you wanted it."

" Well, that a'n't a bad un," replied the other, who was a horse-dealer from Islington.

" No ; I'm blessed if it is," interposed the jolly-looking fellow, who, having finished his dinner, was drinking out of the same glass as his wife, in truly conjugal harmony, some hot gin-and-water. The faithful partner of his cares had brought a plentiful supply of the anti-temperance fluid in a large flat stone bottle, which looked like a half-gallon jar that had been successfully tapped for the dropsy. " You're a rum chap, you are, Mr. Walker—will you dip your beak into this, sir ? "

" Thank'ee, sir," replied Mr. Walker, leaving his box, and advancing to the other to accept the proffered glass. " Here's your health, sir, and your good 'ooman's here. Gentlemen all—yours, and better luck still. Well, Mr. Willis," continued the facetious prisoner, addressing the young man with the cigar, " you seem rather down to-day—floored, as one may say. What's the matter, sir ? Never say die, you know."

" Oh ! I'm all right," replied the smoker. " I shall be bailed out to-morrow."

" Shall you, though ? " inquired the other. " Damme, I wish I could say the same. I am as regularly over head and ears as the Royal George, and stand about as much chance of being *bailed out*. Ha! ha! ha!"

"Why," said the young man, stopping short, and speaking in a very loud key, "look at me. What d'ye think I've stopped here two days for?"

"'Cause you couldn't get out, I suppose," interrupted Mr. Walker, winking to the company. "Not that you're exactly obliged to stop here, only you can't help it. No compulsion, you know, only you must—eh?"

"A'n't he a rum un?" inquired the delighted individual, who had offered the gin-and-water, of his wife.

"Oh, he just is!" replied the lady, who was quite overcome by these flashes of imagination.

"Why, my case," frowned the victim, throwing the end of his cigar into the fire, and illustrating his argument by knocking the bottom of the pot on the table, at intervals,— "my case is a very singular one. My father's a man of large property, and I am his son."

"That's a very strange circumstance!" interrupted the jocose Mr. Walker, *en passant*.

"—I am his son, and have received a liberal education. I don't owe no man nothing—not the value of a' farthing, but I was induced, you see, to put my name to some bills for a friend—bills to a large amount, I may say a very large amount, for which I didn't receive no consideration. What's the consequence?"

"Why, I suppose the bills went out, and you came in. The acceptances weren't taken up, and you were, eh?" inquired Walker.

"To be sure," replied the liberally educated young gentleman. "To be sure; and so here I am, locked up for a matter of twelve hundred pound."

"Why don't you ask your old governor to stump up?" inquired Walker, with a somewhat sceptical air.

"Oh! bless you, he'd never do it," replied the other, in a tone of expostulation—"Never!"

"Well, it is very odd to—be—sure," interposed the owner of the flat bottle, mixing another glass, "but I've been in difficulties, as one may say, now for thirty year. I went to pieces when I was in a milk-walk, thirty year ago; arterwards, when I was a fruiterer, and kept a spring wan; and arter that again in the coal and 'tatur line—but all that time I never see a youngish chap come into a place of this kind, who wasn't going out again directly, and who hadn't been arrested on bills which he'd given a friend and for which he'd received nothing whatsomever—not a fraction."

"Oh! it's always the cry," said Walker. "I can't see the use on it; that's what makes me so wild. Why, I should have a much better opinion of an individual, if he'd say at once in an honourable and gentlemanly manner as he'd done everybody he possibly could."

"Ay, to be sure," interposed the horse-dealer, with whose notions of bargain and sale the axiom perfectly coincided, "so should I."

The young gentleman, who had given rise to these observations, was on the point of offering a rather angry reply to these sneers, but the rising of the young man before noticed, and of the female who had been sitting by him, to leave the room, interrupted the conversation. She had been weeping bitterly, and the noxious atmosphere of the room acting upon her excited feelings and delicate frame, rendered the support of her companion necessary as they quitted it together.

There was an air of superiority about them both, and something in their appearance so unusual in such a place, that a respectful silence was observed until the *whirr—r— bang* of the spring door announced that they were out of hearing. It was broken by the wife of the ex-fruiterer.

"Poor creetur!" said she, quenching a sigh in a rivulet of gin-and-water. "She's very young."

"She's a nice-looking 'ooman too," added the horse-dealer.

"What's he in for, Ikey?" inquired Walker, of an individual who was spreading a cloth with numerous blotches of mustard upon it, on one of the tables, and whom Mr. Gabriel Parsons had no difficulty in recognising as the man who had called upon him in the morning.

"Vy," responded the factotum, "it's one of the rummiest rigs you ever heard on. He come in here last Vensday, which by-the-bye he's a-going over the water to-night—hows'ever that's neither here nor there. You see I've been a going back'ards and for'ards about his business, and ha' managed to pick up some of his story from the servants and them; and so far as I can make it out, it seems to be summat to this here effect——"

"Cut it short, old fellow," interrupted Walker, who knew from former experience that he of the top-boots was neither very concise nor intelligible in his narratives.

"Let me alone," replied Ikey, "and I'll ha' vound up, and made my lucky in five seconds. This here young gen'lm'n's father—so I'm told, mind ye—and the father o' the young voman, have always been on very bad, out-and-out, rig'lar knock-me-down sort o' terms; but somehow or another, when he was a wisitin' at some gentlefolk's house, as he knowed at college, he came into contract with the young lady. He seed her several times, and then he up and said he'd keep company with her, if so be as she vos agreeable. Vell, she vos as sweet upon him as he vos upon her, and so I s'pose they made it all right; for they got married 'bout six months arterwards, unbeknown, mind ye, to the two fathers—leastways so I'm told. When they heard on it—my eyes, there was such a combustion! Starvation vos the very least that vos to be done to 'em. The young gen'lm'n's father cut him off vith a bob, 'cos he'd cut himself off vith a wife; and the young lady's father he behaved even worser and more unnat'ral, for he not only blow'd her up dreadful, and swore he'd never see her again, but he employed a chap as I knows—and as you knows, Mr. Valker, a precious sight too well—to go about and buy up the bills and them things on which the young husband, thinking his governor 'ud come round agin, had raised the vind just to blow himself on vith for a time ; besides vich, he made all the interest he could to set other people agin him. Consequence vos, that he paid as long as he could ; but things he never expected to have to meet till he'd had time to turn himself round, come fast upon him, and he vos nabbed. He vos brought here, as I said afore, last Vensday, and I think there's about—ah, half-a-dozen detainers agin him down-stairs now. I have been," added Ikey, "in the purfession these fifteen year, and I never met vith such windictiveness afore ! "

" Poor creeturs ! " exclaimed the coal-dealer's wife once more : again resorting to the same excellent prescription for nipping a sigh in the bud. " Ah ! when they've seen as much trouble as I and my old man here have, they'll be as comfortable under it as we are."

" The young lady's a pretty creature," said Walker, " only she's a little too delicate for my taste—there ain't enough of her. As to the young cove, he may be very respectable and what not, but he's too down in the mouth for me—he ain't game."

" Game ! " exclaimed Ikey, who had been altering the position of a green-handled knife and fork at least a dozen times, in order that he might remain in the room under the pretext of having something to do. " He's game enough ven there's anything to be fierce about ; but who could be game as you call it, Mr. Walker, with a pale young creetur like that, hanging about him ?—It's enough to drive any man's heart into his boots to see 'em together—and no mistake at all about it. I never shall forget her first comin' here ; he wrote to her on the Thursday to come—I know he did, 'cos I took the letter. Uncommon fidgety he was all day to be sure, and in the evening he goes down into the office, and he says to Jacobs, says he, ' Sir, can I have the loan of a private room for a few minutes this evening, without incurring any additional expense—just to see my wife in?' says he. Jacobs looked as much as to say—'Strike me bountiful if you ain't one of the modest sort!' but as the gen'lm'n who had been in the back parlour had just gone out, and had paid for it for that day, he says—werry grave—'Sir,' says he, 'it's agin our rules to let private rooms to our lodgers on gratis terms, but,' says he, 'for a gentleman, I don't mind breaking through them for once.' So then he turns round to me, and says, ' Ikey, put two mould candles in the back parlour, and charge 'em to this gen'lm'n's account, 'vich I did. Vell, by-and-by a hackney-coach comes up to the door, and there, sure enough, was the young lady, wrapped up in a hopera-cloak, as it might be, and all alone. I opened the gate that night, so I went up when the coach come, and he vos a waitin' at the parlour door—and wasn't he a trembling, neither? The poor creetur see him, and could hardly walk to meet him. 'Oh, Harry!' she says, 'that it should have come to this; and all for my sake,' says she, putting her hand upon his shoulder. So he puts his arm round her pretty little waist, and leading her gently a little way into the room, so that he might be able to shut the door, he says, so kind and soft-like—'Why, Kate,' says he——"

"Here's the gentleman you want," said Ikey, abruptly breaking off in his story, and introducing Mr. Gabriel Parsons to the crest-fallen Watkins Tottle, who at that moment entered the room. Watkins advanced with a wooden expression of passive endurance, and accepted the hand which Mr. Gabriel Parsons held out.

"I want to speak to you," said Gabriel, with a look strongly expressive of his dislike of the company.

"This way," replied the imprisoned one, leading the way to the front drawing-room, where rich debtors did the luxurious at the rate of a couple of guineas a day.

"Well, here I am," said Mr. Watkins, as he sat down on the sofa; and placing the palms of his hands on his knees, anxiously glanced at his friend's countenance.

"Yes; and here you're likely to be," said Gabriel, coolly, as he rattled the money in his unmentionable pockets, and looked out of the window.

"What's the amount with the costs?" inquired Parsons, after an awkward pause.

"37*l*. 3*s*. 10*d*."

"Have you any money?"

"Nine and sixpence halfpenny."

Mr. Gabriel Parsons walked up and down the room for a few seconds, before he could make up his mind to disclose the plan he had formed; he was accustomed to drive hard bargains, but was always most anxious to conceal his avarice. At length he stopped short, and said, "Tottle, you owe me fifty pounds."

"I do."

"And from all I see, I infer that you are likely to owe it to me."

"I fear I am."

"Though you have every disposition to pay me if you could?"

"Certainly."

"Then," said Mr. Gabriel Parsons, "listen: here's my proposition. You know my way of old. Accept it—yes or no—I will or I won't. I'll pay the debt and costs, and I'll lend you 10*l*. more (which, added to your annuity, will enable you to carry on the war well) if you'll give me your note of hand to pay me one hundred and fifty pounds within six months after you are married to Miss Lillerton."

"My dear——"

"Stop a minute—on one condition; and that is, that you propose to Miss Lillerton at once."

"At once! My dear Parsons, consider."

"It's for you to consider, not me. She knows you well from reputation, though she did not know you personally until lately. Notwithstanding all her maiden modesty, I think she'd be devilish glad to get married out of hand with as little delay as possible. My wife has sounded her on the subject, and she has confessed."

140

" What—what ? " eagerly interrupted the enamoured Watkins.

" Why," replied Parsons, " to say exactly what she has confessed, would be rather difficult, because they only spoke in hints, and so forth; but my wife, who is no bad judge in these cases, declared to me that what she had confessed was as good as to say that she was not insensible of your merits —in fact, that no other man should have her."

Mr. Watkins Tottle rose hastily from his seat, and rang the bell.

" What's that for ? " inquired Parsons.

" I want to send the man for the bill stamp," replied Mr. Watkins Tottle.

" Then you've made up your mind ? "

" I have,"—and they shook hands most cordially. The note of hand was given—the debt and costs were paid—Ikey was satisfied for his trouble, and the two friends soon found themselves on that side of Mr. Solomon Jacobs's establishment, on which most of his visitors were very happy when they found themselves once again—to wit, the *out*side.

" Now," said Mr. Gabriel Parsons, as they drove to Norwood together—" you shall have an opportunity to make the disclosure to-night, and mind you speak out, Tottle."

" I will—I will ! " replied Watkins, valorously.

" How I should like to see you together," ejaculated Mr. Gabriel Parsons.—" What fun ! " and he laughed so long and so loudly, that he disconcerted Mr. Watkins Tottle, and frightened the horse.

" There's Fanny and your intended walking about on the lawn," said Gabriel, as they approached the house. " Mind your eye, Tottle."

" Never fear," replied Watkins, resolutely, as he made his way to the spot where the ladies were walking.

" Here's Mr. Tottle, my dear," said Mrs. Parsons, addressing Miss Lillerton. The lady turned quickly round, and acknowledged his courteous salute with the same sort of confusion that Watkins had noticed on their first interview, but with something like a slight expression of disappointment or carelessness.

"Did you see how glad she was to see you?" whispered Parsons to his friend.

"Why, I really thought she looked as if she would rather have seen somebody else," replied Tottle.

"Pooh, nonsense!" whispered Parsons again—"it's always the way with the women, young or old. They never show how delighted they are to see those whose presence makes their hearts beat. It's the way with the whole sex, and no man should have lived to your time of life without knowing it. Fanny confessed it to me, when we were first married, over and over again—see what it is to have a wife."

"Certainly," whispered Tottle, whose courage was vanishing fast.

"Well, now, you'd better begin to pave the way," said Parsons, who, having invested some money in the speculation, assumed the office of director.

"Yes, yes, I will—presently," replied Tottle, greatly flurried.

"Say something to her, man," urged Parsons again. "Confound it! pay her a compliment, can't you?"

"No! not till after dinner," replied the bashful Tottle, anxious to postpone the evil moment.

"Well, gentlemen," said Mrs. Parsons, "you are really very polite; you stay away the whole morning, after promising to take us out, and when you do come home, you stand whispering together and take no notice of us."

"We were talking of the *business*, my dear, which detained us this morning," replied Parsons, looking significantly at Tottle.

"Dear me! how very quickly the morning has gone," said Miss Lillerton, referring to the gold watch, which was wound up on state occasions, whether it required it or not.

"*I* think it has passed very slowly," mildly suggested Tottle.

("That's right—bravo!") whispered Parsons.

"Indeed!" said Miss Lillerton, with an air of majestic surprise.

"I can only impute it to my unavoidable absence from your society, madam," said Watkins, "and that of Mrs. Parsons."

During this short dialogue, the ladies had been leading the way to the house.

"What the deuce did you stick Fanny into that last compliment for?" inquired Parsons, as they followed together; "it quite spoilt the effect."

"Oh! it really would have been too broad without," replied Watkins Tottle, "much too broad!"

"He's mad!" Parsons whispered his wife, as they entered the drawing-room, "mad from modesty."

"Dear me!" ejaculated the lady, "I never heard of such a thing."

"You'll find we have quite a family dinner, Mr. Tottle," said Mrs. Parsons, when they sat down to table: "Miss Lillerton is one of us, and, of course, we make no stranger of you."

Mr. Watkins Tottle expressed a hope that the Parsons family never would make a stranger of him; and wished internally that his bashfulness would allow him to feel a little less like a stranger himself.

"Take off the covers, Martha," said Mrs. Parsons, directing the shifting of the scenery with great anxiety. The order was obeyed, and a pair of boiled fowls, with tongue and et ceteras, were displayed at the top, and a fillet of veal at the bottom. On one side of the table two green saucetureens, with ladles of the same, were setting to each other in a green dish; and on the other was a curried rabbit, in a brown suit, turned up with lemon.

"Miss Lillerton, my dear," said Mrs. Parsons, "shall I assist you?"

"Thank you, no; I think I'll trouble Mr. Tottle."

Watkins started—trembled—helped the rabbit—and broke a tumbler. The countenance of the lady of the house, which had been all smiles previously, underwent an awful change.

"Extremely sorry," stammered Watkins, assisting himself to currie and parsley and butter, in the extremity of his confusion.

"Not the least consequence," replied Mrs. Parsons, in a tone which implied that it was of the greatest consequence possible,—directing aside the researches of the boy, who was groping under the table for the bits of broken glass.

"I presume," said Miss Lillerton, "that Mr. Tottle is aware of the interest which bachelors usually pay in such cases; a dozen glasses for one is the lowest penalty."

Mr. Gabriel Parsons gave his friend an admonitory tread on the toe. Here was a clear hint that the sooner he ceased to be a bachelor and emancipated himself from such penalties, the better. Mr. Watkins Tottle viewed the observation in the same light, and challenged Mrs. Parsons to take wine, with a degree of presence of mind, which, under all the circumstances, was really extraordinary.

"Miss Lillerton," said Gabriel, "may I have the pleasure?"

"I shall be most happy."

"Tottle, will you assist Miss Lillerton, and pass the decanter. Thank you." (The usual pantomimic ceremony of nodding and sipping gone through)—

"Tottle, were you ever in Suffolk?" inquired the master of the house, who was burning to tell one of his seven stock stories.

"No," responded Watkins, adding, by way of a saving clause, "but I've been in Devonshire."

"Ah!" replied Gabriel, "it was in Suffolk that a rather singular circumstance happened to me many years ago. Did you ever happen to hear me mention it?"

Mr. Watkins Tottle *had* happened to hear his friend mention it some four hundred times. Of course he expressed great curiosity, and evinced the utmost impatience to hear the story again. Mr. Gabriel Parsons forthwith attempted to proceed, in spite of the interruptions to which, as our readers must frequently have observed, the master of the house is often exposed in such cases. We will attempt to give them an idea of our meaning.

"When I was in Suffolk——" said Mr. Gabriel Parsons.

"Take off the fowls first, Martha," said Mrs. Parsons. "I beg your pardon, my dear."

"When I was in Suffolk," resumed Mr. Parsons, with an impatient glance at his wife, who pretended not to observe it, "which is now some years ago, business led me to the town of Bury St. Edmund's. I had to stop at the principal places in my way, and therefore, for the sake of convenience, I travelled in a gig. I left Sudbury one dark night—it was winter time—about nine o'clock; the rain poured in torrents, the wind howled among the trees that skirted the roadside, and I was obliged to proceed at a foot-pace, for I could hardly see my hand before me, it was so dark——"

"John," interrupted Mrs. Parsons, in a low, hollow voice, "don't spill that gravy."

"Fanny," said Parsons impatiently, "I wish you'd defer these domestic reproofs to some more suitable time. Really, my dear, these constant interruptions are very annoying."

"My dear, I didn't interrupt you," said Mrs. Parsons.

"But, my dear, you *did* interrupt me," remonstrated Mr. Parsons.

"How very absurd you are, my love! I must give directions to the servants; I am quite sure that if I sat here and allowed John to spill the gravy over the new carpet, you'd be the first to find fault when you saw the stain to-morrow morning."

"Well," continued Gabriel with a resigned air, as if he knew there was no getting over the point about the carpet, "I was just saying, it was so dark that I could hardly see my hand before me. The road was very lonely, and I assure you, Tottle (this was a device to arrest the wandering attention of that individual, which was distracted by a confidential communication between Mrs. Parsons and Martha, accompanied by the delivery of a large bunch of keys), I assure you, Tottle, I became somehow impressed with a sense of the loneliness of my situation——"

"Pie to your master," interrupted Mrs. Parsons, again directing the servant.

"Now, pray, my dear," remonstrated Parsons once more, very pettishly. Mrs. P. turned up her hands and eyebrows, and appealed in dumb show to Miss Lillerton. "As I turned a corner of the road," resumed Gabriel, "the horse stopped short, and reared tremendously. I pulled up, jumped out, ran to his head, and found a man lying on his back in the middle of the road, with his eyes fixed on the sky. I thought he was dead; but no, he was alive, and there appeared to be nothing the matter with him. He jumped up, and putting his hand to his chest, and fixing upon me the most earnest gaze you can imagine, exclaimed——"

"Pudding here," said Mrs. Parsons.

"Oh! it's no use," exclaimed the host, now rendered desperate. "Here, Tottle; a glass of wine. It's useless to attempt relating anything when Mrs. Parsons is present."

This attack was received in the usual way. Mrs. Parsons talked *to* Miss Lillerton and *at* her better half; expatiated on the impatience of men generally; hinted that her husband was peculiarly vicious in this respect, and wound up by insinuating that she must be one of the best tempers that ever existed, or she never could put up with it. Really what she had to endure sometimes, was more than any one who saw her in every-day life could by possibility suppose.—The story was now a painful subject, and therefore Mr. Parsons declined to enter into any details, and contented himself by stating that the man was a maniac, who had escaped from a neighbouring mad-house.

The cloth was removed; the ladies soon afterwards retired,

and Miss Lillerton played the piano in the drawing-room overhead, very loudly, for the edification of the visitor. Mr. Watkins Tottle and Mr. Gabriel Parsons sat chatting comfortably enough, until the conclusion of the second bottle, when the latter, in proposing an adjournment to the drawing-room, informed Watkins that he had concerted a plan with his wife, for leaving him and Miss Lillerton alone, soon after tea.

"I say," said Tottle, as they went up-stairs, "don't you think it would be better if we put it off till—till—to-morrow?"

"Don't *you* think it would have been much better if I had left you in that wretched hole I found you in this morning?" retorted Parsons bluntly.

"Well—well—I only made a suggestion," said poor Watkins Tottle, with a deep sigh.

Tea was soon concluded, and Miss Lillerton, drawing a small work-table on one side of the fire, and placing a little wooden frame upon it, something like a miniature clay-mill without the horse, was soon busily engaged in making a watch-guard with brown silk.

"God bless me!" exclaimed Parsons, starting up with well-feigned surprise, "I've forgotten those confounded letters. Tottle, I know you'll excuse me."

If Tottle had been a free agent, he would have allowed no one to leave the room on any pretence, except himself. As it was, however, he was obliged to look cheerful when Parsons quitted the apartment.

He had scarcely left, when Martha put her head into the room, with—"Please, ma'am, you're wanted."

Mrs. Parsons left the room, shut the door carefully after her, and Mr. Watkins Tottle was left alone with Miss Lillerton.

For the first five minutes there was a dead silence.—Mr. Watkins Tottle was thinking how he should begin, and Miss Lillerton appeared to be thinking of nothing. The fire was

147

burning low; Mr. Watkins Tottle stirred it, and put some coals on.

"Hem!" coughed Miss Lillerton; Mr. Watkins Tottle thought the fair creature had spoken. "I beg your pardon," said he.

"Eh?"

"I thought you spoke."

"No."

"Oh!"

"There are some books on the sofa, Mr. Tottle, if you would like to look at them," said Miss Lillerton, after the lapse of another five minutes.

"No, thank you," returned Watkins; and then he added, with a courage which was perfectly astonishing, even to himself, "Madam, that is Miss Lillerton, I wish to speak to you."

"To me!" said Miss Lillerton, letting the silk drop from her hands, and sliding her chair back a few paces.—"Speak —to me!"

"To you, madam—and on the subject of the state of your affections." The lady hastily rose and would have left the room; but Mr. Watkins Tottle gently detained her by the hand, and holding it as far from him as the joint length of their arms would permit, he thus proceeded: "Pray do not misunderstand me, or suppose that I am led to address you, after so short an acquaintance, by any feeling of my own merits—for merits I have none which could give me a claim to your hand. I hope you will acquit me of any presumption when I explain that I have been acquainted through Mrs. Parsons, with the state—that is, that Mrs. Parsons has told me—at least, not Mrs. Parsons, but——" here Watkins began to wander, but Miss Lillerton relieved him.

"Am I to understand, Mr. Tottle, that Mrs. Parsons has acquainted you with my feeling—my affection—I mean my respect, for an individual of the opposite sex?"

"She has."

"Then, what?" inquired Miss Lillerton, averting her face,

with a girlish air, "what could induce *you* to seek such an interview as this? What can your object be? How can I promote your happiness, Mr. Tottle?"

Here was the time for a flourish—"By allowing me," replied Watkins, falling bump on his knees, and breaking two brace-buttons and a waistcoat-string, in the act—"By allowing me to be your slave, your servant—in short, by unreservedly making me the confidant of your heart's feelings —may I say for the promotion of your own happiness—may I say, in order that you may become the wife of a kind and affectionate husband?"

"Disinterested creature!" exclaimed Miss Lillerton, hiding her face in a white pocket-handkerchief with an eyelet-hole border.

Mr. Watkins Tottle thought that if the lady knew all, she might possibly alter her opinion on this last point. He raised the tip of her middle finger ceremoniously to his lips, and got off his knees, as gracefully as he could. "My information was correct?" he tremulously inquired, when he was once more on his feet.

"It was." Watkins elevated his hands, and looked up to the ornament in the centre of the ceiling, which had been made for a lamp, by way of expressing his rapture.

"Our situation, Mr. Tottle," resumed the lady, glancing at him through one of the eyelet-holes, "is a most peculiar and delicate one."

"It is," said Mr. Tottle.

"Our acquaintance has been of *so* short duration," said Miss Lillerton.

"Only a week," assented Watkins Tottle.

"Oh! more than that," exclaimed the lady, in a tone of surprise.

"Indeed!" said Tottle.

"More than a month—more than two months!" said Miss Lillerton.

"Rather odd, this," thought Watkins.

"Oh!" he said, recollecting Parsons's assurance that she had known him from report, "I understand. But, my dear madam, pray, consider. The longer this acquaintance has existed, the less reason is there for delay now. Why not at once fix a period for gratifying the hopes of your devoted admirer?"

"It has been represented to me again and again that this is the course I ought to pursue," replied Miss Lillerton, "but pardon my feelings of delicacy, Mr. Tottle—pray excuse this embarrassment—I have peculiar ideas on such subjects, and I am quite sure that I never could summon up fortitude enough to name the day to my future husband."

"Then allow *me* to name it," said Tottle eagerly.

"I should like to fix it myself," replied Miss Lillerton, bashfully, "but I cannot do so without at once resorting to a third party."

"A third party!" thought Watkins Tottle; "who the deuce is that to be, I wonder!"

"Mr. Tottle," continued Miss Lillerton, "you have made me a most disinterested and kind offer—that offer I accept. Will you at once be the bearer of a note from me to—to Mr. Timson?"

"Mr. Timson!" said Watkins.

"After what has passed between us," responded Miss Lillerton, still averting her head, "you must understand whom I mean; Mr. Timson, the—the—clergyman."

"Mr. Timson, the clergyman!" ejaculated Watkins Tottle, in a state of inexpressible beatitude, and positive wonder at his own success. "Angel! Certainly—this moment!"

"I'll prepare it immediately," said Miss Lillerton, making for the door; "the events of this day have flurried me so much, Mr. Tottle, that I shall not leave my room again this evening; I will send you the note by the servant."

"Stay,—stay," cried Watkins Tottle, still keeping a most respectful distance from the lady; "when shall we meet again?"

"Oh! Mr. Tottle," replied Miss Lillerton, coquettishly,

"when *we* are married, I can never see you too often, nor thank you too much;" and she left the room.

Mr. Watkins Tottle flung himself into an arm-chair, and indulged in the most delicious reveries of future bliss, in which the idea of "Five hundred pounds per annum, with an uncontrolled power of disposing of it by her last will and testament," was somehow or other the foremost. He had gone through the interview so well, and it had terminated so admirably, that he almost began to wish he had expressly stipulated for the settlement of the annual five hundred on himself.

"May I come in?" said Mr. Gabriel Parsons, peeping in at the door.

"You may," replied Watkins.

"Well, have you done it?" anxiously inquired Gabriel.

"Have I done it!" said Watkins Tottle. "Hush—I'm going to the clergyman."

"No!" said Parsons. "How well you have managed it!"

"Where does Timson live?" inquired Watkins.

"At his uncle's," replied Gabriel, "just round the lane. He's waiting for a living, and has been assisting his uncle here for the last two or three months. But how well you have done it—I didn't think you could have carried it off so!"

Mr. Watkins Tottle was proceeding to demonstrate that the Richardsonian principle was the best on which love could possibly be made, when he was interrupted by the entrance of Martha, with a little pink note folded like a fancy cocked-hat.

"Miss Lillerton's compliments," said Martha, as she delivered it into Tottle's hands, and vanished.

"Do you observe the delicacy?" said Tottle, appealing to Mr. Gabriel Parsons. "*Compliments*, not *love*, by the servant, eh?"

Mr. Gabriel Parsons didn't exactly know what reply to make, so he poked the forefinger of his right hand between the third and fourth ribs of Mr. Watkins Tottle.

" Come," said Watkins, when the explosion of mirth, consequent on this practical jest, had subsided, " we'll be off at once—let's lose no time."

" Capital ! " echoed Gabriel Parsons; and in five minutes they were at the garden-gate of the villa tenanted by the uncle of Mr. Timson.

" Is Mr. Charles Timson at home ? " inquired Mr. Watkins Tottle of Mr. Charles Timson's uncle's man.

" Mr. Charles *is* at home," replied the man, stammering; " but he desired me to say he couldn't be interrupted, sir, by any of the parishioners."

" *I* am not a parishioner," replied Watkins.

" Is Mr. Charles writing a sermon, Tom ? " inquired Parsons, thrusting himself forward.

" No, Mr. Parsons, sir; he's not exactly writing a sermon, but he is practising the violoncello in his own bedroom, and gave strict orders not to be disturbed."

" Say I'm here," replied Gabriel, leading the way across the garden ; " Mr. Parsons and Mr. Tottle, on private and particular business."

They were shown into the parlour, and the servant departed to deliver his message. The distant groaning of the violoncello ceased ; footsteps were heard on the stairs ; and Mr. Timson presented himself, and shook hands with Parsons with the utmost cordiality.

" How do you do, sir ? " said Watkins Tottle, with great solemnity.

" How do *you* do, sir ? " replied Timson, with as much coldness as if it were a matter of perfect indifference to him how he did, as it very likely was.

" I beg to deliver this note to you," said Watkins Tottle, producing the cocked-hat.

" From Miss Lillerton ! " said Timson, suddenly changing colour. " Pray sit down."

Mr. Watkins Tottle sat down ; and while Timson perused the note, fixed his eyes on an oyster-sauce-coloured portrait of the Archbishop of Canterbury, which hung over the fireplace.

Mr. Timson rose from his seat when he had concluded the note, and looked dubiously at Parsons. "May I ask," he inquired, appealing to Watkins Tottle, "whether our friend here is acquainted with the object of your visit?"

"Our friend is in *my* confidence," replied Watkins, with considerable importance.

"Then, sir," said Timson, seizing both Tottle's hands, "allow me in his presence to thank you most unfeignedly and cordially, for the noble part you have acted in this affair."

"He thinks I recommended him," thought Tottle. "Confound these fellows! they never think of anything but their fees."

"I deeply regret having misunderstood your intentions, my dear sir," continued Timson. "Disinterested and manly, indeed! There are very few men who would have acted as you have done."

Mr. Watkins Tottle could not help thinking that this last remark was anything but complimentary. He therefore inquired, rather hastily, "When is it to be?"

"On Thursday," replied Timson,—"on Thursday morning at half-past eight."

"Uncommonly early," observed Watkins Tottle, with an air of triumphant self-denial. "I shall hardly be able to get down here by that hour." (This was intended for a joke.)

"Never mind, my dear fellow," replied Timson, all suavity, shaking hands with Tottle again most heartily, "so long as we see you to breakfast, you know——"

"Eh!" said Parsons, with one of the most extraordinary expressions of countenance that ever appeared in a human face.

"What!" ejaculated Watkins Tottle, at the same moment.

"I say that so long as we see you to breakfast," replied Timson, "we will excuse your being absent from the ceremony, though of course your presence at it would give us the utmost pleasure."

Mr. Watkins Tottle staggered against the wall, and fixed his eyes on Timson with appalling perseverance.

"Timson," said Parsons, hurriedly brushing his hat with his left arm, "when you say 'us,' whom do you mean?"

Mr. Timson looked foolish in his turn, when he replied, "Why—Mrs. Timson that will be this day week : Miss Lillerton that is—— "

"Now don't stare at that idiot in the corner," angrily exclaimed Parsons, as the extraordinary convulsions of Watkins Tottle's countenance excited the wondering gaze of Timson,—"but have the goodness to tell me in three words the contents of that note?"

"This note," replied Timson, "is from Miss Lillerton, to whom I have been for the last five weeks regularly engaged. Her singular scruples and strange feeling on some points have hitherto prevented my bringing the engagement to that termination which I so anxiously desire. She informs me here, that she sounded Mrs. Parsons with the view of making her her confidante and go-between, that Mrs. Parsons informed this elderly gentleman, Mr. Tottle, of the circumstance, and that he, in the most kind and delicate terms, offered to assist us in any way, and even undertook to convey this note, which contains the promise I have long sought in vain—an act of kindness for which I can never be sufficiently grateful."

"Good night, Timson," said Parsons, hurrying off, and carrying the bewildered Tottle with him.

"Won't you stay—and have something?" said Timson.

"No, thank ye," replied Parsons ; "I've had quite enough ; " and away he went, followed by Watkins Tottle in a state of stupefaction.

Mr. Gabriel Parsons whistled until they had walked some quarter of a mile past his own gate, when he suddenly stopped, and said—

"You are a clever fellow, Tottle, ain't you?"

"I don't know," said the unfortunate Watkins.

"I suppose you'll say this is Fanny's fault, won't you?" inquired Gabriel.

"I don't know anything about it," replied the bewildered Tottle.

"Well," said Parsons, turning on his heel to go home, "the next time you make an offer, you had better speak plainly, and don't throw a chance away. And the next time you're locked up in a spunging-house, just wait there till I come and take you out, there's a good fellow."

How, or at what hour, Mr. Watkins Tottle returned to Cecil-street is unknown. His boots were seen outside his bedroom-door next morning; but we have the authority of his landlady for stating that he neither emerged therefrom nor accepted sustenance for four-and-twenty hours. At the expiration of that period, and when a council of war was being held in the kitchen on the propriety of summoning the parochial beadle to break his door open, he rang his bell, and demanded a cup of milk-and-water. The next morning he went through the formalities of eating and drinking as usual, but a week afterwards he was seized with a relapse, while perusing the list of marriages in a morning paper, from which he never perfectly recovered.

A few weeks after the last-named occurrence, the body of a gentleman unknown, was found in the Regent's canal. In the trousers-pockets were four shillings and threepence half-penny; a matrimonial advertisement from a lady, which appeared to have been cut out of a Sunday paper: a tooth-pick, and a card-case, which it is confidently believed would have led to the identification of the unfortunate gentleman, but for the circumstance of there being none but blank cards in it. Mr. Watkins Tottle absented himself from his lodgings shortly before. A bill, which has not been taken up, was presented next morning; and a bill, which has not been taken down, was soon afterwards affixed in his parlour-window.

CHAPTER XI

MR. NICODEMUS DUMPS, or, as his acquaintance called him, "long Dumps," was a bachelor, six feet high, and fifty years old: cross, cadaverous, odd, and ill-natured. He was never happy but when he was miserable; and always miserable when he had the best reason to be happy. The only real comfort of his existence was to make everybody about him wretched—then he might be truly said to enjoy life. He was afflicted with a situation in the Bank worth five hundred a-year, and he rented a "first-floor furnished," at Pentonville, which he originally took because it commanded a dismal prospect of an adjacent churchyard. He was familiar with the face of every tombstone, and the burial service seemed to excite his strongest sympathy. His friends said he was surly—he insisted he was nervous; they thought him a lucky dog, but he protested that he was "the most unfortunate man in the world." Cold as he was, and wretched as he declared himself to be, he was not wholly unsusceptible of attachments. He revered the memory of Hoyle, as he was himself an admirable and imperturbable whist-player, and he chuckled with delight at a fretful and impatient adversary. He adored King Herod for his massacre of the innocents; and if he hated one thing more than another, it was a child. However, he could hardly be said to hate anything in particular, because he disliked everything

156

Bloomsbury Christening

in general; but perhaps his greatest antipathies were cabs, old women, doors that would not shut, musical amateurs, and omnibus cads. He subscribed to the "Society for the Suppression of Vice" for the pleasure of putting a stop to any harmless amusements; and he contributed largely towards the support of two itinerant methodist parsons, in the amiable hope that if circumstances rendered any people happy in this world, they might perchance be rendered miserable by fears for the next.

Mr. Dumps had a nephew who had been married about a year, and who was somewhat of a favourite with his uncle, because he was an admirable subject to exercise his misery-creating powers upon. Mr. Charles Kitterbell was a small, sharp, spare man, with a very large head, and a broad, good-humoured countenance. He looked like a faded giant, with the head and face partially restored; and he had a cast in his eye which rendered it quite impossible for any one with whom he conversed to know where he was looking. His eyes appeared fixed on the wall, and he was staring you out of countenance; in short, there was no catching his eye, and perhaps it is a merciful dispensation of Providence that such eyes are not catching. In addition to these characteristics, it may be added that Mr. Charles Kitterbell was one of the most credulous and matter-of-fact little personages that ever took *to* himself a wife, and *for* himself a house in Great Russell-street, Bedford-square. (Uncle Dumps always dropped the "Bedford-square," and inserted in lieu thereof the dreadful words "Tottenham-court-road.")

"No, but, uncle, 'pon my life you must—you must promise to be godfather," said Mr. Kitterbell, as he sat in conversation with his respected relative one morning.

"I cannot, indeed I cannot," returned Dumps.

"Well, but why not? Jemima will think it very unkind. It's very little trouble."

"As to the trouble," rejoined the most unhappy man in existence, "I don't mind that; but my nerves are in that state—I cannot go through the ceremony. You know I don't like going out.—For God's sake, Charles, don't fidget with that stool so; you'll drive me mad." Mr. Kitterbell, quite regardless of his uncle's nerves, had occupied himself for some ten minutes in describing a circle on the floor with one leg of the office-stool on which he was seated, keeping the other three up in the air, and holding fast on by the desk.

"I beg your pardon, uncle," said Kitterbell, quite abashed, suddenly releasing his hold of the desk, and bringing the three wandering legs back to the floor, with a force sufficient to drive them through it.

"But come, don't refuse. If it's a boy, you know, we must have two godfathers."

"*If* it's a boy!" said Dumps; "why can't you say at once whether it *is* a boy or not?"

"I should be very happy to tell you, but it's impossible I can undertake to say whether it's a girl or a boy, if the child isn't born yet."

"Not born yet!" echoed Dumps, with a gleam of hope lighting up his lugubrious visage. "Oh, well, it *may* be a girl, and then you won't want me; or if it is a boy, it *may* die before it is christened."

"I hope not," said the father that expected to be, looking very grave.

"I hope not," acquiesced Dumps, evidently pleased with the subject. He was beginning to get happy. "*I* hope not, but distressing cases frequently occur during the first two or three days of a child's life; fits, I am told, are exceedingly common, and alarming convulsions are almost matters of course."

"Lord, uncle!" ejaculated little Kitterbell, gasping for breath.

"Yes; my landlady was confined—let me see—last Tuesday: an uncommonly fine boy. On the Thursday night the nurse was sitting with him upon her knee before the fire, and he was as well as possible. Suddenly he became black in the face, and alarmingly spasmodic. The medical man was instantly sent for, and every remedy was tried, but——"

" How frightful ! " interrupted the horror-stricken Kitterbell.

" The child died, of course. However, your child *may* not die ; and if it should be a boy, and should *live* to be christened, why I suppose I must be one of the sponsors." Dumps was evidently good-natured on the faith of his anticipations.

" Thank you, uncle," said his agitated nephew, grasping his hand as warmly as if he had done him some essential service. " Perhaps I had better not tell Mrs. K. what you have mentioned."

" Why, if she's low-spirited, perhaps you had better not mention the melancholy case to her," returned Dumps, who of course had invented the whole story ; " though perhaps it would be but doing your duty as a husband to prepare her for the *worst.*"

A day or two afterwards, as Dumps was perusing a morning paper at the chop-house which he regularly frequented, the following paragraph met his eyes :—

" *Births.*—On Saturday, the 18th inst., in Great Russell-street, the lady of Charles Kitterbell, Esq., of a son."

" It *is* a boy ! " he exclaimed, dashing down the paper, to the astonishment of the waiters. " It *is* a boy ! " But he speedily regained his composure as his eye rested on a paragraph quoting the number of infant deaths from the bills of mortality.

Six weeks passed away, and as no communication had been received from the Kitterbells, Dumps was beginning to flatter himself that the child was dead, when the following note painfully resolved his doubts :—

> " *Great Russell-street,*
> *Monday morning.*

" Dear Uncle,—You will be delighted to hear that my dear Jemima has left her room, and that your future godson is getting on capitally. He was very thin at first, but he is getting much larger, and nurse says he is filling out every day. He cries a good deal, and is a very singular colour, which made Jemima and me rather uncomfortable; but as nurse says it's natural, and as of course we know nothing about these things yet, we are quite satisfied with what nurse says. We think he will be a sharp child; and nurse says she's sure he will, because he never goes to sleep. You will readily believe that we are all very happy, only we're a little worn out for want of rest, as he keeps us awake all night; but this we must expect, nurse says, for the first six or eight months. He has been vaccinated, but in consequence of the operation being rather awkwardly performed, some small particles of glass were introduced into the arm with the matter. Perhaps this may in some degree account for his being rather fractious; at least, so nurse says. We propose to have him christened at twelve o'clock on Friday, at Saint George's church, in Hart-street, by the name of Frederick Charles William. Pray don't be later than a quarter before twelve. We shall have a very few friends in the evening, when of course we shall see you. I am sorry to say that the dear boy appears rather restless and uneasy to-day: the cause, I fear, is fever.

" Believe me, dear Uncle,

" Yours affectionately,

" CHARLES KITTERBELL.

" P.S.—I open this note to say that we have just discovered the cause of little Frederick's restlessness. It is not fever, as I apprehended, but a small pin, which nurse accidentally stuck in his leg yesterday evening. We have taken it out, and he appears more composed, though he still sobs a good deal."

It is almost unnecessary to say that the perusal of the above interesting statement was no great relief to the mind of the hypochondriacal Dumps. It was impossible to recede, however, and so he put the best face—that is to say, an uncommonly miserable one—upon the matter ; and purchased a handsome silver mug for the infant Kitterbell, upon which he ordered the initials " F. C. W. K.," with the customary untrained grape-vine-looking flourishes, and a large full stop, to be engraved forthwith.

Monday was a fine day, Tuesday was delightful, Wednesday was equal to either, and Thursday was finer than ever ; four successive fine days in London ! Hackney-coachmen became revolutionary, and crossing-sweepers began to doubt the existence of a First Cause. The *Morning Herald* informed its readers that an old woman in Camden Town had been heard to say that the fineness of the season was " unprecedented in the memory of the oldest inhabitant ; " and Islington clerks, with large families and small salaries, left off their black gaiters, disdained to carry their once green cotton umbrellas, and walked to town in the conscious pride of white stockings and cleanly brushed Bluchers. Dumps beheld all this with an eye of supreme contempt—his triumph was at hand. He knew that if it had been fine for four weeks instead of four days, it would rain when he went out ; he was lugubriously happy in the conviction that Friday would be a wretched day—and so it was. " I knew how it would be," said Dumps, as he turned round opposite the Mansion-house at half-past eleven o'clock on the Friday morning. " I knew how it would be. *I* am concerned, and that's enough ; "—and certainly the appearance of the day was sufficient to depress the spirits of a much more buoyant-hearted individual than himself. It had rained, without a moment's cessation, since eight o'clock ; everybody that passed up Cheapside, and down Cheapside, looked wet, cold, and dirty. All sorts of forgotten and long-concealed umbrellas had been put into requisition. Cabs whisked about, with the " fare " as carefully boxed up behind two glazed calico curtains as any mysterious picture in any one of Mrs. Radcliffe's castles ; omnibus horses smoked like steam-engines ; nobody thought of " standing up " under doorways or arches ; they were painfully convinced it was a hopeless case; and so everybody went hastily along, jumbling and jostling, and swearing and perspiring, and slipping about, like amateur skaters behind wooden chairs on the Serpentine on a frosty Sunday.

Dumps paused; he could not think of walking, being rather smart for the christening. If he took a cab he was sure to be spilt, and a hackney-coach was too expensive for his economical ideas. An omnibus was waiting at the opposite corner—it was a desperate case—he had never heard of an omnibus upsetting or running away, and if the cad did knock him down, he could "pull him up" in return.

"Now, sir!" cried the young gentleman who officiated as "cad" to the "Lads of the Village," which was the name of the machine just noticed. Dumps crossed.

"This vay, sir!" shouted the driver of the "Hark-away," pulling up his vehicle immediately across the door of the opposition—"This vay, sir—he's full." Dumps hesitated, whereupon the "Lads of the Village" commenced pouring out a torrent of abuse against the "Hark-away;" but the conductor of the "Admiral Napier" settled the contest in a most satisfactory manner, for all parties, by seizing Dumps round the waist, and thrusting him into the middle of his vehicle which had just come up and only wanted the sixteenth inside.

"All right," said the "Admiral," and off the thing thundered, like a fire-engine at full gallop, with the kid-napped customer inside, standing in the position of a half doubled-up bootjack, and falling about with every jerk of the machine, first on the one side, and then on the other, like a "Jack-in-the-green," on May-day, setting to the lady with a brass ladle.

"For Heaven's sake, where am I to sit?" inquired the miserable man of an old gentleman, into whose stomach he had just fallen for the fourth time.

"Anywhere but on my *chest*, sir," replied the old gentleman in a surly tone.

"Perhaps the *box* would suit the gentleman better," suggested a very damp lawyer's clerk, in a pink shirt, and a smirking countenance.

After a great deal of struggling and falling about, Dumps at last managed to squeeze himself into a seat, which, in addition to the slight disadvantage of being between a window that would not shut, and a door that must be open, placed him in close contact with a passenger, who had been walking about all the morning without an umbrella, and who looked as if he had spent the day in a full water-butt—only wetter.

"Don't bang the door so," said Dumps to the conductor, as he shut it after letting out four of the passengers; "I am very nervous—it destroys me."

"Did any gen'lm'n say anythink?" replied the cad, thrusting in his head, and trying to look as if he didn't understand the request.

"I told you not to bang the door so!" repeated Dumps, with an expression of countenance like the knave of clubs, in convulsions.

"Oh! vy, it's rather a sing'ler circumstance about this here door, sir, that it von't shut without banging," replied the conductor; and he opened the door very wide, and shut it again with a terrific bang, in proof of the assertion.

"I beg your pardon, sir," said a little prim, wheezing old gentleman, sitting opposite Dumps, "I beg your pardon; but have you ever observed, when you have been in an omnibus on a wet day, that four people out of five always come in with large cotton umbrellas, without a handle at the top, or the brass spike at the bottom?"

"Why, sir," returned Dumps, as he heard the clock strike twelve, "it never struck me before; but now you mention it, I——Hollo! hollo!" shouted the persecuted individual, as the omnibus dashed past Drury-lane, where he had directed to be set down.—"Where is the cad?"

"I think he's on the box, sir," said the young gentleman

before noticed in the pink shirt, which looked like a white one ruled with red ink.

"I want to be set down!" said Dumps in a faint voice, overcome by his previous efforts.

"I think these cads want to be *set down*," returned the attorney's clerk, chuckling at his sally.

"Hollo!" cried Dumps again.

"Hollo!" echoed the passengers. The omnibus passed St. Giles's church.

"Hold hard!" said the conductor; "I'm blowed if we ha'n't forgot the gen'lm'n as vas to be set down at Doory-lane. —Now, sir, make haste, if you please," he added, opening the door, and assisting Dumps out with as much coolness as if it was "all right." Dumps's indignation was for once getting the better of his cynical equanimity. "Drury-lane!" he gasped, with the voice of a boy in a cold bath for the first time.

"Doory-lane, sir?—yes, sir,—third turning on the right-hand side, sir."

Dumps's passion was paramount: he clutched his umbrella, and was striding off with the firm determination of not paying the fare. The cad, by a remarkable coincidence, happened to entertain a directly contrary opinion, and Heaven knows how far the altercation would have proceeded, if it had not been most ably and satisfactorily brought to a close by the driver.

"Hollo!" said that respectable person, standing up on the box, and leaning with one hand on the roof of the omnibus. "Hollo, Tom! tell the gentleman if so be as he feels aggrieved, we will take him up to the Edge-er (Edgeware) Road for nothing, and set him down at Doory-lane when we comes back. He can't reject that, anyhow."

The argument was irresistible: Dumps paid the disputed sixpence, and in a quarter of an hour was on the staircase of No. 14, Great Russell-street.

Everything indicated that preparations were making for

the reception of "a few friends" in the evening. Two dozen extra tumblers, and four ditto wine-glasses—looking anything but transparent, with little bits of straw in them—were on the slab in the passage, just arrived. There was a great smell of nutmeg, port wine, and almonds, on the staircase; the covers were taken off the stair-carpet, and the figure of Venus on the first landing looked as if she were ashamed of the composition-candle in her right hand, which contrasted beautifully with the lamp-blacked drapery of the goddess of love. The female servant (who looked very warm and bustling) ushered Dumps into a front drawing-room, very prettily furnished, with a plentiful sprinkling of little baskets, paper table-mats, china watchmen, pink and gold albums, and rainbow-bound little books on the different tables.

"Ah, uncle!" said Mr. Kitterbell, "how d'ye do? Allow me—Jemima, my dear—my uncle. I think you've seen Jemima before, sir?"

"Have had the *pleasure*," returned big Dumps, his tone and look making it doubtful whether in his life he had ever experienced the sensation.

"I'm sure," said Mrs. Kitterbell, with a languid smile, and a slight cough. "I'm sure—hem—any friend—of Charles's—hem—much less a relation, is——"

"I knew you'd say so, my love," said little Kitterbell, who, while he appeared to be gazing on the opposite houses, was looking at his wife with a most affectionate air: "Bless you!" The last two words were accompanied with a simper, and a squeeze of the hand, which stirred up all Uncle Dumps's bile.

"Jane, tell nurse to bring down baby," said Mrs. Kitterbell, addressing the servant. Mrs. Kitterbell was a tall, thin young lady, with very light hair, and a particularly white face—one of those young women who almost invariably, though one hardly knows why, recall to one's mind the idea of a cold fillet of veal. Out went the servant, and in came the nurse, with a remarkably small parcel in her arms, packed up in a blue mantle trimmed with white fur.—This was the baby.

"Now, uncle," said Mr. Kitterbell, lifting up that part of the mantle which covered the infant's face, with an air of great triumph, " *Who* do you think he's like?"

"He! he! Yes, who?" said Mrs. K., putting her arm through her husband's, and looking up into Dumps's face with an expression of as much interest as she was capable of displaying.

"Good God, how small he is!" cried the amiable uncle, starting back with well-feigned surprise; "*remarkably* small indeed."

"Do you think so?" inquired poor little Kitterbell, rather alarmed. "He's a monster to what he was—ain't he, nurse?"

"He's a dear," said the nurse, squeezing the child, and evading the question—not because she scrupled to disguise the fact, but because she couldn't afford to throw away the chance of Dumps's half-crown.

"Well, but who is he like?" inquired little Kitterbell.

Dumps looked at the little pink heap before him, and only thought at the moment of the best mode of mortifying the youthful parents.

"I really don't know *who* he's like," he answered, very well knowing the reply expected of him.

"Don't you think he's like *me?*" inquired his nephew with a knowing air.

"Oh, *decidedly* not!" returned Dumps, with an emphasis not to be misunderstood. "Decidedly not like you.—Oh, certainly not."

"Like Jemima?" asked Kitterbell, faintly.

"Oh, dear no; not in the least. I'm no judge, of course, in such cases; but I really think he's more like one of those little carved representations that one sometimes sees blowing a trumpet on a tombstone!" The nurse stooped down over the child, and with great difficulty prevented an explosion of mirth. Pa and ma looked almost as miserable as their amiable uncle.

"Well!" said the disappointed little father, "you'll be

better able to tell what he's like by-and-by. You shall see him this evening with his mantle off."

"Thank you," said Dumps, feeling particularly grateful.

"Now, my love," said Kitterbell to his wife, "it's time we were off. We're to meet the other godfather and the godmother at the church, uncle,—Mr. and Mrs. Wilson from over the way—uncommonly nice people. My love, are you well wrapped up?"

"Yes, dear."

"Are you sure you won't have another shawl?" inquired the anxious husband.

"No, sweet," returned the charming mother, accepting Dumps's proffered arm; and the little party entered the hackney-coach that was to take them to the church; Dumps amusing Mrs. Kitterbell by expatiating largely on the danger of measles, thrush, teeth-cutting, and other interesting diseases to which children are subject.

The ceremony (which occupied about five minutes) passed off without anything particular occurring. The clergyman had to dine some distance from town, and had two churchings, three christenings, and a funeral to perform in something less than an hour. The godfathers and godmother, therefore, promised to renounce the devil and all his works—"and all that sort of thing"—as little Kitterbell said—"in less than no time;" and with the exception of Dumps nearly letting the child fall into the font when he handed it to the clergyman, the whole affair went off in the usual business-like and matter-of-course manner, and Dumps re-entered the Bank-gates at two o'clock with a heavy heart, and the painful conviction that he was regularly booked for an evening party.

Evening came—and so did Dumps's pumps, black silk stockings, and white cravat which he had ordered to be forwarded, per boy, from Pentonville. The depressed godfather dressed himself at a friend's counting-house, from whence, with his spirits fifty degrees below proof, he sallied forth—as the weather had cleared up, and the evening was

167

tolerably fine—to walk to Great Russell-street. Slowly he paced up Cheapside, Newgate-street, down Snow-hill, and up Holborn ditto, looking as grim as the figure-head of a man-of-war, and finding out fresh causes of misery at every step. As he was crossing the corner of Hatton-garden, a man apparently intoxicated, rushed against him, and would have knocked him down, had he not been providentially caught by a very genteel young man, who happened to be close to him at the time. The shock so disarranged Dumps's nerves, as well as his dress, that he could hardly stand. The gentleman took his arm, and in the kindest manner walked with him as far as Furnival's Inn. Dumps, for about the first time in his life, felt grateful and polite; and he and the gentlemanly-looking young man parted with mutual expressions of good will.

"There are at least some well-disposed men in the world," ruminated the misanthropical Dumps, as he proceeded towards his destination.

Rat—tat—ta-ra-ra-ra-ra-rat—knocked a hackney-coachman at Kitterbell's door, in imitation of a gentleman's servant, just as Dumps reached it; and out came an old lady in a large toque, and an old gentleman in a blue coat, and three female copies of the old lady in pink dresses, and shoes to match.

"It's a large party," sighed the unhappy godfather, wiping the perspiration from his forehead, and leaning against the area-railings. It was some time before the miserable man could muster up courage to knock at the door, and when he did, the smart appearance of a neighbouring greengrocer (who had been hired to wait for seven and sixpence, and whose calves alone were worth double the money), the lamp in the passage, and the Venus on the landing, added to the hum of many voices, and the sound of a harp and two violins, painfully convinced him that his surmises were but too well founded.

"How are you?" said little Kitterbell, in a greater bustle

than ever, bolting out of the little back parlour with a cork-screw in his hand, and various particles of sawdust, looking like so many inverted commas, on his inexpressibles.

"Good God!" said Dumps, turning into the aforesaid parlour to put his shoes on, which he had brought in his coat-pocket, and still more appalled by the sight of seven fresh-drawn corks, and a corresponding number of decanters. "How many people are there up-stairs?"

"Oh, not above thirty-five. We've had the carpet taken up in the back drawing-room, and the piano and the card-tables are in the front. Jemima thought we'd better have a regular sit-down supper in the front parlour, because of the speechi-fying, and all that. But, Lord! uncle, what's the matter?" continued the excited little man, as Dumps stood with one shoe on, rummaging his pockets with the most frightful distor-tion of visage. "What have you lost? Your pocket-book?"

"No," returned Dumps, diving first into one pocket and then into the other, and speaking in a voice like Desdemona with the pillow over her mouth.

"Your card-case? snuff-box? the key of your lodgings?" continued Kitterbell, pouring question on question with the rapidity of lightning.

"No! no!" ejaculated Dumps, still diving eagerly into his empty pockets.

"Not—not—the *mug* you spoke of this morning?"

"Yes, the *mug!*" replied Dumps, sinking into a chair.

"How *could* you have done it?" inquired Kitterbell. "Are you sure you brought it out?"

"Yes! yes! I see it all!" said Dumps, starting up as the idea flashed across his mind; "miserable dog that I am—I was born to suffer. I see it all: it was the gentlemanly-looking young man!"

"Mr. Dumps!" shouted the greengrocer in a stentorian voice, as he ushered the somewhat recovered godfather into the drawing-room half an hour after the above declaration. "Mr. Dumps!"—everybody looked at the door, and in came

Dumps, feeling about as much out of place as a salmon might be supposed to be on a gravel-walk.

"Happy to see you again," said Mrs. Kitterbell, quite unconscious of the unfortunate man's confusion and misery; "you must allow me to introduce you to a few of our friends: —my mamma, Mr. Dumps—my papa and sisters." Dumps seized the hand of the mother as warmly as if she was his own parent, bowed *to* the young ladies, and *against* a gentleman behind him, and took no notice whatever of the father, who had been bowing incessantly for three minutes and a quarter.

"Uncle," said little Kitterbell, after Dumps had been introduced to a select dozen or two, "you must let me lead you to the other end of the room, to introduce you to my friend Danton. Such a splendid fellow!—I'm sure you'll like him —this way,"—Dumps followed as tractably as a tame bear.

Mr. Danton was a young man of about five-and-twenty, with a considerable stock of impudence, and a very small share of ideas: he was a great favourite, especially with young ladies of from sixteen to twenty-six years of age, both inclusive. He could imitate the French-horn to admiration, sang comic songs most inimitably, and had the most insinuating way of saying impertinent nothings to his doting female admirers. He had acquired, somehow or other, the reputation of being a great wit, and, accordingly, whenever he opened his mouth, everybody who knew him laughed very heartily.

The introduction took place in due form. Mr. Danton bowed, and twirled a lady's handkerchief, which he held in his hand, in a most comic way. Everybody smiled.

"Very warm," said Dumps, feeling it necessary to say something.

"Yes. It was warmer yesterday," returned the brilliant Mr. Danton.—A general laugh.

"I have great pleasure in congratulating you on your first appearance in the character of a father, sir," he continued, addressing Dumps—"godfather, I mean."—The young ladies were convulsed, and the gentlemen in ecstasies.

THE BABY ADMIRED

A general hum of admiration interrupted the conversation, and announced the entrance of nurse with the baby. An universal rush of the young ladies immediately took place. (Girls are always *so* fond of babies in company.)

"Oh, you dear!" said one.

"How sweet!" cried another, in a low tone of the most enthusiastic admiration.

"Heavenly!" added a third.

"Oh! what dear little arms!" said a fourth, holding up an arm and fist about the size and shape of the leg of a fowl cleanly picked.

"Did you ever!"—said a little coquette with a large bustle, who looked like a French lithograph, appealing to a gentleman in three waistcoats—"Did you ever!"

"Never, in my life," returned her admirer, pulling up his collar.

"Oh! *do* let me take it, nurse," cried another young lady. "The love!"

"Can it open its eyes, nurse?" inquired another, affecting the utmost innocence.—Suffice it to say, that the single ladies unanimously voted him an angel, and that the married ones, *nem. con.*, agreed that he was decidedly the finest baby they had ever beheld—except their own.

The quadrilles were resumed with great spirit. Mr. Danton was universally admitted to be beyond himself; several young ladies enchanted the company and gained admirers by singing "We met"—"I saw her at the Fancy Fair"—and other equally sentimental and interesting ballads. "The young men," as Mrs. Kitterbell said, "made themselves very agreeable;" the girls did not lose their opportunity; and the evening promised to go off excellently. Dumps didn't mind it: he had devised a plan for himself—a little bit of fun in his own way—and he was almost happy! He played a rubber and lost every point. Mr. Danton said he could not have lost every point, because he made a point of losing: everybody laughed tremendously. Dumps retorted with a better

171

joke, and nobody smiled, with the exception of the host, who seemed to consider it his duty to laugh till he was black in the face, at everything. There was only one drawback—the musicians did not play with quite as much spirit as could have been wished. The cause, however, was satisfactorily explained; for it appeared, on the testimony of a gentleman who had come up from Gravesend in the afternoon, that they had been engaged on board a steamer all day, and had played almost without cessation all the way to Gravesend, and all the way back again.

The "sit-down supper" was excellent; there were four barley-sugar temples on the table, which would have looked beautiful if they had not melted away when the supper began; and a water-mill, whose only fault was that instead of going round, it ran over the table-cloth. Then there were fowls, and tongue, and trifle, and sweets, and lobster salad, and potted beef—and everything. And little Kitterbell kept calling out for clean plates, and the clean plates did not come: and then the gentlemen who wanted the plates said they didn't mind, they'd take a lady's; and then Mrs. Kitterbell applauded their gallantry, and the greengrocer ran about till he thought his seven and sixpence was very hardly earned; and the young ladies didn't eat much for fear it shouldn't look romantic, and the married ladies eat as much as possible, for fear they shouldn't have enough; and a great deal of wine was drunk, and everybody talked and laughed considerably.

"Hush! hush!" said Mr. Kitterbell, rising and looking very important. "My love (this was addressed to his wife at the other end of the table), take care of Mrs. Maxwell, and your mamma, and the rest of the married ladies; the gentlemen will persuade the young ladies to fill their glasses, I am sure."

"Ladies and gentlemen," said long Dumps, in a very sepulchral voice and rueful accent, rising from his chair like the ghost in Don Juan, "will you have the kindness to charge your glasses? I am desirous of proposing a toast."

A dead silence ensued, and the glasses were filled—everybody looked serious.

"Ladies and gentlemen," slowly continued the ominous Dumps, "I"—(here Mr. Danton imitated two notes from the French-horn, in a very loud key, which electrified the nervous toast-proposer, and convulsed his audience).

"Order! order!" said little Kitterbell, endeavouring to suppress his laughter.

"Order!" said the gentlemen.

"Danton, be quiet," said a particular friend on the opposite side of the table.

"Ladies and gentlemen," resumed Dumps, somewhat recovered, and not much disconcerted, for he was always a pretty good hand at a speech—"In accordance with what is, I believe, the established usage on these occasions, I, as one of the godfathers of Master Frederick Charles William Kitterbell—(here the speaker's voice faltered, for he remembered the mug)—venture to rise to propose a toast. I need hardly say that it is the health and prosperity of that young gentleman, the particular event of whose early life we are here met to celebrate—(applause). Ladies and gentlemen, it is impossible to suppose that our friends here, whose sincere well-wishers we all are, can pass through life without some trials, considerable suffering, severe affliction, and heavy losses!"—Here the arch-traitor paused, and slowly drew forth a long, white pocket-handkerchief—his example was followed by several ladies. "That these trials may be long spared them is my most earnest prayer, my most fervent wish (a distinct sob from the grandmother). I hope and trust, ladies and gentlemen, that the infant whose christening we have this evening met to celebrate, may not be removed from the arms of his parents by premature decay (several cambrics were in requisition): that his young and now *apparently* healthy form, may not be wasted by lingering disease. (Here Dumps cast a sardonic glance around, for a great sensation was manifest among the married ladies.) You, I am sure, will concur with

173

me in wishing that he may live to be a comfort and a blessing to his parents. ('Hear, hear!' and an audible sob from Mr. Kitterbell.) But should he not be what we could wish—should he forget in after times the duty which he owes to them—should they unhappily experience that distracting truth, 'how sharper than a serpent's tooth it is to have a thankless child'"—Here Mrs. Kitterbell, with her handkerchief to her eyes, and accompanied by several ladies, rushed from the room, and went into violent hysterics in the passage, leaving her better half in almost as bad a condition, and a general impression in Dumps's favour; for people like sentiment, after all.

It need hardly be added, that this occurrence quite put a stop to the harmony of the evening. Vinegar, hartshorn, and cold water, were now as much in request as negus, rout-cakes, and *bon-bons* had been a short time before. Mrs. Kitterbell was immediately conveyed to her apartment, the musicians were silenced, flirting ceased, and the company slowly departed. Dumps left the house at the commencement of the bustle, and walked home with a light step, and (for him) a cheerful heart. His landlady, who slept in the next room, has offered to make oath that she heard him laugh, in his peculiar manner, after he had locked his door. The assertion, however, is so improbable, and bears on the face of it such strong evidence of untruth, that it has never obtained credence to this hour.

The family of Mr. Kitterbell has considerably increased since the period to which we have referred; he has now two sons and a daughter; and as he expects, at no distant period, to have another addition to his blooming progeny, he is anxious to secure an eligible godfather for the occasion. He is determined, however, to impose upon him two conditions. He must bind himself, by a solemn obligation, not to make any speech after supper; and it is indispensable that he should be in no way connected with "the most miserable man in the world."

CHAPTER XII

THE DRUNKARD'S DEATH

WE will be bold to say, that there is scarcely a man in the constant habit of walking, day after day, through any of the crowded thoroughfares of London, who cannot recollect among the people whom he "knows by sight," to use a familiar phrase, some being of abject and wretched appearance whom he remembers to have seen in a very different condition, whom he has observed sinking lower and lower, by almost imperceptible degrees, and the shabbiness and utter destitution of whose appearance, at last, strike forcibly and painfully upon him, as he passes by. Is there any man who has mixed much with society, or whose avocations have caused him to mingle, at one time or other, with a great number of people, who cannot call to mind the time when some shabby, miserable wretch, in rags and filth, who shuffles past him now in all the squalor of disease and poverty, was a respectable tradesman, or clerk, or a man following some thriving pursuit, with good prospects, and decent means?—or cannot any of our readers call to mind from among the list of their *quondam* acquaintance, some fallen and degraded man, who lingers about the pavement in hungry misery—from whom every one turns coldly away, and who preserves himself from sheer starvation, nobody knows how? Alas! such cases are of too frequent occurrence to be rare items in any man's experience; and but too often arise from one cause—drunkenness—that

175

fierce rage for the slow, sure poison, that oversteps every other consideration; that casts aside wife, children, friends, happiness, and station; and hurries its victims madly on to degradation and death.

Some of these men have been impelled, by misfortune and misery, to the vice that has degraded them. The ruin of worldly expectations, the death of those they loved, the sorrow that slowly consumes, but will not break the heart, has driven them wild; and they present the hideous spectacle of mad-men, slowly dying by their own hands. But by far the greater part have wilfully, and with open eyes, plunged into the gulf from which the man who once enters it never rises more, but into which he sinks deeper and deeper down, until recovery is hopeless.

Such a man as this once stood by the bedside of his dying wife, while his children knelt around, and mingled low bursts of grief with their innocent prayers. The room was scantily and meanly furnished; and it needed but a glance at the pale form from which the light of life was fast passing away, to know that grief, and want, and anxious care, had been busy at the heart for many a weary year. An elderly woman, with her face bathed in tears, was supporting the head of the dying woman—her daughter—on her arm. But it was not towards her that the wan face turned; it was not her hand that the cold and trembling fingers clasped; they pressed the husband's arm; the eyes so soon to be closed in death rested on his face, and the man shook beneath their gaze. His dress was slovenly and disordered, his face inflamed, his eyes blood-shot and heavy. He had been summoned from some wild debauch to the bed of sorrow and death.

A shaded lamp by the bed-side cast a dim light on the figures around, and left the remainder of the room in thick, deep shadow. The silence of night prevailed without the house, and the stillness of death was in the chamber. A watch hung over the mantel-shelf; its low ticking was the only sound that broke the profound quiet, but it was a solemn one, for well they knew, who heard it, that before it had recorded the passing of another hour, it would beat the knell of a departed spirit.

It is a dreadful thing to wait and watch for the approach of death; to know that hope is gone, and recovery impossible; and to sit and count the dreary hours through long, long nights—such nights as only watchers by the bed of sickness know. It chills the blood to hear the dearest secrets of the heart—the pent-up, hidden secrets of many years—poured forth by the unconscious, helpless being before you; and to think how little the reserve and cunning of a whole life will avail, when fever and delirium tear off the mask at last. Strange tales have been told in the wanderings of dying men; tales so full of guilt and crime, that those who stood by the sick person's couch have fled in horror and affright, lest they should be scared to madness by what they heard and saw; and many a wretch has died alone, raving of deeds the very name of which has driven the boldest man away.

But no such ravings were to be heard at the bed-side by which the children knelt. Their half-stifled sobs and moanings alone broke the silence of the lonely chamber. And when at last the mother's grasp relaxed, and, turning one look from the children to the father, she vainly strove to speak, and fell backward on the pillow, all was so calm and tranquil that she seemed to sink to sleep. They leant over her; they called upon her name, softly at first, and then in the loud and piercing tones of desperation. But there was no reply. They listened for her breath, but no sound came. They felt for the palpitation of the heart, but no faint throb responded to the touch. That heart was broken, and she was dead!

The husband sunk into a chair by the bed-side, and clasped his hands upon his burning forehead. He gazed from child to child, but when a weeping eye met his, he quailed beneath its look. No word of comfort was whispered in his ear, no look of kindness lighted on his face. All shrunk from and avoided him; and when at last he staggered from the room, no one sought to follow or console the widower.

The time had been when many a friend would have crowded round him in his affliction, and many a heartfelt condolence would have met him in his grief. Where were they now? One by one, friends, relations, the commonest acquaintance even, had fallen off from and deserted the drunkard. His wife alone had clung to him in good and evil, in sickness and poverty, and how had he rewarded her? He had reeled from the tavern to her bed-side in time to see her die.

He rushed from the house, and walked swiftly through the streets. Remorse, fear, shame, all crowded on his mind. Stupefied with drink, and bewildered with the scene he had just witnessed, he re-entered the tavern he had quitted shortly before. Glass succeeded glass. His blood mounted, and his brain whirled round. Death! Every one must die, and why not *she?* She was too good for him; her relations had often told him so. Curses on them! Had they not deserted her, and left her to whine away the time at home? Well—she was dead, and happy perhaps. It was better as it was. Another glass—one more! Hurrah! It was a merry life while it lasted; and he would make the most of it.

Time went on; the three children who were left to him, grew up, and were children no longer. The father remained the same—poorer, shabbier, and more dissolute-looking, but the same confirmed and irreclaimable drunkard. The boys had, long ago, run wild in the streets, and left him; the girl alone remained, but she worked hard, and words or blows could always procure him something for the tavern. So he went on in the old course, and a merry life he led.

One night, as early as ten o'clock—for the girl had been sick for many days, and there was, consequently, little to spend at the public-house—he bent his steps homeward, bethinking himself that if he would have her able to earn money, it would be as well to apply to the parish surgeon, or, at all events, to take the trouble of inquiring what ailed her, which he had not yet thought it worth while to do. It was a wet December night; the wind blew piercing cold, and the rain poured heavily down. He begged a few halfpence from a passer-by, and having bought a small loaf (for it was his interest to keep the girl alive, if he could), he shuffled onwards as fast as the wind and rain would let him.

At the back of Fleet-street, and lying between it and the water-side, are several mean and narrow courts, which form a portion of Whitefriars: it was to one of these that he directed his steps.

The alley into which he turned, might, for filth and misery, have competed with the darkest corner of this ancient sanctuary in its dirtiest and most lawless time. The houses, varying from two stories in height to four, were stained with every indescribable hue that long exposure to the weather, damp, and rottenness can impart to tenements composed originally of the roughest and coarsest materials. The windows were patched with paper, and stuffed with the foulest rags; the doors were falling from their hinges; poles with lines on which to dry clothes, projected from every casement, and sounds of quarrelling or drunkenness issued from every room.

The solitary oil lamp in the centre of the court had been blown out, either by the violence of the wind or the act of some inhabitant who had excellent reasons for objecting to his residence being rendered too conspicuous; and the only light which fell upon the broken and uneven pavement, was derived from the miserable candles that here and there twinkled in the rooms of such of the more fortunate residents as could afford to indulge in so expensive a luxury. A gutter ran down the centre of the alley—all the sluggish odours of which had been called forth by the rain; and as the wind whistled through the old houses, the doors and shutters creaked upon their hinges, and the windows shook in their frames, with a violence which every moment seemed to threaten the destruction of the whole place.

The man whom we have followed into this den, walked on in the darkness, sometimes stumbling into the main gutter, and at others into some branch repositories of garbage which had been formed by the rain, until he reached the last house in the court. The door, or rather what was left of it, stood ajar, for the convenience of the numerous lodgers; and he proceeded to grope his way up the old and broken stair, to the attic story.

He was within a step or two of his room door, when it opened, and a girl, whose miserable and emaciated appearance was only to be equalled by that of the candle which she shaded with her hand, peeped anxiously out.

"Is that you, father?" said the girl.

"Who else should it be?" replied the man gruffly. "What are you trembling at? It's little enough that I've had to drink to-day, for there's no drink without money, and no money without work. What the devil's the matter with the girl?"

"I am not well, father—not at all well," said the girl, bursting into tears.

"Ah!" replied the man, in the tone of a person who is compelled to admit a very unpleasant fact, to which he would rather remain blind, if he could. "You must get better somehow, for we must have money. You must go to the parish doctor, and make him give you some medicine. They're paid for it, damn 'em. What are you standing before the door for? Let me come in, can't you?"

"Father," whispered the girl, shutting the door behind her, and placing herself before it, "William has come back."

"Who!" said the man with a start.

"Hush," replied the girl, "William; brother William."

"And what does he want?" said the man, with an effort at composure—"money? meat? drink? He's come to the wrong shop for that, if he does. Give me the candle—give me the candle, fool—I ain't going to hurt him." He snatched the candle from her hand, and walked into the room.

Sitting on an old box, with his head resting on his hand, and his eyes fixed on a wretched cinder fire that was smouldering on the hearth, was a young man of about two-and-twenty, miserably clad in an old coarse jacket and trousers. He started up when his father entered.

"Fasten the door, Mary," said the young man hastily— "Fasten the door. You look as if you didn't know me, father. It's long enough, since you drove me from home; you may well forget me."

"And what do you want here, now?" said the father, seating himself on a stool, on the other side of the fireplace. "What do you want here, now?"

"Shelter," replied the son. "I'm in trouble: that's enough. If I'm caught I shall swing; that's certain. Caught I shall be, unless I stop here; that's *as* certain. And there's an end of it."

"You mean to say, you've been robbing, or murdering, then?" said the father.

"Yes, I do," replied the son. "Does it surprise you, father?" He looked steadily in the man's face, but he withdrew his eyes, and bent them on the ground.

"Where's your brothers?" he said, after a long pause.

"Where they'll never trouble you," replied his son: "John's gone to America, and Henry's dead."

"Dead!" said the father, with a shudder, which even he could not express.

"Dead," replied the young man. "He died in my arms —shot like a dog, by a gamekeeper. He staggered back, I caught him, and his blood trickled down my hands. It poured out from his side like water. He was weak, and it blinded him, but he threw himself down on his knees, on the grass, and prayed to God. that if his mother was in heaven,

He would hear her prayers for pardon for her youngest son. 'I was her favourite boy, Will,' he said, ' and I am glad to think, now, that when she was dying, though I was a very young child then, and my little heart was almost bursting, I knelt down at the foot of the bed, and thanked God for having made me so fond of her as to have never once done anything to bring the tears into her eyes. O Will, why was she taken away, and father left?' There's his dying words, father," said the young man; "make the best you can of 'em. You struck him across the face, in a drunken fit, the morning we ran away; and here's the end of it."

The girl wept aloud; and the father, sinking his head upon his knees, rocked himself to and fro.

"If I am taken," said the young man, "I shall be carried back into the country, and hung for that man's murder. They cannot trace me here, without your assistance, father. For aught I know, you may give me up to justice; but unless you do, here I stop, until I can venture to escape abroad."

For two whole days, all three remained in the wretched room, without stirring out. On the third evening, however, the girl was worse than she had been yet, and the few scraps of food they had were gone. It was indispensably necessary that somebody should go out; and as the girl was too weak and ill, the father went, just at nightfall.

He got some medicine for the girl, and a trifle in the way of pecuniary assistance. On his way back, he earned sixpence by holding a horse; and he turned homewards with enough money to supply their most pressing wants for two or three days to come. He had to pass the public-house. He lingered for an instant, walked past it, turned back again, lingered once more, and finally slunk in. Two men whom he had not observed, were on the watch. They were on the point of giving up their search in despair, when his loitering attracted their attention ; and when he entered the public-house, they followed him.

" You'll drink with me, master," said one of them, proffering him a glass of liquor.

" And me too," said the other, replenishing the glass as soon as it was drained of its contents.

The man thought of his hungry children, and his son's danger. But they were nothing to the drunkard. He *did* drink ; and his reason left him.

" A wet night, Warden," whispered one of the men in his ear, as he at length turned to go away, after spending in liquor one-half of the money on which, perhaps, his daughter's life depended.

" The right sort of night for our friends in hiding, Master Warden," whispered the other.

" Sit down here," said the one who had spoken first, drawing him into a corner. " We have been looking arter the young un. We came to tell him, it's all right now, but we couldn't find him 'cause we hadn't got the precise direction. But that ain't strange, for I don't think he know'd it himself, when he come to London, did he ? "

" No, he didn't," replied the father.

The two men exchanged glances.

" There's a vessel down at the docks, to sail at midnight, when it's high water," resumed the first speaker, " and we'll put him on board. His passage is taken in another name, and what's better than that, it's paid for. It's lucky we met you."

" Very," said the second.

" Capital luck," said the first, with a wink to his companion.

" Great," replied the second, with a slight nod of intelligence.

" Another glass here ; quick "—said the first speaker. And in five minutes more, the father had unconsciously yielded up his own son into the hangman's hands.

Slowly and heavily the time dragged along, as the brother and sister, in their miserable hiding-place, listened in anxious suspense to the slightest sound. At length, a heavy footstep was heard upon the stair; it approached nearer; it reached the landing; and the father staggered into the room.

The girl saw that he was intoxicated, and advanced with the candle in her hand to meet him; she stopped short, gave a loud scream, and fell senseless on the ground. She had caught sight of the shadow of a man reflected on the floor. They both rushed in, and in another instant the young man was a prisoner, and handcuffed.

"Very quietly done," said one of the men to his companion, "thanks to the old man. Lift up the girl, Tom—come, come, it's no use crying, young woman. It's all over now, and can't be helped."

The young man stooped for an instant over the girl, and then turned fiercely round upon his father, who had reeled against the wall, and was gazing on the group with drunken stupidity.

"Listen to me, father," he said, in a tone that made the drunkard's flesh creep. "My brother's blood, and mine, is on your head: I never had kind look, or word, or care, from you, and alive or dead, I never will forgive you. Die when you will, or how, I will be with you. I speak as a dead man now, and I warn you, father, that as surely as you must one day stand before your Maker, so surely shall your children be there, hand in hand, to cry for judgment against you." He raised his manacled hands in a threatening attitude, fixed his eyes on his shrinking parent, and slowly left the room; and neither father nor sister ever beheld him more, on this side of the grave.

When the dim and misty light of a winter's morning penetrated into the narrow court, and struggled through the begrimed window of the wretched room, Warden awoke from his heavy sleep, and found himself alone. He rose, and looked round him; the old flock mattress on the floor was undisturbed; everything was just as he remembered to have seen it last: and there were no signs of any one, save himself, having occupied the room during the night. He inquired of the other lodgers, and of the neighbours; but his daughter had not been seen or heard of. He rambled through the streets, and scrutinised each wretched face among the crowds that thronged them, with anxious eyes. But his search was fruitless, and he returned to his garret when night came on, desolate and weary.

For many days he occupied himself in the same manner, but no trace of his daughter did he meet with, and no word of her reached his ears. At length he gave up the pursuit as hopeless. He had long thought of the probability of her leaving him, and endeavouring to gain her bread in quiet, elsewhere. She had left him at last to starve alone. He ground his teeth, and cursed her!

He begged his bread from door to door. Every halfpenny he could wring from the pity or credulity of those to whom he addressed himself, was spent in the old way. A year passed over his head; the roof of a jail was the only one that had sheltered him for many months. He slept under archways, and in brickfields—anywhere, where there was some warmth or shelter from the cold and rain. But in the last stage of poverty, disease, and houseless want, he was a drunkard still.

At last, one bitter night, he sunk down on a door-step faint and ill. The premature decay of vice and profligacy had worn him to the bone. His cheeks were hollow and livid; his eyes were sunken, and their sight was dim. His legs trembled beneath his weight, and a cold shiver ran through every limb.

And now the long-forgotten scenes of a misspent life crowded thick and fast upon him. He thought of the time when he had a home—a happy, cheerful home—and of those who peopled it, and flocked about him then, until the forms of his elder children seemed to rise from the grave, and stand about him—so plain, so clear, and so distinct they were that he could touch and feel them. Looks that he had long forgotten were fixed upon him once more; voices long since hushed in death sounded in his ears like the music of village bells. But it was only for an instant. The rain beat heavily upon him; and cold and hunger were gnawing at his heart again.

He rose, and dragged his feeble limbs a few paces further. The street was silent and empty; the few passengers who passed by, at that late hour, hurried quickly on, and his tremulous voice was lost in the violence of the storm. Again that heavy chill struck through his frame, and his blood seemed to stagnate beneath it. He coiled himself up in a projecting doorway, and tried to sleep.

But sleep had fled from his dull and glazed eyes. His mind wandered strangely, but he was awake, and conscious. The well-known shout of drunken mirth sounded in his ear, the glass was at his lips, the board was covered with choice rich food—they were before him : he could see them all, he had but to reach out his hand, and take them—and, though the illusion was reality itself, he knew that he was sitting alone in the deserted street, watching the rain-drops as they pattered on the stones; that death was coming upon him by inches—and that there were none to care for or help him.

Suddenly he started up, in the extremity of terror. He had heard his own voice shouting in the night air, he knew not what, or why. Hark! A groan!—another! His senses were leaving him : half-formed and incoherent words burst from his lips; and his hands sought to tear and lacerate his flesh. He was going mad, and he shrieked for help till his voice failed him.

He raised his head, and looked up the long dismal street. He recollected that outcasts like himself, condemned to wander day and night in those dreadful streets, had some-times gone distracted with their own loneliness. He re-membered to have heard many years before that a homeless wretch had once been found in a solitary corner, sharpening a rusty knife to plunge into his own heart, preferring death to that endless, weary, wandering to and fro. In an instant his resolve was taken, his limbs received new life; he ran quickly from the spot, and paused not for breath until he reached the river-side.

He crept softly down the steep stone stairs that lead from the commencement of Waterloo Bridge, down to the water's level. He crouched into a corner, and held his breath, as the patrol passed. Never did prisoner's heart throb with the hope of liberty and life half so eagerly as did that of the wretched man at the prospect of death. The watch passed close to him, but he remained unobserved; and after waiting till the sound of footsteps had died away in the distance, he cautiously descended, and stood beneath the gloomy arch that forms the landing-place from the river.

The tide was in, and the water flowed at his feet. The rain had ceased, the wind was lulled, and all was, for the moment, still and quiet—so quiet, that the slightest sound on the opposite bank, even the rippling of the water against the barges that were moored there, was distinctly audible to his ear. The stream stole languidly and sluggishly on. Strange and fantastic forms rose to the surface, and beckoned him to approach; dark gleaming eyes peered from the water, and seemed to mock his hesitation, while hollow murmurs from behind, urged him onwards. He retreated a few paces, took a short run, desperate leap, and plunged into the river.

Not five seconds had passed when he rose to the water's surface—but what a change had taken place in that short time, in all his thoughts and feelings! Life—life in any form, poverty, misery, starvation—anything but death. He fought and struggled with the water that closed over his head, and screamed in agonies of terror. The curse of his own son rang in his ears. The shore—but one foot of dry ground — he could almost touch the step. One hand's breadth nearer, and he was saved—but the tide bore him onward, under the dark arches of the bridge, and he sank to the bottom.

187

Again he rose, and struggled for life. For one instant—for one brief instant—the buildings on the river's banks, the lights on the bridge through which the current had borne him, the black water, and the fast-flying clouds, were distinctly visible—once more he sunk, and once again he rose. Bright flames of fire shot up from earth to heaven, and reeled before his eyes, while the water thundered in his ears, and stunned him with its furious roar.

A week afterwards the body was washed ashore, some miles down the river, a swollen and disfigured mass. Unrecognised and unpitied, it was borne to the grave; and there it has long since mouldered away !

SKETCHES OF
YOUNG GENTLEMEN

TO THE YOUNG LADIES

OF THE

United Kingdom of Great Britain and Ireland;

ALSO

THE YOUNG LADIES

OF

THE PRINCIPALITY OF WALES,

AND LIKEWISE

THE YOUNG LADIES

RESIDENT IN THE ISLES OF

Guernsey, Jersey, Alderney, and Sark,

THE HUMBLE DEDICATION OF THEIR DEVOTED ADMIRER,

SHEWETH,—

THAT your Dedicator has perused, with feelings of virtuous indignation, a work purporting to be "Sketches of Young Ladies;" written by Quiz, illustrated by Phiz, and published in one volume, square twelvemo.

THAT after an attentive and vigilant perusal of the said work, your Dedicator is humbly of opinion that so many libels, upon your Honourable sex, were never contained in any previously published work, in twelvemo or any other mo.

191

DEDICATION

THAT in the title page and preface to the said work, your Honourable sex are described and classified as animals; and although your Dedicator is not at present prepared to deny that you *are* animals, still he humbly submits that it is not polite to call you so.

THAT in the aforesaid preface, your Honourable sex are also described as Troglodites, which, being a hard word, may, for aught your Honourable sex or your Dedicator can say to the contrary, be an injurious and disrespectful appellation.

THAT the author of the said work applied himself to his task in malice prepense and with wickedness aforethought; a fact which, your Dedicator contends, is sufficiently demonstrated, by his assuming the name of Quiz, which, your Dedicator submits, denotes a foregone conclusion, and implies an intention of quizzing.

THAT in the execution of his evil design, the said Quiz, or author of the said work, must have betrayed some trust or confidence reposed in him by some members of your Honourable sex, otherwise he never could have acquired so much information relative to the manners and customs of your Honourable sex in general.

THAT actuated by these considerations, and further moved by various slanders and insinuations respecting your Honourable sex contained in the said work, square twelvemo, entitled "Sketches of Young Ladies," your Dedicator ventures to produce another work, square twelvemo, entitled "Sketches of Young Gentlemen," of which he now solicits your acceptance and approval.

DEDICATION

THAT as the Young Ladies are the best companions of the Young Gentlemen, so the Young Gentlemen should be the best companions of the Young Ladies; and extending the comparison from animals (to quote the disrespectful language of the said Quiz) to inanimate objects, your Dedicator humbly suggests, that such of your Honourable sex as purchased the bane should possess themselves of the antidote, and that those of your Honourable sex who were not rash enough to take the first, should lose no time in swallowing the last, —prevention being in all cases better than cure, as we are informed upon the authority, not only of general acknowledgment, but also of traditionary wisdom.

THAT with reference to the said bane and antidote, your Dedicator has no further remarks to make, than are comprised in the printed directions issued with Doctor Morison's pills; namely, that whenever your Honourable sex take twenty-five of Number 1, you will be pleased to take fifty of Number 2, without delay.

And your Dedicator shall ever pray, &c.

THE BASHFUL YOUNG GENTLEMAN

We found ourself seated at a small dinner party the other day, opposite a stranger of such singular appearance and manner, that he irresistibly attracted our attention.

This was a fresh-coloured young gentleman, with as good a promise of light whisker as one might wish to see, and possessed of a very velvet-like, soft-looking countenance. We do not use the latter term invidiously, but merely to denote a pair of smooth, plump, highly-coloured cheeks of capacious dimensions, and a mouth rather remarkable for the fresh hue of the lips than for any marked or striking expression it presented. His whole face was suffused with a crimson blush, and bore that downcast, timid, retiring look, which betokens a man ill at ease with himself.

There was nothing in these symptoms to attract more than a passing remark, but our attention had been originally drawn to the bashful young gentleman, on his first appearance in the drawing-room above-stairs, into which he was no sooner introduced, than making his way towards us who were standing in a window, and wholly neglecting several persons who warmly accosted him, he seized our hand with visible emotion, and pressed it with a convulsive grasp for a good couple of minutes, after which he dived in a nervous manner across the room, oversetting in his way a fine little girl of six years and a quarter old—and shrouding himself behind some hangings, was seen no more, until the eagle eye of the hostess detecting him in his concealment, on the announcement of dinner, he was requested to pair off with a lively single lady, of two or three and thirty.

This most flattering salutation from a perfect stranger, would have gratified us not a little as a token of his having held us in high respect, and for that reason been desirous of our acquaintance, if we had not suspected from the first, that the young gentleman, in making a desperate effort to get through the ceremony of introduction, had, in the bewilderment of his ideas, shaken hands with us at random. This impression was fully confirmed by the subsequent behaviour of the bashful young gentleman in question, which we noted particularly, with the view of ascertaining whether we were right in our conjecture.

The young gentleman seated himself at table with evident misgivings, and turning sharp round to pay attention to some observation of his loquacious neighbour, overset his bread. There was nothing very bad in this, and if he had had the presence of mind to let it go, and say nothing about it, nobody but the man who had laid the cloth would have been a bit the wiser; but the young gentleman in various semi-successful attempts to prevent its fall, played with it a little, as gentlemen in the streets may be seen to do with their hats on a windy day, and then giving the roll a smart rap in his anxiety to catch it, knocked it with great adroitness into a tureen of white soup at some distance, to the unspeakable terror and disturbance of a very amiable bald gentleman, who was dispensing the contents. We thought the bashful young gentleman would have gone off in an apoplectic fit, consequent upon the violent rush of blood to his face at the occurrence of this catastrophe.

THE BASHFUL YOUNG GENTLEMAN

From this moment we perceived, in the phraseology of the fancy, that it was "all up" with the bashful young gentleman, and so indeed it was. Several benevolent persons endeavoured to relieve his embarrassment by taking wine with him, but finding that it only augmented his sufferings, and that after mingling sherry, champagne, hock, and moselle together, he applied the greater part of the mixture externally, instead of internally, they gradually dropped off, and left him to the exclusive care of the talkative lady, who, not noting the wildness of his eye, firmly believed she had secured a listener. He broke a glass or two in the course of the meal, and disappeared shortly afterwards; it is inferred that he went away in some confusion, inasmuch as he left the house in another gentleman's coat, and the footman's hat.

This little incident led us to reflect upon the most prominent characteristics of bashful young gentlemen in the abstract; and as this portable volume will be the great text-book of young ladies in all future generations, we record them here for their guidance and behoof.

If the bashful young gentleman, in turning a street corner, chance to stumble suddenly upon two or three young ladies of his acquaintance, nothing can exceed his confusion and agitation. His first impulse is to make a great variety of bows, and dart past them, which he does until, observing that they wish to stop, but are uncertain whether to do so or not, he makes several feints of returning, which causes them to do the same; and at length, after a great quantity of unnecessary dodging and falling up against the other passengers, he returns and shakes hands most affectionately with all of them, in doing which he knocks out of their grasp sundry little parcels, which he hastily picks up, and returns very muddy and disordered. The chances are that the bashful young gentleman then observes it is very fine weather, and being reminded that it has only just left off raining for the first time these three days, he blushes very much, and smiles as if he had said a very good thing. The young lady who was most anxious to speak, here inquires, with an air of great commiseration, how his dear sister Harriet is to-day; to which the young gentleman, without the slightest consideration, replies with many thanks, that she is remarkably well. "Well, Mr. Hopkins!" cries the young lady, "why, we heard she was bled yesterday evening, and have been perfectly miserable about her." "Oh, ah," says the young gentleman, "so she was. Oh, she's very ill, very ill indeed." The young gentleman then shakes his head, and looks very desponding (he has been smiling perpetually up to this time), and after a short pause, gives his glove a great wrench at the wrist, and says, with a strong emphasis on the adjective, "*Good* morning, *good* morning." And making a great number of bows in acknowledgment of several little messages to his sister, walks backward a few paces, and comes with great violence against a lamp-post, knocking his hat off in the contact, which in his mental confusion and bodily pain he is going to walk away without, until a great roar from a carter attracts his attention, when he picks it up, and tries to smile cheerfully to the young ladies, who are looking back, and who, he has the satisfaction of seeing, are all laughing heartily.

At a quadrille party, the bashful young gentleman always remains as near the entrance of the room as possible, from which position he smiles at the people he knows as they come in, and sometimes steps forward to shake hands with more intimate friends: a process which on each repetition seems to turn him a deeper scarlet than before. He declines dancing the first set or two, observing, in a faint voice, that he would rather wait a little; but at length is absolutely compelled to allow himself to be introduced to a partner, when he is led, in a great heat and blushing furiously, across the room to a spot where half-a-dozen unknown ladies are congregated together.

"Miss Lambert, let me introduce Mr. Hopkins for the next quadrille." Miss Lambert inclines her head graciously. Mr. Hopkins bows, and his fair conductress disappears, leaving

Mr. Hopkins, as he too well knows, to make himself agreeable. The young lady more than half expects that the bashful young gentleman will say something, and the bashful young gentleman feeling this, seriously thinks whether he has got anything to say, which, upon mature reflection, he is rather disposed to conclude he has not, since nothing occurs to him. Meanwhile, the young lady, after several inspections of her *bouquet*, all made in the expectation that the bashful young gentleman is going to talk, whispers her mamma, who is sitting next her, which whisper the bashful young gentleman immediately suspects (and possibly with very good reason) must be about *him*. In this comfortable condition he remains until it is time to "stand up," when murmuring a "Will you allow me?" he gives the young lady his arm, and after inquiring where she will stand, and receiving a reply that she has no choice, conducts her to the remotest corner of the quadrille, and making one attempt at conversation, which turns out a desperate failure, preserves a profound silence until it is all over, when he walks her twice round the room, deposits her in her old seat, and retires in confusion.

A married bashful gentleman—for these bashful gentlemen *do* get married sometimes; how it is ever brought about, is a mystery to us—a married bashful gentleman either causes his wife to appear bold by contrast, or merges her proper importance in his own insignificance. Bashful young gentlemen should be cured, or avoided. They are never hopeless, and never will be, while female beauty and attractions retain their influence, as any young lady will find, who may think it worth while on this confident assurance to take a patient in hand.

THE OUT-AND-OUT YOUNG GENTLEMAN

OUT-AND-OUT young gentlemen may be divided into two classes—those who have something to do, and those who have nothing. I shall commence with the former, because that species come more frequently under the notice of young ladies, whom it is our province to warn and to instruct.

The out-and-out young gentleman is usually no great dresser, his instructions to his tailor being all comprehended in the one general direction to " make that what's-a-name a regular bang-up sort of thing." For some years past, the favourite costume of the out-and-out young gentleman has been a rough pilot coat, with two gilt hooks and eyes to the velvet collar; buttons somewhat larger than crown-pieces; a black or fancy neckerchief, loosely tied; a wide-brimmed hat, with a low crown; tightish inexpressibles, and iron-shod boots. Out of doors he sometimes carries a large ash stick, but only on special occasions, for he prefers keeping his hands in his coat pockets. He smokes at all hours, of course, and swears considerably.

The out-and-out young gentleman is employed in a city counting-house or solicitor's office, in which he does as little as he possibly can: his chief places of resort are, the streets, the taverns, and the theatres. In the streets at evening time, out-and-out young gentlemen have a pleasant custom

The Out-and-Out Young Gentleman

of walking six or eight abreast, thus driving females and other inoffensive persons into the road, which never fails to afford them the highest satisfaction, especially if there be any immediate danger of their being run over, which enhances the fun of the thing materially. In all places of public resort, the out-and-outers are careful to select each a seat to himself, upon which he lies at full length, and (if the weather be very dirty, but not in any other case) he lies with his knees up, and the soles of his boots planted firmly on the cushion, so that if any low fellow should ask him to make room for a lady, he takes ample revenge upon her dress, without going at all out of his way to do it. He always sits with his hat on, and flourishes his stick in the air while the play is proceeding, with a dignified contempt of the perform-ance; if it be possible for one or two out-and-out young gentlemen to get up a little crowding in the passages, they are quite in their element, squeezing, pushing, whooping, and shouting in the most humorous manner possible. If they can only succeed in irritating the gentleman who has a family of daughters under his charge, they are like to die with laughing, and boast of it among their companions for a week afterwards, adding, that one or two of them were " devilish fine girls," and that they really thought the youngest would have fainted, which was the only thing wanted to render the joke complete.

If the out-and-out young gentleman have a mother and sisters, of course he treats them with becoming contempt, inasmuch as they (poor things!) having no notion of life or gaiety, are far too weak-spirited and moping for him. Some-times, however, on a birth-day or at Christmas-time, he' cannot very well help accompanying them to a party at some old friend's, with which view he comes home when they have been dressed an hour or two, smelling very strongly of tobacco and spirits, and after exchanging his rough coat for some more suitable attire (in which however he loses nothing of the out-and-outer), gets into the coach and grumbles all the way at his own good nature: his bitter reflections aggravated by the recollection, that Tom Smith has taken the chair at a little impromptu dinner at a fighting man's, and that a set-to was to take place on a dining-table, between the fighting man and his brother-in-law, which is probably "coming off" at that very instant.

As the out-and-out young gentleman is by no means at his ease in ladies' society, he shrinks into a corner of the drawing-room when they reach the friend's, and unless one of his sisters is kind enough to talk to him, remains there without being much troubled by the attentions of other people, until he espies, lingering outside the door, another gentleman, whom he at once knows, by his air and manner (for there is a kind of free-masonry in the craft), to be a brother out-and-outer, and towards whom he accordingly makes his way. Conversation being soon opened by some casual remark, the second out-and-outer confidentially informs the first, that he is one of the rough sort and hates that kind of thing, only he couldn't very well be off coming; to which the other replies, that that's just his case—"and I'll tell you what," continues the out-and-outer in a whisper, "I should like a glass of warm brandy and water just now," —"Or a pint of stout and a pipe," suggests the other out-and-outer.

The discovery is at once made that they are sympathetic souls ; each of them says at the same moment, that he sees the other understands what's what: and they become fast friends at once, more especially when it appears, that the second out-and-outer is no other than a gentleman, long favourably known to his familiars as "Mr. Warmint Blake," who upon divers occasions has distinguished himself in a manner that would not have disgraced the fighting man, and who—having been a pretty long time about town—had the honour of once shaking hands with the celebrated Mr. Thurtell himself.

At supper, these gentlemen greatly distinguish themselves,

brightening up very much when the ladies leave the table, and proclaiming aloud their intention of beginning to spend the evening—a process which is generally understood to be satisfactorily performed, when a great deal of wine is drunk and a great deal of noise made, both of which feats the out-and-out young gentlemen execute to perfection. Having protracted their sitting until long after the host and the other guests have adjourned to the drawing-room, and finding that they have drained the decanters empty, they follow them thither with complexions rather heightened, and faces rather bloated with wine; and the agitated lady of the house whispers her friends as they waltz together, to the great terror of the whole room, that "both Mr. Blake and Mr. Dummins are very nice sort of young men in their way, only they are eccentric persons, and unfortunately *rather too wild!*"

The remaining class of out-and-out young gentlemen is composed of persons, who, having no money of their own and a soul above earning any, enjoy similar pleasures, nobody knows how. These respectable gentlemen, without aiming quite so much at the out-and-out in external appearance, are distinguished by all the same amiable and attractive characteristics, in an equal or perhaps greater degree, and now and then find their way into society, through the medium of the other class of out-and-out young gentlemen, who will sometimes carry them home, and who usually pay their tavern bills. As they are equally gentlemanly, clever, witty, intelligent, wise, and well-bred, we need scarcely have recommended them to the peculiar consideration of the young ladies, if it were not that some of the gentle creatures whom we hold in such high respect, are perhaps a little too apt to confound a great many heavier terms with the light word eccentricity, which we beg them henceforth to take in a strictly Johnsonian sense, without any liberality or latitude of construction.

THE VERY FRIENDLY YOUNG
GENTLEMAN

WE know—and all people know—so many specimens of
this class, that in selecting the few heads our limits enable
us to take from a great number, we have been induced to
give the very friendly young gentleman the preference over
many others, to whose claims upon a more cursory view of
the question we had felt disposed to assign the priority.

The very friendly young gentleman is very friendly to
everybody, but he attaches himself particularly to two, or at
most to three families: regulating his choice by their dinners,
their circle of acquaintance, or some other criterion in which
he has an immediate interest. He is of any age between
twenty and forty, unmarried of course, must be fond of
children, and is expected to make himself generally useful if
possible. Let us illustrate our meaning by an example,
which is the shortest mode and the clearest.

We encountered one day, by chance, an old friend of whom
we had lost sight for some years, and who—expressing a
strong anxiety to renew our former intimacy—urged us to
dine with him on an early day, that we might talk over old
times. We readily assented, adding, that we hoped we
should be alone. "Oh, certainly, certainly," said our friend,
"not a soul with us but Mincin." "And who is Mincin?"
was our natural inquiry. "O don't mind him," replied our

friend, "he's a most particular friend of mine, and a very friendly fellow you will find him;" and so he left us.

We thought no more about Mincin until we duly presented ourselves at the house next day, when, after a hearty welcome, our friend motioned towards a gentleman who had been previously showing his teeth by the fireplace, and gave us to understand that it was Mr. Mincin, of whom he had spoken. It required no great penetration on our part to discover at once that Mr. Mincin was in every respect a very friendly young gentleman.

"I am delighted," said Mincin, hastily advancing, and pressing our hand warmly between both of his, "I am delighted, I am sure, to make your acquaintance—(here he smiled)—very much delighted indeed—(here he exhibited a little emotion)—I assure you that I have looked forward to it anxiously for a very long time:" here he released our hands, and rubbing his own, observed, that the day was severe, but that he was delighted to perceive from our appearance that it agreed with us wonderfully; and then went on to observe, that, notwithstanding the coldness of the weather, he had that morning seen in the paper an exceedingly curious paragraph, to the effect, that there was now in the garden of Mr. Wilkins of Chichester, a pumpkin, measuring four feet in height, and eleven feet seven inches in circumference, which he looked upon as a very extraordinary piece of intelligence. We ventured to remark, that we had a dim recollection of having once or twice before observed a similar paragraph in the public prints, upon which Mr. Mincin took us confidentially by the button, and said, Exactly, exactly, to be sure, we were very right, and he wondered what the editors meant by putting in such things. Who the deuce, he should like to know, did they suppose cared about them? that struck him as being the best of it.

The lady of the house appeared shortly afterwards, and Mr. Mincin's friendliness, as will readily be supposed, suffered no diminution in consequence; he exerted much strength and skill in wheeling a large easy-chair up to the fire, and the lady being seated in it, carefully closed the door, stirred the fire, and looked to the windows to see that they admitted no air; having satisfied himself upon all these points, he expressed himself quite easy in his mind, and begged to know how she found herself to-day. Upon the lady's replying very well, Mr. Mincin (who it appeared was a medical gentleman) offered some general remarks upon the nature and treatment of colds in the head, which occupied us agreeably until dinner-time. During the meal, he devoted himself to complimenting everybody, not forgetting himself, so that we were an uncommonly agreeable quartette.

"I'll tell you what, Capper," said Mr. Mincin to our host, as he closed the room door after the lady had retired, "you have very great reason to be fond of your wife. Sweet woman, Mrs. Capper, sir!" "Nay, Mincin—I beg," interposed the host, as we were about to reply that Mrs. Capper unquestionably was particularly sweet. "Pray, Mincin, don't." "Why not?" exclaimed Mr. Mincin, "why not? Why should you feel any delicacy before your old friend—*our* old friend, if I may be allowed to call you so, sir; why should you, I ask?" We of course wished to know why he should also, upon which our friend admitted that Mrs. Capper *was* a very sweet woman, at which admission Mr. Mincin cried "Bravo!" and begged to propose Mrs. Capper with heartfelt enthusiasm, whereupon our host said, "Thank you, Mincin," with deep feeling; and gave us, in a low voice, to understand, that Mincin had saved Mrs. Capper's cousin's life no less than fourteen times in a year and a half, which he considered no common circumstance—an opinion to which we most cordially subscribed.

Now that we three were left to entertain ourselves with conversation, Mr. Mincin's extreme friendliness became every moment more apparent; he was so amazingly friendly, indeed, that it was impossible to talk about anything in which he had not the chief concern. We happened to allude to some affairs in which our friend and we had been mutually engaged nearly fourteen years before, when Mr. Mincin was all at once reminded of a joke which our friend had made on that day four years, which he positively must insist upon telling— and which he did tell accordingly, with many pleasant recollections of what he said, and what Mrs. Capper said, and how he well remembered that they had been to the play with orders on the very night previous, and had seen Romeo and Juliet, and the pantomime, and how Mrs. Capper being faint had been led into the lobby, where she smiled, said it was nothing after all, and went back again, with many other interesting and absorbing particulars: after which the friendly young gentleman went on to assure us, that our friend had experienced a marvellously prophetic opinion of that same pantomime, which was of such an admirable kind, that two morning papers took the same view next day: to this our friend replied, with a little triumph, that in that instance he had some reason to think he had been correct, which gave the friendly young gentleman occasion to believe that our friend was always correct; and so we went on, until our friend, filling a bumper, said he must drink one glass to his dear friend Mincin, than whom he would say no man saved the lives of his acquaintances more, or had a more friendly heart. Finally, our friend having emptied his glass, said, "God bless you, Mincin,"—and Mr. Mincin and he shook hands across the table with much affection and earnestness.

But great as the friendly young gentleman is, in a limited scene like this, he plays the same part on a larger scale with increased *éclat*. Mr. Mincin is invited to an evening party with his dear friends the Martins, where he meets his dear friends the Cappers, and his dear friends the Watsons, and a hundred other dear friends too numerous to mention. He is as much at home with the Martins as with the Cappers; but how exquisitely he balances his attentions, and divides them among his dear friends! If he flirts with one of the Miss Watsons, he has one little Martin on the sofa pulling his hair, and the other little Martin on the carpet riding on his foot. He carries Mrs. Watson down to supper on one arm, and Miss Martin on the other, and takes wine so judiciously, and in such exact order, that it is impossible for the most punctilious old lady to consider herself neglected. If any young lady, being prevailed upon to sing, become nervous afterwards, Mr. Mincin leads her tenderly into the next room, and restores her with port wine, which she must take medicinally. If any gentleman be standing by the piano during the progress of the ballad, Mr. Mincin seizes him by the arm at one point of the melody, and softly beating time the while with his head, expresses in dumb show his intense perception of the delicacy of the passage. If anybody's self-love is to be flattered, Mr. Mincin is at hand. If anybody's overweening vanity is to be pampered, Mr. Mincin will surfeit it. What wonder that people of all stations and ages recognise Mr. Mincin's friendliness; that he is universally allowed to be handsome as amiable; that mothers think him an oracle, daughters a dear, brothers a beau, and fathers a wonder! And who would not have the reputation of the very friendly young gentleman?

THE MILITARY YOUNG GENTLEMAN

WE are rather at a loss to imagine how it has come to pass that military young gentlemen have obtained so much favour in the eyes of the young ladies of this kingdom. We cannot think so lightly of them as to suppose that the mere circumstance of a man's wearing a red coat ensures him a ready passport to their regard; and even if this were the case, it would be no satisfactory explanation of the circumstance, because, although the analogy may in some degree hold good in the case of mail coachmen and guards, still general postmen wear red coats, and *they* are not to our knowledge better received than other men; nor are firemen either, who wear (or used to wear) not only red coats, but very resplendent and massive badges besides—much larger than epaulettes. Neither do the twopenny post-office boys, if the result of our inquiries be correct, find any peculiar favour in woman's eyes, although they wear very bright red jackets, and have the additional advantage of constantly appearing in public on horseback, which last circumstance may be naturally supposed to be greatly in their favour.

We have sometimes thought that this phenomenon may take its rise in the conventional behaviour of captains and colonels and other gentlemen in red coats on the stage, where they are invariably represented as fine swaggering fellows, talking of nothing but charming girls, their king and country, their honour, and their debts, and crowing over the inferior classes of the community, whom they occasionally treat with a little gentlemanly swindling, no less to the improvement and pleasure of the audience, than to the satisfaction and approval of the choice spirits who consort with them. But we will not devote these pages to our speculations upon the subject, inasmuch as our business at the present moment is not so much with the young ladies who are bewitched by her Majesty's livery as with the young gentlemen whose heads are turned by it. For "heads" we had written "brains;" but upon consideration, we think the former the more appropriate word of the two.

These young gentlemen may be divided into two classes— young gentlemen who are actually in the army, and young gentlemen who, having an intense and enthusiastic admiration for all things appertaining to a military life, are compelled by adverse fortune or adverse relations to wear out their existence in some ignoble counting-house. We will take this latter description of military young gentlemen first.

The whole heart and soul of the military young gentleman are concentrated in his favourite topic. There is nothing that he is so learned upon as uniforms; he will tell you, without faltering for an instant, what the habiliments of any one regiment are turned up with, what regiment wear stripes down the outside and inside of the leg, and how many buttons the Tenth had on their coats; he knows to a fraction how many yards and odd inches of gold lace it takes to make an ensign in the Guards; is deeply read in the comparative merits of different bands, and the apparelling of trumpeters; and is very luminous indeed in descanting upon "crack regiments," and the "crack" gentlemen who compose them, of whose mightiness and grandeur he is never tired of telling.

We were suggesting to a military young gentleman only the other day, after he had related to us several dazzling instances of the profusion of half-a-dozen honourable ensign somebodies or nobodies in the articles of kid gloves and polished boots, that possibly "cracked" regiments would be

The Military Young Gentleman

an improvement upon " crack," as being a more expressive and appropriate designation, when he suddenly interrupted us by pulling out his watch, and observing that he must hurry off to the Park in a cab, or he would be too late to hear the band play. Not wishing to interfere with so important an engagement, and being in fact already slightly overwhelmed by the anecdotes of the honourable ensigns afore-mentioned, we made no attempt to detain the military young gentleman, but parted company with ready good-will.

Some three or four hours afterwards, we chanced to be walking down Whitehall, on the Admiralty side of the way, when, as we drew near to one of the little stone places in which a couple of horse soldiers mount guard in the day-time, we were attracted by the motionless appearance and eager gaze of a young gentleman, who was devouring both man and horse with his eyes, so eagerly, that he seemed deaf and blind to all that was passing around him. We were not much surprised at the discovery that it was our friend, the military young gentleman, but we *were* a little astonished when we returned from a walk to South Lambeth to find him still there, looking on with the same intensity as before. As it was a very windy day, we felt bound to awaken the young gentleman from his reverie, when he inquired of us with great enthusiasm, whether " that was not a glorious spectacle," and proceeded to give us a detailed account of the weight of every article of the spectacle's trappings, from the man's gloves to the horse's shoes.

We have made it a practice since, to take the Horse Guards in our daily walk, and we find it is the custom of military young gentlemen to plant themselves opposite the sentries, and contemplate them at leisure, in periods varying from fifteen minutes to fifty, and averaging twenty-five. We were much struck a day or two since, by the behaviour of a very promising young butcher who (evincing an interest in the service, which cannot be too strongly commended or encouraged), after a prolonged inspection of the sentry, proceeded to handle his boots with great curiosity, and as much composure and indifference as if the man were wax-work.

But the really military young gentleman is waiting all this time, and at the very moment that an apology rises to our lips, he emerges from the barrack gate (he is quartered in a garrison town), and takes the way towards the high street. He wears his undress uniform, which somewhat mars the glory of his outward man; but still how great, how grand, he is! What a happy mixture of ease and ferocity in his gait and carriage, and how lightly he carries that dreadful sword under his arm, making no more ado about it than if it were a silk umbrella! The lion is sleeping: only think if an enemy were in sight, how soon he'd whip it out of the scabbard, and what a terrible fellow he would be!

But he walks on, thinking of nothing less than blood and slaughter; and now he comes in sight of three other military young gentlemen, arm-in-arm, who are bearing down towards him, clanking their iron heels on the pavement, and clashing their swords with a noise, which should cause all peaceful men to quail at heart. They stop to talk. See how the flaxen-haired young gentleman with the weak legs—he who has his pocket-handkerchief thrust into the breast of his coat —glares upon the faint-hearted civilians who linger to look upon his glory; how the next young gentleman elevates his head in the air, and majestically places his arms a-kimbo, while the third stands with his legs very wide apart, and clasps his hands behind him. Well may we inquire—not in familiar jest, but in respectful earnest—if you call that nothing. Oh! if some encroaching foreign power—the Emperor of Russia, for instance, or any of those deep fellows, could only see those military young gentlemen as they move on together towards the billiard-room over the way, wouldn't he tremble a little!

And then, at the Theatre at night, when the performances are by command of Colonel Fitz-Sordust and the officers of the garrison—what a splendid sight it is! How sternly the defenders of their country look round the house as if in mute assurance to the audience, that they may make themselves comfortable regarding any foreign invasion, for they (the military young gentlemen) are keeping a sharp look-out, and are ready for anything. And what a contrast between them, and that stage-box full of grey-headed officers with tokens of many battles about them, who have nothing at all in common with the military young gentlemen, and who—but for an old-fashioned kind of manly dignity in their looks and bearing—might be common hard-working soldiers for anything they take the pains to announce to the contrary!

Ah! here is a family just come in who recognise the flaxen-headed young gentleman; and the flaxen-headed young gentleman recognises them too, only he doesn't care to show it just now. Very well done indeed! He talks louder to the little group of military young gentlemen who are standing by him, and coughs to induce some ladies in the next box but one to look round, in order that their faces may undergo the same ordeal of criticism to which they have subjected, in not a wholly inaudible tone, the majority of the female portion of the audience. Oh! a gentleman in the same box looks round as if he were disposed to resent this as an impertinence; and the flaxen-headed young gentleman sees his friends at once, and hurries away to them with the most charming cordiality.

Three young ladies, one young man, and the mamma of the party, receive the military young gentleman with great warmth and politeness, and in five minutes afterwards the military young gentleman, stimulated by the mamma, introduces the two other military young gentlemen with whom he was walking in the morning, who take their seats behind the young ladies and commence conversation; whereat the mamma bestows a triumphant bow upon a rival mamma, who has not succeeded in decoying any military young gentlemen, and prepares to consider her visitors from that moment three of the most elegant and superior young gentlemen in the whole world.

THE POLITICAL YOUNG GENTLEMAN

ONCE upon a time—*not* in the days when pigs drank wine, but in a more recent period of our history—it was customary to banish politics when ladies were present. If this usage still prevailed, we should have had no chapter for political young gentlemen, for ladies would have neither known nor cared what kind of monster a political young gentleman was. But as this good custom in common with many others has "gone out," and left no word when it is likely to be home again; as political young ladies are by no means rare, and political young gentlemen the very reverse of scarce, we are bound in the strict discharge of our most responsible duty not to neglect this natural division of our subject.

If the political young gentleman be resident in a country town (and there *are* political young gentlemen in country towns sometimes), he is wholly absorbed in his politics; as a pair of purple spectacles communicate the same uniform tint to all objects near and remote, so the political glasses, with which the young gentleman assists his mental vision, give to everything the hue and tinge of party feeling. The political young gentleman would as soon think of being struck with the beauty of a young lady in the opposite interest, as he would dream of marrying his sister to the opposite member.

If the political young gentleman be a Conservative, he has usually some vague ideas about Ireland and the Pope which he cannot very clearly explain, but which he knows are the right sort of thing, and not to be very easily got over by the other side. He has also some choice sentences regarding church and state, culled from the banners in use at the last election, with which he intersperses his conversation at intervals with surprising effect. But his great topic is the constitution, upon which he will declaim, by the hour together, with much heat and fury; not that he has any particular information on the subject, but because he knows that the constitution is somehow church and state, and church and state somehow the constitution, and that the fellows on the other side say it isn't, which is quite a sufficient reason for him to say it is, and to stick to it.

Perhaps his greatest topic of all, though, is the people. If a fight takes place in a populous town, in which many noses are broken, and a few windows, the young gentleman throws down the newspaper with a triumphant air, and exclaims, "Here's your precious people!" if half-a-dozen boys run across the course at race time, when it ought to be kept clear, the young gentleman looks indignantly round, and begs you to observe the conduct of the people; if the gallery demand a hornpipe between the play and the afterpiece, the same young gentleman cries "No" and "Shame" till he is hoarse, and then inquires with a sneer what you think of popular moderation *now;* in short, the people form a never-failing theme for him; and when the attorney, on the side of his candidate, dwells upon it with great power of eloquence at election time, as he never fails to do, the young gentleman and his friends, and the body they head, cheer with great violence against *the other people*, with whom, of course, they have no possible connexion. In much the same manner the audience at a theatre never fail to be highly amused with any jokes at the expense of the public—always laughing heartily at some other public, and never at themselves.

If the political young gentleman be a Radical, he is usually a very profound person indeed, having great store of theoretical questions to put to you, with an infinite variety of possible cases and logical deductions therefrom. If he be of the utilitarian school, too, which is more than probable, he is particularly pleasant company, having many ingenious remarks to offer upon the voluntary principle and various cheerful disquisitions connected with the population of the country, the position of Great Britain in the scale of nations, and the balance of power. Then he is exceedingly well versed in all doctrines of political economy as laid down in the newspapers, and knows a great many parliamentary speeches by heart ; nay, he has a small stock of aphorisms, none of them exceeding a couple of lines in length, which will settle the toughest question and leave you nothing to say. He gives all the young ladies to understand, that Miss Martineau is the greatest woman that ever lived ; and when they praise the good looks of Mr. Hawkins the new member, says he's very well for a representative, all things considered, but he wants a little calling to account, and he is more than half afraid it will be necessary to bring him down on his knees for that vote on the miscellaneous estimates. At this, the young ladies express much wonderment, and say surely a Member of Parliament is not to be brought upon his knees so easily ; in reply to which the political young gentleman smiles sternly, and throws out dark hints regarding the speedy arrival of that day, when Members of Parliament will be paid salaries, and required to render weekly accounts of their proceedings, at which the young ladies utter many expressions of astonishment and incredulity, while their ladymothers regard the prophecy as little else than blasphemous.

It is extremely improving and interesting to hear two political young gentlemen, of diverse opinions, discuss some great question across a dinner-table ; such as, whether, if the public were admitted to Westminster Abbey for nothing, they would or would not convey small chisels and hammers in their pockets, and immediately set about chipping all the noses off the statues ; or whether, if they once got into the

Tower for a shilling, they would not insist upon trying the crown on their own heads, and loading and firing off all the small arms in the armoury, to the great discomposure of Whitechapel and the Minories. Upon these, and many other momentous questions which agitate the public mind in these desperate days, they will discourse with great vehemence and irritation for a considerable time together, both leaving off precisely where they began, and each thoroughly persuaded that he has got the better of the other.

In society, at assemblies, balls, and playhouses, these political young gentlemen are perpetually on the watch for a political allusion, or anything which can be tortured or construed into being one; when, thrusting themselves into the very smallest openings for their favourite discourse, they fall upon the unhappy company tooth and nail. They have recently had many favourable opportunities of opening in churches, but as there the clergyman has it all his own way, and must not be contradicted, whatever politics he preaches, they are fain to hold their tongues until they reach the outer door, though at the imminent risk of bursting in the effort.

As such discussions can please nobody but the talkative parties concerned, we hope they will henceforth take the hint and discontinue them, otherwise we now give them warning, that the ladies have our advice to discountenance such talkers altogether.

THE DOMESTIC YOUNG GENTLEMAN

Let us make a slight sketch of our amiable friend, Mr. Felix Nixon. We are strongly disposed to think, that if we put him in this place, he will answer our purpose without another word of comment.

Felix, then, is a young gentleman who lives at home with his mother, just within the twopenny-post office circle of three miles from St. Martin-le-Grand. He wears India-rubber goloshes when the weather is at all damp, and always has a silk handkerchief neatly folded up in the right-hand pocket of his great-coat, to tie over his mouth when he goes home at night; moreover, being rather near-sighted, he carries spectacles for particular occasions, and has a weakish tremulous voice, of which he makes great use, for he talks as much as any old lady breathing.

The two chief subjects of Felix's discourse, are himself and his mother, both of whom would appear to be very wonderful and interesting persons. As Felix and his mother are seldom apart in body, so Felix and his mother are scarcely ever separate in spirit. If you ask Felix how he finds himself to-day, he prefaces his reply with a long and minute bulletin of his mother's state of health; and the good lady in her turn, edifies her acquaintance with a circumstantial and alarming account, how he sneezed four times and coughed once after being out in the rain the other night, but having his feet

The Domestic Young Gentleman

promptly put into hot water, and his head into a flannel-something, which we will not describe more particularly than by this delicate allusion, was happily brought round by the next morning, and enabled to go to business as usual.

Our friend is not a very adventurous or hot-headed person, but he has passed through many dangers, as his mother can testify: there is one great story in particular, concerning a hackney coachman who wanted to overcharge him one night for bringing them home from the play, upon which Felix gave the aforesaid coachman a look which his mother thought would have crushed him to the earth, but which did not crush him quite, for he continued to demand another six-pence, notwithstanding that Felix took out his pocket-book, and, with the aid of a flat candle, pointed out the fare in print, which the coachman obstinately disregarding, he shut the street-door with a slam which his mother shudders to think of; and then, roused to the most appalling pitch of passion by the coachman knocking a double knock to show that he was by no means convinced, he broke with uncontrollable force from his parent and the servant girl, and running into the street without his hat, actually shook his fist at the coachman, and came back again with a face as white, Mrs. Nixon says, looking about her for a simile, as white as that ceiling. She never will forget his fury that night, Never!

To this account Felix listens with a solemn face, occasionally looking at you to see how it affects you, and when his mother has made an end of it, adds that he looked at every coachman he met for three weeks afterwards, in hopes that he might see the scoundrel; whereupon Mrs. Nixon, with an exclamation of terror, requests to know what he would have done to him if he *had* seen him, at which Felix smiling darkly and clenching his right fist, she exclaims, " Goodness gracious! " with a distracted air, and insists upon extorting a promise that he never will on any account do anything so rash, which her dutiful son—it being something more than three years since the offence was committed—reluctantly concedes, and his mother, shaking her head prophetically, fears with a sigh that his spirit will lead him into something violent yet. The discourse then, by an easy transition, turns upon the spirit which glows within the bosom of Felix, upon which point Felix himself becomes eloquent, and relates a thrilling anecdote of the time when he used to sit up till two o'clock in the morning reading French, and how his mother used to say, "Felix, you will make yourself ill, I know you will;" and how *he* used to say, "Mother, I don't care —I will do it;" and how at last his mother privately procured a doctor to come and see him, who declared, the moment he felt his pulse, that if he had gone on reading one night more —only one night more—he must have put a blister on each temple, and another between his shoulders; and who, as it was, sat down upon the instant, and writing a prescription for a blue pill, said it must be taken immediately, or he wouldn't answer for the consequences. The recital of these and many other moving perils of the like nature, constantly harrows up the feelings of Mr. Nixon's friends.

Mrs. Nixon has a tolerably extensive circle of female acquaintance, being a good-humoured, talkative, bustling little body, and to the unmarried girls among them she is constantly vaunting the virtues of her son, hinting that she will be a very happy person who wins him, but that they must mind their P's and Q's, for he is very particular, and terribly severe upon young ladies. At this last caution the young ladies resident in the same row, who happen to be spending the evening there, put their pocket-handkerchiefs before their mouths, and are troubled with a short cough; just then Felix knocks at the door, and his mother drawing the tea-table nearer the fire, calls out to him as he takes off his boots in the back parlour that he needn't mind coming in in his slippers, for there are only the two Miss Greys and Miss Thompson, and she is quite sure they will excuse *him*, and nodding to the two Miss Greys, she adds, in a whisper, that

THE DOMESTIC YOUNG GENTLEMAN

Julia Thompson is a great favourite with Felix, at which intelligence the short cough comes again, and Miss Thompson in particular is greatly troubled with it, till Felix coming in, very faint for want of his tea, changes the subject of discourse, and enables her to laugh out boldly and tell Amelia Grey not to be so foolish. Here they all three laugh, and Mrs. Nixon says they are giddy girls; in which stage of the proceedings, Felix, who has by this time refreshened himself with the grateful herb that "cheers but not inebriates," removes his cup from his countenance and says with a knowing smile, that all girls are; whereat his admiring mamma pats him on the back and tells him not to be sly, which calls forth a general laugh from the young ladies, and another smile from Felix, who, thinking he looks very sly indeed, is perfectly satisfied.

Tea being over, the young ladies resume their work, and Felix insists upon holding a skein of silk while Miss Thompson winds it on a card. This process having been performed to the satisfaction of all parties, he brings down his flute in compliance with a request from the youngest Miss Grey, and plays divers tunes out of a very small music-book till supper-time, when he is very facetious and talkative indeed. Finally, after half a tumblerful of warm sherry and water, he gallantly puts on his goloshes over his slippers, and telling Miss Thompson's servant to run on first and get the door open, escorts that young lady to her house, five doors off: the Miss Greys who live in the next house but one stopping to peep with merry faces from their own door till he comes back again, when they call out "Very well, Mr. Felix," and trip into the passage with a laugh more musical than any flute that was ever played.

Felix is rather prim in his appearance, and perhaps a little priggish about his books and flute, and so forth, which have all their peculiar corners of peculiar shelves in his bedroom; indeed all his female acquaintance (and they are good judges) have long ago set him down as a thorough old bachelor.

THE DOMESTIC YOUNG GENTLEMAN

He is a favourite with them however, in a certain way, as an honest, inoffensive, kind-hearted creature; and as his peculiarities harm nobody, not even himself, we are induced to hope that many who are not personally acquainted with him will take our good word in his behalf, and be content to leave him to a long continuance of his harmless existence

THE
CENSORIOUS YOUNG GENTLEMAN

THERE is an amiable kind of young gentleman going about in society, upon whom, after much experience of him, and considerable turning over of the subject in our mind, we feel it our duty to affix the above appellation. Young ladies mildly call him a "sarcastic" young gentleman, or a "severe" young gentleman. We, who know better, beg to acquaint them with the fact, that he is merely a censorious young gentleman, and nothing else.

The censorious young gentleman has the reputation among his familiars of a remarkably clever person, which he maintains by receiving all intelligence and expressing all opinions with a dubious sneer, accompanied with a half smile, expressive of anything you please but good-humour. This sets people about thinking what on earth the censorious young gentleman means, and they speedily arrive at the conclusion that he means something very deep indeed; for they reason in this way—"This young gentleman looks so very knowing that he must mean something, and as I am by no means a dull individual, what a very deep meaning he must have if *I* can't find it out!" It is extraordinary how soon a censorious young gentleman may make a reputation in his own small circle if he bear this in his mind, and regulate his proceedings accordingly.

THE CENSORIOUS YOUNG GENTLEMAN

As young ladies are generally—not curious, but laudably desirous to acquire information, the censorious young gentleman is much talked about among them, and many surmises are hazarded regarding him. " I wonder," exclaims the eldest Miss Greenwood, laying down her work to turn up the lamp, " I wonder whether Mr. Fairfax will ever be married." " Bless me, dear," cries Miss Marshall, " what ever made you think of him?" "Really I hardly know," replies Miss Greenwood; " he is such a very mysterious person, that I often wonder about him." " Well, to tell you the truth," replies Miss Marshall, "and so do I." Here two other young ladies profess that they are constantly doing the like, and all present appear in the same condition except one young lady, who, not scrupling to state that she considers Mr. Fairfax " a horror," draws down all the opposition of the others, which having been expressed in a great many ejaculatory passages, such as " Well, did I ever ! "—and " Lor, Emily, dear ! " ma takes up the subject, and gravely states, that she must say she does not think Mr. Fairfax by any means a horror, but rather takes him to be a young man of very great ability; "and I am quite sure," adds the worthy lady, " he always means a great deal more than he says."

The door opens at this point of the discourse, and who of all people alive walks into the room, but the very Mr. Fairfax, who has been the subject of conversation ! " Well, it really is curious," cries ma, " we were at that very moment talking about you." " You did me great honour," replies Mr. Fairfax ; " may I venture to ask what you were saying?" " Why, if you must know," returns the eldest girl, " we were remarking what a very mysterious man you are." " Ay, ay ! " observes Mr. Fairfax, " Indeed ! " Now Mr. Fairfax says this ay, ay, and indeed, which are slight words enough in themselves, with so very unfathomable an air, and accompanies them with such a very equivocal smile, that ma and the young ladies are more than ever convinced that he means an immensity, and so tell him he is a very dangerous man, and

seems to be always thinking ill of somebody, which is precisely
the sort of character the censorious young gentleman is most
desirous to establish; wherefore he says, "Oh, dear, no," in
a tone, obviously intended to mean, "You have me there,"
and which gives them to understand that they have hit the
right nail on the very centre of its head.

When the conversation ranges from the mystery overhang-
ing the censorious young gentleman's behaviour, to the general
topics of the day, he sustains his character to admiration.
He considers the new tragedy well enough *for* a new tragedy,
but Lord bless us—well, no matter; he could say a great
deal on that point, but he would rather not, lest he should
be thought ill-natured, as he knows he would be. "But is
not Mr. So-and-So's performance truly charming?" inquires
a young lady. "Charming!" replies the censorious young
gentleman. "Oh, dear, yes, certainly; very charming—oh,
very charming indeed." After this, he stirs the fire, smiling
contemptuously all the while: and a modest young gentleman,
who has been a silent listener, thinks what a great thing it
must be, to have such a critical judgment. Of music, pictures,
books, and poetry, the censorious young gentleman has an
equally fine conception. As to men and women, he can tell
all about them at a glance. "Now let us hear your opinion
of young Mrs. Barker," says some great believer in the powers
of Mr. Fairfax, "but don't be too severe." "I never am
severe," replies the censorious young gentleman. "Well,
never mind that now. She is very lady-like, is she not?"
"Lady-like!" repeats the censorious young gentleman (for
he always repeats when he is at a loss for anything to say).
"Did you observe her manner? Bless my heart and soul,
Mrs. Thompson, did you observe her manner?—that's all I
ask." "I thought I had done so," rejoins the poor lady,
much perplexed; "I did not observe it very closely perhaps."
"Oh, not very closely," rejoins the censorious young gentleman, triumphantly. "Very good; then *I* did. Let us talk no
more about her." The censorious young gentleman purses up

his lips, and nods his head sagely, as he says this; and it is forthwith whispered about, that Mr. Fairfax (who, though he is a little prejudiced, must be admitted to be a very excellent judge) has observed something exceedingly odd in Mrs. Barker's manner.

THE FUNNY YOUNG GENTLEMAN

As one funny young gentleman will serve as a sample of all funny young gentlemen, we purpose merely to note down the conduct and behaviour of an individual specimen of this class, whom we happened to meet at an annual family Christmas party in the course of this very last Christmas that ever came.

We were all seated round a blazing fire which crackled pleasantly as the guests talked merrily and the urn steamed cheerily—for, being an old-fashioned party, there *was* an urn, and a teapot besides—when there came a postman's knock at the door, so violent and sudden, that it startled the whole circle, and actually caused two or three very interesting and most unaffected young ladies to scream aloud and to exhibit many afflicting symptoms of terror and distress, until they had been several times assured by their respective adorers, that they were in no danger. We were about to remark that it was surely beyond post-time, and must have been a runaway knock, when our host, who had hitherto been paralysed with wonder, sank into a chair in a perfect ecstasy of laughter, and offered to lay twenty pounds that it was that droll dog Griggins. He had no sooner said this, than the majority of the company and all the children of the house burst into a roar of laughter too, as if some inimitable joke flashed upon them simultaneously, and gave vent to various exclamations of—To be sure it must be Griggins, and

How like him that was, and What spirits he was always in !
with many other commendatory remarks of the like nature.

Not having the happiness to know Griggins, we became
extremely desirous to see so pleasant a fellow, the more
especially as a stout gentleman with a powdered head, who
was sitting with his breeches buckles almost touching the
hob, whispered us he was a wit of the first water, when the
door opened, and Mr. Griggins being announced, presented
himself, amidst another shout of laughter and a loud clapping
of hands from the younger branches. This welcome he acknowledged by sundry contortions of countenance, imitative
of the clown in one of the new pantomimes, which were so
extremely successful, that one stout gentleman rolled upon
an ottoman in a paroxysm of delight, protesting, with many
gasps, that if somebody didn't make that fellow Griggins
leave off, he would be the death of him, he knew. At this
the company only laughed more boisterously than before, and
as we always like to accommodate our tone and spirit if
possible to the humour of any society in which we find ourself, we laughed with the rest, and exclaimed, " Oh ! capital,
capital ! " as loud as any of them.

When he had quite exhausted all beholders, Mr. Griggins
received the welcomes and congratulations of the circle, and
went through the needful introductions with much ease and
many puns. This ceremony over, he avowed his intention of
sitting in somebody's lap unless the young ladies made room
for him on the sofa, which being done, after a great deal of
tittering and pleasantry, he squeezed himself among them,
and likened his condition to that of love among the roses.
At this novel jest we all roared once more. " You should
consider yourself highly honoured, sir," said we. " Sir,"
replied Mr. Griggins, " you do me proud." Here everybody
laughed again ; and the stout gentleman by the fire whispered
in our ear that Griggins was making a dead set at us.

The tea-things having been removed, we all sat down to a
round game, and here Mr. Griggins shone forth with peculiar

The Funny Young Gentleman

brilliancy, abstracting other people's fish, and looking over their hands in the most comical manner. He made one most excellent joke in snuffing a candle, which was neither more nor less than setting fire to the hair of a pale young gentleman who sat next him, and afterwards begging his pardon with considerable humour. As the young gentleman could not see the joke however, possibly in consequence of its being on the top of his own head, it did not go off quite as well as it might have done ; indeed, the young gentleman was heard to murmur some general references to "imperti- nence," and a "rascal," and to state the number of his lodgings in an angry tone—a turn of the conversation which might have been productive of slaughterous consequences, if a young lady, betrothed to the young gentleman, had not used her immediate influence to bring about a reconciliation : emphatically declaring in an agitated whisper, intended for his peculiar edification but audible to the whole table, that if he went on in that way, she never would think of him otherwise than as a friend, though as that she must always regard him. At this terrible threat the young gentleman became calm, and the young lady, overcome by the revulsion of feeling, instantaneously fainted.

Mr. Griggins's spirits were slightly depressed for a short period by this unlooked-for result of such a harmless pleasantry, but being promptly elevated by the attentions of the host and several glasses of wine, he soon recovered, and became even more vivacious than before, insomuch that the stout gentleman previously referred to, assured us that although he had known him since he was *that* high (some- thing smaller than a nutmeg-grater), he had never beheld him in such excellent cue.

When the round game and several games at blind man's buff which followed it were all over, and we were going down to supper, the inexhaustible Mr. Griggins produced a small sprig of mistletoe from his waistcoat pocket, and commenced a general kissing of the assembled females, which occasioned great commotion and much excitement. We observed that several young gentlemen—including the young gentleman with the pale countenance—were greatly scandalised at this indecorous proceeding, and talked very big among themselves in corners; and we observed too, that several young ladies when remonstrated with by the aforesaid young gentlemen, called each other to witness how they had struggled, and protested vehemently that it was very rude, and that they were surprised at Mrs. Brown's allowing it, and that they couldn't bear it, and had no patience with such impertinence. But such is the gentle and forgiving nature of woman, that although we looked very narrowly for it, we could not detect the slightest harshness in the subsequent treatment of Mr. Griggins. Indeed, upon the whole, it struck us that among the ladies he seemed rather more popular than before!

To recount all the drollery of Mr. Griggins at supper, would fill such a tiny volume as this,* to the very bottom of the outside cover. How he drank out of other people's glasses, and ate of other people's bread, how he frightened into screaming convulsions a little boy who was sitting up to supper in a high chair, by sinking below the table and suddenly reappearing with a mask on; how the hostess was really surprised that anybody could find a pleasure in tormenting children, and how the host frowned at the hostess, and felt convinced that Mr. Griggins had done it with the very best intentions; how Mr. Griggins explained, and how everybody's good-humour was restored but the child's;—to tell these and a hundred other things ever so briefly, would occupy more of our room and our readers' patience, than either they or we can conveniently spare. Therefore we change the subject, merely observing that we have offered no description of the funny young gentleman's personal appearance, believing that almost every society has a Griggins of its own, and leaving all readers to supply the deficiency, according to the particular circumstances of their particular case.

* [In its original form.]

THE
THEATRICAL YOUNG GENTLEMAN

ALL gentlemen who love the drama—and there are few gentlemen who are not attached to the most intellectual and rational of all our amusements—do not come within this definition. As we have no mean relish for theatrical entertainments ourself, we are disinterestedly anxious that this should be perfectly understood.

The theatrical young gentleman has early and important information on all theatrical topics. "Well," says he, abruptly, when you meet him in the street, "here's a pretty to-do. Flimkins has thrown up his part in the melodrama at the Surrey."—"And what's to be done?" you inquire with as much gravity as you can counterfeit. "Ah, that's the point," replies the theatrical young gentleman, looking very serious; "Boozle declines it; positively declines it. From all I am told, I should say it was decidedly in Boozle's line, and that he would be very likely to make a great hit in it; but he objects on the ground of Flimkins having been put up in the part first, and says no earthly power shall induce him to take the character. It's a fine part, too— excellent business, I'm told. He has to kill six people in the course of the piece, and to fight over a bridge in red fire, which is as safe a card, you know, as can be. Don't mention it; but I hear that the last scene, when he is first poisoned, and then stabbed, by Mrs. Flimkins as Vengedora, will be the greatest thing that has been done these many years." With this piece of news, and laying his finger on his lips as a caution for you not to excite the town with it, the theatrical young gentleman hurries away.

The theatrical young gentleman, from often frequenting the different theatrical establishments, has pet and familiar names for them all. Thus Covent-Garden is the garden, Drury-Lane the lane, the Victoria the vic, and the Olympic the pic. Actresses, too, are always designated by their surnames only, as Taylor, Nisbett, Faucit, Honey; that talented and lady-like girl Sheriff, that clever little creature Horton, and so on. In the same manner he prefixes Christian names when he mentions the actors, as Charley Young, Jemmy Buckstone, Fred. Yates, Paul Bedford. When he is at a loss for a Christian name, the word "old" applied indiscriminately answers quite as well: as old Charley Matthews at Vestris's, old Harley, and old Braham. He has a great knowledge of the private proceedings of actresses, especially of their getting married, and can tell you in a breath half-a-dozen who have changed their names without avowing it. Whenever an alteration of this kind is made in the playbills, he will remind you that he let you into the secret six months ago.

The theatrical young gentleman has a great reverence for all that is connected with the stage department of the different theatres. He would, at any time, prefer going a street or two out of his way, to omitting to pass a stage-entrance, into which he always looks with a curious and searching eye. If he can only identify a popular actor in the street, he is in a perfect transport of delight; and no sooner meets him, than he hurries back, and walks a few paces in front of him, so that he can turn round from time to time, and have a good stare at his features. He looks upon a theatrical-fund dinner as one of the most enchanting festivities ever known; and thinks that to be a member of the Garrick Club, and see so many actors in their plain clothes, must be one of the highest gratifications the world can bestow.

232

THE THEATRICAL YOUNG GENTLEMAN

The theatrical young gentleman is a constant half-price visitor at one or other of the theatres, and has an infinite relish for all pieces which display the fullest resources of the establishment. He likes to place implicit reliance upon the play-bills when he goes to see a show-piece, and works himself up to such a pitch of enthusiasm, as not only to believe (if the bills say so) that there are three hundred and seventy-five people on the stage at one time in the last scene, but is highly indignant with you, unless you believe it also. He considers that if the stage be opened from the foot-lights to the back wall, in any new play, the piece is a triumph of dramatic writing, and applauds accordingly. He has a great notion of trap-doors too; and thinks any character going down or coming up a trap (no matter whether he be an angel or a demon—they both do it occasionally) one of the most interesting feats in the whole range of scenic illusion.

Besides these acquirements, he has several veracious accounts to communicate of the private manners and customs of different actors, which, during the pauses of a quadrille, he usually communicates to his partner, or imparts to his neighbour at a supper table. Thus he is advised, that Mr. Liston always had a footman in gorgeous livery waiting at the side-scene with a brandy bottle and tumbler, to administer half a pint or so of spirit to him every time he came off, without which assistance he must infallibly have fainted. He knows for a fact, that, after an arduous part, Mr. George Bennett is put between two feather beds, to absorb the perspiration; and is credibly informed, that Mr. Baker has, for many years, submitted to a course of lukewarm toast-and-water, to qualify him to sustain his favourite characters. He looks upon Mr. Fitz Ball as the principal dramatic genius and poet of the day; but holds that there are great writers extant besides him,—in proof whereof he refers you to various dramas and melo-dramas recently produced, of which he takes in all the sixpenny and threepenny editions as fast as they appear.

THE THEATRICAL YOUNG GENTLEMAN

The theatrical young gentleman is a great advocate for violence of emotion and redundancy of action. If a father has to curse a child upon the stage, he likes to see it done in the thorough-going style, with no mistake about it: to which end it is essential that the child should follow the father on her knees, and be knocked violently over on her face by the old gentleman as he goes into a small cottage, and shuts the door behind him. He likes to see a blessing invoked upon the young lady, when the old gentleman repents, with equal earnestness, and accompanied by the usual conventional forms, which consist of the old gentleman looking anxiously up into the clouds, as if to see whether it rains, and then spreading an imaginary tablecloth in the air over the young lady's head—soft music playing all the while. Upon these, and other points of a similar kind, the theatrical young gentleman is a great critic indeed. He is likewise very acute in judging of natural expressions of the passions, and knows precisely the frown, wink, nod, or leer, which stands for any one of them, or the means by which it may be converted into any other: as jealousy, with a good stamp of the right foot, becomes anger; or wildness, with the hands clasped before the throat, instead of tearing the wig, is passionate love. If you venture to express a doubt of the accuracy of any of these portraitures, the theatrical young gentleman assures you, with a haughty smile, that it always has been done in that way, and he supposes they are not going to change it at this time of day to please you; to which, of course, you meekly reply that you suppose not.

There are innumerable disquisitions of this nature, in which the theatrical young gentleman is very profound, especially to ladies whom he is most in the habit of entertaining with them; but as we have no space to recapitulate them at greater length, we must rest content with calling the attention of the young ladies in general to the theatrical young gentlemen of their own acquaintance.

THE POETICAL YOUNG GENTLEMAN

TIME was, and not very long ago either, when a singular epidemic raged among the young gentlemen, vast numbers of whom, under the influence of the malady, tore off their neckerchiefs, turned down their shirt collars, and exhibited themselves in the open streets with bare throats and dejected countenances, before the eyes of an astonished public. These were poetical young gentlemen. The custom was gradually found to be inconvenient, as involving the necessity of too much clean linen and too large washing bills, and these outward symptoms have consequently passed away; but we are disposed to think, notwithstanding, that the number of poetical young gentlemen is considerably on the increase.

We know a poetical young gentleman—a very poetical young gentleman. We do not mean to say that he is troubled with the gift of poesy in any remarkable degree, but his countenance is of a plaintive and melancholy cast, his manner is abstracted and bespeaks affliction of soul: he seldom has his hair cut, and often talks about being an outcast and wanting a kindred spirit; from which, as well as from many general observations in which he is wont to indulge, concerning mysterious impulses, and yearnings of the heart, and the supremacy of intellect gilding all earthly things with the glowing magic of immortal verse, it is clear to all his friends that he has been stricken poetical.

THE POETICAL YOUNG GENTLEMAN

The favourite attitude of the poetical young gentleman is lounging on a sofa with his eyes fixed upon the ceiling, or sitting bolt upright in a high-backed chair, staring with very round eyes at the opposite wall. When he is in one of these positions, his mother, who is a worthy, affectionate old soul, will give you a nudge to bespeak your attention without disturbing the abstracted one, and whisper with a shake of the head, that John's imagination is at some extraordinary work or other, you may take her word for it. Hereupon John looks more fiercely intent upon vacancy than before, and suddenly snatching a pencil from his pocket, puts down three words, and a cross on the back of a card, sighs deeply, paces once or twice across the room, inflicts a most unmerciful slap upon his head, and walks moodily up to his dormitory.

The poetical young gentleman is apt to acquire peculiar notions of things too, which plain ordinary people, unblessed with a poetical obliquity of vision, would suppose to be rather distorted. For instance, when the sickening murder and mangling of a wretched woman was affording delicious food wherewithal to gorge the insatiable curiosity of the public, our friend the poetical young gentleman was in ecstasies— not of disgust, but admiration. "Heavens!" cried the poetical young gentleman, "how grand; how great!" We ventured deferentially to inquire upon whom these epithets were bestowed: our humble thoughts oscillating between the police officer who found the criminal, and the lock-keeper who found the head. "Upon whom!" exclaimed the poetical young gentleman in a frenzy of poetry, "Upon whom should they be bestowed but upon the murderer!"—and thereupon it came out, in a fine torrent of eloquence, that the murderer was a great spirit, a bold creature full of daring and nerve, a man of dauntless heart and determined courage, and withal a great casuist and able reasoner, as was fully demonstrated in his philosophical colloquies with the great and noble of the land. We held our peace, and meekly signified our indisposition to controvert these opinions– firstly, because we

The Poetical Young Gentleman

were no match at quotation for the poetical young gentleman ; and secondly, because we felt it would be of little use our entering into any disputation, if we were: being perfectly convinced that the respectable and immoral hero in question is not the first and will not be the last hanged gentleman upon whom false sympathy or diseased curiosity will be plentifully expended.

This was a stern mystic flight of the poetical young gentleman. In his milder and softer moments he occasionally lays down his neckcloth, and pens stanzas, which sometimes find their way into a Lady's Magazine, or the " Poets' Corner " of some country newspaper ; or which, in default of either vent for his genius, adorn the rainbow leaves of a lady's album. These are generally written upon some such occasions as contemplating the Bank of England by midnight, or beholding Saint Paul's in a snow-storm ; and when these gloomy objects fail to afford him inspiration, he pours forth his soul in a touching address to a violet, or a plaintive lament that he is no longer a child, but has gradually grown up.

The poetical young gentleman is fond of quoting passages from his favourite authors, who are all of the gloomy and desponding school. He has a great deal to say too about the world, and is much given to opining, especially if he has taken anything strong to drink, that there is nothing in it worth living for. He gives you to understand, however, that for the sake of society, he means to bear his part in the tiresome play, manfully resisting the gratification of his own strong desire to make a premature exit; and consoles himself with the reflection, that immortality has some chosen nook for himself and the other great spirits whom earth has chafed and wearied.

When the poetical young gentleman makes use of adjectives, they are all superlatives. Everything is of the grandest, greatest, noblest, mightiest, loftiest ; or the lowest, meanest, obscurest, vilest, and most pitiful. He knows no medium :

for enthusiasm is the soul of poetry ; and who so enthusiastic as a poetical young gentleman ? " Mr. Milkwash," says a young lady as she unlocks her album to receive the young gentleman's original impromptu contribution, " how very silent you are ! I think you must be in love." " Love ! " cries the poetical young gentleman, starting from his seat by the fire and terrifying the cat who scampers off at full speed, " Love ! that burning, consuming passion ; that ardour of the soul, that fierce glowing of the heart. Love ! The withering, blighting influence of hope misplaced and affection slighted. Love did you say ! Ha ! ha ! ha ! "

With this, the poetical young gentleman laughs a laugh belonging only to poets and Mr. O. Smith of the Adelphi Theatre, and sits down, pen in hand, to throw off a page or two of verse in the biting, semi-atheistical demoniac style, which, like the poetical young gentleman himself, is full of sound and fury, signifying nothing.

THE "THROWING-OFF" YOUNG
GENTLEMAN

THERE is a certain kind of impostor—a bragging, vaunting, puffing young gentleman—against whom we are desirous to warn that fairer part of the creation, to whom we more peculiarly devote these our labours. And we are particularly induced to lay especial stress upon this division of our subject, by a little dialogue we held some short time ago, with an esteemed young lady of our acquaintance, touching a most gross specimen of this class of men. We had been urging all the absurdities of his conduct and conversation, and dwelling upon the impossibilities he constantly recounted—to which indeed we had not scrupled to prefix a certain hard little word of one syllable and three letters—when our fair friend, unable to maintain the contest any longer, reluctantly cried, "Well; he certainly has a habit of throwing-off, but then—" What then? Throw him off yourself, said we. And so she did, but not at our instance, for other reasons appeared, and it might have been better if she had done so at first.

The throwing-off young gentleman has so often a father possessed of vast property in some remote district of Ireland, that we look with some suspicion upon all young gentlemen who volunteer this description of themselves. The deceased grandfather of the throwing-off young gentleman was a man

239

of immense possessions, and untold wealth ; the throwing-off young gentleman remembers, as well as if it were only yesterday, the deceased baronet's library, with its long rows of scarce and valuable books in superbly embossed bindings, arranged in cases, reaching from the lofty ceiling to the oaken floor ; and the fine antique chairs and tables, and the noble old castle of Ballykillbabaloo, with its splendid prospect of hill and dale, and wood, and rich wild scenery, and the fine hunting stables and the spacious court-yards, " and— and—everything upon the same magnificent scale," says the throwing-off young gentleman, "princely; quite princely. Ah !" And he sighs as if mourning over the fallen fortunes of his noble house.

The throwing-off young gentleman is a universal genius; at walking, running, rowing, swimming, and skating, he is unrivalled; at all games of chance or skill, at hunting, shooting, fishing, riding, driving, or amateur theatricals, no one can touch him—that is *could* not, because he gives you carefully to understand, lest there should be any opportunity of testing his skill, that he is quite out of practice just now, and has been for some years. If you mention any beautiful girl of your common acquaintance in his hearing, the throwing-off young gentleman starts, smiles, and begs you not to mind him, for it was quite involuntary : people do say indeed that they were once engaged, but no—although she is a very fine girl, he was so situated at that time that he couldn't possibly encourage the—" but it's of no use talking about it !" he adds, interrupting himself. " She has got over it now, and I firmly hope and trust is happy." With this benevolent aspiration he nods his head in a mysterious manner, and whistling the first part of some popular air, thinks perhaps it will be better to change the subject.

There is another great characteristic of the throwing-off young gentleman, which is, that he " happens to be acquainted " with a most extraordinary variety of people in all parts of the world. Thus in all disputed questions, when the throwing-off young gentleman has no argument to bring forward, he invariably happens to be acquainted with some distant person, intimately connected with the subject, whose testimony decides the point against you, to the great—may we say it—to the great admiration of three young ladies out of every four, who consider the throwing-off young gentleman a very highly-connected young man, and a most charming person.

Sometimes the throwing-off young gentleman happens to look in upon a little family circle of young ladies who are quietly spending the evening together, and then indeed is he at the very height and summit of his glory; for it is to be observed that he by no means shines to equal advantage in the presence of men as in the society of over-credulous young ladies, which is his proper element. It is delightful to hear the number of pretty things the throwing-off young gentleman gives utterance to, during tea, and still more so to observe the ease with which, from long practice and study, he delicately blends one compliment to a lady with two for himself. "Did you ever see a more lovely blue than this flower, Mr. Caveton?" asks a young lady who, truth to tell, is rather smitten with the throwing-off young gentleman. "Never," he replies, bending over the object of admiration, "never but in your eyes." "Oh, Mr. Caveton," cries the young lady, blushing of course. "Indeed I speak the truth," replies the throwing-off young gentleman, "I never saw any approach to them. I used to think my cousin's blue eyes lovely, but they grow dim and colourless beside yours." "Oh! a beautiful cousin, Mr. Caveton!" replies the young lady, with that perfect artlessness which is the distinguishing characteristic of all young ladies; "an affair, of course." "No; indeed, indeed you wrong me," rejoins the throwing-off young gentleman with great energy. "I fervently hope that her attachment towards me may be nothing but the natural result of our close intimacy in childhood, and that in change of scene and among new faces she may soon overcome it. _I_ love her! Think not so meanly of me, Miss Lowfield,

I beseech, as to suppose that title, lands, riches, and beauty, can influence *my* choice. The heart, the heart, Miss Lowfield." Here the throwing-off young gentleman sinks his voice to a still lower whisper; and the young lady duly proclaims to all the other young ladies when they go up-stairs, to put their bonnets on, that Mr. Caveton's relations are all immensely rich, and that he is hopelessly beloved by title, lands, riches, and beauty.

We have seen a throwing-off young gentleman who, to our certain knowledge, was innocent of a note of music, and scarcely able to recognise a tune by ear, volunteer a Spanish air upon the guitar when he had previously satisfied himself that there was not such an instrument within a mile of the house.

We have heard another throwing-off young gentleman, after striking a note or two upon the piano, and accompanying it correctly (by dint of laborious practice) with his voice, assure a circle of wondering listeners that so acute was his ear that he was wholly unable to sing out of tune, let him try as he would. We have lived to witness the unmasking of another throwing-off young gentleman, who went out a visiting in a military cap with a gold band and tassel, and who, after passing successfully for a captain and being lauded to the skies for his red whiskers, his bravery, his soldierly bearing and his pride, turned out to be the dishonest son of an honest linen-draper in a small country town, and whom, if it were not for this fortunate exposure, we should not yet despair of encountering as the fortunate husband of some rich heiress. Ladies, ladies, the throwing-off young gentlemen are often swindlers, and always fools. So pray you avoid them.

THE
YOUNG LADIES' YOUNG GENTLEMAN

This young gentleman has several titles. Some young ladies consider him "a nice young man," others "a fine young man," others "quite a lady's man," others "a handsome man," others "a remarkably good-looking young man." With some young ladies he is "a perfect angel," and with others "quite a love." He is likewise a charming creature, a duck, and a dear.

The young ladies' young gentleman has usually a fresh colour and very white teeth, which latter articles, of course, he displays on every possible opportunity. He has brown or black hair, and whiskers of the same, if possible; but a slight tinge of red, or the hue which is vulgarly known as *sandy*, is not considered an objection. If his head and face be large, his nose prominent, and his figure square, he is an uncommonly fine young man, and worshipped accordingly. Should his whiskers meet beneath his chin, so much the better, though this is not absolutely insisted on; but he must wear an under-waistcoat, and smile constantly.

There was a great party got up by some party-loving friends of ours last summer, to go and dine in Epping Forest. As we hold that such wild expeditions should never be indulged in, save by people of the smallest means, who have no dinner at home, we should indubitably have excused ourself from attending, if we had not recollected that the projectors of

243

the excursion were always accompanied on such occasions by a choice sample of the young ladies' young gentleman, whom we were very anxious to have an opportunity of meeting. This determined us, and we went.

We were to make for Chigwell in four glass coaches, each with a trifling company of six or eight inside, and a little boy belonging to the projectors on the box—and to start from the residence of the projectors, Woburn-place, Russell-square, at half-past ten precisely. We arrived at the place of rendezvous at the appointed time, and found the glass coaches and the little boys quite ready, and divers young ladies and young gentlemen looking anxiously over the break-fast-parlour blinds, who appeared by no means so much gratified by our approach as we might have expected, but evidently wished we had been somebody else. Observing that our arrival in lieu of the unknown occasioned some dis-appointment, we ventured to inquire who was yet to come, when we found from the hasty reply of a dozen voices, that it was no other than the young ladies' young gentleman.

"I cannot imagine," said the mamma, "what has become of Mr. Balim—always so punctual, always so pleasant and agreeable. I am sure I can-*not* think." As these last words were uttered in that measured, emphatic manner which painfully announces that the speaker has not quite made up his or her mind what to say, but is determined to talk on nevertheless, the eldest daughter took up the subject, and hoped no accident had happened to Mr. Balim, upon which there was a general chorus of "Dear Mr. Balim!" and one young lady, more adventurous than the rest, proposed that an express should be straightway sent to dear Mr. Balim's lodgings. This, however, the papa resolutely opposed, observing, in what a short young lady behind us termed "quite a bearish way," that if Mr. Balim didn't choose to come, he might stop at home. At this all the daughters raised a murmur of "Oh pa!" except one sprightly little girl of eight or ten years old, who, taking advantage of a pause

The Young Ladies' Young Gentleman

in the discourse, remarked, that perhaps Mr. Balim might have been married that morning—for which impertinent suggestion she was summarily ejected from the room by her eldest sister.

We were all in a state of great mortification and uneasiness, when one of the little boys, running into the room as airily as little boys usually run who have an unlimited allowance of animal food in the holidays, and keep their hands constantly forced down to the bottoms of very deep trouser-pockets when they take exercise, joyfully announced that Mr. Balim was at that moment coming up the street in a hackney-cab; and the intelligence was confirmed beyond all doubt a minute afterwards by the entry of Mr. Balim himself, who was received with repeated cries of "Where have you been, you naughty creature?" whereunto the naughty creature replied, that he had been in bed, in consequence of a late party the night before, and had only just risen. The acknowledgment awakened a variety of agonizing fears that he had taken no breakfast; which appearing after a slight cross-examination to be the real state of the case, breakfast for one was immediately ordered, notwithstanding Mr. Balim's repeated protestations that he couldn't think of it. He did think of it though, and thought better of it too, for he made a remarkably good meal when it came, and was assiduously served by a select knot of young ladies. It was quite delightful to see how he ate and drank, while one pair of fair hands poured out his coffee, and another put in the sugar, and another the milk; the rest of the company ever and anon casting angry glances at their watches, and the glass coaches,—and the little boys looking on in an agony of apprehension lest it should begin to rain before we set out; it might have rained all day, after we were once too far to turn back again, and welcome, for aught they cared.

However, the cavalcade moved at length, every coachman being accommodated with a hamper between his legs something larger than a wheelbarrow; and the company being packed as closely as they possibly could in the carriages, "according," as one married lady observed, "to the immemorial custom, which was half the diversion of gipsy parties." Thinking it very likely it might be (we have never been able to discover the other half), we submitted to be stowed away with a cheerful aspect, and were fortunate enough to occupy one corner of a coach in which were one old lady, four young ladies, and the renowned Mr. Balim the young ladies' young gentleman.

We were no sooner fairly off, than the young ladies' young gentleman hummed a fragment of an air, which induced a young lady to inquire whether he had danced to that the night before. "By Heaven, then, I did," replied the young gentleman, "and with a lovely heiress; a superb creature, with twenty thousand pounds." "You seem rather struck," observed another young lady. "'Gad she was a sweet creature," returned the young gentleman, arranging his hair. "Of course *she* was struck too?" inquired the first young lady. "How can you ask, love?" interposed the second; "could she fail to be?" "Well, honestly I think she was," observed the young gentleman. At this point of the dialogue, the young lady who had spoken first, and who sat on the young gentleman's right, struck him a severe blow on the arm with a rosebud, and said he was a vain man—whereupon the young gentleman insisted on having the rosebud, and the young lady appealing for help to the other young ladies, a charming struggle ensued, terminating in the victory of the young gentleman, and the capture of the rosebud. This little skirmish over, the married lady, who was the mother of the rosebud, smiled sweetly upon the young gentleman, and accused him of being a flirt; the young gentleman pleading not guilty, a most interesting discussion took place upon the important point whether the young gentleman was a flirt or not, which being an agreeable conversation of a light kind, lasted a considerable time. At length, a short silence occurring, the young ladies on either side of the young gentleman fell suddenly fast asleep; and the young gentleman, winking upon us to preserve silence, won a pair of gloves from each, thereby causing them to wake with equal suddenness and to scream very loud. The lively conversation to which this pleasantry gave rise, lasted for the remainder of the ride, and would have eked out a much longer one.

We dined rather more comfortably than people usually do under such circumstances, nothing having been left behind but the corkscrew and the bread. The married gentlemen were unusually thirsty, which they attributed to the heat of the weather; the little boys ate to inconvenience; mammas were very jovial, and their daughters very fascinating; and the attendants being well-behaved men, got exceedingly drunk at a respectful distance.

We had our eye on Mr. Balim at dinner-time, and perceived that he flourished wonderfully, being still surrounded by a little group of young ladies, who listened to him as an oracle, while he ate from their plates and drank from their glasses in a manner truly captivating from its excessive playfulness. His conversation, too, was exceedingly brilliant. In fact, one elderly lady assured us, that in the course of a little lively *badinage* on the subject of ladies' dresses, he had evinced as much knowledge as if he had been born and bred a milliner.

As such of the fat people who did not happen to fall asleep after dinner entered upon a most vigorous game at ball, we slipped away alone into a thicker part of the wood, hoping to fall in with Mr. Balim, the greater part of the young people having dropped off in twos and threes, and the young ladies' young gentleman among them. Nor were we disappointed, for we had not walked far, when, peeping through the trees, we discovered him before us, and truly it was a pleasant thing to contemplate his greatness.

The young ladies' young gentleman was seated upon the ground, at the feet of a few young ladies who were reclining on a bank; he was so profusely decked with scarfs, ribands, flowers, and other pretty spoils, that he looked like a lamb

247

—or perhaps a calf would be a better simile—adorned for the sacrifice. One young lady supported a parasol over his interesting head, another held his hat, and a third his neck-cloth, which in romantic fashion he had thrown off; the young gentleman himself, with his hand upon his breast, and his face moulded into an expression of the most honeyed sweet-ness, was warbling forth some choice specimens of vocal music in praise of female loveliness, in a style so exquisitely perfect, that we burst into an involuntary shout of laughter, and made a hasty retreat.

What charming fellows these young ladies' young gentlemen are! Ducks, dears, loves, angels, are all terms inadequate to express their merit. They are such amazingly, uncommonly, wonderfully, nice men.

CONCLUSION

As we have placed before the young ladies so many specimens of young gentlemen, and have also in the dedication of
this volume given them to understand how much we reverence
and admire their numerous virtues and perfections; as we
have given them such strong reasons to treat us with confidence, and to banish, in our case, all that reserve and distrust
of the male sex which, as a point of general behaviour, they
cannot do better than preserve and maintain—we say, as we
have done all this, we feel that now, when we have arrived
at the close of our task, they may naturally press upon us
the inquiry, what particular description of young gentlemen
we can conscientiously recommend.

Here we are at a loss. We look over our list, and can
neither recommend the bashful young gentleman, nor the
out-and-out young gentleman, nor the very friendly young
gentleman, nor the military young gentleman, nor the
political young gentleman, nor the domestic young gentleman, nor the censorious young gentleman, nor the funny
young gentleman, nor the theatrical young gentleman, nor
the poetical young gentleman, nor the throwing-off young
gentleman, nor the young ladies' young gentleman.

As there are some good points about many of them, which
still are not sufficiently numerous to render any one among
them eligible, as a whole, our respectful advice to the young

ladies is, to seek for a young gentleman who unites in himself the best qualities of all, and the worst weaknesses of none, and to lead him forthwith to the hymeneal altar, whether he will or no. And to the young lady who secures him, we beg to tender one short fragment of matrimonial advice, selected from many sound passages of a similar tendency, to be found in a letter written by Dean Swift to a young lady on her marriage.

"The grand affair of your life will be, to gain and preserve the esteem of your husband. Neither good-nature nor virtue will suffer him to *esteem* you against his judgment; and although he is not capable of using you ill, yet you will in time grow a thing indifferent and perhaps contemptible; unless you can supply the loss of youth and beauty with more durable qualities. You have but a very few years to be young and handsome in the eyes of the world; and as few months to be so in the eyes of a husband who is not a fool; for I hope you do not still dream of charms and raptures, which marriage ever did, and ever will, put a sudden end to."

From the anxiety we express for the proper behaviour of the fortunate lady after marriage, it may possibly be inferred that the young gentleman to whom we have so delicately alluded, is no other than ourself. Without in any way committing ourself upon this point, we have merely to observe, that we are ready to receive sealed offers containing a full specification of age, temper, appearance, and condition ; but we beg it to be distinctly understood that we do not pledge ourself to accept the highest bidder.

These offers may be forwarded to the Publishers, Messrs. Chapman and Hall, London; to whom all pieces of plate and other testimonials of approbation from the young ladies generally, are respectfully requested to be addressed.

SKETCHES OF YOUNG COUPLES

An Urgent Remonstrance, &c.

TO THE GENTLEMEN OF ENGLAND,

(BEING BACHELORS OR WIDOWERS,)

THE REMONSTRANCE OF THEIR FAITHFUL FELLOW-SUBJECT,

SHEWETH,—

THAT Her Most Gracious Majesty, Victoria, by the Grace of God of the United Kingdom of Great Britain and Ireland Queen, Defender of the Faith, did, on the 23rd day of November last past, declare and pronounce to Her Most Honourable Privy Council, Her Majesty's Most Gracious intention of entering into the bonds of wedlock.

THAT Her Most Gracious Majesty, in so making known Her Most Gracious intention to Her Most Honourable Privy Council as aforesaid, did use and employ the words—" It is my intention to ally myself in marriage with Prince Albert of Saxe Coburg and Gotha."

THAT the present is Bissextile, or Leap Year, in which it is held and considered lawful for any lady to offer and submit

253

proposals of marriage to any gentleman, and to enforce and insist upon acceptance of the same, under pain of a certain fine or penalty ; to wit, one silk or satin dress of the first quality, to be chosen by the lady and paid (or owed) for, by the gentleman.

THAT these and other the horrors and dangers with which the said Bissextile, or Leap Year, threatens the gentlemen of England on every occasion of its periodical return, have been greatly aggravated and augmented by the terms of Her Majesty's said Most Gracious communication, which have filled the heads of divers young ladies in this Realm with certain new ideas destructive to the peace of mankind, that never entered their imagination before.

THAT a case has occurred in Camberwell, in which a young lady informed her Papa that "she intended to ally herself in marriage" with Mr. Smith of Stepney ; and that another, and a very distressing case, has occurred at Tottenham, in which a young lady not only stated her intention of allying herself in marriage with her cousin John, but, taking violent possession of her said cousin, actually married him.

THAT similar outrages are of constant occurrence, not only in the capital and its neighbourhood, but throughout the kingdom, and that unless the excited female populace be speedily checked and restrained in their lawless proceedings, most deplorable results must ensue therefrom ; among which may be anticipated a most alarming increase in the population of the country, with which no efforts of the agricultural or manufacturing interest can possibly keep pace.

AN URGENT REMONSTRANCE

THAT there is strong reason to suspect the existence of a most extensive plot, conspiracy, or design, secretly contrived by vast numbers of single ladies in the United Kingdom of Great Britain and Ireland, and now extending its ramifications in every quarter of the land; the object and intent of which plainly appears to be the holding and solemnising of an enormous and unprecedented number of marriages, on the day on which the nuptials of Her said Most Gracious Majesty are performed.

THAT such plot, conspiracy, or design, strongly savours of Popery, as tending to the discomfiture of the Clergy of the Established Church, by entailing upon them great mental and physical exhaustion; and that such Popish plots are fomented and encouraged by Her Majesty's Ministers, which clearly appears—not only from Her Majesty's principal Secretary of State for Foreign Affairs traitorously getting married while holding office under the Crown; but from Mr. O'Connell having been heard to declare and avow that, if he had a daughter to marry, she should be married on the same day as Her said Most Gracious Majesty.

THAT such arch plots, conspiracies, and designs, besides being fraught with danger to the Established Church, and (consequently) to the State, cannot fail to bring ruin and bankruptcy upon a large class of Her Majesty's subjects; as a great and sudden increase in the number of married men occasioning the comparative desertion (for a time) of Taverns, Hotels, Billiard-rooms, and Gaming-Houses, will deprive the Proprietors of their accustomed profits and returns. And in further proof of the depth and baseness of such designs, it may be here observed, that all proprietors of Taverns, Hotels,

Billiard-rooms, and Gaming-Houses, are (especially the last) solemnly devoted to the Protestant religion.

> For all these reasons, and many others of no less gravity and import, an urgent appeal is made to the gentlemen of England (being bachelors or widowers) to take immediate steps for convening a Public meeting; To consider of the best and surest means of averting the dangers with which they are threatened by the recurrence of Bissextile, or Leap Year, and the additional sensation created among single ladies by the terms of Her Majesty's Most Gracious Declaration; To take measures, without delay, for resisting the said single Ladies, and counteracting their evil designs; And to pray Her Majesty to dismiss her present Ministers, and to summon to her Councils those distinguished Gentlemen in various Honourable Professions who, by insulting on all occasions the only Lady in England who can be insulted with safety, have given a sufficient guarantee to Her Majesty's Loving Subjects that they, at least, are qualified to make war with women, and are already expert in the use of those weapons which are common to the lowest and most abandoned of the sex.

THE YOUNG COUPLE

THERE is to be a wedding this morning at the corner house in the terrace. The pastry-cook's people have been there half-a-dozen times already; all day yesterday there was a great stir and bustle, and they were up this morning as soon as it was light. Miss Emma Fielding is going to be married to young Mr. Harvey.

Heaven alone can tell in what bright colours this marriage is painted upon the mind of the little housemaid at number six, who has hardly slept a wink all night with thinking of it, and now stands on the unswept door-steps leaning upon her broom, and looking wistfully towards the enchanted house. Nothing short of omniscience can divine what visions of the baker, or the green-grocer, or the smart and most insinuating butterman, are flitting across her mind—what thoughts of how she would dress on such an occasion, if she were a lady—of how she would dress, if she were only a bride —of how cook would dress, being bridesmaid, conjointly with her sister "in place" at Fulham, and how the clergyman, deeming them so many ladies, would be quite humbled and respectful. What day-dreams of hope and happiness—of life being one perpetual holiday, with no master and no mistress to grant or withhold it—of every Sunday being a Sunday out —of pure freedom as to curls and ringlets, and no obligation to hide fine heads of hair in caps—what pictures of happiness, vast and immense to her, but utterly ridiculous to us, bewilder the brain of the little housemaid at number six, all called into existence by the wedding at the corner!

We smile at such things, and so we should, though perhaps for a better reason than commonly presents itself. It should be pleasant to us to know that there are notions of happiness so moderate and limited, since upon those who entertain them, happiness and lightness of heart are very easily bestowed.

But the little housemaid is awakened from her reverie, for forth from the door of the magical corner house there runs towards her, all fluttering in smart new dress and streaming ribands, her friend Jane Adams, who comes all out of breath to redeem a solemn promise of taking her in, under cover of the confusion, to see the breakfast table spread forth in state, and—sight of sights!—her young mistress ready dressed for church.

And there, in good truth, when they have stolen up-stairs on tiptoe and edged themselves in at the chamber-door— there is Miss Emma "looking like the sweetest picter," in a white chip bonnet and orange flowers, and all other elegancies becoming a bride, (with the make, shape, and quality of every article of which the girl is perfectly familiar in one moment, and never forgets to her dying day)—and there is Miss Emma's mamma in tears, and Miss Emma's papa comforting her, and saying how that of course she has been long looking forward to this, and how happy she ought to be— and there too is Miss Emma's sister with her arms round her neck, and the other bridesmaid all smiles and tears, quieting the children, who would cry more but that they are so finely dressed, and yet sob for fear sister Emma should be taken away—and it is all so affecting, that the two servant-girls cry more than anybody; and Jane Adams, sitting down upon the stairs, when they have crept away, declares that her legs tremble so that she don't know what to do, and that she will say for Miss Emma, that she never had a hasty word from her, and that she does hope and pray she may be happy.

But Jane soon comes round again, and then surely there never was anything like the breakfast table, glittering with plate and china, and set out with flowers and sweets, and long-necked bottles, in the most sumptuous and dazzling manner. In the centre, too, is the mighty charm, the cake, glistening with frosted sugar, and garnished beautifully. They agree that there ought to be a little Cupid under one of the barley-sugar temples, or at least two hearts and an arrow; but, with this exception, there is nothing to wish for, and a table could not be handsomer. As they arrive at this conclusion, who should come in but Mr. John! to whom Jane says that it's only Anne from number six; and John says *he* knows, for he's often winked his eye down the area, which causes Anne to blush and look confused. She is going away, indeed; when Mr. John will have it that she must drink a glass of wine, and he says never mind it's being early in the morning, it won't hurt her: so they shut the door and pour out the wine; and Anne drinking Jane's health, and adding, "and here's wishing you yours, Mr. John," drinks it in a great many sips,—Mr. John all the time making jokes appropriate to the occasion. At last Mr. John, who has waxed bolder by degrees, pleads the usage at weddings, and claims the privilege of a kiss, which he obtains after a great scuffle; and footsteps being now heard on the stairs, they disperse suddenly.

By this time a carriage has driven up to convey the bride to church, and Anne of number six prolonging the process of "cleaning her door," has the satisfaction of beholding the bride and bridesmaids, and the papa and mamma, hurry into the same and drive rapidly off. Nor is this all, for soon other carriages begin to arrive with a posse of company all beautifully dressed, at whom she could stand and gaze for ever; but having something else to do, is compelled to take one last long look and shut the street-door.

And now the company have gone down to breakfast, and tears have given place to smiles, for all the corks are out of the long-necked bottles, and their contents are disappearing rapidly. Miss Emma's papa is at the top of the table; Miss Emma's mamma at the bottom; and beside the latter are Miss Emma herself and her husband,—admitted on all hands to be the handsomest and most interesting young couple ever known. All down both sides of the table, too, are various young ladies, beautiful to see, and various young gentlemen who seem to think so; and there, in a post of honour, is an unmarried aunt of Miss Emma's, reported to possess unheard-of riches, and to have expressed vast testamentary intentions respecting her favourite niece and new nephew. This lady has been very liberal and generous already, as the jewels worn by the bride abundantly testify, but that is nothing to what she means to do, or even to what she has done, for she put herself in close communication with the dress-maker three months ago, and prepared a wardrobe (with some articles worked by her own hands) fit for a Princess. People may call her an old maid, and so she may be, but she is neither cross nor ugly for all that; on the contrary, she is very cheerful and pleasant-looking, and very kind and tender-hearted: which is no matter of surprise except to those who yield to popular prejudices without thinking why, and will never grow wiser and never know better.

Of all the company though, none are more pleasant to behold or better pleased with themselves than two young children, who, in honour of the day, have seats among the guests. Of these, one is a little fellow of six or eight years old, brother to the bride,—and the other a girl of the same age, or something younger, whom he calls "his wife." The real bride and bridegroom are not more devoted than they:

he all love and attention, and she all blushes and fondness, toying with a little bouquet which he gave her this morning, and placing the scattered rose-leaves in her bosom with nature's own coquettishness. They have dreamt of each other in their quiet dreams, these children, and their little hearts have been nearly broken when the absent one has been dispraised in jest. When will there come in after-life a passion so earnest, generous, and true as theirs; what, even in its gentlest realities, can have the grace and charm that hover round such fairy lovers!

By this time the merriment and happiness of the feast have gained their height; certain ominous looks begin to be exchanged between the bridesmaids, and somehow it gets whispered about that the carriage which is to take the young couple into the country has arrived. Such members of the party as are most disposed to prolong its enjoyments, affect to consider this a false alarm, but it turns out too true, being speedily confirmed, first by the retirement of the bride and a select file of intimates who are to prepare her for the journey, and secondly by the withdrawal of the ladies generally. To this there ensues a particularly awkward pause, in which everybody essays to be facetious, and nobody succeeds; at length the bridegroom makes a mysterious disappearance in obedience to some equally mysterious signal; and the table is deserted.

Now, for at least six weeks last past it has been solemnly devised and settled that the young couple should go away in secret; but they no sooner appear without the door than the drawing-room windows are blocked up with ladies waving their handkerchiefs and kissing their hands, and the dining-room panes with gentlemen's faces beaming farewell in every queer variety of its expression. The hall and steps are crowded with servants in white favours, mixed up with particular friends and relations who have darted out to say good bye; and foremost in the group are the tiny lovers arm in arm, thinking, with fluttering hearts, what happiness it would be to dash away together in that gallant coach, and never part again.

The bride has barely time for one hurried glance at her old home, when the steps rattle, the door slams, the horses clatter on the pavement, and they have left it far away.

A knot of women servants still remain clustered in the hall, whispering among themselves, and there of course is Anne from number six, who has made another escape on some plea or other, and been an admiring witness of the departure. There are two points on which Anne expatiates over and over again, without the smallest appearance of fatigue or intending to leave off; one is, that she " never see in all her life such a—oh such a angel of a gentleman as Mr. Harvey "—and the other, that she " can't tell how it is, but it don't seem a bit like a work-a-day, or a Sunday neither —it's all so unsettled and unregular."

Departure of the Young Couple

THE FORMAL COUPLE

THE formal couple are the most prim, cold, immovable, and unsatisfactory people on the face of the earth. Their faces, voices, dress, house, furniture, walk, and manner, are all the essence of formality, unrelieved by one redeeming touch of frankness, heartiness, or nature.

Everything with the formal couple resolves itself into a matter of form. They don't call upon you on your account, but their own; not to see how you are, but to show how they are: it is not a ceremony to do honour to you, but to themselves,—not due to your position, but to theirs. If one of a friend's children die, the formal couple are as sure and punctual in sending to the house as the undertaker; if a friend's family be increased, the monthly nurse is not more attentive than they. The formal couple, in fact, joyfully seize all occasions of testifying their good-breeding and precise observance of the little usages of society; and for you, who are the means to this end, they care as much as a man does for the tailor who has enabled him to cut a figure, or a woman for the milliner who has assisted her to a conquest.

Having an extensive connexion among that kind of people who make acquaintances and eschew friends, the formal gentleman attends from time to time a great many funerals, to which he is formally invited, and to which he formally

goes, as returning a call for the last time. Here his deportment is of the most faultless description; he knows the exact
pitch of voice it is proper to assume, the sombre look he
ought to wear, the melancholy tread which should be his gait
for the day. He is perfectly acquainted with all the dreary
courtesies to be observed in a mourning-coach; knows when
to sigh, and when to hide his nose in the white handkerchief;
and looks into the grave and shakes his head when the
ceremony is concluded, with the sad formality of a mute.

"What kind of funeral was it?" says the formal lady,
when he returns home. "Oh!" replies the formal gentleman,
"there never was such a gross and disgusting impropriety;
there were no feathers." "No feathers!" cries the lady, as
if on wings of black feathers dead people fly to Heaven, and,
lacking them, they must of necessity go elsewhere. Her
husband shakes his head; and further adds, that they had
seed-cake instead of plum-cake, and that it was all white
wine. "All white wine!" exclaims his wife. "Nothing but
sherry and madeira," says the husband. "What! no port?"
"Not a drop." No port, no plums, and no feathers! "You
will recollect, my dear," says the formal lady, in a voice of
stately reproof, "that when we first met this poor man who
is now dead and gone, and he took that very strange course
of addressing me at dinner without being previously introduced, I ventured to express my opinion that the family were
quite ignorant of etiquette, and very imperfectly acquainted
with the decencies of life. You have now had a good
opportunity of judging for yourself, and all I have to say is,
that I trust you will never go to a funeral *there* again." "My
dear," replies the formal gentleman, "I never will." So the
informal deceased is cut in his grave; and the formal couple,
when they tell the story of the funeral, shake their heads,
and wonder what some people's feelings *are* made of, and
what their notions of propriety *can* be!

If the formal couple have a family (which they sometimes
have), they are not children, but little, pale, sour, sharp-nosed

men and women; and so exquisitely brought up, that they might be very old dwarfs for anything that appeareth to the contrary. Indeed, they are so acquainted with forms and conventionalities, and conduct themselves with such strict decorum, that to see the little girl break a looking-glass in some wild outbreak, or the little boy kick his parents, would be to any visitor an unspeakable relief and consolation.

The formal couple are always sticklers for what is rigidly proper, and have a great readiness in detecting hidden impropriety of speech or thought, which by less scrupulous people would be wholly unsuspected. Thus, if they pay a visit to the theatre, they sit all night in a perfect agony lest anything improper or immoral should proceed from the stage; and if anything should happen to be said which admits of a double construction, they never fail to take it up directly, and to express by their looks the great outrage which their feelings have sustained. Perhaps this is their chief reason for absenting themselves almost entirely from places of public amusement. They go sometimes to the Exhibition of the Royal Academy;—but that is often more shocking than the stage itself, and the formal lady thinks that it really is high time Mr. Etty was prosecuted and made a public example of.

We made one at a christening party not long since, where there were amongst the guests a formal couple, who suffered the acutest torture from certain jokes, incidental to such an occasion, cut—and very likely dried also—by one of the godfathers; a red-faced elderly gentleman, who, being highly popular with the rest of the company, had it all his own way, and was in great spirits. It was at supper-time that this gentleman came out in full force. We—being of a grave and quiet demeanour—had been chosen to escort the formal lady down-stairs, and, sitting beside her, had a favourable opportunity of observing her emotions.

We have a shrewd suspicion that, in the very beginning, and in the first blush—literally the first blush—of the matter, the formal lady had not felt quite certain whether the being present at such a ceremony, and encouraging, as it were, the public exhibition of a baby, was not an act involving some degree of indelicacy and impropriety; but certain we are, that when that baby's health was drunk, and allusions were made, by a grey-headed gentleman proposing it, to the time when he had dandled in his arms the young Christian's mother, —certain we are that then the formal lady took the alarm, and recoiled from the old gentleman as from a hoary profligate. Still she bore it; she fanned herself with an indignant air, but still she bore it. A comic song was sung, involving a confession from some imaginary gentleman that he had kissed a female, and yet the formal lady bore it. But when at last, the health of the godfather before-mentioned being drunk, the godfather rose to return thanks, and in the course of his observations darkly hinted at babies yet unborn, and even contemplated the possibility of the subject of that festival having brothers and sisters, the formal lady could endure no more, but, bowing slightly round, and sweeping haughtily past the offender, left the room in tears, under the protection of the formal gentleman.

THE LOVING COUPLE

There cannot be a better practical illustration of the wise saw and ancient instance, that there may be too much of a good thing, than is presented by a loving couple. Undoubtedly it is meet and proper that two persons joined together in holy matrimony should be loving, and unquestionably it is pleasant to know and see that they are so; but there is a time for all things, and the couple who happen to be always in a loving state before company, are well-nigh intolerable.

And in taking up this position we would have it distinctly understood that we do not seek alone the sympathy of bachelors, in whose objection to loving couples we recognise interested motives and personal considerations. We grant that to that unfortunate class of society there may be something very irritating, tantalising, and provoking, in being compelled to witness those gentle endearments and chaste interchanges which to loving couples are quite the ordinary business of life. But while we recognise the natural character of the prejudice to which these unhappy men are subject, we can neither receive their biassed evidence, nor address ourself to their inflamed and angered minds. Dispassionate experience is our only guide; and in these moral essays we seek no less to reform hymeneal offenders than to hold out a timely warning to all rising couples, and even to those who have not yet set forth upon their pilgrimage towards the matrimonial altar.

THE LOVING COUPLE

Let all couples, present or to come, therefore profit by the example of Mr. and Mrs. Leaver, themselves a loving couple in the first degree.

Mr. and Mrs. Leaver are pronounced by Mrs. Starling, a widow lady who lost her husband when she was young, and lost herself about the same time—for by her own count she has never since grown five years older—to be a perfect model of wedded felicity. "You would suppose," says the romantic lady, "that they were lovers only just now engaged. Never was such happiness! They are so tender, so affectionate, so attached to each other, so enamoured, that positively nothing can be more charming!"

"Augusta, my soul," says Mr. Leaver. "Augustus, my life," replies Mrs. Leaver. "Sing some little ballad, darling," quoth Mr. Leaver. "I couldn't, indeed, dearest," returns Mrs. Leaver. "Do, my dove," says Mr. Leaver. "I couldn't possibly, my love," replies Mrs. Leaver; "and it's very naughty of you to ask me." "Naughty, darling!" cries Mr. Leaver. "Yes, very naughty, and very cruel," returns Mrs. Leaver, "for you know I have a sore throat, and that to sing would give me great pain. You're a monster, and I hate you. Go away!" Mrs. Leaver has said "go away," because Mr. Leaver has tapped her under the chin: Mr. Leaver not doing as he is bid, but. on the contrary, sitting down beside her, Mrs. Leaver slaps Mr. Leaver; and Mr. Leaver in return slaps Mrs. Leaver, and it being now time for all persons present to look the other way, they look the other way, and hear a still small sound as of kissing, at which Mrs. Starling is thoroughly enraptured, and whispers her neighbour that if all married couples were like that, what a heaven this earth would be!

The loving couple are at home when this occurs, and maybe only three or four friends are present, but, unaccustomed to reserve upon this interesting point, they are pretty much the same abroad. Indeed upon some occasions, such as a pic-nic or a water-party, their lovingness is even more

The Loving Couple

developed, as we had an opportunity last summer of observing in person.

There was a great water-party made up to go to Twicken-ham and dine, and afterwards dance in an empty villa by the river-side, hired expressly for the purpose. Mr. and Mrs. Leaver were of the company; and it was our fortune to have a seat in the same boat, which was an eight-oared galley, manned by amateurs, with a blue striped awning of the same pattern as their Guernsey shirts, and a dingy red flag of the same shade as the whiskers of the stroke oar. A coxswain being appointed, and all other matters adjusted, the eight gentlemen threw themselves into strong paroxysms, and pulled up with the tide, stimulated by the compassionate remarks of the ladies, who one and all exclaimed, that it seemed an immense exertion—as indeed it did. At first we raced the other boat, which came alongside in gallant style; but this being found an unpleasant amusement, as giving rise to a great quantity of splashing, and rendering the cold pies and other viands very moist, it was unanimously voted down, and we were suffered to shoot a-head, while the second boat followed ingloriously in our wake.

It was at this time that we first recognised Mr. Leaver. There were two firemen-watermen in the boat, lying by until somebody was exhausted; and one of them, who had taken upon himself the direction of affairs, was heard to cry in a gruff voice, "Pull away, number two—give it her, number two—take a longer reach, number two—now, number two, sir, think you're winning a boat." The greater part of the company had no doubt begun to wonder which of the striped Guernseys it might be that stood in need of such encourage-ment, when a stifled shriek from Mrs. Leaver confirmed the doubtful and informed the ignorant; and Mr. Leaver, still further disguised in a straw hat and no neckcloth, was observed to be in a fearful perspiration, and failing visibly. Nor was the general consternation diminished at this instant by the same gentleman (in the performance of an accidental aquatic feat, termed "catching a crab") plunging suddenly backward, and displaying nothing of himself to the company, but two violently struggling legs. Mrs. Leaver shrieked again several times, and cried piteously—"Is he dead? Tell me the worst. Is he dead?"

Now, a moment's reflection might have convinced the loving wife, that unless her husband were endowed with some most surprising powers of muscular action, he never could be dead while he kicked so hard; but still Mrs. Leaver cried, "Is he dead? is he dead?" and still everybody else cried—"No, no, no," until such time as Mr. Leaver was replaced in a sitting posture, and his oar (which had been going through all kinds of wrong-headed performances on its own account) was once more put in his hand, by the exertions of the two firemen-watermen. Mrs. Leaver then exclaimed, "Augustus, my child, come to me;" and Mr. Leaver said, "Augusta, my love, compose yourself, I am not injured." But Mrs. Leaver cried again more piteously than before, "Augustus, my child, come to me;" and now the company generally, who seemed to be apprehensive that if Mr. Leaver remained where he was, he might contribute more than his proper share towards the drowning of the party, disinterestedly took part with Mrs. Leaver, and said he really ought to go, and that he was not strong enough for such violent exercise, and ought never to have undertaken it. Reluctantly, Mr. Leaver went, and laid himself down at Mrs. Leaver's feet, and Mrs. Leaver stooping over him, said, "Oh Augustus, how could you terrify me so?" and Mr. Leaver said, "Augusta, my sweet, I never meant to terrify you;" and Mrs. Leaver said, "You are faint, my dear;" and Mr. Leaver said, "I am rather so, my love;" and they were very loving indeed under Mrs. Leaver's veil, until at length Mr. Leaver came forth again, and pleasantly asked if he had not heard something said about bottled stout and sandwiches.

Mrs. Starling, who was one of the party, was perfectly delighted with this scene, and frequently murmured half-aside,

THE LOVING COUPLE

"What a loving couple you are!" or "How delightful it is to see man and wife so happy together!" To us she was quite poetical, (for we are a kind of cousins,) observing that hearts beating in unison like that made life a paradise of sweets; and that when kindred creatures were drawn together by sympathies so fine and delicate, what more than mortal happiness did not our souls partake! To all this we answered "Certainly," or "Very true," or merely sighed, as the case might be. At every new act of the loving couple, the widow's admiration broke out afresh; and when Mrs. Leaver would not permit Mr. Leaver to keep his hat off, lest the sun should strike to his head, and give him a brain fever, Mrs. Starling actually shed tears, and said it reminded her of Adam and Eve.

The loving couple were thus loving all the way to Twickenham, but when we arrived there (by which time the amateur crew looked very thirsty and vicious) they were more playful than ever, for Mrs. Leaver threw stones at Mr. Leaver, and Mr. Leaver ran after Mrs. Leaver on the grass, in a most innocent and enchanting manner. At dinner, too, Mr. Leaver *would* steal Mrs. Leaver's tongue, and Mrs. Leaver *would* retaliate upon Mr. Leaver's fowl; and when Mrs. Leaver was going to take some lobster salad, Mr. Leaver wouldn't let her have any, saying that it made her ill, and she was always sorry for it afterwards, which afforded Mrs. Leaver an opportunity of pretending to be cross, and showing many other prettinesses. But this was merely the smiling surface of their loves, not the mighty depths of the stream, down to which the company, to say the truth, dived rather unexpectedly, from the following accident. It chanced that Mr. Leaver took upon himself to propose the bachelors who had first originated the notion of that entertainment, in doing which, he affected to regret that he was no longer of their body himself, and pretended grievously to lament his fallen state. This Mrs. Leaver's feelings could not brook, even in jest, and consequently, exclaiming aloud, "He loves me not, he loves

271

me not!" she fell in a very pitiable state into the arms of
Mrs. Starling, and, directly becoming insensible, was conveyed
by that lady and her husband into another room. Presently
Mr. Leaver came running back to know if there was a medical
gentleman in company, and as there was, (in what company
is there not?) both Mr. Leaver and the medical gentleman
hurried away together.

The medical gentleman was the first who returned, and
among his intimate friends he was observed to laugh and
wink, and look as unmedical as might be; but when Mr.
Leaver came back he was very solemn, and in answer to all
inquiries, shook his head, and remarked that Augusta was
far too sensitive to be trifled with—an opinion which the
widow subsequently confirmed. Finding that she was in no
imminent peril, however, the rest of the party betook themselves to dancing on the green, and very merry and happy
they were, and a vast quantity of flirtation there was; the
last circumstance being no doubt attributable, partly to the
fineness of the weather, and partly to the locality, which is
well known to be favourable to all harmless recreations.

In the bustle of the scene, Mr. and Mrs. Leaver stole down
to the boat, and disposed themselves under the awning, Mrs.
Leaver reclining her head upon Mr. Leaver's shoulder, and
Mr. Leaver grasping her hand with great fervour, and looking
in her face from time to time with a melancholy and sympathetic aspect. The widow sat apart, feigning to be occupied
with a book, but stealthily observing them from behind her
fan; and the two firemen-watermen, smoking their pipes on
the bank hard by, nudged each other, and grinned in enjoyment of the joke. Very few of the party missed the loving
couple; and the few who did, heartily congratulated each
other on their disappearance.

THE CONTRADICTORY COUPLE

ONE would suppose that two people who are to pass their whole lives together, and must necessarily be very often alone with each other, could find little pleasure in mutual contradiction; and yet what is more common than a contradictory couple?

The contradictory couple agree in nothing but contradiction. They return home from Mrs. Bluebottle's dinner-party, each in an opposite corner of the coach, and do not exchange a syllable until they have been seated for at least twenty minutes by the fireside at home, when the gentleman, raising his eyes from the stove, all at once breaks silence:

"What a very extraordinary thing it is," says he, "that you *will* contradict, Charlotte!" "*I* contradict!" cries the lady, "but that's just like you." "What's like me?" says the gentleman sharply. "Saying that I contradict you," replies the lady. "Do you mean to say that you do *not* contradict me?" retorts the gentleman; "do you mean to say that you have not been contradicting me the whole of this day? Do you mean to tell me now, that you have not?" "I mean to tell you nothing of the kind," replies the lady quietly; "when you are wrong, of course I shall contradict you."

During this dialogue the gentleman has been taking his brandy-and-water on one side of the fire, and the lady, with her dressing-case on the table, has been curling her hair on the other. She now lets down her back hair, and proceeds to brush it; preserving at the same time an air of conscious rectitude and suffering virtue, which is intended to exasperate the gentleman—and does so.

"I do believe," he says, taking the spoon out of his glass, and tossing it on the table, "that of all the obstinate, positive, wrong-headed creatures that were ever born, you are the most so, Charlotte." "Certainly, certainly, have it your own way, pray. You see how much *I* contradict you," rejoins the lady. "Of course, you didn't contradict me at dinner-time—oh no, not you!" says the gentleman. "Yes, I did," says the lady. "Oh, you did," cries the gentleman; "you admit that?" "If you call that contradiction, I do," the lady answers; "and I say again, Edward, that when I know you are wrong, I will contradict you. I am not your slave." "Not my slave!" repeats the gentleman bitterly; "and you still mean to say that in the Blackburns' new house there are not more than fourteen doors, including the door of the wine-cellar!" "I mean to say," retorts the lady, beating time with her hair-brush on the palm of her hand, "that in that house there are fourteen doors and no more." "Well then—" cries the gentleman, rising in despair, and pacing the room with rapid strides. "By G—, this is enough to destroy a man's intellect, and drive him mad!"

By and by the gentleman comes-to a little, and passing his hand gloomily across his forehead, reseats himself in his former chair. There is a long silence, and this time the lady begins. "I appealed to Mr. Jenkins, who sat next to me on the sofa in the drawing-room during tea—" "Morgan, you mean," interrupts the gentleman. "I do not mean anything of the kind," answers the lady. "Now, by all that is aggravating and impossible to bear," cries the gentleman, clenching his hands and looking upwards in agony, "she is going to insist upon it that Morgan is Jenkins!" "Do you take me for a perfect fool?" exclaims the lady; "do you suppose I don't know the one from the other? Do you suppose I don't

know that the man in the blue coat was Mr. Jenkins?"
"Jenkins in a blue coat!" cries the gentleman with a groan;
"Jenkins in a blue coat! a man who would suffer death
rather than wear anything but brown!" "Do you dare to
charge me with telling an untruth?" demands the lady,
bursting into tears. "I charge you, ma'am," retorts the
gentleman, starting up, "with being a monster of contradiction, a monster of aggravation, a—a—a—Jenkins in a blue
coat!—what have I done that I should be doomed to hear
such statements!"

Expressing himself with great scorn and anguish, the
gentleman takes up his candle and stalks off to bed, where
feigning to be fast asleep when the lady comes up-stairs
drowned in tears, murmuring lamentations over her hard fate
and indistinct intentions of consulting her brothers, he under-
goes the secret torture of hearing her exclaim between whiles,
"I know there are only fourteen doors in the house, I know
it was Mr. Jenkins, I know he had a blue coat on, and I
would say it as positively as I do now, if they were the last
words I had to speak!"

If the contradictory couple are blessed with children, they
are not the less contradictory on that account. Master
James and Miss Charlotte present themselves after dinner,
and being in perfect good humour, and finding their parents
in the same amiable state, augur from these appearances half
a glass of wine a-piece and other extraordinary indulgences.
But unfortunately Master James, growing talkative upon
such prospects, asks his mamma how tall Mrs. Parsons is, and
whether she is not six feet high; to which his mamma replies,
"Yes, she should think she was, for Mrs. Parsons is a very
tall lady indeed; quite a giantess." "For Heaven's sake,
Charlotte," cries her husband, "do not tell the child such
preposterous nonsense. Six feet high!" "Well," replies the
lady, "surely I may be permitted to have an opinion; my
opinion is, that she is six feet high—at least six feet." "Now
you know, Charlotte," retorts the gentleman sternly, "that

that is *not* your opinion—that you have no such idea—and that you only say this for the sake of contradiction." "You are exceedingly polite," his wife replies; "to be wrong about such a paltry question as anybody's height, would be no great crime; but I say again, that I believe Mrs. Parsons to be six feet—more than six feet; nay, I believe you know her to be full six feet, and only say she is not, because I say she is." This taunt disposes the gentleman to become violent, but he checks himself, and is content to mutter, in a haughty tone, "Six feet—ha! ha! Mrs. Parsons six feet!" and the lady answers, "Yes, six feet. I am sure I am glad you are amused, and I'll say it again—six feet." Thus the subject gradually drops off, and the contradiction begins to be forgotten, when Master James, with some undefined notion of making himself agreeable, and putting things to rights again, unfortunately asks his mamma what the moon's made of; which gives her occasion to say that he had better not ask her, for she is always wrong and never can be right; that he only exposes her to contradiction by asking any question of her; and that he had better ask his papa, who is infallible, and never can be wrong. Papa, smarting under this attack, gives a terrible pull at the bell, and says, that if the conversation is to proceed in this way, the children had better be removed. Removed they are, after a few tears and many struggles; and Pa having looked at Ma sideways for a minute or two, with a baleful eye, draws his pocket-handkerchief over his face, and composes himself for his after-dinner nap.

The friends of the contradictory couple often deplore their frequent disputes, though they rather make light of them at the same time: observing, that there is no doubt they are very much attached to each other, and that they never quarrel except about trifles. But neither the friends of the contradictory couple, nor the contradictory couple themselves, reflect, that as the most stupendous objects in nature are but vast collections of minute particles, so the slightest and least considered trifles make up the sum of human happiness or misery.

THE COUPLE WHO DOTE UPON
THEIR CHILDREN

The couple who dote upon their children have usually a great many of them: six or eight at least. The children are either the healthiest in all the world, or the most unfortunate in existence. In either case, they are equally the theme of their doting parents, and equally a source of mental anguish and irritation to their doting parents' friends.

The couple who dote upon their children recognise no dates but those connected with their births, accidents, illnesses, or remarkable deeds. They keep a mental almanack with a vast number of Innocents'-days, all in red letters. They recollect the last coronation, because on that day little Tom fell down the kitchen stairs; the anniversary of the Gunpowder Plot, because it was on the fifth of November that Ned asked whether wooden legs were made in heaven and cocked hats grew in gardens. Mrs. Whiffler will never cease to recollect the last day of the old year as long as she lives, for it was on that day that the baby had the four red spots on its nose which they took for measles: nor Christmas-day, for twenty-one days after Christmas-day the twins were born ; nor Good Friday, for it was on a Good Friday that she was frightened by the donkey-cart when she was in the family way with Georgiana. The movable feasts have no motion for Mr. and Mrs. Whiffler, but remain pinned down tight and fast to the shoulders of some small child, from whom they can never be separated any more. Time was made, according to their creed, not for slaves but for girls and boys; the restless sands in his glass are but little children at play.

As we have already intimated, the children of this couple can know no medium. They are either prodigies of good health or prodigies of bad health; whatever they are, they must be prodigies. Mr. Whiffler must have to describe at his office such excruciating agonies constantly undergone by his eldest boy, as nobody else's eldest boy ever underwent; or he must be able to declare that there never was a child endowed with such amazing health, such an indomitable constitution, and such a cast-iron frame, as his child. His children must be, in some respect or other, above and beyond the children of all other people. To such an extent is this feeling pushed, that we were once slightly acquainted with a lady and gentleman who carried their heads so high and became so proud after their youngest child fell out of a two-pair-of-stairs window without hurting himself much, that the greater part of their friends were obliged to forego their acquaintance. But perhaps this may be an extreme case, and one not justly entitled to be considered as a precedent of general application.

If a friend happen to dine in a friendly way with one of these couples who dote upon their children, it is nearly impossible for him to divert the conversation from their favourite topic. Everything reminds Mr. Whiffler of Ned, or Mrs. Whiffler of Mary Anne, or of the time before Ned was born, or the time before Mary Anne was thought of. The slightest remark, however harmless in itself, will awaken slumbering recollections of the twins. It is impossible to steer clear of them. They will come uppermost, let the poor man do what he may. Ned has been known to be lost sight of for half an hour, Dick has been forgotten, the name of Mary Anne has not been mentioned, but the twins will out. Nothing can keep down the twins.

The Couple who dote upon their Children

"It's a very extraordinary thing, Saunders," says Mr. Whiffler to the visitor, "but—you have seen our little babies, the—the—twins?" The friend's heart sinks within him as he answers, "Oh, yes—often." "Your talking of the Pyramids," says Mr. Whiffler, quite as a matter of course, "reminds me of the twins. It's a very extraordinary thing about those babies—what colour should you say their eyes were?" "Upon my word," the friend stammers, "I hardly know how to answer"—the fact being, that except as the friend does not remember to have heard of any departure from the ordinary course of nature in the instance of these twins, they might have no eyes at all for aught he has observed to the contrary. "You wouldn't say they were red, I suppose?" says Mr. Whiffler. The friend hesitates, and rather thinks they are; but inferring from the expression of Mr. Whiffler's face that red is not the colour, smiles with some confidence, and says, "No, no! very different from that." "What should you say to blue?" says Mr. Whiffler. The friend glances at him, and observing a different expression in his face, ventures to say, "I should say they *were* blue—a decided blue." "To be sure!" cries Mr. Whiffler, triumphantly, "I knew you would! But what should you say if I was to tell you that the boy's eyes are blue and the girl's hazel, eh?" "Impossible!" exclaims the friend, not at all knowing why it should be impossible. "A fact, notwithstanding," cries Mr. Whiffler; "and let me tell you, Saunders, *that's* not a common thing in twins, or a circumstance that'll happen every day."

In this dialogue Mrs. Whiffler, as being deeply responsible for the twins, their charms and singularities, has taken no share; but she now relates, in broken English, a witticism of little Dick's bearing upon the subject just discussed, which delights Mr. Whiffler beyond measure, and causes him to declare that he would have sworn that was Dick's if he had heard it anywhere. Then he requests that Mrs. Whiffler will tell Saunders what Tom said about mad bulls; and Mrs. Whiffler relating the anecdote, a discussion ensues upon the

different character of Tom's wit and Dick's wit, from which
it appears that Dick's humour is of a lively turn, while Tom's
style is the dry and caustic. This discussion being enlivened
by various illustrations, lasts a long time, and is only stopped
by Mrs. Whiffler instructing the footman to ring the nursery
bell, as the children were promised that they should come
down and taste the pudding.

The friend turns pale when this order is given, and paler
still when it is followed up by a great pattering on the
staircase, (not unlike the sound of rain upon a skylight,) a
violent bursting open of the dining-room door, and the tumul-
tuous appearance of six small children, closely succeeded by a
strong nursery-maid with a twin in each arm. As the whole
eight are screaming, shouting, or kicking—some influenced by
a ravenous appetite, some by a horror of the stranger, and
some by a conflict of the two feelings—a pretty long space
elapses before all their heads can be ranged round the table
and anything like order restored; in bringing about which
happy state of things both the nurse and footman are severely
scratched. At length Mrs. Whiffler is heard to say, "Mr.
Saunders, shall I give you some pudding?" A breathless
silence ensues, and sixteen small eyes are fixed upon the guest
in expectation of his reply. A wild shout of joy proclaims
that he has said "No, thank you." Spoons are waved in the
air, legs appear above the table-cloth in uncontrollable ecstasy,
and eighty short fingers dabble in damson syrup.

While the pudding is being disposed of, Mr. and Mrs.
Whiffler look on with beaming countenances, and Mr.
Whiffler nudging his friend Saunders, begs him to take notice
of Tom's eyes, or Dick's chin, or Ned's nose, or Mary Anne's
hair, or Emily's figure, or little Bob's calves, or Fanny's
mouth, or Carry's head, as the case may be. Whatever the
attention of Mr. Saunders is called to, Mr. Saunders admires
of course; though he is rather confused about the sex of the
youngest branches and looks at the wrong children, turning
to a girl when Mr. Whiffler directs his attention to a boy,

and falling into raptures with a boy when he ought to be enchanted with a girl. Then the dessert comes, and there is a vast deal of scrambling after fruit, and sudden spirting forth of juice out of tight oranges into infant eyes, and much screeching and wailing in consequence. At length it becomes time for Mrs. Whiffler to retire, and all the children are by force of arms compelled to kiss and love Mr. Saunders before going up-stairs, except Tom, who, lying on his back in the hall, proclaims that Mr. Saunders "is a naughty beast;" and Dick, who having drunk his father's wine when he was looking another way, is found to be intoxicated and is carried out, very limp and helpless.

Mr. Whiffler and his friend are left alone together, but Mr. Whiffler's thoughts are still with his family, if his family are not with him. "Saunders," says he, after a short silence, "if you please, we'll drink Mrs. Whiffler and the children." Mr. Saunders feels this to be a reproach against himself for not proposing the same sentiment, and drinks it in some confusion. "Ah!" Mr. Whiffler sighs, "these children, Saunders, make one quite an old man." Mr. Saunders thinks that if they were his, they would make him a very old man; but he says nothing. "And yet," pursues Mr. Whiffler, "what can equal domestic happiness? what can equal the engaging ways of children! Saunders, why don't *you* get married?" Now, this is an embarrassing question, because Mr. Saunders has been thinking that if he had at any time entertained matrimonial designs, the revelation of that day would surely have routed them for ever. "I am glad, however," says Mr. Whiffler, "that you *are* a bachelor,—glad on one account, Saunders; a selfish one, I admit. Will you do Mrs. Whiffler and myself a favour?" Mr. Saunders is surprised—evidently surprised; but he replies, "with the greatest pleasure." "Then, will you, Saunders," says Mr. Whiffler, in an impressive manner, "will you cement and consolidate our friendship by coming into the family (so to speak) as a godfather?" "I shall be proud and delighted," replies Mr. Saunders: "which of the children is it? really, I thought they were all christened; or— " "Saunders," Mr. Whiffler interposes, "they *are* all christened; you are right. The fact is, that Mrs. Whiffler is—in short, we expect another." "Not a ninth!" cries the friend, all aghast at the idea. "Yes, Saunders," rejoins Mr. Whiffler, solemnly, "a ninth. Did we drink Mrs. Whiffler's health? Let us drink it again, Saunders, and wish her well over it!"

Doctor Johnson used to tell a story of a man who had but one idea, which was a wrong one. The couple who dote upon their children are in the same predicament: at home or abroad, at all times, and in all places, their thoughts are bound up in this one subject, and have no sphere beyond. They relate the clever things their offspring say or do, and weary every company with their prolixity and absurdity. Mr. Whiffler takes a friend by the button at a street corner on a windy day to tell him a *bon mot* of his youngest boy's; and Mrs. Whiffler, calling to see a sick acquaintance, entertains her with a cheerful account of all her own past sufferings and present expectations. In such cases the sins of the fathers indeed descend upon the children; for people soon come to regard them as predestined little bores. The couple who dote upon their children cannot be said to be actuated by a general love for these engaging little people (which would be a great excuse); for they are apt to underrate and entertain a jealousy of any children but their own. If they examined their own hearts, they would, perhaps, find at the bottom of all this, more self-love and egotism than they think of. Self-love and egotism are bad qualities, of which the unrestrained exhibition, though it may be sometimes amusing, never fails to be wearisome and unpleasant. Couples who dote upon their children, therefore, are best avoided.

THE COOL COUPLE

THERE is an old-fashioned weather-glass representing a house with two doorways, in one of which is the figure of a gentleman, in the other the figure of a lady. When the weather is to be fine the lady comes out and the gentleman goes in; when wet, the gentleman comes out and the lady goes in. They never seek each other's society, are never elevated and depressed by the same cause, and have nothing in common. They are the model of a cool couple, except that there is something of politeness and consideration about the behaviour of the gentleman in the weather-glass, in which, neither of the cool couple can be said to participate.

The cool couple are seldom alone together, and when they are, nothing can exceed their apathy and dulness: the gentleman being for the most part drowsy, and the lady silent. If they enter into conversation, it is usually of an ironical or recriminatory nature. Thus, when the gentleman has indulged in a very long yawn and settled himself more snugly in his easy-chair, the lady will perhaps remark, " Well, I am sure, Charles ! I hope you're comfortable." To which the gentleman replies, "Oh yes, he's quite comfortable—quite." " There are not many married men, I hope," returns the lady, " who seek comfort in such selfish gratifications as you do." " Nor many wives who seek comfort in such selfish gratifications as *you* do, I hope," retorts the gentleman. " Whose fault is that?" demands the lady. The gentleman becoming more sleepy, returns no answer. "Whose fault is that?" the lady repeats. The gentleman still returning no answer, she goes on to say that she believes there never was in all this world anybody so attached to her home, so thoroughly domestic, so unwilling to seek a moment's gratification or pleasure beyond her own fireside as she. God knows that before she was married she never thought or dreamt of such a thing; and she remembers that her poor papa used to say again and again, almost every day of his life, "Oh, my dear Louisa, if you only marry a man who understands you, and takes the trouble to consider your happiness and accommodate himself a very little to your disposition, what a treasure he will find in you!" She supposes her papa knew what her disposition was—he had known her long enough—he ought to have been acquainted with it, but what can she do? If her home is always dull and lonely, and her husband is always absent and finds no pleasure in her society, she is naturally sometimes driven (seldom enough, she is sure) to seek a little recreation elsewhere; she is not expected to pine and mope to death, she hopes. "Then come, Louisa," says the gentleman, waking up as suddenly as he fell asleep, "stop at home this evening, and so will I." "I should be sorry to suppose, Charles, that you took a pleasure in aggravating me," replies the lady; "but you know as well as I do that I am particularly engaged to Mrs. Mortimer, and that it would be an act of the grossest rudeness and ill-breeding, after accepting a seat in her box and preventing her from inviting anybody else, not to go." "Ah! there it is!" says the gentleman, shrugging his shoulders, "I knew that perfectly well. I knew you couldn't devote an evening to your own home. Now all I have to say, Louisa, is this—recollect that *I* was quite willing to stay at home, and that it's no fault of *mine* we are not oftener together."

With that the gentleman goes away to keep an old appointment at his club, and the lady hurries off to dress for

Mrs. Mortimer's; and neither thinks of the other until by some odd chance they find themselves alone again.

But it must not be supposed that the cool couple are habitually a quarrelsome one. Quite the contrary. These differences are only occasions for a little self-excuse,—nothing more. In general they are as easy and careless, and dispute as seldom, as any common acquaintances may; for it is neither worth their while to put each other out of the way, nor to ruffle themselves.

When they meet in society, the cool couple are the best-bred people in existence. The lady is seated in a corner among a little knot of lady friends, one of whom exclaims, "Why, I vow and declare there is your husband, my dear!" "Whose?—mine?" she says, carelessly. "Ay, yours, and coming this way too." "How very odd!" says the lady, in a languid tone, "I thought he had been at Dover." The gentleman coming up, and speaking to all the other ladies and nodding slightly to his wife, it turns out that he has been at Dover, and has just now returned. "What a strange creature you are!" cries his wife; "and what on earth brought you here, I wonder?" "I came to look after you, *of course*," rejoins her husband. This is so pleasant a jest that the lady is mightily amused, as are all the other ladies similarly situated who are within hearing; and while they are enjoying it to the full, the gentleman nods again, turns upon his heel, and saunters away.

There are times, however, when his company is not so agreeable, though equally unexpected; such as when the lady has invited one or two particular friends to tea and scandal, and he happens to come home in the very midst of their diversion. It is a hundred chances to one that he remains in the house half an hour, but the lady is rather disturbed by the intrusion, notwithstanding, and reasons within herself,—"I am sure I never interfere with him, and why should he interfere with me? It can scarcely be accidental; it never happens that I have a particular reason for not wishing him to come home, but he always comes. It's very provoking and tiresome; and I am sure when he leaves me so much alone for his own pleasure, the least he could do would be to do as much for mine." Observing what passes in her mind, the gentleman, who has come home for his own accommodation, makes a merit of it with himself; arrives at the conclusion that it is the very last place in which he can hope to be comfortable; and determines, as he takes up his hat and cane, never to be so virtuous again.

Thus a great many cool couples go on until they are cold couples, and the grave has closed over their folly and indifference. Loss of name, station, character, life itself, has ensued from causes as slight as these, before now; and when gossips tell such tales, and aggravate their deformities, they elevate their hands and eyebrows, and call each other to witness what a cool couple Mr. and Mrs. So-and-So always were, even in the best of times.

THE PLAUSIBLE COUPLE

THE plausible couple have many titles. They are "a delightful couple," an "affectionate couple," "a most agreeable
couple," "a good-hearted couple," and "the best-natured
couple in existence." The truth is, that the plausible couple
are people of the world; and either the way of pleasing the
world has grown much easier than it was in the days of the
old man and his ass, or the old man was but a bad hand
at it, and knew very little of the trade.

"But is it really possible to please the world!" says some
doubting reader. It is indeed. Nay, it is not only very
possible, but very easy. The ways are crooked, and sometimes foul and low. What then? A man need but crawl
upon his hands and knees, know when to close his eyes and
when his ears, when to stoop and when to stand upright;
and if by the world is meant that atom of it in which he
moves himself, he shall please it, never fear.

Now, it will be readily seen, that if a plausible man or
woman have an easy means of pleasing the world by an
adaptation of self to all its twistings and twinings, a plausible
man *and* woman, or, in other words, a plausible couple, playing into each other's hands, and acting in concert, have
a manifest advantage. Hence it is that plausible couples
scarcely ever fail of success on a pretty large scale; and hence
it is that if the reader, laying down this unwieldy volume

at the next full stop, will have the goodness to review his or her circle of acquaintance, and to search particularly for some man and wife with a large connexion and a good name, not easily referable to their abilities or their wealth, he or she (that is, the male or female reader) will certainly find that gentleman or lady, on a very short reflection, to be a plausible couple.

The plausible couple are the most ecstatic people living: the most sensitive people—to merit—on the face of the earth. Nothing clever or virtuous escapes them. They have microscopic eyes for such endowments, and can find them anywhere. The plausible couple never fawn—oh no ! They don't even scruple to tell their friends of their faults. One is too generous, another too candid ; a third has a tendency to think all people like himself, and to regard mankind as a company of angels ; a fourth is kind-hearted to a fault. " We never flatter, my dear Mrs. Jackson," say the plausible couple ; " we speak our minds. Neither you nor Mr. Jackson have faults enough. It may sound strangely, but it is true. You have not faults enough. You know our way,—we must speak out, and always do. Quarrel with us for saying so, if you will ; but we repeat it,—you have not faults enough ! "

The plausible couple are no less plausible to each other than to third parties. They are always loving and harmonious. The plausible gentleman calls his wife " darling," and the plausible lady addresses him as " dearest." If it be Mr. and Mrs. Bobtail Widger, Mrs. Widger is " Lavinia, darling," and Mr. Widger is " Bobtail, dearest." Speaking of each other, they observe the same tender form. Mrs. Widger relates what " Bobtail " said, and Mr. Widger recounts what " darling " thought and did.

If you sit next to the plausible lady at a dinner-table, she takes the earliest opportunity of expressing her belief that you are acquainted with the Clickits ; she is sure she has heard the Clickits speak of you—she must not tell you in what terms, or you will take her for a flatterer. You admit a knowledge of the Clickits; the plausible lady immediately launches out in their praise. She quite loves the Clickits. Were there ever such true-hearted, hospitable, excellent people—such a gentle, interesting little woman as Mrs. Clickit, or such a frank, unaffected creature as Mr. Clickit? were there ever two people, in short, so little spoiled by the world as they are? "As who, darling?" cries Mr. Widger, from the opposite side of the table. "The Clickits, dearest," replies Mrs. Widger. "Indeed you are right, darling," Mr. Widger rejoins; "the Clickits are a very high-minded, worthy, estimable couple." Mrs. Widger remarking that Bobtail always grows quite eloquent upon this subject, Mr. Widger admits that he feels very strongly whenever such people as the Clickits and some other friends of his (here he glances at the host and hostess) are mentioned; for they are an honour to human nature, and do one good to think of. " *You* know the Clickits, Mrs. Jackson?" he says, addressing the lady of the house. "No, indeed; we have not that pleasure," she replies. "You astonish me!" exclaims Mr. Widger: "not know the Clickits! why, you are the very people of all others who ought to be their bosom friends. You are kindred beings; you are one and the same thing: —not know the Clickits! Now *will* you know the Clickits? Will you make a point of knowing them? Will you meet them in a friendly way at our house one evening, and be acquainted with them?" Mrs. Jackson will be quite delighted; nothing would give her more pleasure. "Then, Lavinia, my darling," says Mr. Widger, "mind you don't lose sight of that; now, pray take care that Mr. and Mrs. Jackson know the Clickits without loss of time. Such people ought not to be strangers to each other." Mrs. Widger books both families as the centre of attraction for her next party; and Mr. Widger, going on to expatiate upon the virtues of the Clickits, adds to their other moral qualities, that they keep one of the neatest phaetons in town, and have two thousand a year.

THE PLAUSIBLE COUPLE

As the plausible couple never laud the merits of any absent person, without dexterously contriving that their praises shall reflect upon somebody who is present, so they never depreciate anything or anybody, without turning their depreciation to the same account. Their friend, Mr. Slummery, say they, is unquestionably a clever painter, and would no doubt be very popular, and sell his pictures at a very high price, if that cruel Mr. Fithers had not forestalled him in his department of art, and made it thoroughly and completely his own;—Fithers, it is to be observed, being present and within hearing, and Slummery elsewhere. Is Mrs. Tabblewick really as beautiful as people say? Why, there indeed you ask them a very puzzling question, because there is no doubt that she is a very charming woman, and they have long known her intimately. She is no doubt beautiful, very beautiful; they once thought her the most beautiful woman ever seen; still if you press them for an honest answer, they are bound to say that this was before they had ever seen our lovely friend on the sofa, (the sofa is hard by, and our lovely friend can't help hearing the whispers in which this is said;) since that time, perhaps, they have been hardly fair judges; Mrs. Tabblewick is no doubt extremely handsome,—very like our friend, in fact, in the form of the features,—but in point of expression, and soul, and figure, and air altogether—oh dear!

But while the plausible couple depreciate, they are still careful to preserve their character for amiability and kind feeling; indeed the depreciation itself is often made to grow out of their excessive sympathy and good will. The plausible lady calls on a lady who dotes upon her children, and is sitting with a little girl upon her knee, enraptured by her artless replies, and protesting that there is nothing she delights in so much as conversing with these fairies; when the other lady inquires if she has seen young Mrs. Finching lately, and whether the baby has turned out a finer one than it promised to be. "Oh dear!" cries the plausible lady, "you can-not think how often Bobtail and I have talked about poor Mrs. Finching—she is such a dear soul, and was so anxious that the baby should be a fine child—and very naturally, because she was very much here at one time, and there is, you know, a natural emulation among mothers—that it is impossible to tell you how much we have felt for her." "Is it weak or plain, or what?" inquires the other. "Weak or plain, my love," returns the plausible lady, "it's a fright —a perfect little fright; you ne-ver saw such a miserable creature in all your days. Positively you must not let her see one of these beautiful dears again, or you'll break her heart, you will indeed.—Heaven bless this child, see how she is looking in my face! can you conceive anything prettier than that? If poor Mrs. Finching could only hope—but that's impossible—and the gifts of Providence, you know— What *did* I do with my pocket-handkerchief!"

What prompts the mother, who dotes upon her children, to comment to her lord that evening on the plausible lady's engaging qualities and feeling heart, and what is it that procures Mr. and Mrs. Bobtail Widger an immediate invitation to dinner?

THE NICE LITTLE COUPLE

A CUSTOM once prevailed in old-fashioned circles, that when a lady or gentleman was unable to sing a song, he or she should enliven the company with a story. As we find ourself in the predicament of not being able to describe (to our own satisfaction) nice little couples in the abstract, we purpose telling in this place a little story about a nice little couple of our acquaintance.

Mr. and Mrs. Chirrup are the nice little couple in question. Mr. Chirrup has the smartness, and something of the brisk, quick manner of a small bird. Mrs. Chirrup is the prettiest of all little women, and has the prettiest little figure conceivable. She has the neatest little foot, and the softest little voice, and the pleasantest little smile, and the tidiest little curls, and the brightest little eyes, and the quietest little manner, and is, in short, altogether one of the most engaging of all little women, dead or alive. She is a condensation of all the domestic virtues,—a pocket edition of the young man's best companion,—a little woman at a very high pressure, with an amazing quantity of goodness and usefulness in an exceedingly small space. Little as she is, Mrs. Chirrup might furnish forth matter for the moral equipment of a score of housewives, six feet high in their stockings—if, in the presence of ladies, we may be allowed the expression— and of corresponding robustness.

The Nice Little Couple

THE NICE LITTLE COUPLE

Nobody knows all this better than Mr. Chirrup, though he rather takes on that he don't. Accordingly he is very proud of his better-half, and evidently considers himself, as all other people consider him, rather fortunate in having her to wife. We say evidently, because Mr. Chirrup is a warm-hearted little fellow; and if you catch his eye when he has been slyly glancing at Mrs. Chirrup in company, there is a certain complacent twinkle in it, accompanied, perhaps, by a half-expressed toss of the head, which as clearly indicates what has been passing in his mind as if he had put it into words, and shouted it out through a speaking-trumpet. Moreover, Mr. Chirrup has a particularly mild and bird-like manner of calling Mrs. Chirrup "my dear;" and—for he is of a jocose turn—of cutting little witticisms upon her, and making her the subject of various harmless pleasantries, which nobody enjoys more thoroughly than Mrs. Chirrup herself. Mr. Chirrup, too, now and then affects to deplore his bachelor-days, and to bemoan (with a marvellously con-tented and smirking face) the loss of his freedom, and the sorrow of his heart at having been taken captive by Mrs. Chirrup—all of which circumstances combine to show the secret triumph and satisfaction of Mr. Chirrup's soul.

We have already had occasion to observe that Mrs. Chirrup is an incomparable housewife. In all the arts of domestic arrangement and management, in all the mysteries of con-fectionery-making, pickling, and preserving, never was such a thorough adept as that nice little body. She is, besides, a cunning worker in muslin and fine linen, and a special hand at marketing to the very best advantage. But if there be one branch of housekeeping in which she excels to an utterly unparalleled and unprecedented extent, it is in the important one of carving. A roast goose is universally allowed to be the great stumbling-block in the way of young aspirants to perfection in this department of science; many promising carvers, beginning with legs of mutton, and preserving a good reputation through fillets of veal, sirloins of beef, quarters of lamb, fowls, and even ducks, have sunk before a roast goose, and lost caste and character for ever. To Mrs. Chirrup the resolving a goose into its smallest component parts is a pleasant pastime—a practical joke—a thing to be done in a minute or so, without the smallest interruption to the conversation of the time. No handing the dish over to an unfortunate man upon her right or left, no wild sharpening of the knife, no hacking and sawing at an unruly joint, no noise, no splash, no heat, no leaving off in despair; all is confidence and cheerfulness. The dish is set upon the table, the cover is removed; for an instant, and only an instant, you observe that Mrs. Chirrup's attention is distracted; she smiles, but heareth not. You proceed with your story; meanwhile the glittering knife is slowly upraised, both Mrs. Chirrup's wrists are slightly but not ungracefully agitated, she compresses her lips for an instant, then breaks into a smile, and all is over. The legs of the bird slide gently down into a pool of gravy, the wings seem to melt from the body, the breast separates into a row of juicy slices, the smaller and more complicated parts of his anatomy are perfectly developed, a cavern of stuffing is revealed, and the goose is gone!

To dine with Mr. and Mrs. Chirrup is one of the pleasantest things in the world. Mr. Chirrup has a bachelor friend, who lived with him in his own days of single blessedness, and to whom he is mightily attached. Contrary to the usual custom, this bachelor friend is no less a friend of Mrs. Chirrup's, and, consequently, whenever you dine with Mr. and Mrs. Chirrup, you meet the bachelor friend. It would put any reasonably-conditioned mortal into good-humour to observe the entire unanimity which subsists between these three; but there is a quiet welcome dimpling in Mrs. Chirrup's face, a bustling hospitality oozing as it were out of the waistcoat-pockets of Mr. Chirrup, and a patronising enjoyment of their cordiality and satisfaction on the part of the bachelor friend, which is quite delightful. On these occasions Mr. Chirrup usually takes an opportunity of rally-ing the friend on being single, and the friend retorts on Mr. Chirrup for being married, at which moments some single young ladies present are like to die of laughter; and we have more than once observed them bestow looks upon the friend, which convinces us that his position is by no means a safe one, as, indeed, we hold no bachelor's to be who visits married friends and cracks jokes on wedlock, for certain it is that such men walk among traps and nets and pitfalls innumerable, and often find themselves down upon their knees at the altar rails, taking M. or N. for their wedded wives, before they know anything about the matter.

However, this is no business of Mr. Chirrup's, who talks, and laughs, and drinks his wine, and laughs again, and talks more, until it is time to repair to the drawing-room, where, coffee served and over, Mrs. Chirrup prepares for a round game, by sorting the nicest possible little fish into the nicest possible little pools, and calling Mr. Chirrup to assist her, which Mr. Chirrup does. As they stand side by side, you find that Mr. Chirrup is the least possible shadow of a shade taller than Mrs. Chirrup, and that they are the neatest and best-matched little couple that can be, which the chances are ten to one against your observing with such effect at any other time, unless you see them in the street arm-in-arm, or meet them some rainy day trotting along under a very small umbrella. The round game (at which Mr. Chirrup is the merriest of the party) being done and over, in course of time a nice little tray appears, on which is a nice little supper; and when that is finished likewise, and you have said "Good night," you find yourself repeating a dozen times, as you ride home, that there never was such a nice little couple as Mr. and Mrs. Chirrup.

Whether it is that pleasant qualities, being packed more closely in small bodies than in large, come more readily to hand than when they are diffused over a wider space, and have to be gathered together for use, we don't know, but as a general rule,—strengthened like all other rules by its exceptions,—we hold that little people are sprightly and good-natured. The more sprightly and good-natured people we have, the better; therefore, let us wish well to all nice little couples, and hope that they may increase and multiply.

THE EGOTISTICAL COUPLE

EGOTISM in couples is of two kinds.—It is our purpose to show this by two examples.

The egotistical couple may be young, old, middle-aged, well to do, or ill to do; they may have a small family, a large family, or no family at all. There is no outward sign by which an egotistical couple may be known and avoided. They come upon you unawares; there is no guarding against them. No man can of himself be forewarned or forearmed against an egotistical couple.

The egotistical couple have undergone every calamity, and experienced every pleasurable and painful sensation of which our nature is susceptible. You cannot by possibility tell the egotistical couple anything they don't know, or describe to them anything they have not felt. They have been everything but dead. Sometimes we are tempted to wish they had been even that, but only in our uncharitable moments, which are few and far between.

We happened the other day, in the course of a morning call, to encounter an egotistical couple, nor were we suffered to remain long in ignorance of the fact, for our very first inquiry of the lady of the house brought them into active and vigorous operation. The inquiry was of course touching the lady's health, and the answer happened to be, that she had not been very well. " Oh, my dear ! " said the egotistical lady, "don't talk of not being well. We have been in *such* a state since we saw you last!"—The lady of the house happening to remark that her lord had not been well either, the egotistical gentleman struck in: "Never let Briggs complain of not being well—never let Briggs complain, my dear Mrs. Briggs, after what I have undergone within these six weeks. He doesn't know what it is to be ill, he hasn't the least idea of it; not the faintest conception."—"My dear," interposed his wife smiling, "you talk as if it were almost a crime in Mr. Briggs not to have been as ill as we have been, instead of feeling thankful to Providence that both he and our dear Mrs. Briggs are in such blissful ignorance of real suffering."—"My love," returned the egotistical gentleman, in a low and pious voice, "you mistake me;—I feel grateful —very grateful. I trust our friends may never purchase their experience as dearly as we have bought ours; I hope they never may!"

Having put down Mrs. Briggs upon this theme, and settled the question thus, the egotistical gentleman turned to us, and, after a few preliminary remarks, all tending towards and leading up to the point he had in his mind, inquired if we happened to be acquainted with the Dowager Lady Snorflerer. On our replying in the negative, he presumed we had often met Lord Slang, or beyond all doubt, that we were on intimate terms with Sir Chipkins Glogwog. Finding that we were equally unable to lay claim to either of these distinctions, he expressed great astonishment, and turning to his wife with a retrospective smile, inquired who it was that had told that capital story about the mashed potatoes. "Who, my dear?" returned the egotistical lady, "why Sir Chipkins, of course; how can you ask! Don't you remember his applying it to our cook, and saying that you and I were so like the Prince and Princess, that he could almost have sworn we were they?" "To be sure, I remember that," said the egotistical gentleman, "but are you quite certain that didn't apply to the other anecdote about the Emperor of

Austria and the pump?" "Upon my word then, I think it did," replied his wife. "To be sure it did," said the egotistical gentleman, "it was Slang's story, I remember now, perfectly." However, it turned out, a few seconds afterwards, that the egotistical gentleman's memory was rather treacherous, as he began to have a misgiving that the story had been told by the Dowager Lady Snorflerer the very last time they dined there; but there appearing, on further consideration, strong circumstantial evidence tending to show that this couldn't be, inasmuch as the Dowager Lady Snorflerer had been, on the occasion in question, wholly engrossed by the egotistical lady, the egotistical gentleman recanted this opinion; and after laying the story at the doors of a great many great people, happily left it at last with the Duke of Scuttlewig:—observing that it was not extraordinary he had forgotten his Grace hitherto, as it often happened that the names of those with whom we were upon the most familiar footing were the very last to present themselves to our thoughts.

It not only appeared that the egotistical couple knew everybody, but that scarcely any event of importance or notoriety had occurred for many years with which they had not been in some way or other connected. Thus we learned that when the well-known attempt upon the life of George the Third was made by Hatfield in Drury Lane theatre, the egotistical gentleman's grandfather sat upon his right hand and was the first man who collared him; and that the egotistical lady's aunt, sitting within a few boxes of the royal party, was the only person in the audience who heard his Majesty exclaim, "Charlotte, Charlotte, don't be frightened don't be frightened; they're letting off squibs, they're letting off squibs." When the fire broke out, which ended in the destruction of the two Houses of Parliament, the egotistical couple, being at the time at a drawing-room window on Blackheath, then and there simultaneously exclaimed, to the astonishment of a whole party—"It's the House of Lords!"

Nor was this a solitary instance of their peculiar discernment, for chancing to be (as by a comparison of dates and circumstances they afterwards found) in the same omnibus with Mr. Greenacre, when he carried his victim's head about town in a blue bag, they both remarked a singular twitching in the muscles of his countenance; and walking down Fish Street Hill, a few weeks since, the egotistical gentleman said to his lady—slightly casting up his eyes to the top of the Monument—" There's a boy up there, my dear, reading a Bible. It's very strange. I don't like it.—In five seconds afterwards, Sir," says the egotistical gentleman, bringing his hands together with one violent clap—" the lad was over!"

Diversifying these topics by the introduction of many others of the same kind, and entertaining us between whiles with a minute account of what weather and diet agreed with them, and what weather and diet disagreed with them, and at what time they usually got up, and at what time went to bed, with many other particulars of their domestic economy too numerous to mention; the egotistical couple at length took their leave, and afforded us an opportunity of doing the same.

Mr. and Mrs. Sliverstone are an egotistical couple of another class, for all the lady's egotism is about her husband, and all the gentleman's about his wife. For example:—Mr. Sliverstone is a clerical gentleman, and occasionally writes sermons, as clerical gentlemen do. If you happen to obtain admission at the street-door while he is so engaged, Mrs. Sliverstone appears on tip-toe, and speaking in a solemn whisper, as if there were at least three or four particular friends up-stairs, all upon the point of death, implores you to be very silent, for Mr. Sliverstone is composing, and she need not say how very important it is that he should not be disturbed. Unwilling to interrupt anything so serious, you hasten to withdraw, with many apologies; but this Mrs. Sliverstone will by no means allow, observing, that she knows you would like to see him, as it is very natural you should, and that she is

determined to make a trial for you, as you are a great favourite.
So you are led up-stairs—still on tip-toe—to the door of a
little back room, in which, as the lady informs you in a
whisper, Mr. Sliverstone always writes. No answer being
returned to a couple of soft taps, the lady opens the door,
and there, sure enough, is Mr. Sliverstone, with dishevelled
hair, powdering away with pen, ink, and paper, at a rate
which, if he has any power of sustaining it, would settle the
longest sermon in no time. At first he is too much absorbed
to be roused by this intrusion ; but presently looking up, says
faintly, " Ah ! " and pointing to his desk with a weary and
languid smile, extends his hand, and hopes you'll forgive him.
Then Mrs. Sliverstone sits down beside him, and taking his
hand in hers, tells you how that Mr. Sliverstone has been
shut up there ever since nine o'clock in the morning, (it is
by this time twelve at noon,) and how she knows it cannot
be good for his health, and is very uneasy about it. Unto
this Mr. Sliverstone replies firmly, that " It must be done ; "
which agonizes Mrs. Sliverstone still more, and she goes on
to tell you that such were Mr. Sliverstone's labours last week
—what with the buryings, marryings, churchings, christenings,
and all together,—that when he was going up the pulpit
stairs on Sunday evening, he was obliged to hold on by the
rails, or he would certainly have fallen over into his own pew.
Mr. Sliverstone, who has been listening and smiling meekly,
says, " Not quite so bad as that, not quite so bad ! " he admits
though, on cross-examination, that he *was* very near falling
upon the verger who was following him up to bolt the door ;
but adds, that it was his duty as a Christian to fall upon
him, if need were, and that he, Mr. Sliverstone, and (possibly
the verger too) ought to glory in it.

This sentiment communicates new impulse to Mrs. Sliverstone, who launches into new praises of Mr. Sliverstone's
worth and excellence, to which he listens in the same meek
silence, save when he puts in a word of self-denial relative
to some question of fact, as—" Not seventy-two christenings

that week, my dear. Only seventy-one, only seventy-one."
At length his lady has quite concluded, and then he says,
Why should he repine, why should he give way, why should
he suffer his heart to sink within him? Is it he alone who
toils and suffers? What has she gone through, he should
like to know? What does she go through every day for him
and for society?

With such an exordium Mr. Sliverstone launches out into
glowing praises of the conduct of Mrs. Sliverstone in the
production of eight young children, and the subsequent rearing
and fostering of the same; and thus the husband magnifies
the wife, and the wife the husband.

This would be well enough if Mr. and Mrs. Sliverstone
kept it to themselves, or even to themselves and a friend or
two; but they do not. The more hearers they have, the
more egotistical the couple become, and the more anxious they
are to make believers in their merits. Perhaps this is the
worst kind of egotism. It has not even the poor excuse of
being spontaneous, but is the result of a deliberate system
and malice aforethought. Mere empty-headed conceit excites
our pity, but ostentatious hypocrisy awakens our disgust.

THE COUPLE WHO CODDLE
THEMSELVES

Mrs. Merrywinkle's maiden name was Chopper. She was the only child of Mr. and Mrs. Chopper. Her father died when she was, as the play-books express it, "yet an infant;" and so old Mrs. Chopper, when her daughter married, made the house of her son-in-law her home from that time henceforth, and set up her staff of rest with Mr. and Mrs. Merrywinkle.

Mr. and Mrs. Merrywinkle are a couple who coddle themselves; and the venerable Mrs. Chopper is an aider and abettor in the same.

Mr. Merrywinkle is a rather lean and long-necked gentleman, middle-aged and middle-sized, and usually troubled with a cold in the head. Mrs. Merrywinkle is a delicate-looking lady, with very light hair, and is exceedingly subject to the same unpleasant disorder. The venerable Mrs. Chopper—who is strictly entitled to the appellation, her daughter not being very young, otherwise than by courtesy, at the time of her marriage, which was some years ago—is a mysterious old lady who lurks behind a pair of spectacles, and is afflicted with a chronic disease, respecting which she has taken a vast deal of medical advice, and referred to a vast number of medical books, without meeting any definition of symptoms that at all suits her, or enables her to say, "That's my

303

complaint." Indeed, the absence of authentic information upon the subject of this complaint would seem to be Mrs. Chopper's greatest ill, as in all other respects she is an uncommonly hale and hearty gentlewoman.

Both Mr. and Mrs. Chopper wear an extraordinary quantity of flannel, and have a habit of putting their feet in hot water to an unnatural extent. They likewise indulge in chamomile tea and such-like compounds, and rub themselves on the slightest provocation with camphorated spirits and other lotions applicable to mumps, sore-throat, rheumatism, or lumbago.

Mr. Merrywinkle's leaving home to go to business on a damp or wet morning is a very elaborate affair. He puts on wash-leather socks over his stockings, and India-rubber shoes above his boots, and wears under his waistcoat a cuirass of hare-skin. Besides these precautions, he winds a thick shawl round his throat, and blocks up his mouth with a large silk handkerchief. Thus accoutred, and furnished besides with a great-coat and umbrella, he braves the dangers of the streets; travelling in severe weather at a gentle trot, the better to preserve the circulation, and bringing his mouth to the surface to take breath, but very seldom, and with the utmost caution. His office-door opened, he shoots past his clerk at the same pace, and diving into his own private room, closes the door, examines the window-fastenings, and gradually unrobes himself: hanging his pocket-handkerchief on the fender to air, and determining to write to the newspapers about the fog, which, he says, "has really got to that pitch that it is quite unbearable."

In this last opinion Mrs. Merrywinkle and her respected mother fully concur; for though not present, their thoughts and tongues are occupied with the same subject, which is their constant theme all day. If anybody happens to call, Mrs. Merrywinkle opines that they must assuredly be mad, and her first salutation is, "Why, what in the name of goodness can bring you out in such weather? You know

The Couple who coddle themselves

you *must* catch your death." This assurance is corroborated by Mrs. Chopper, who adds, in further confirmation, a dismal legend concerning an individual of her acquaintance who, making a call under precisely parallel circumstances, and being then in the best health and spirits, expired in forty-eight hours afterwards, of a complication of inflammatory disorders. The visitor, rendered not altogether comfortable perhaps by this and other precedents, inquires very affectionately after Mr. Merrywinkle, but by so doing brings about no change of the subject; for Mr. Merrywinkle's name is inseparably connected with his complaints, and his complaints are inseparably connected with Mrs. Merrywinkle's; and when these are done with, Mrs. Chopper, who has been biding her time, cuts in with the chronic disorder—a subject upon which the amiable old lady never leaves off speaking until she is left alone, and very often not then.

But Mr. Merrywinkle comes home to dinner. He is received by Mrs. Merrywinkle and Mrs. Chopper, who, on his remarking that he thinks his feet are damp, turn pale as ashes and drag him up-stairs, imploring him to have them rubbed directly with a dry coarse towel. Rubbed they are, one by Mrs. Merrywinkle and one by Mrs. Chopper, until the friction causes Mr. Merrywinkle to make horrible faces, and look as if he had been smelling very powerful onions; when they desist, and the patient, provided for his better security with thick worsted stockings and list slippers, is borne down-stairs to dinner. Now, the dinner is always a good one, the appetites of the diners being delicate, and re-quiring a little of what Mrs. Merrywinkle calls " tittivation ; " the secret of which is understood to lie in good cookery and tasteful spices, and which process is so successfully performed in the present instance, that both Mr. and Mrs. Merrywinkle eat a remarkably good dinner, and even the afflicted Mrs. Chopper wields her knife and fork with much of the spirit and elasticity of youth. But Mr. Merrywinkle, in his desire to gratify his appetite, is not unmindful of his health, for he has a bottle of carbonate of soda with which to qualify his porter, and a little pair of scales in which to weigh it out. Neither in his anxiety to take care of his body is he unmindful of the welfare of his immortal part, as he always prays that for what he is going to receive he may be made truly thankful; and in order that he may be as thankful as possible, eats and drinks to the utmost.

Either from eating and drinking so much, or from being the victim of this constitutional infirmity, among others, Mr. Merrywinkle, after two or three glasses of wine, falls fast asleep; and he has scarcely closed his eyes, when Mrs. Merrywinkle and Mrs. Chopper fall asleep likewise. It is on awakening at tea-time that their most alarming symptoms prevail; for then Mr. Merrywinkle feels as if his temples were tightly bound round with the chain of the street-door, and Mrs. Merrywinkle as if she had made a hearty dinner of half-hundredweights, and Mrs. Chopper as if cold water were running down her back, and oyster-knives with sharp points were plunging of their own accord into her ribs. Symptoms like these are enough to make people peevish, and no wonder that they remain so until supper-time, doing little more than doze and complain, unless Mr. Merrywinkle calls out very loudly to a servant "to keep that draught out," or rushes into the passage to flourish his fist in the countenance of the twopenny-postman, for daring to give such a knock as he had just performed at the door of a private gentleman with nerves.

Supper, coming after dinner, should consist of some gentle provocative; and therefore the tittivating art is again in requisition, and again done honour to by Mr. and Mrs. Merrywinkle, still comforted and abetted by Mrs. Chopper. After supper, it is ten to one but the last-named old lady becomes worse, and is led off to bed with the chronic complaint in full vigour. Mr. and Mrs. Merrywinkle, having administered to her a warm cordial, which is something of the strongest, then repair to their own room, where Mr.

THE COUPLE WHO CODDLE THEMSELVES

Merrywinkle, with his legs and feet in hot water, superintends the mulling of some wine which he is to drink at the very moment he plunges into bed, while Mrs. Merrywinkle, in garments whose nature is unknown to and unimagined by all but married men, takes four small pills with a spasmodic look between each, and finally comes to something hot and fragrant out of another little saucepan, which serves as her composing-draught for the night.

There is another kind of couple who coddle themselves, and who do so at a cheaper rate and on more spare diet, because they are niggardly and parsimonious; for which reason they are kind enough to coddle their visitors too. It is unnecessary to describe them, for our readers may rest assured of the accuracy of these general principles :—that all couples who coddle themselves are selfish and slothful,—that they charge upon every wind that blows, every rain that falls, and every vapour that hangs in the air, the evils which arise from their own imprudence or the gloom which is engendered in their own tempers,—and that all men and women, in couples or otherwise, who fall into exclusive habits of self-indulgence, and forget their natural sympathy and close connexion with everybody and everything in the world around them, not only neglect the first duty of life, but, by a happy retributive justice, deprive themselves of its truest and best enjoyment.

THE OLD COUPLE

THEY are grandfather and grandmother to a dozen grown people and have great-grandchildren besides; their bodies are bent, their hair is grey, their step tottering and infirm. Is this the lightsome pair whose wedding was so merry, and have the young couple indeed grown old so soon!

It seems but yesterday—and yet what a host of cares and griefs are crowded into the intervening time which, reckoned by them, lengthens out into a century! How many new associations have wreathed themselves about their hearts since then! The old time is gone, and a new time has come for others—not for them. They are but the rusting link that feebly joins the two, and is silently loosening its hold and dropping asunder.

It seems but yesterday—and yet three of their children have sunk into the grave, and the tree that shades it has grown quite old. One was an infant—they wept for him; the next a girl, a slight young thing too delicate for earth— her loss was hard indeed to bear. The third, a man. That was the worst of all, but even that grief is softened now.

It seems but yesterday—and yet how the gay and laughing faces of that bright morning have changed and vanished from above ground! Faint likenesses of some remain about them yet, but they are very faint and scarcely to be traced. The rest are only seen in dreams, and even they are unlike what they were, in eyes so old and dim.

The Old Couple

THE OLD COUPLE

One or two dresses from the bridal wardrobe are yet preserved. They are of a quaint and antique fashion, and seldom seen except in pictures. White has turned yellow, and brighter hues have faded. Do you wonder, child? The wrinkled face was once as smooth as yours, the eyes as bright, the shrivelled skin as fair and delicate. It is the work of hands that have been dust these many years.

Where are the fairy lovers of that happy day whose annual return comes upon the old man and his wife, like the echo of some village bell which has long been silent? Let yonder peevish bachelor, racked by rheumatic pains, and quarrelling with the world, let him answer to the question. He recollects something of a favourite playmate; her name was Lucy—so they tell him. He is not sure whether she was married, or went abroad, or died. It is a long while ago, and he don't remember.

Is nothing as it used to be; does no one feel, or think, or act, as in days of yore? Yes. There is an aged woman who once lived servant with the old lady's father, and is sheltered in an alms-house not far off. She is still attached to the family, and loves them all; she nursed the children in her lap, and tended in their sickness those who are no more. Her old mistress has still something of youth in her eyes; the young ladies are like what she was but not quite so handsome, nor are the gentlemen as stately as Mr. Harvey used to be. She has seen a great deal of trouble; her husband and her son died long ago; but she has got over that, and is happy now—quite happy.

If ever her attachment to her old protectors were disturbed by fresher cares and hopes, it has long since resumed its former current. It has filled the void in the poor creature's heart, and replaced the love of kindred. Death has not left her alone, and this, with a roof above her head, and a warm hearth to sit by, makes her cheerful and contented. Does she remember the marriage of great-grandmamma? Ay, that she does, as well—as if it was only yesterday. You wouldn't think it to look at her now, and perhaps she ought not to say so of herself, but she was as smart a young girl then as you'd wish to see. She recollects she took a friend of hers up-stairs to see Miss Emma dressed for church ; her name was—ah ! she forgets the name, but she remembers that she was a very pretty girl, and that she married not long afterwards, and lived—it has quite passed out of her mind where she lived, but she knows she had a bad husband who used her ill, and that she died in Lambeth workhouse. Dear, dear, in Lambeth workhouse !

And the old couple—have they no comfort or enjoyment of existence ? See them among their grandchildren and great-grandchildren ; how garrulous they are, how they compare one with another, and insist on likenesses which no one else can see ; how gently the old lady lectures the girls on points of breeding and decorum, and points the moral by anecdotes of herself in her young days—how the old gentleman chuckles over boyish feats and roguish tricks, and tells long stories of a "barring-out" achieved at the school he went to : which was very wrong, he tells the boys, and never to be imitated of course, but which he cannot help letting them know was very pleasant too—especially when he kissed the master's niece. This last, however, is a point on which the old lady is very tender, for she considers it a shocking and indelicate thing to talk about, and always says so whenever it is mentioned, never failing to observe that he ought to be very penitent for having been so sinful. So the old gentleman gets no further, and what the schoolmaster's niece said afterwards (which he is always going to tell) is lost to posterity.

The old gentleman is eighty years old, to-day—"Eighty years old, Crofts, and never had a headache," he tells the barber who shaves him (the barber being a young fellow, and very subject to that complaint). "That's a great age, Crofts," says the old gentleman. "I don't think it's sich a wery great age, Sir," replied the barber. "Crofts," rejoins the old gentleman, "you're talking nonsense to me. Eighty not a great age?" "It's a wery great age, Sir, for a gentleman to be as healthy and active as you are," returns the barber; "but my grandfather, Sir, he was ninety-four." "You don't mean that, Crofts?" says the old gentleman. "I do indeed, Sir," retorts the barber, "and as wiggerous as Julius Cæsar, my grandfather was." The old gentleman muses a little time, and then says, "What did he die of, Crofts?" "He died accidentally, Sir," returns the barber; "he didn't mean to do it. He always would go a running about the streets—walking never satisfied *his* spirit—and he run against a post and died of a hurt in his chest." The old gentleman says no more until the shaving is concluded, and then he gives Crofts half-a-crown to drink his health. He is a little doubtful of the barber's veracity afterwards, and telling the anecdote to the old lady, affects to make very light of it—though to be sure (he adds) there was old Parr, and in some parts of England, ninety-five or so is a common age, quite a common age.

This morning the old couple are cheerful but serious, recalling old times as well as they can remember them, and dwelling upon many passages in their past lives which the day brings to mind. The old lady reads aloud, in a tremulous voice, out of a great Bible, and the old gentleman with his hand to his ear, listens with profound respect. When the book is closed, they sit silent for a short space, and afterwards resume their conversation, with a reference perhaps to their dead children, as a subject not unsuited to that they have just left. By degrees they are led to consider which of those who survive are the most like those dearly-remembered objects, and so they fall into a less solemn strain, and become cheerful again.

How many people in all, grandchildren, great-grandchildren, and one or two intimate friends of the family, dine together to-day at the eldest son's to congratulate the old couple, and wish them many happy returns, is a calculation beyond our powers: but this we know, that the old couple no sooner present themselves, very sprucely and carefully attired, than there is a violent shouting and rushing forward of the younger branches with all manner of presents, such as pocket-books, pencil-cases, pen-wipers, watch-papers, pincushions, sleeve-buckles, worked-slippers, watch-guards, and even a nutmeg-grater: the latter article being presented by a very chubby and very little boy, who exhibits it in great triumph as an extraordinary variety. The old couple's emotion at these tokens of remembrance occasions quite a pathetic scene, of which the chief ingredients are a vast quantity of kissing and hugging, and repeated wipings of small eyes and noses with small square pocket-handkerchiefs, which don't come at all easily out of small pockets. Even the peevish bachelor is moved, and he says, as he presents the old gentleman with a queer sort of antique ring from his own finger, that he'll be de'ed if he doesn't think he looks younger than he did ten years ago.

But the great time is after dinner, when the dessert and wine are on the table, which is pushed back to make plenty of room, and they are all gathered in a large circle round the fire, for it is then—the glasses being filled, and everybody ready to drink the toast—that two great-grandchildren rush out at a given signal, and presently return, dragging in old Jane Adams leaning upon her crutched stick, and trembling with age and pleasure. Who so popular as poor old Jane, nurse and story-teller in ordinary to two generations; and who so happy as she, striving to bend her stiff limbs into a curtsey, while tears of pleasure steal down her withered cheeks!

The old couple sit side by side, and the old time seems like yesterday indeed. Looking back upon the path they have travelled, its dust and ashes disappear; the flowers that withered long ago, show brightly again upon its borders, and they grow young once more in the youth of those about them.

CONCLUSION

WE have taken for the subjects of the foregoing moral essays, twelve samples of married couples, carefully selected from a large stock on hand, open to the inspection of all comers. These samples are intended for the benefit of the rising generation of both sexes, and, for their more easy and pleasant information, have been separately ticketed and labelled in the manner they have seen.

We have purposely excluded from consideration the couple in which the lady reigns paramount and supreme, holding such cases to be of a very unnatural kind, and like hideous births and other monstrous deformities, only to be discreetly and sparingly exhibited.

And here our self-imposed task would have ended, but that to those young ladies and gentlemen who are yet revolving singly round the church, awaiting the advent of that time when the mysterious laws of attraction shall draw them towards it in couples, we are desirous of addressing a few last words.

Before marriage and afterwards, let them learn to centre all their hopes of real and lasting happiness in their own fireside; let them cherish the faith that in home, and all the English virtues which the love of home engenders, lies the only true source of domestic felicity; let them believe that round the household gods, contentment and tranquillity cluster

313

CONCLUSION

in their gentlest and most graceful forms; and that many weary hunters of happiness through the noisy world, have learnt this truth too late, and found a cheerful spirit and a quiet mind only at home at last.

How much may depend on the education of daughters and the conduct of mothers; how much of the brightest part of our old national character may be perpetuated by their wisdom or frittered away by their folly—how much of it may have been lost already, and how much more in danger of vanishing every day—are questions too weighty for discussion here, but well deserving a little serious consideration from all young couples nevertheless.

To that one young couple on whose bright destiny the thoughts of nations are fixed, may the youth of England look, and not in vain, for an example. From that one young couple, blessed and favoured as they are, may they learn that even the glare and glitter of a court, the splendour of a palace, and the pomp and glory of a throne, yield in their power of conferring happiness, to domestic worth and virtue. From that one young couple may they learn that the crown of a great empire, costly and jewelled though it be, gives place in the estimation of a Queen to the plain gold ring that links her woman's nature to that of tens of thousands of her humble subjects, and guards in her woman's heart one secret store of tenderness, whose proudest boast shall be that it knows no Royalty save Nature's own, and no pride of birth but being the child of heaven!

So shall the highest young couple in the land for once hear the truth, when men throw up their caps, and cry with loving shouts—

GOD BLESS THEM.

THE MUDFOG AND OTHER
SKETCHES

PUBLIC LIFE OF MR. TULRUMBLE,

ONCE MAYOR OF MUDFOG

MUDFOG is a pleasant town—a remarkably pleasant town—
situated in a charming hollow by the side of a river, from
which river, Mudfog derives an agreeable scent of pitch, tar,
coals, and rope-yarn, a roving population in oilskin hats, a
pretty steady influx of drunken bargemen, and a great many
other maritime advantages. There is a good deal of water
about Mudfog, and yet it is not exactly the sort of town for
a watering-place, either. Water is a perverse sort of element
at the best of times, and in Mudfog it is particularly so.
In winter, it comes oozing down the streets and tumbling
over the fields,—nay, rushes into the very cellars and kitchens
of the houses, with a lavish prodigality that might well be
dispensed with ; but in the hot summer weather it *will* dry
up, and turn green : and, although green is a very good
colour in its way, especially in grass, still it certainly is not
becoming to water ; and it cannot be denied that the beauty
of Mudfog is rather impaired, even by this trifling circumstance. Mudfog is a healthy place—very healthy ;—damp,
perhaps, but none the worse for that. It's quite a mistake

to suppose that damp is unwholesome: plants thrive best in damp situations, and why shouldn't men? The inhabitants of Mudfog are unanimous in asserting that there exists not a finer race of people on the face of the earth; here we have an indisputable and veracious contradiction of the vulgar error at once. So, admitting Mudfog to be damp, we distinctly state that it is salubrious.

The town of Mudfog is extremely picturesque. Limehouse and Ratcliff Highway are both something like it, but they give you a very faint idea of Mudfog. There are a great many more public-houses in Mudfog—more than in Ratcliff Highway and Limehouse put together. The public buildings, too, are very imposing. We consider the town-hall one of the finest specimens of shed architecture, extant: it is a combination of the pig-sty and tea-garden-box orders; and the simplicity of its design is of surpassing beauty. The idea of placing a large window on one side of the door, and a small one on the other, is particularly happy. There is a fine old Doric beauty, too, about the padlock and scraper, which is strictly in keeping with the general effect.

In this room do the mayor and corporation of Mudfog assemble together in solemn council for the public weal. Seated on the massive wooden benches, which, with the table in the centre, form the only furniture of the whitewashed apartment, the sage men of Mudfog spend hour after hour in grave deliberation. Here they settle at what hour of the night the public-houses shall be closed, at what hour of the morning they shall be permitted to open, how soon it shall be lawful for people to eat their dinner on church-days, and other great political questions; and sometimes, long after silence has fallen on the town, and the distant lights from the shops and houses have ceased to twinkle, like far-off stars, to the sight of the boatmen on the river, the illumination in the two unequal-sized windows of the town-hall, warns the inhabitants of Mudfog that its little body of legislators, like a larger and better-known body of the same genus, a great deal more noisy, and not a whit more profound, are patriotically dozing away in company, far into the night, for their country's good.

Among this knot of sage and learned men, no one was so eminently distinguished, during many years, for the quiet modesty of his appearance and demeanour, as Nicholas Tulrumble, the well-known coal-dealer. However exciting the subject of discussion, however animated the tone of the debate, or however warm the personalities exchanged, (and even in Mudfog we get personal sometimes,) Nicholas Tulrumble was always the same. To say truth, Nicholas, being an industrious man, and always up betimes, was apt to fall asleep when a debate began, and to remain asleep till it was over, when he would wake up very much refreshed, and give his vote with the greatest complacency. The fact was, that Nicholas Tulrumble, knowing that everybody there had made up his mind beforehand, considered the talking as just a long botheration about nothing at all; and to the present hour it remains a question, whether, on this point at all events, Nicholas Tulrumble was not pretty near right.

Time, which strews a man's head with silver, sometimes fills his pockets with gold. As he gradually performed one good office for Nicholas Tulrumble, he was obliging enough, not to omit the other. Nicholas began life in a wooden tenement of four feet square, with a capital of two and ninepence, and a stock in trade of three bushels and a-half of coals, exclusive of the large lump which hung, by way of sign-board, outside. Then he enlarged the shed, and kept a truck; then he left the shed, and the truck too, and started a donkey and a Mrs. Tulrumble; then he moved again and set up a-cart; the cart was soon afterwards exchanged for a waggon; and so he went on like his great predecessor Whittington—only without a cat for a partner—increasing in wealth and fame, until at last he gave up business altogether, and retired with Mrs. Tulrumble and family to Mudfog Hall, which he had himself erected, on something which he attempted to delude himself into the belief was a hill, about a quarter of a mile distant from the town of Mudfog.

About this time, it began to be murmured in Mudfog that Nicholas Tulrumble was growing vain and haughty; that prosperity and success had corrupted the simplicity of his manners, and tainted the natural goodness of his heart; in short, that he was setting up for a public character, and a great gentleman, and affected to look down upon his old companions with compassion and contempt. Whether these reports were at the time well-founded, or not, certain it is that Mrs. Tulrumble very shortly afterwards started a four-wheel chaise, driven by a tall postilion in a yellow cap,—that Mr. Tulrumble junior took to smoking cigars, and calling the footman a "feller,"—and that Mr. Tulrumble from that time forth, was no more seen in his old seat in the chimney-corner of the Lighterman's Arms at night. This looked bad; but, more than this, it began to be observed that Mr. Nicholas Tulrumble attended the corporation meetings more frequently than heretofore; and he no longer went to sleep as he had done for so many years, but propped his eyelids open with his two forefingers; that he read the newspapers by himself at home; and that he was in the habit of indulging abroad in distant and mysterious allusions to "masses of people," and "the property of the country," and "productive power," and "the monied interest:" all of which denoted and proved that Nicholas Tulrumble was either mad, or worse; and it puzzled the good people of Mudfog amazingly.

At length, about the middle of the month of October, Mr. Tulrumble and family went up to London; the middle of October being, as Mrs. Tulrumble informed her acquaintance in Mudfog, the very height of the fashionable season.

Somehow or other, just about this time, despite the health-preserving air of Mudfog, the Mayor died. It was a most extraordinary circumstance; he had lived in Mudfog for eighty-five years. The corporation didn't understand it at all; indeed it was with great difficulty that one old gentleman, who was a great stickler for forms, was dissuaded from proposing a vote of censure on such unaccountable conduct. Strange as it was, however, die he did, without taking the slightest notice of the corporation; and the corporation were imperatively called upon to elect his successor. So, they met for the purpose; and being very full of Nicholas Tulrumble just then, and Nicholas Tulrumble being a very important man, they elected him, and wrote off to London by the very next post to acquaint Nicholas Tulrumble with his new elevation.

Now, it being November time, and Mr. Nicholas Tulrumble being in the capital, it fell out that he was present at the Lord Mayor's show and dinner, at sight of the glory and splendour whereof, he, Mr. Tulrumble, was greatly mortified, inasmuch as the reflection would force itself on his mind, that, had he been born in London instead of in Mudfog, he might have been a Lord Mayor too, and have patronized the judges, and been affable to the Lord Chancellor, and friendly with the Premier, and coldly condescending to the Secretary to the Treasury, and have dined with a flag behind his back, and done a great many other acts and deeds which unto Lord Mayors of London peculiarly appertain. The more he thought of the Lord Mayor, the more enviable a personage he seemed. To be a King was all very well; but what was the King to the Lord Mayor! When the King made a speech, everybody knew it was somebody else's writing; whereas here was the Lord Mayor, talking away for half an hour—all out of his own head—amidst the enthusiastic applause of the whole company, while it was notorious that the King might talk to his parliament till he was black in the face without getting so much as a single cheer. As all these reflections passed through the mind of Mr. Nicholas Tulrumble, the Lord Mayor of London appeared to him the greatest sovereign on the face of the earth, beating the Emperor of Russia all to nothing, and leaving the Great Mogul immeasurably behind.

321

Mr. Nicholas Tulrumble was pondering over these things, and inwardly cursing the fate which had pitched his coal-shed in Mudfog, when the letter of the corporation was put into his hand. A crimson flush mantled over his face as he read it, for visions of brightness were already dancing before his imagination.

"My dear," said Mr. Tulrumble to his wife, "they have elected me, Mayor of Mudfog."

"Lor-a-mussy!" said Mrs. Tulrumble: "why what's become of old Sniggs?"

"The late Mr. Sniggs, Mrs. Tulrumble," said Mr. Tulrumble sharply, for he by no means approved of the notion of unceremoniously designating a gentleman who filled the high office of Mayor, as "Old Sniggs,"—"The late Mr. Sniggs, Mrs. Tulrumble, is dead."

The communication was very unexpected; but Mrs. Tulrumble only ejaculated "Lor-a-mussy!" once again, as if a Mayor were a mere ordinary Christian, at which Mr. Tulrumble frowned gloomily.

"What a pity 'tan't in London, ain't it?" said Mrs. Tulrumble, after a short pause; "what a pity 'tan't in London, where you might have had a show."

"I *might* have a show in Mudfog, if I thought proper, I apprehend," said Mr. Tulrumble mysteriously.

"Lor! so you might, I declare," replied Mrs. Tulrumble.

"And a good one too," said Mr. Tulrumble.

"Delightful!" exclaimed Mrs. Tulrumble.

"One which would rather astonish the ignorant people down there," said Mr. Tulrumble.

"It would kill them with envy," said Mrs. Tulrumble.

So it was agreed that his Majesty's lieges in Mudfog should be astonished with splendour, and slaughtered with envy, and that such a show should take place as had never been seen in that town, or in any other town before,—no, not even in London itself.

On the very next day after the receipt of the letter, down

came the tall postilion in a post-chaise,—not upon one of the horses, but inside—actually inside the chaise,—and, driving up to the very door of the town-hall, where the corporation were assembled, delivered a letter, written by the Lord knows who, and signed by Nicholas Tulrumble, in which Nicholas said, all through four sides of closely-written, gilt-edged, hot-pressed, Bath post letter paper, that he responded to the call of his fellow-townsmen with feelings of heartfelt delight; that he accepted the arduous office which their confidence had imposed upon him; that they would never find him shrinking from the discharge of his duty; that he would endeavour to execute his functions with all that dignity which their magni-tude and importance demanded; and a great deal more to the same effect. But even this was not all. The tall postilion produced from his right-hand top-boot, a damp copy of that afternoon's number of the county paper; and there, in large type, running the whole length of the very first column, was a long address from Nicholas Tulrumble to the inhabitants of Mudfog, in which he said that he cheerfully complied with their requisition, and, in short, as if to prevent any mistake about the matter, told them over again what a grand fellow he meant to be, in very much the same terms as those in which he had already told them all about the matter in his letter.

The corporation stared at one another very hard at all this, and then looked as if for explanation to the tall postilion, but as the tall postilion was intently contemplating the gold tassel on the top of his yellow cap, and could have afforded no explanation whatever, even if his thoughts had been entirely disengaged, they contented themselves with coughing very dubiously, and looking very grave. The tall postilion then delivered another letter, in which Nicholas Tulrumble informed the corporation, that he intended repairing to the town-hall, in grand state and gorgeous procession, on the Monday after-noon next ensuing. At this the corporation looked still more solemn; but, as the epistle wound up with a formal invitation

323

to the whole body to dine with the Mayor on that day, at Mudfog Hall, Mudfog Hill, Mudfog, they began to see the fun of the thing directly, and sent back their compliments, and they'd be sure to come.

Now there happened to be in Mudfog, as somehow or other there does happen to be, in almost every town in the British dominions, and perhaps in foreign dominions too—we think it very likely, but, being no great traveller, cannot distinctly say—there happened to be, in Mudfog, a merry-tempered, pleasant-faced, good-for-nothing sort of vagabond, with an invincible dislike to manual labour, and an unconquerable attachment to strong beer and spirits, whom everybody knew, and nobody, except his wife, took the trouble to quarrel with, who inherited from his ancestors the appellation of Edward Twigger, and rejoiced in the *sobriquet* of Bottle-nosed Ned. He was drunk upon the average once a day, and penitent upon an equally fair calculation once a month; and when he was penitent, he was invariably in the very last stage of maudlin intoxication. He was a ragged, roving, roaring kind of fellow, with a burly form, a sharp wit, and a ready head, and could turn his hand to anything when he chose to do it. He was by no means opposed to hard labour on principle, for he would work away at a cricket-match by the day together, —running, and catching, and batting, and bowling, and revelling in toil which would exhaust a galley-slave. He would have been invaluable to a fire-office; never was a man with such a natural taste for pumping engines, running up ladders, and throwing furniture out of two-pair-of-stairs' windows: nor was this the only element in which he was at home; he was a humane society in himself, a portable drag, an animated life-preserver, and had saved more people, in his time, from drowning, than the Plymouth life-boat, or Captain Manby's apparatus. With all these qualifications, notwithstanding his dissipation, Bottle-nosed Ned was a general favourite; and the authorities of Mudfog, remembering his numerous services to the population, allowed him in return to get drunk in his own way, without the fear of stocks, fine, or imprisonment. He had a general licence, and he showed his sense of the compliment by making the most of it.

We have been thus particular in describing the character and avocations of Bottle-nosed Ned, because it enables us to introduce a fact politely, without hauling it into the reader's presence with indecent haste by the head and shoulders, and brings us very naturally to relate, that on the very same evening on which Mr. Nicholas Tulrumble and family returned to Mudfog, Mr. Tulrumble's new secretary, just imported from London, with a pale face and light whiskers, thrust his head down to the very bottom of his neckcloth-tie, in at the tap-room door of the Lighterman's Arms, and inquiring whether one Ned Twigger was luxuriating within, announced himself as the bearer of a message from Nicholas Tulrumble, Esquire, requiring Mr. Twigger's immediate attendance at the hall, on private and particular business. It being by no means Mr. Twigger's interest to affront the Mayor, he rose from the fireplace with a slight sigh, and followed the light-whiskered secretary through the dirt and wet of Mudfog streets, up to Mudfog Hall, without further ado.

Mr. Nicholas Tulrumble was seated in a small cavern with a skylight, which he called his library, sketching out a plan of the procession on a large sheet of paper; and into the cavern the secretary ushered Ned Twigger.

"Well, Twigger!" said Nicholas Tulrumble, condescendingly.

There was a time when Twigger would have replied, "Well, Nick!" but that was in the days of the truck, and a couple of years before the donkey; so, he only bowed.

"I want you to go into training, Twigger," said Mr. Tulrumble.

"What for, sir?" inquired Ned, with a stare.

"Hush, hush, Twigger!" said the Mayor. "Shut the door, Mr. Jennings. Look here, Twigger."

As the Mayor said this, he unlocked a high closet, and disclosed a complete suit of brass armour, of gigantic dimensions.

"I want you to wear this next Monday, Twigger," said the Mayor.

"Bless your heart and soul, sir!" replied Ned, "you might as well ask me to wear a seventy-four pounder, or a cast-iron boiler."

"Nonsense, Twigger, nonsense!" said the Mayor.

"I couldn't stand under it, sir," said Twigger; "it would make mashed potatoes of me, if I attempted it."

"Pooh, pooh, Twigger!" returned the Mayor. "I tell you I have seen it done with my own eyes, in London, and the man wasn't half such a man as you are, either."

"I should as soon have thought of a man's wearing the case of an eight-day clock to save his linen," said Twigger, casting a look of apprehension at the brass suit.

"It's the easiest thing in the world," rejoined the Mayor.

"It's nothing," said Mr. Jennings.

"When you're used to it," added Ned.

"You do it by degrees," said the Mayor. "You would begin with one piece to-morrow, and two the next day, and so on, till you had got it all on. Mr. Jennings, give Twigger a glass of rum. Just try the breast-plate, Twigger. Stay; take another glass of rum first. Help me to lift it, Mr. Jennings. Stand firm, Twigger! There!—it isn't half as heavy as it looks, is it?"

Twigger was a good strong, stout fellow; so, after a great deal of staggering, he managed to keep himself up, under the breast-plate, and even contrived, with the aid of another glass of rum, to walk about in it, and the gauntlets into the bargain. He made a trial of the helmet, but was not equally successful, inasmuch as he tipped over instantly,—an accident which Mr. Tulrumble clearly demonstrated to be occasioned by his not having a counteracting weight of brass on his legs.

"Now, wear that with grace and propriety on Monday next," said Tulrumble, "and I'll make your fortune."

"I'll try what I can do, sir," said Twigger.

"It must be kept a profound secret," said Tulrumble.

"Of course, sir," replied Twigger.

"And you must be sober," said Tulrumble; "perfectly sober."

Mr. Twigger at once solemnly pledged himself to be as sober as a judge, and Nicholas Tulrumble was satisfied, although, had we been Nicholas, we should certainly have exacted some promise of a more specific nature; inasmuch as, having attended the Mudfog assizes in the evening more than once, we can solemnly testify to having seen judges with very strong symptoms of dinner under their wigs. However, that's neither here nor there.

The next day, and the day following, and the day after that, Ned Twigger was securely locked up in the small cavern with the skylight, hard at work at the armour. With every additional piece he could manage to stand upright in, he had an additional glass of rum; and at last, after many partial suffocations, he contrived to get on the whole suit, and to stagger up and down the room in it, like an intoxicated effigy from Westminster Abbey.

Never was man so delighted as Nicholas Tulrumble; never was woman so charmed as Nicholas Tulrumble's wife. Here was a sight for the common people of Mudfog! A live man in brass armour! Why, they would go wild with wonder!

The day—*the* Monday—arrived.

If the morning had been made to order, it couldn't have been better adapted to the purpose. They never showed a better fog in London on Lord Mayor's day, than enwrapped the town of Mudfog on that eventful occasion. It had risen slowly and surely from the green and stagnant water with the first light of morning, until it reached a little above the lamp-post tops; and there it had stopped, with a sleepy, sluggish obstinacy, which bade defiance to the sun, who had got up very blood-shot about the eyes, as if he had been at a drinking-party over-night, and was doing his day's work with the worst possible grace. The thick damp mist hung over the town like a huge gauze curtain. All was dim and dismal. The church steeples had bidden a temporary adieu to the world below; and every object of lesser importance — houses, barns, hedges, trees, and barges—had all taken the veil.

The church-clock struck one. A cracked trumpet from the front garden of Mudfog Hall produced a feeble flourish, as if some asthmatic person had coughed into it accidentally; the gate flew open, and out came a gentleman, on a moist-sugar coloured charger, intended to represent a herald, but bearing a much stronger resemblance to a court-card on horseback. This was one of the Circus people, who always came down to Mudfog at that time of the year, and who had been engaged by Nicholas Tulrumble expressly for the occasion. There was the horse, whisking his tail about, balancing himself on his hind-legs, and flourishing away with his fore-feet, in a manner which would have gone to the hearts and souls of any reasonable crowd. But a Mudfog crowd never was a reasonable one, and in all probability never will be. Instead of scattering the very fog with their shouts, as they ought most indubitably to have done, and were fully intended to do, by Nicholas Tulrumble, they no sooner recognized the herald, than they began to growl forth the most unqualified disapprobation at the bare notion of his riding like any other man. If he had come out on his head indeed, or jumping through a hoop, or flying through a red-hot drum, or even standing on one leg with his other foot in his mouth, they might have had something to say to him; but for a professional gentleman to sit astride in the saddle, with his feet in the stirrups, was rather too good a joke. So, the herald was a decided failure, and the crowd hooted with great energy, as he pranced ingloriously away.

On the procession came. We are afraid to say how many supernumeraries there were, in striped shirts and black velvet caps, to imitate the London watermen, or how many base imitations of running-footmen, or how many banners, which, owing to the heaviness of the atmosphere, could by no means be prevailed on to display their inscriptions: still less do we feel disposed to relate how the men who played the wind instruments, looking up into the sky (we mean the fog) with musical fervour, walked through pools of water and hillocks of mud, till they covered the powdered heads of the running-footmen aforesaid with splashes, that looked curious, but not ornamental; or how the barrel-organ performer put on the wrong stop, and played one tune while the band played another; or how the horses, being used to the arena, and not to the streets, would stand still and dance, instead of going on and prancing;—all of which are matters which might be dilated upon to great advantage, but which we have not the least intention of dilating upon, notwithstanding.

Oh! it was a grand and beautiful sight to behold a corporation in glass coaches, provided at the sole cost and charge of Nicholas Tulrumble, coming rolling along, like a funeral out of mourning, and to watch the attempts the corporation made to look great and solemn, when Nicholas Tulrumble himself, in the four-wheel chaise, with the tall postilion, rolled out after them, with Mr. Jennings on one side to look like a chaplain, and a supernumerary on the other, with an old life-guardsman's sabre, to imitate the sword-bearer; and to see the tears rolling down the faces of the mob as they screamed with merriment. This was beautiful! and so was the appearance of Mrs. Tulrumble and son, as they bowed with grave dignity out of their coach-window to all the dirty faces that were laughing around them: but it is not even with this that we have to do, but with the sudden stopping of the procession at another blast of the trumpet, whereat, and whereupon, a profound silence ensued, and all eyes were turned towards Mudfog Hall, in the confident anticipation of some new wonder.

"They won't laugh now, Mr. Jennings," said Nicholas Tulrumble.

"I think not, sir," said Mr. Jennings.

"See how eager they look," said Nicholas Tulrumble.

"Aha! the laugh will be on our side now; eh, Mr. Jennings?"

"No doubt of that, sir," replied Mr. Jennings; and Nicholas Tulrumble, in a state of pleasurable excitement, stood up in the four-wheel chaise, and telegraphed gratification to the Mayoress behind.

While all this was going forward, Ned Twigger had descended into the kitchen of Mudfog Hall for the purpose of indulging the servants with a private view of the curiosity that was to burst upon the town; and, somehow or other, the footman was so companionable, and the housemaid so kind, and the cook so friendly, that he could not resist the offer of the first-mentioned to sit down and take something—just to drink success to master in.

So, down Ned Twigger sat himself in his brass livery on the top of the kitchen-table; and in a mug of something strong, paid for by the unconscious Nicholas Tulrumble, and provided by the companionable footman, drank success to the Mayor and his procession; and, as Ned laid by his helmet to imbibe the something strong, the companionable footman put it on his own head, to the immeasurable and unrecordable delight of the cook and housemaid. The companionable footman was very facetious to Ned, and Ned was very gallant to the cook and housemaid by turns. They were all very cosy and comfortable; and the something strong went briskly round.

At last Ned Twigger was loudly called for, by the procession people: and, having had his helmet fixed on, in a very complicated manner, by the companionable footman, and the kind housemaid, and the friendly cook, he walked gravely forth, and appeared before the multitude.

The crowd roared—it was not with wonder, it was not with surprise; it was most decidedly and unquestionably with laughter.

"What!" said Mr. Tulrumble, starting up in the four-wheel chaise. "Laughing? If they laugh at a man in real

Ned Twigger in the Kitchen of Mudfog Hall

brass armour, they'd laugh when their own fathers were dying. Why doesn't he go into his place, Mr. Jennings? What's he rolling down towards us for? he has no business here!"

"I am afraid, sir——" faltered Mr. Jennings.

"Afraid of what, sir?" said Nicholas Tulrumble, looking up into the secretary's face.

"I am afraid he's drunk, sir," replied Mr. Jennings.

Nicholas Tulrumble took one look at the extraordinary figure that was bearing down upon them; and then, clasping his secretary by the arm, uttered an audible groan in anguish of spirit.

It is a melancholy fact that Mr. Twigger having full licence to demand a single glass of rum on the putting on of every piece of the armour, got, by some means or other, rather out of his calculation in the hurry and confusion of preparation, and drank about four glasses to a piece instead of one, not to mention the something strong which went on the top of it. Whether the brass armour checked the natural flow of perspiration, and thus prevented the spirit from evaporating, we are not scientific enough to know; but, whatever the cause was, Mr. Twigger no sooner found himself outside the gate of Mudfog Hall, than he also found himself in a very considerable state of intoxication; and hence his extraordinary style of progressing. This was bad enough, but, as if fate and fortune had conspired against Nicholas Tulrumble, Mr. Twigger, not having been penitent for a good calendar month, took it into his head to be most especially and particularly sentimental, just when his repentance could have been most conveniently dispensed with. Immense tears were rolling down his cheeks, and he was vainly endeavouring to conceal his grief by applying to his eyes a blue cotton pocket-hand-kerchief with white spots,—an article not strictly in keeping with a suit of armour some three hundred years old, or thereabouts.

"Twigger, you villain!" said Nicholas Tulrumble, quite forgetting his dignity, "go back."

"Never," said Ned. "I'm a miserable wretch. I'll never leave you."

The by-standers of course received this declaration with acclamations of "That's right, Ned; don't!"

"I don't intend it," said Ned, with all the obstinacy of a very tipsy man. "I'm very unhappy. I'm the wretched father of an unfortunate family; but I am very faithful, sir. I'll never leave you." Having reiterated this obliging promise, Ned proceeded in broken words to harangue the crowd upon the number of years he had lived in Mudfog, the excessive respectability of his character, and other topics of the like nature.

"Here! will anybody lead him away?" said Nicholas: "if they'll call on me afterwards, I'll reward them well."

Two or three men stepped forward, with the view of bearing Ned off, when the secretary interposed.

"Take care! take care!" said Mr. Jennings. "I beg your pardon, sir; but they'd better not go too near him, because, if he falls over, he'll certainly crush somebody."

At this hint the crowd retired on all sides to a very respectful distance, and left Ned, like the Duke of Devonshire, in a little circle of his own.

"But, Mr. Jennings," said Nicholas Tulrumble, "he'll be suffocated."

"I'm very sorry for it, sir," replied Mr. Jennings; "but nobody can get that armour off, without his own assistance. I'm quite certain of it from the way he put it on."

Here Ned wept dolefully, and shook his helmeted head, in a manner that might have touched a heart of stone; but the crowd had not hearts of stone, and they laughed heartily.

"Dear me, Mr. Jennings," said Nicholas, turning pale at the possibility of Ned's being smothered in his antique costume —"Dear me, Mr. Jennings, can nothing be done with him?"

"Nothing at all," replied Ned, "nothing at all. Gentlemen, I'm an unhappy wretch. I'm a body, gentlemen, in a brass coffin." At this poetical idea of his own conjuring up,

Ned cried so much that the people began to get sympathetic, and to ask what Nicholas Tulrumble meant by putting a man into such a machine as that; and one individual in a hairy waistcoat like the top of a trunk, who had previously expressed his opinion that if Ned hadn't been a poor man, Nicholas wouldn't have dared do it, hinted at the propriety of breaking the four-wheel chaise, or Nicholas's head, or both, which last compound proposition the crowd seemed to consider a very good notion.

It was not acted upon, however, for it had hardly been broached, when Ned Twigger's wife made her appearance abruptly in the little circle before noticed, and Ned no sooner caught a glimpse of her face and form, than from the mere force of habit he set off towards his home just as fast as his legs could carry him; and that was not very quick in the present instance either, for, however ready they might have been to carry *him*, they couldn't get on very well under the brass armour. So, Mrs. Twigger had plenty of time to denounce Nicholas Tulrumble to his face: to express her opinion that he was a decided monster; and to intimate that, if her ill-used husband sustained any personal damage from the brass armour, she would have the law of Nicholas Tulrumble for manslaughter. When she had said all this with due vehemence, she posted after Ned, who was dragging himself along as best he could, and deploring his unhappiness in most dismal tones.

What a wailing and screaming Ned's children raised when he got home at last! Mrs. Twigger tried to undo the armour, first in one place, and then in another, but she couldn't manage it; so she tumbled Ned into bed, helmet, armour, gauntlets, and all. Such a creaking as the bedstead made, under Ned's weight in his new suit! It didn't break down though; and there Ned lay, like the anonymous vessel in the Bay of Biscay, till next day, drinking barley-water, and looking miserable: and every time he groaned, his good lady said it served him right, which was all the consolation Ned Twigger got.

Nicholas Tulrumble and the gorgeous procession went on together to the town-hall, amid the hisses and groans of all the spectators, who had suddenly taken it into their heads to consider poor Ned a martyr. Nicholas was formally installed in his new office, in acknowledgment of which ceremony he delivered himself of a speech, composed by the secretary, which was very long, and no doubt very good, only the noise of the people outside prevented anybody from hearing it, but Nicholas Tulrumble himself. After which, the procession got back to Mudfog Hall any how it could; and Nicholas and the corporation sat down to dinner.

But the dinner was flat, and Nicholas was disappointed. They were such dull sleepy old fellows, that corporation. Nicholas made quite as long speeches as the Lord Mayor of London had done, nay, he said the very same things that the Lord Mayor of London had said, and the deuce a cheer the corporation gave him. There was only one man in the party who was thoroughly awake; and he was insolent, and called him Nick. Nick! What would be the consequence, thought Nicholas, of anybody presuming to call the Lord Mayor of London "Nick!" He should like to know what the sword-bearer would say to that; or the recorder, or the toast-master, or any other of the great officers of the city. They'd nick him.

But these were not the worst of Nicholas Tulrumble's doings. If they had been, he might have remained a Mayor to this day, and have talked till he lost his voice. He contracted a relish for statistics, and got philosophical; and the statistics and the philosophy together, led him into an act which increased his unpopularity and hastened his downfall.

At the very end of the Mudfog High-street, and abutting on the river-side, stands the Jolly Boatmen, an old-fashioned low-roofed, bay-windowed house, with a bar, kitchen, and tap-room all in one, and a large fireplace with a kettle to correspond, round which the working men have congregated time out of mind on a winter's night, refreshed by draughts of good strong beer, and cheered by the sounds of a fiddle and tambourine : the Jolly Boatmen having been duly licensed by the Mayor and corporation, to scrape the fiddle and thumb the tambourine from time, whereof the memory of the oldest inhabitants goeth not to the contrary. Now Nicholas Tulrumble had been reading pamphlets on crime, and parliamentary reports,—or had made the secretary read them to him, which is the same thing in effect,—and he at once perceived that this fiddle and tambourine must have done more to demoralize Mudfog, than any other operating causes that ingenuity could imagine. So he read up for the subject, and determined to come out on the corporation with a burst, the very next time the licence was applied for.

The licensing day came, and the red-faced landlord of the Jolly Boatmen walked into the town-hall, looking as jolly as need be, having actually put on an extra fiddle for that night, to commemorate the anniversary of the Jolly Boatmen's music licence. It was applied for in due form, and was just about to be granted as a matter of course, when up rose Nicholas Tulrumble, and drowned the astonished corporation in a torrent of eloquence. He descanted in glowing terms upon the increasing depravity of his native town of Mudfog, and the excesses committed by its population. Then, he related how shocked he had been, to see barrels of beer sliding down into the cellar of the Jolly Boatmen week after week ; and how he had sat at a window opposite the Jolly Boatmen for two days together, to count the people who went in for beer between the hours of twelve and one o'clock alone—which, by-the-bye, was the time at which the great majority of the Mudfog people dined. Then, he went on to state, how the number of people who came out with beer-jugs, averaged twenty-one in five minutes, which, being multiplied by twelve, gave two hundred and fifty-two people with beer-jugs in an hour, and multiplied again by fifteen (the number of hours during which the house was open daily) yielded three thousand seven hundred and eighty people with beer-jugs per day, or twenty-six thousand four hundred and sixty people with beer-jugs, per week. Then he proceeded to show that a tambourine and moral degradation were synonymous terms, and a fiddle and vicious propensities wholly inseparable. All these arguments he strengthened and demonstrated by frequent references to a large book with a blue cover, and sundry quotations from the Middlesex magistrates; and in the end, the corporation, who were posed with the figures, and sleepy with the speech, and sadly in want of dinner into the bargain, yielded the palm to Nicholas Tulrumble, and refused the music licence to the Jolly Boatmen.

But although Nicholas triumphed, his triumph was short. He carried on the war against beer-jugs and fiddles, forgetting the time when he was glad to drink out of the one, and to dance to the other, till the people hated, and his old friends shunned him. He grew tired of the lonely magnificence of Mudfog Hall, and his heart yearned towards the Lighterman's Arms. He wished he had never set up as a public man, and sighed for the good old times of the coal-shop, and the chimney corner.

At length old Nicholas, being thoroughly miserable, took heart of grace, paid the secretary a quarter's wages in advance, and packed him off to London by the next coach. Having taken this step, he put his hat on his head, and his pride in his pocket, and walked down to the old room at the Lighterman's Arms. There were only two of the old fellows there, and they looked coldly on Nicholas as he proffered his hand.

"Are you going to put down pipes, Mr. Tulrumble?" said one.

"Or trace the progress of crime to 'bacca?" growled another.

"Neither," replied Nicholas Tulrumble, shaking hands with them both, whether they would or not. "I've come down to say that I'm very sorry for having made a fool of myself, and that I hope you'll give me up the old chair, again."

The old fellows opened their eyes, and three or four more

old fellows opened the door, to whom Nicholas, with tears in his eyes, thrust out his hand too, and told the same story. They raised a shout of joy, that made the bells in the ancient church-tower vibrate again, and wheeling the old chair into the warm corner, thrust old Nicholas down into it, and ordered in the very largest-sized bowl of hot punch, with an unlimited number of pipes, directly.

The next day, the Jolly Boatmen got the licence, and the next night, old Nicholas and Ned Twigger's wife led off a dance to the music of the fiddle and tambourine, the tone of which seemed mightily improved by a little rest, for they never had played so merrily before. Ned Twigger was in the very height of his glory, and he danced hornpipes, and balanced chairs on his chin, and straws on his nose, till the whole company, including the corporation, were in raptures of admiration at the brilliancy of his acquirements.

Mr. Tulrumble, junior, couldn't make up his mind to be anything but magnificent, so he went up to London and drew bills on his father; and when he had overdrawn, and got into debt, he grew penitent, and came home again.

As to old Nicholas, he kept his word, and having had six weeks of public life, never tried it any more. He went to sleep in the town-hall at the very next meeting; and, in full proof of his sincerity, has requested us to write this faithful narrative. We wish it could have the effect of reminding the Tulrumbles of another sphere, that puffed-up conceit is not dignity, and that snarling at the little pleasures they were once glad to enjoy, because they would rather forget the times when they were of lower station, renders them objects of contempt and ridicule.

This is the first time we have published any of our gleanings from this particular source. Perhaps, at some future period, we may venture to open the chronicles of Mudfog.

FULL REPORT OF THE FIRST MEETING
OF THE MUDFOG ASSOCIATION
FOR THE ADVANCEMENT OF EVERYTHING

WE have made the most unparalleled and extraordinary exertions to place before our readers a complete and accurate account of the proceedings at the late grand meeting of the Mudfog Association, holden in the town of Mudfog; it affords us great happiness to lay the result before them, in the shape of various communications received from our able, talented, and graphic correspondent, expressly sent down for the purpose, who has immortalized us, himself, Mudfog, and the association, all at one and the same time. We have been, indeed, for some days unable to determine who will transmit the greatest name to posterity; ourselves, who sent our correspondent down; our correspondent, who wrote an account of the matter; or the association, who gave our correspondent something to write about. We rather incline to the opinion that we are the greatest man of the party, inasmuch as the notion of an exclusive and authentic report originated with us; this may be prejudice: it may arise from a prepossession on our part in our own favour. Be it so. We have no doubt that every gentleman concerned in this mighty assemblage is troubled with the same complaint in a greater or less degree; and it is a consolation to us to know that we have at least this feeling in common with the great scientific stars, the brilliant and extraordinary luminaries, whose speculations we record.

We give our correspondent's letters in the order in which they reached us. Any attempt at amalgamating them into one beautiful whole, would only destroy that glowing tone, that dash of wildness, and rich vein of picturesque interest, which pervade them throughout.

" Mudfog, Monday night, seven o'clock.

" WE are in a state of great excitement here. Nothing is spoken of, but the approaching meeting of the association. The inn-doors are thronged with waiters anxiously looking for the expected arrivals; and the numerous bills which are wafered up in the windows of private houses, intimating that there are beds to let within, give the streets a very animated and cheerful appearance, the wafers being of a great variety of colours, and the monotony of printed inscriptions being relieved by every possible size and style of hand-writing. It is confidently rumoured that Professors Snore, Doze, and Wheezy have engaged three beds and a sitting-room at the Pig and Tinder-box. I give you the rumour as it has reached me; but I cannot, as yet, vouch for its accuracy. The moment I have been enabled to obtain any certain information upon this interesting point, you may depend upon receiving it."

" Half-past seven.

" I HAVE just returned from a personal interview with the landlord of the Pig and Tinder-box. He speaks confidently of the probability of Professors Snore, Doze, and Wheezy taking up their residence at his house during the sitting of the association, but denies that the beds have been yet engaged; in which representation he is confirmed by the chambermaid—a girl of artless manners, and interesting appearance. The boots denies that it is at all likely that Professors Snore, Doze, and Wheezy will put up here; but I have reason to believe that this man has been suborned by the proprietor of the Original Pig, which is the opposition hotel. Amidst such conflicting testimony it is difficult to arrive at the real truth ; but you may depend upon receiving authentic information upon this point the moment the fact is ascertained. The excitement still continues. A boy fell through the window of the pastrycook's shop at the corner of the High-street about half an hour ago, which has occasioned much confusion. The general impression is, that it was an accident. Pray heaven it may prove so ! "

"*Tuesday, noon.*

"AT an early hour this morning the bells of all the churches struck seven o'clock ; the effect of which, in the present lively state of the town, was extremely singular. While I was at breakfast, a yellow gig, drawn by a dark grey horse, with a patch of white over his right eyelid, proceeded at a rapid pace in the direction of the Original Pig stables; it is currently reported that this gentleman has arrived here for the purpose of attending the association, and, from what I have heard, I consider it extremely probable, although nothing decisive is yet known regarding him. You may conceive the anxiety with which we are all looking forward to the arrival of the four o'clock coach this afternoon.

"Notwithstanding the excited state of the populace, no outrage has yet been committed, owing to the admirable discipline and discretion of the police, who are nowhere to be seen. A barrel-organ is playing opposite my window, and groups of people, offering fish and vegetables for sale, parade the streets. With these exceptions everything is quiet, and I trust will continue so."

"*Five o'clock.*

"IT is now ascertained, beyond all doubt, that Professors Snore, Doze, and Wheezy will *not* repair to the Pig and Tinder-box, but have actually engaged apartments at the

Original Pig. This intelligence is *exclusive*; and I leave you and your readers to draw their own inferences from it. Why Professor Wheezy, of all people in the world, should repair to the Original Pig in preference to the Pig and Tinder-box, it is not easy to conceive. The professor is a man who should be above all such petty feelings. Some people here openly impute treachery, and a distinct breach of faith to Professors Snore and Doze; while others, again, are disposed to acquit them of any culpability in the transaction, and to insinuate that the blame rests solely with Professor Wheezy. I own that I incline to the latter opinion; and although it gives me great pain to speak in terms of censure or disapprobation of a man of such transcendent genius and acquirements, still I am bound to say that, if my suspicions be well founded, and if all the reports which have reached my ears be true, I really do not well know what to make of the matter.

" Mr. Slug, so celebrated for his statistical researches, arrived this afternoon by the four o'clock stage. His complexion is a dark purple, and he has a habit of sighing constantly. He looked extremely well, and appeared in high health and spirits. Mr. Woodensconce also came down in the same conveyance. The distinguished gentleman was fast asleep on his arrival, and I am informed by the guard that he had been so the whole way. He was, no doubt, preparing for his approaching fatigues; but what gigantic visions must those be that flit through the brain of such a man when his body is in a state of torpidity !

" The influx of visitors increases every moment. I am told (I know not how truly) that two post-chaises have arrived at the Original Pig within the last half-hour, and I myself observed a wheelbarrow, containing three carpet bags and a bundle, entering the yard of the Pig and Tinder-box no longer ago than five minutes since. The people are still quietly pursuing their ordinary occupations; but there is a wildness in their eyes, and an unwonted rigidity in the

341

muscles of their countenances, which shows to the observant spectator that their expectations are strained to the very utmost pitch. I fear, unless some very extraordinary arrivals take place to-night, that consequences may arise from this popular ferment, which every man of sense and feeling would deplore."

" Twenty minutes past six.

" I HAVE just heard that the boy who fell through the pastrycook's window last night has died of the fright. He was suddenly called upon to pay three and sixpence for the damage done, and his constitution, it seems, was not strong enough to bear up against the shock. The inquest, it is said, will be held to-morrow."

" Three-quarters past seven.

" PROFESSORS Muff and Nogo have just driven up to the hotel door; they at once ordered dinner with great condescension. We are all very much delighted with the urbanity of their manners, and the ease with which they adapt themselves to the forms and ceremonies of ordinary life. Immediately on their arrival they sent for the head waiter, and privately requested him to purchase a live dog, —as cheap a one as he could meet with,—and to send him up after dinner, with a pie-board, a knife and fork, and a clean plate. It is conjectured that some experiments will be tried upon the dog to-night; if any particulars should transpire, I will forward them by express."

" Half-past eight.

" THE animal has been procured. He is a pug-dog, of rather intelligent appearance, in good condition, and with very short legs. He has been tied to a curtain-peg in a dark room, and is howling dreadfully."

" Ten minutes to nine.

" THE dog has just been rung for. With an instinct which would appear almost the result of reason, the sagacious animal seized the waiter by the calf of the leg when he approached to take him, and made a desperate, though ineffectual resistance. I have not been able to procure admission to the apartment occupied by the scientific gentlemen; but, judging from the sounds which reached my ears when I stood upon the landing-place outside the door, just now, I should be disposed to say that the dog had retreated growling beneath some article of furniture, and was keeping the professors at bay. This conjecture is confirmed by the testimony of the ostler, who, after peeping through the key-hole, assures me that he distinctly saw Professor Nogo on his knees, holding forth a small bottle of prussic acid, to which the animal, who was crouched beneath an arm-chair, obstinately declined to smell. You cannot imagine the feverish state of irritation we are in, lest the interests of science should be sacrificed to the prejudices of a brute creature, who is not endowed with sufficient sense to foresee the incalculable benefits which the whole human race may derive from so very slight a concession on his part."

" Nine o'clock.

" THE dog's tail and ears have been sent down-stairs to be washed; from which circumstance we infer that the animal is no more. His forelegs have been delivered to the boots to be brushed, which strengthens the supposition."

" Half after ten.

" MY feelings are so overpowered by what has taken place in the course of the last hour and a half, that I have scarcely strength to detail the rapid succession of events which have quite bewildered all those who are cognizant of their occurrence. It appears that the pug-dog mentioned in my last was surreptitiously obtained,—stolen, in fact,—by some person attached to the stable department, from an unmarried lady resident in this town. Frantic on discovering the loss of her favourite, the lady rushed distractedly into the street, calling in the most heart-rending and pathetic manner upon the passengers to restore her, her Augustus,—for so the deceased was named, in affectionate remembrance of a former lover of his mistress, to whom he bore a striking personal resemblance, which renders the circumstances additionally affecting. I am not yet in a condition to inform you what circumstance induced the bereaved lady to direct her steps to the hotel which had witnessed the last struggles of her *protégé*. I can only state that she arrived there, at the very instant when his detached members were passing through the passage on a small tray. Her shrieks still reverberate in my ears! I grieve to say that the expressive features of Professor Muff were much scratched and lacerated by the injured lady; and that Professor Nogo, besides sustaining several severe bites, has lost some handfuls of hair from the same cause. It must be some consolation to these gentlemen to know that their ardent attachment to scientific pursuits has alone occasioned these unpleasant consequences ; for which the sympathy of a grateful country will sufficiently reward them. The unfortunate lady remains at the Pig and Tinder-box, and up to this time is reported in a very precarious state.

" I need scarcely tell you that this unlooked-for catastrophe has cast a damp and gloom upon us in the midst of our exhilaration ; natural in any case, but greatly enhanced in this, by the amiable qualities of the deceased animal, who appears to have been much and deservedly respected by the whole of his acquaintance."

" Twelve o'clock.

" I TAKE the last opportunity before sealing my parcel to inform you that the boy who fell through the pastrycook's window is not dead, as was universally believed, but alive and well. The report appears to have had its origin in his mysterious disappearance. He was found half an hour since on the premises of a sweet-stuff maker, where a raffle had been announced for a second-hand seal-skin cap and a tambourine ; and where—a sufficient number of members not having been obtained at first—he had patiently waited until the list was completed. This fortunate discovery has in some degree restored our gaiety and cheerfulness. It is proposed to get up a subscription for him without delay.

"Everybody is nervously anxious to see what to-morrow will bring forth. If any one should arrive in the course of the night, I have left strict directions to be called immediately. I should have sat up, indeed, but the agitating events of this day have been too much for me.

"No news yet of either of the Professors Snore, Doze, or Wheezy. It is very strange!"

" Wednesday afternoon.

"ALL is now over; and, upon one point at least, I am at length enabled to set the minds of your readers at rest. The three professors arrived at ten minutes after two o'clock, and, instead of taking up their quarters at the Original Pig, as it was universally understood in the course of yesterday that they would assuredly have done, drove straight to the Pig and Tinder-box, where they threw off the mask at once, and openly announced their intention of remaining. Professor Wheezy *may* reconcile this very extraordinary conduct with *his* notions of fair and equitable dealing, but I would recommend Professor Wheezy to be cautious how he presumes too far upon his well-earned reputation. How such a man as Professor Snore, or, which is still more extraordinary, such an individual as Professor Doze, can quietly allow himself to be mixed up with such proceedings as these, you will naturally inquire. Upon this head, rumour is silent; I have my speculations, but forbear to give utterance to them just now."

" Four o'clock.

"THE town is filling fast; eighteenpence has been offered for a bed and refused. Several gentlemen were under the necessity last night of sleeping in the brick fields, and on the steps of doors, for which they were taken before the magistrates in a body this morning, and committed to prison as vagrants for various terms. One of these persons I understand to be a highly-respectable tinker, of great practical skill, who had forwarded a paper to the President of Section D. Mechanical Science, on the construction of pipkins with copper bottoms and safety-valves, of which report speaks highly. The incarceration of this gentleman is greatly to be regretted, as his absence will preclude any discussion on the subject.

"The bills are being taken down in all directions, and lodgings are being secured on almost any terms. I have heard of fifteen shillings a week for two rooms, exclusive of coals and attendance, but I can scarcely believe it. The excitement is dreadful. I was informed this morning that the civil authorities, apprehensive of some outbreak of popular feeling, had commanded a recruiting sergeant and two corporals to be under arms; and that, with the view of not irritating the people unnecessarily by their presence, they had been requested to take up their position before daybreak in a turnpike, distant about a quarter of a mile from the town. The vigour and promptness of these measures cannot be too highly extolled.

"Intelligence has just been brought me, that an elderly female, in a state of inebriety, has declared in the open street her intention to 'do' for Mr. Slug. Some statistical returns compiled by that gentleman, relative to the consumption of raw spirituous liquors in this place, are supposed to be the cause of the wretch's animosity. It is added that this declaration was loudly cheered by a crowd of persons who had assembled on the spot; and that one man had the boldness to designate Mr. Slug aloud by the opprobrious epithet of 'Stick-in-the-mud!' It is earnestly to be hoped that now, when the moment has arrived for their interference, the magistrates will not shrink from the exercise of that power which is vested in them by the constitution of our common country."

" Half-past ten.

" THE disturbance, I am happy to inform you, has been completely quelled, and the ringleader taken into custody. She had a pail of cold water thrown over her, previous to being locked up, and expresses great contrition and uneasiness. We are all in a fever of anticipation about to-morrow ; but, now that we are within a few hours of the meeting of the association, and at last enjoy the proud consciousness of having its illustrious members amongst us, I trust and hope everything may go off peaceably. I shall send you a full report of to-morrow's proceedings by the night coach."

" Eleven o'clock.

" I OPEN my letter to say that nothing whatever has occurred since I folded it up."

" Thursday.

" THE sun rose this morning at the usual hour. I did not observe anything particular in the aspect of the glorious planet, except that he appeared to me (it might have been a delusion of my heightened fancy) to shine with more than common brilliancy, and to shed a refulgent lustre upon the town, such as I had never observed before. This is the more extraordinary, as the sky was perfectly cloudless, and the atmosphere peculiarly fine. At half-past nine o'clock the general committee assembled, with the last year's president in the chair. The report of the council was read ; and one passage, which stated that the council had corresponded with no less than three thousand five hundred and seventy-one persons, (all of whom paid their own postage,) on no fewer than seven thousand two hundred and forty-three topics, was received with a degree of enthusiasm which no efforts could suppress. The various committees and sections having been appointed, and the more formal business transacted, the great proceedings of the meeting commenced at eleven o'clock precisely. I had the happiness of occupying a most eligible position at that time, in

"SECTION A. —ZOOLOGY AND BOTANY.

GREAT ROOM, PIG AND TINDER-BOX.

President—Professor Snore.   *Vice-Presidents*—Professors Doze and Wheezy.

"The scene at this moment was particularly striking. The sun streamed through the windows of the apartments, and tinted the whole scene with its brilliant rays, bringing out in strong relief the noble visages of the professors and scientific gentlemen, who, some with bald heads, some with red heads, some with brown heads, some with grey heads, some with black heads, some with block heads, presented a *coup d'œil* which no eye-witness will readily forget. In front of these gentlemen were papers and inkstands; and round the room, on elevated benches extending as far as the forms could reach, were assembled a brilliant concourse of those lovely and elegant women for which Mudfog is justly acknowledged to be without a rival in the whole world. The contrast between their fair faces and the dark coats and trousers of the scientific gentlemen I shall never cease to remember while Memory holds her seat.

"Time having been allowed for a slight confusion, occasioned by the falling down of the greater part of the platforms, to subside, the president called on one of the secretaries to read a communication entitled, 'Some remarks on the industrious fleas, with considerations on the importance of establishing infant-schools among that numerous class of society; of directing their industry to useful and practical ends; and of applying the surplus fruits thereof, towards providing for them a comfortable and respectable maintenance in their old age.'

"The author stated, that, having long turned his attention to the moral and social condition of these interesting animals, he had been induced to visit an exhibition in Regent-street, London, commonly known by the designation of 'The Industrious Fleas.' He had there seen many fleas, occupied certainly in various pursuits and avocations, but occupied, he was bound to add, in a manner which no man of well-regulated mind could fail to regard with sorrow and regret. One flea, reduced to the level of a beast of burden, was drawing about a miniature gig, containing a particularly small effigy of His Grace the Duke of Wellington; while another was staggering beneath the weight of a golden model of his great adversary Napoleon Bonaparte. Some, brought up as mountebanks and ballet-dancers, were performing a figure-dance (he regretted to observe, that, of the fleas so employed, several were females); others were in training, in a small card-board box, for pedestrians,—mere sporting characters—and two were actually engaged in the cold-blooded and barbarous occupation of duelling; a pursuit from which humanity recoiled with horror and disgust. He suggested that measures should be immediately taken to employ the labour of these fleas as part and parcel of the productive power of the country, which might easily be done by the establishment among them of infant schools and houses of industry, in which a system of virtuous education, based upon sound principles, should be observed, and moral precepts strictly inculcated. He proposed that every flea who presumed to exhibit, for hire, music, or dancing, or any species of theatrical entertainment, without a licence, should be considered a vagabond, and treated accordingly; in which respect he only placed him upon a level with the rest of mankind. He would further suggest that their labour should be placed under the control and regulation of the state, who should set apart from the profits, a fund for the support of superannuated or disabled fleas, their widows and orphans. With this view, he proposed that liberal premiums should be offered for the three best designs for a general almshouse; from which—as insect architecture was well known to be in a very advanced and perfect state—we might possibly derive many valuable hints for the improvement of our metropolitan universities, national galleries, and other public edifices.

"THE PRESIDENT wished to be informed how the ingenious gentleman proposed to open a communication with fleas generally, in the first instance, so that they might be thoroughly imbued with a sense of the advantages they must necessarily derive from changing their mode of life, and applying themselves to honest labour. This appeared to him, the only difficulty.

"THE AUTHOR submitted that this difficulty was easily overcome, or rather that there was no difficulty at all in the case. Obviously the course to be pursued, if Her Majesty's government could be prevailed upon to take up the plan, would be, to secure at a remunerative salary the individual to whom he had alluded as presiding over the exhibition in Regent-street at the period of his visit. That gentleman would at once be able to put himself in communication with the mass of the fleas, and to instruct them in pursuance of some general plan of education, to be sanctioned by Parliament, until such time as the more intelligent among them were advanced enough to officiate as teachers to the rest.

"The President and several members of the section highly complimented the author of the paper last read, on his most ingenious and important treatise. It was determined that the subject should be recommended to the immediate consideration of the council.

"MR. WIGSBY produced a cauliflower somewhat larger than a chaise-umbrella, which had been raised by no other artificial means than the simple application of highly carbonated soda-water as manure. He explained that by scooping out the head, which would afford a new and delicious species of nourishment for the poor, a parachute, in principle something similar to that constructed by M. Garnerin, was at once obtained; the stalk of course being kept downwards. He added that he was perfectly willing to make a descent from a height of not less than three miles and a quarter; and had in fact already proposed the same to the proprietors of Vauxhall Gardens, who in the handsomest manner at once consented to his wishes, and appointed an early day next summer for the undertaking; merely stipulating that the rim of the cauliflower should be previously broken in three or four places to ensure the safety of the descent.

"THE PRESIDENT congratulated the public on the *grand gala* in store for them, and warmly eulogised the proprietors of the establishment alluded to, for their love of science, and regard for the safety of human life, both of which did them the highest honour.

"A Member wished to know how many thousand additional lamps the royal property would be illuminated with, on the night after the descent.

"MR. WIGSBY replied that the point was not yet finally decided; but he believed it was proposed, over and above the ordinary illuminations, to exhibit in various devices eight millions and a-half of additional lamps.

"The Member expressed himself much gratified with this announcement.

"MR. BLUNDERUM delighted the section with a most interesting and valuable paper 'on the last moments of the learned pig,' which produced a very strong impression on the assembly, the account being compiled from the personal recollections of his favourite attendant. The account stated in the most emphatic terms that the animal's name was not Toby, but Solomon; and distinctly proved that he could have no near relatives in the profession, as many designing persons had falsely stated, inasmuch as his father, mother, brothers and sisters, had all fallen victims to the butcher at different times. An uncle of his indeed, had with very great labour been traced to a sty in Somers Town; but as he was in a very infirm state at the time, being afflicted with measles, and shortly afterwards disappeared, there appeared too much reason to conjecture that he had been converted into sausages.

REPORT OF THE FIRST MEETING

The disorder of the learned pig was originally a severe cold, which, being aggravated by excessive trough indulgence, finally settled upon the lungs, and terminated in a general decay of the constitution. A melancholy instance of a presentiment entertained by the animal of his approaching dissolution, was recorded. After gratifying a numerous and fashionable company with his performances, in which no falling off whatever was visible, he fixed his eyes on the biographer, and, turning to the watch which lay on the floor, and on which he was accustomed to point out the hour, deliberately passed his snout twice round the dial. In precisely four-and-twenty hours from that time he had ceased to exist!

"PROFESSOR WHEEZY inquired whether, previous to his demise, the animal had expressed, by signs or otherwise, any wishes regarding the disposal of his little property.

"MR. BLUNDERUM replied, that, when the biographer took up the pack of cards at the conclusion of the performance, the animal grunted several times in a significant manner, and nodding his head as he was accustomed to do, when gratified. From these gestures it was understood that he wished the attendant to keep the cards, which he had ever since done. He had not expressed any wish relative to his watch, which had accordingly been pawned by the same individual.

"THE PRESIDENT wished to know whether any Member of the section had ever seen or conversed with the pig-faced lady, who was reported to have worn a black velvet mask, and to have taken her meals from a golden trough.

"After some hesitation a Member replied that the pig-faced lady was his mother-in-law, and that he trusted the President would not violate the sanctity of private life.

"THE PRESIDENT begged pardon. He had considered the pig-faced lady a public character. Would the honourable member object to state, with a view to the advancement of science, whether she was in any way connected with the learned pig?

"The Member replied in the same low tone, that, as the question appeared to involve a suspicion that the learned pig might be his half-brother, he must decline answering it.

"SECTION B.—ANATOMY AND MEDICINE.

COACH-HOUSE, PIG AND TINDER-BOX.

President—Dr. Toorell. *Vice-Presidents*—Professors Muff and Nogo.

"DR. KUTANKUMAGEN (of Moscow) read to the section a report of a case which had occurred within his own practice, strikingly illustrative of the power of medicine, as exemplified in his successful treatment of a virulent disorder. He had been called in to visit the patient on the 1st of April, 1837. He was then labouring under symptoms peculiarly alarming to any medical man. His frame was stout and muscular, his step firm and elastic, his cheeks plump and red, his voice loud, his appetite good, his pulse full and round. He was in the constant habit of eating three meals *per diem*, and of drinking at least one bottle of wine, and one glass of spirituous liquors diluted with water, in the course of the four-and-twenty hours. He laughed constantly, and in so hearty a manner that it was terrible to hear him. By dint of powerful medicine, low diet, and bleeding, the symptoms in the course of three days perceptibly decreased. A rigid perseverance in the same course of treatment for only one week, accompanied with small doses of water-gruel, weak broth, and barley-water, led to their entire disappearance. In the course of a month he was sufficiently recovered to be carried down-stairs by two nurses, and to enjoy an airing in a close carriage, supported by soft pillows. At the present moment he was restored so far as to walk about, with the slight assistance of a crutch and a boy. It would perhaps be gratifying to the section to learn that he ate little, drank little, slept little, and was never heard to laugh by any accident whatever.

"DR. W. R. FEE, in complimenting the honourable member

upon the triumphant cure he had effected, begged to ask whether the patient still bled freely?

"Dr. Kutankumagen replied in the affirmative.

"Dr. W. R. Fee.—And you found that he bled freely during the whole course of the disorder?

"Dr. Kutankumagen.—Oh dear, yes; most freely.

"Dr. Neeshawts supposed, that if the patient had not submitted to be bled with great readiness and perseverance, so extraordinary a cure could never, in fact, have been accomplished. Dr. Kutankumagen rejoined, certainly not.

"Mr. Knight Bell (M.R.C.S.) exhibited a wax preparation of the interior of a gentleman who in early life had inadvertently swallowed a door-key. It was a curious fact that a medical student of dissipated habits, being present at the *post mortem* examination, found means to escape unobserved from the room, with that portion of the coats of the stomach upon which an exact model of the instrument was distinctly impressed, with which he hastened to a locksmith of doubtful character, who made a new key from the pattern so shown to him. With this key the medical student entered the house of the deceased gentleman, and committed a burglary to a large amount, for which he was subsequently tried and executed.

"The President wished to know what became of the original key after the lapse of years. Mr. Knight Bell replied that the gentleman was always much accustomed to punch, and it was supposed the acid had gradually devoured it.

"Dr. Neeshawts and several of the members were of opinion that the key must have lain very cold and heavy upon the gentleman's stomach.

"Mr. Knight Bell believed it did at first. It was worthy of remark, perhaps, that for some years the gentleman was troubled with a night-mare, under the influence of which he always imagined himself a wine-cellar door.

"Professor Muff related a very extraordinary and

convincing proof of the wonderful efficacy of the system of infinitesimal doses, which the section were doubtless aware was based upon the theory that the very minutest amount of any given drug, properly dispersed through the human frame, would be productive of precisely the same result as a very large dose administered in the usual manner. Thus, the fortieth part of a grain of calomel was supposed to be equal to a five-grain calomel pill, and so on in proportion throughout the whole range of medicine. He had tried the experiment in a curious manner upon a publican who had been brought into the hospital with a broken head, and was cured upon the infinitesimal system in the incredibly short space of three months. This man was a hard drinker. He (Professor Muff) had dispersed three drops of rum through a bucket of water, and requested the man to drink the whole. What was the result? Before he had drunk a quart, he was in a state of beastly intoxication; and five other men were made dead drunk with the remainder.

"THE PRESIDENT wished to know whether an infinitesimal dose of soda-water would have recovered them? Professor Muff replied that the twenty-fifth part of a teaspoonful, properly administered to each patient, would have sobered him immediately. The President remarked that this was a most important discovery, and he hoped the Lord Mayor and Court of Aldermen would patronize it immediately.

"A Member begged to be informed whether it would be possible to administer—say, the twentieth part of a grain of bread and cheese to all grown-up paupers, and the fortieth part to children, with the same satisfying effect as their present allowance.

"PROFESSOR MUFF was willing to stake his professional reputation on the perfect adequacy of such a quantity of food to the support of human life—in workhouses; the addition of the fifteenth part of a grain of pudding twice a week would render it a high diet.

"PROFESSOR NOGO called the attention of the section to a

very extraordinary case of animal magnetism. A private watchman, being merely looked at by the operator from the opposite side of a wide street, was at once observed to be in a very drowsy and languid state. He was followed to his box, and being once slightly rubbed on the palms of the hands, fell into a sound sleep, in which he continued without intermission for ten hours.

"SECTION C.—STATISTICS.

HAY-LOFT, ORIGINAL PIG.

President—Mr. Woodensconce. *Vice-Presidents*—Mr. Ledbrain and Mr. Timbered.

"MR. SLUG stated to the section the result of some calculations he had made with great difficulty and labour, regarding the state of infant education among the middle classes of London. He found that, within a circle of three miles from the Elephant and Castle, the following were the names and numbers of children's books principally in circulation:—

"Jack the Giant-killer	.	.	.	7,943
Ditto and Bean-stalk	.	.	.	8,621
Ditto and Eleven Brothers	.	.	.	2,845
Ditto and Jill	.	.	.	1,998
Total	.	.	.	21,407

"He found that the proportion of Robinson Crusoes to Philip Quarlls was as four and a half to one; and that the preponderance of Valentine and Orsons over Goody Two Shoeses was as three and an eighth of the former to half a one of the latter; a comparison of Seven Champions with Simple Simons gave the same result. The ignorance that prevailed, was lamentable. One child, on being asked whether he would rather be Saint George of England or a respectable tallow-chandler, instantly replied, 'Taint George of Ingling.' Another, a little boy of eight years old, was found to be firmly impressed with a belief in the existence of dragons, and openly stated that it was his intention when he grew up, to rush forth sword in hand for the deliverance of captive princesses, and the promiscuous slaughter of giants. Not one child among the number interrogated had ever heard of Mungo Park,—some inquiring whether he was at all connected with the black man that swept the crossing; and others whether he was in any way related to the Regent's Park. They had not the slightest conception of the commonest principles of mathematics, and considered Sindbad the Sailor the most enterprising voyager that the world had ever produced.

"A Member strongly deprecating the use of all the other books mentioned, suggested that Jack and Jill might perhaps be exempted from the general censure, inasmuch as the hero and heroine, in the very outset of the tale, were depicted as going *up* a hill to fetch a pail of water, which was a laborious and useful occupation,—supposing the family linen was being washed, for instance.

"MR. SLUG feared that the moral effect of this passage was more than counterbalanced by another in a subsequent part of the poem, in which very gross allusion was made to the mode in which the heroine was personally chastised by her mother

"'For laughing at Jack's disaster;'

besides, the whole work had this one great fault, *it was not true*.

"THE PRESIDENT complimented the honourable member on the excellent distinction he had drawn. Several other Members, too, dwelt upon the immense and urgent necessity of storing the minds of children with nothing but facts and figures; which process the President very forcibly remarked, had made them (the section) the men they were.

"MR. SLUG then stated some curious calculations respecting the dogs'-meat barrows of London. He found that the total number of small carts and barrows engaged in dispensing provision to the cats and dogs of the metropolis was one thousand seven hundred and forty-three. The average number of skewers delivered daily with the provender, by each dogs'-meat cart or barrow, was thirty-six. Now, multiplying the number of skewers so delivered by the number of barrows, a total of sixty-two thousand seven hundred and forty-eight skewers daily would be obtained. Allowing that, of these sixty-two thousand seven hundred and forty-eight skewers, the odd two thousand seven hundred and forty-eight were accidentally devoured with the meat, by the most voracious of the animals supplied, it followed that sixty thousand skewers per day, or the enormous number of twenty-one millions nine hundred thousand skewers annually, were wasted in the kennels and dustholes of London; which, if collected and warehoused, would in ten years' time afford a mass of timber more than sufficient for the construction of a first-rate vessel of war for the use of her Majesty's navy, to be called 'The Royal Skewer,' and to become under that name the terror of all the enemies of this island.

"MR. X. LEDBRAIN read a very ingenious communication, from which it appeared that the total number of legs belonging to the manufacturing population of one great town in Yorkshire was, in round numbers, forty thousand, while the total number of chair and stool legs in their houses was only thirty thousand, which, upon the very favourable average of three legs to a seat, yielded only ten thousand seats in all. From this calculation it would appear,—not taking wooden or cork legs into the account, but allowing two legs to every person,—that ten thousand individuals (one-half of the whole population) were either destitute of any rest for their legs at all, or passed the whole of their leisure time in sitting upon boxes.

"SECTION D.—MECHANICAL SCIENCE.

COACH-HOUSE, ORIGINAL PIG.

President—Mr. Carter. *Vice-Presidents*—Mr. Truck and Mr. Waghorn.

"PROFESSOR QUEERSPECK exhibited an elegant model of a portable railway, neatly mounted in a green case, for the waistcoat pocket. By attaching this beautiful instrument to his boots, any Bank or public-office clerk could transport himself from his place of residence to his place of business, at the easy rate of sixty-five miles an hour, which, to gentlemen of sedentary pursuits, would be an incalculable advantage.

"The President was desirous of knowing whether it was necessary to have a level surface on which the gentleman was to run.

"Professor Queerspeck explained that City gentlemen would run in trains, being handcuffed together to prevent confusion or unpleasantness. For instance, trains would start every morning at eight, nine, and ten o'clock, from Camden Town, Islington, Camberwell, Hackney, and various other places in which City gentlemen are accustomed to reside. It would be necessary to have a level, but he had provided for this difficulty by proposing that the best line that the circumstances would admit of, should be taken through the sewers which undermine the streets of the metropolis, and which, well lighted by jets from the gas pipes which run immediately above them, would form a pleasant and commodious arcade, especially in winter-time, when the inconvenient custom of carrying umbrellas, now so general, could be wholly dispensed with. In reply to another question, Professor Queerspeck stated that no substitute for the purposes to which these arcades were at present devoted had yet occurred to him, but that he hoped no fanciful objection on this head would be allowed to interfere with so great an undertaking.

"Mr. Jobba produced a forcing-machine on a novel plan, for bringing joint-stock railway shares prematurely to a premium. The instrument was in the form of an elegant gilt weather-glass, of most dazzling appearance, and was worked behind, by strings, after the manner of a pantomime trick, the strings being always pulled by the directors of the company to which the machine belonged. The quicksilver was so ingeniously placed, that when the acting directors held shares in their pockets, figures denoting very small expenses and very large returns appeared upon the glass; but the moment the directors parted with these pieces of paper, the estimate of needful expenditure suddenly increased itself to an immense extent, while the statements of certain profits became reduced in the same proportion. Mr. Jobba stated that the machine had been in constant requisition for some months past, and he had never once known it to fail.

"A Member expressed his opinion that it was extremely neat and pretty. He wished to know whether it was not liable to accidental derangement? Mr. Jobba said that the whole machine was undoubtedly liable to be blown up, but that was the only objection to it.

"Professor Nogo arrived from the anatomical section to exhibit a model of a safety fire-escape, which could be fixed at any time, in less than half an hour, and by means of which, the youngest or most infirm persons (successfully resisting the progress of the flames until it was quite ready) could be preserved if they merely balanced themselves for a few minutes on the sill of their bedroom window, and got into the escape without falling into the street. The Professor stated that the number of boys who had been rescued in the daytime by this machine from houses which were not on fire, was almost incredible. Not a conflagration had occurred in the whole of London for many months past to which the escape had not been carried on the very next day, and put in action before a concourse of persons.

"The President inquired whether there was not some difficulty in ascertaining which was the top of the machine, and which the bottom, in cases of pressing emergency.

"Professor Nogo explained that of course it could not be expected to act quite as well when there was a fire, as when there was not a fire; but in the former case he thought it would be of equal service whether the top were up or down."

With the last section our correspondent concludes his most able and faithful Report, which will never cease to reflect credit upon him for his scientific attainments, and upon us for our enterprising spirit. It is needless to take a review of the subjects which have been discussed ; of the mode in which they have been examined ; of the great truths which they have elicited. They are now before the world, and we leave them to read, to consider, and to profit.

The place of meeting for next year has undergone discussion, and has at length been decided, regard being had to, and evidence being taken upon, the goodness of its wines, the supply of its markets, the hospitality of its inhabitants, and the quality of its hotels. We hope at this next meeting our correspondent may again be present, and that we may be once more the means of placing his communications before the world. Until that period we have been prevailed upon to allow this number of our Miscellany to be retailed to the public, or wholesaled to the trade, without any advance upon our usual price.

We have only to add, that the committees are now broken up, and that Mudfog is once again restored to its accustomed tranquillity,—that Professors and Members have had balls, and *soirées*, and suppers, and great mutual complimentations, and have at length dispersed to their several homes,—whither all good wishes and joys attend them, until next year !

Signed **Boz.**

FULL REPORT OF THE SECOND MEETING
OF THE MUDFOG ASSOCIATION

FOR THE ADVANCEMENT OF EVERYTHING

In October last, we did ourselves the immortal credit of re-
cording, at an enormous expense, and by dint of exertions
unparalleled in the history of periodical publication, the proceedings of the Mudfog Association for the Advancement of
Everything, which in that month held its first great half-
yearly meeting, to the wonder and delight of the whole
empire. We announced at the conclusion of that extraordinary and most remarkable Report, that when the Second
Meeting of the Society should take place, we should be found
again at our post, renewing our gigantic and spirited
endeavours, and once more making the world ring with the
accuracy, authenticity, immeasurable superiority, and intense
remarkability of our account of its proceedings. In redemp-
tion of this pledge, we caused to be despatched per steam to
Oldcastle (at which place this second meeting of the Society
was held on the 20th instant), the same superhumanly-
endowed gentleman who furnished the former report, and
who,—gifted by nature with transcendent abilities, and
furnished by us with a body of assistants scarcely·inferior to
himself,—has forwarded a series of letters, which, for faith-
fulness of description, power of language, fervour of thought,
happiness of expression, and importance of subject-matter,

have no equal in the epistolary literature of any age or country. We give this gentleman's correspondence entire, and in the order in which it reached our office.

" Saloon of Steamer, Thursday night, half-past eight.

" WHEN I left New Burlington Street this evening in the hackney cabriolet, number four thousand two hundred and eighty-five, I experienced sensations as novel as they were oppressive. A sense of the importance of the task I had undertaken, a consciousness that I was leaving London, and, stranger still, going somewhere else, a feeling of loneliness and a sensation of jolting, quite bewildered my thoughts, and for a time rendered me even insensible to the presence of my carpet-bag and hat-box. I shall ever feel grateful to the driver of a Blackwall omnibus who, by thrusting the pole of his vehicle through the small door of the cabriolet, awakened me from a tumult of imaginings that are wholly indescribable. But of such materials is our imperfect nature composed !

" I am happy to say that I am the first passenger on board, and shall thus be enabled to give you an account of all that happens in the order of its occurrence. The chimney is smoking a good deal, and so are the crew ; and the captain, I am informed, is very drunk in a little house upon deck, something like a black turnpike. I should infer from all I hear that he has got the steam up.

" You will readily guess with what feelings I have just made the discovery that my berth is in the same closet with those engaged by Professor Woodensconce, Mr. Slug, and Professor Grime. Professor Woodensconce has taken the shelf above me, and Mr. Slug and Professor Grime the two shelves opposite. Their luggage has already arrived. On Mr. Slug's bed is a long tin tube of about three inches in diameter, carefully closed at both ends. What can this contain ? Some powerful instrument of a new construction, doubtless."

REPORT OF THE SECOND MEETING

" Ten minutes past nine.

"NOBODY has yet arrived, nor has anything fresh come in my way except several joints of beef and mutton, from which I conclude that a good plain dinner has been provided for to-morrow. There is a singular smell below, which gave me some uneasiness at first; but as the steward says it is always there, and never goes away, I am quite comfortable again. I learn from this man that the different sections will be distributed at the Black Boy and Stomach-ache, and the Boot-jack and Countenance. If this intelligence be true (and I have no reason to doubt it), your readers will draw such conclusions as their different opinions may suggest.

"I write down these remarks as they occur to me, or as the facts come to my knowledge, in order that my first impressions may lose nothing of their original vividness. I shall despatch them in small packets as opportunities arise."

" Half-past nine.

"SOME dark object has just appeared upon the wharf. I think it is a travelling carriage."

" A quarter to ten.

"No, it isn't."

" Half-past ten.

"THE passengers are pouring in every instant. Four omnibuses full have just arrived upon the wharf, and all is bustle and activity. The noise and confusion are very great. Cloths are laid in the cabins, and the steward is placing blue plates-full of knobs of cheese at equal distances down the centre of the tables. He drops a great many knobs; but, being used to it, picks them up again with great dexterity, and, after wiping them on his sleeve, throws them back into the plates. He is a young man of exceedingly prepossessing appearance—either dirty or a mulatto, but I think the former.

"An interesting old gentleman, who came to the wharf in an omnibus, has just quarrelled violently with the porters, and is staggering towards the vessel with a large trunk in his arms. I trust and hope that he may reach it in safety; but the board he has to cross is narrow and slippery. Was that a splash? Gracious powers!

"I have just returned from the deck. The trunk is standing upon the extreme brink of the wharf, but the old gentleman is nowhere to be seen. The watchman is not sure whether he went down or not, but promises to drag for him the first thing to-morrow morning. May his humane efforts prove successful!

"Professor Nogo has this moment arrived with his nightcap on under his hat. He has ordered a glass of cold brandy and water, with a hard biscuit and a basin, and has gone straight to bed. What can this mean?

"The three other scientific gentlemen to whom I have already alluded have come on board, and have all tried their beds, with the exception of Professor Woodensconce, who sleeps in one of the top ones, and can't get into it. Mr. Slug, who sleeps in the other top one, is unable to get out of his, and is to have his supper handed up by a boy. I have had the honour to introduce myself to these gentlemen, and we have amicably arranged the order in which we shall retire to rest; which it is necessary to agree upon, because, although the cabin is very comfortable, there is not room for more than one gentleman to be out of bed at a time, and even he must take his boots off in the passage.

"As I anticipated, the knobs of cheese were provided for the passengers' supper, and are now in course of consumption. Your readers will be surprised to hear that Professor Woodensconce has abstained from cheese for eight years, although he takes butter in considerable quantities. Professor Grime having lost several teeth, is unable, I observe, to eat his crusts without previously soaking them in his bottled porter. How interesting are these peculiarities!"

" *Half-past eleven.*

"PROFESSORS Woodensconce and Grime, with a degree of good humour that delights us all, have just arranged to toss for a bottle of mulled port. There has been some discussion whether the payment should be decided by the first toss or the best out of three. Eventually the latter course has been determined on. Deeply do I wish that both gentlemen could win; but that being impossible, I own that my personal aspirations (I speak as an individual, and do not compromise either you or your readers by this expression of feeling) are with Professor Woodensconce. I have backed that gentleman to the amount of eighteenpence."

" Twenty minutes to twelve.

"PROFESSOR Grime has inadvertently tossed his half-crown out of one of the cabin-windows, and it has been arranged that the steward shall toss for him. Bets are offered on any side to any amount, but there are no takers.

"Professor Woodensconce has just called 'woman;' but the coin having lodged in a beam, is a long time coming down again. The interest and suspense of this one moment are beyond anything that can be imagined."

" Twelve o'clock.

"THE mulled port is smoking on the table before me, and Professor Grime has won. Tossing is a game of chance; but on every ground, whether of public or private character, intellectual endowments, or scientific attainments, I cannot help expressing my opinion that Professor Woodensconce *ought* to have come off victorious. There is an exultation about Professor Grime incompatible, I fear, with true greatness."

" A quarter past twelve.

"PROFESSOR Grime continues to exult, and to boast of his victory in no very measured terms, observing that he always does win, and that he knew it would be a 'head' beforehand, with many other remarks of a similar nature. Surely this gentleman is not so lost to every feeling of decency and propriety as not to feel and know the superiority of Professor Woodensconce? Is Professor Grime insane? or does he wish to be reminded in plain language of his true position in society, and the precise level of his acquirements and abilities? Professor Grime will do well to look to this."

"*One o'clock.*

"I AM writing in bed. The small cabin is illuminated by the feeble light of a flickering lamp suspended from the ceiling; Professor Grime is lying on the opposite shelf on the broad of his back, with his mouth wide open. The scene is indescribably solemn. The rippling of the tide, the noise of the sailors' feet overhead, the gruff voices on the river, the dogs on the shore, the snoring of the passengers, and a constant creaking of every plank in the vessel, are the only sounds that meet the ear. With these exceptions, all is profound silence.

"My curiosity has been within the last moment very much excited. Mr. Slug, who lies above Professor Grime, has cautiously withdrawn the curtains of his berth, and, after looking anxiously out, as if to satisfy himself that his companions are asleep, has taken up the tin tube of which I have before spoken, and is regarding it with great interest. What rare mechanical combination can be contained in that mysterious case? It is evidently a profound secret to all."

"*A quarter past one.*

"THE behaviour of Mr. Slug grows more and more mysterious. He has unscrewed the top of the tube, and now renews his observations upon his companions, evidently to make sure that he is wholly unobserved. He is clearly on the eve of some great experiment. Pray heaven that it be not a dangerous one; but the interests of science must be promoted, and I am prepared for the worst."

"*Five minutes later.*

"HE has produced a large pair of scissors, and drawn a roll of some substance, not unlike parchment in appearance, from the tin case. The experiment is about to begin. I must strain my eyes to the utmost, in the attempt to follow its minutest operation."

" Twenty minutes before two.

" I HAVE at length been enabled to ascertain that the tin tube contains a few yards of some celebrated plaster, recommended—as I discover on regarding the label attentively through my eye-glass—as a preservative against sea-sickness. Mr. Slug has cut it up into small portions, and is now sticking it over himself in every direction."

" Three o'clock.

" PRECISELY a quarter of an hour ago we weighed anchor, and the machinery was suddenly put in motion with a noise so appalling, that Professor Woodensconce (who had ascended to his berth by means of a platform of carpet-bags arranged by himself on geometrical principles) darted from his shelf head foremost, and, gaining his feet with all the rapidity of extreme terror, ran wildly into the ladies' cabin, under the impression that we were sinking, and uttering loud cries for aid. I am assured that the scene which ensued baffles all description. There were one hundred and forty-seven ladies in their respective berths at the time.

" Mr. Slug has remarked, as an additional instance of the extreme ingenuity of the steam-engine as applied to purposes of navigation, that in whatever part of the vessel a passenger's berth may be situated, the machinery always appears to be exactly under his pillow. He intends stating this very beautiful, though simple discovery, to the association."

" Half-past three.

" WE are still in smooth water; that is to say, in as smooth water as a steam-vessel ever can be, for, as Professor Woodensconce (who has just woke up) learnedly remarks, another great point of ingenuity about a steamer is, that it always carries a little storm with it. You can scarcely conceive how exciting the jerking pulsation of the ship becomes. It is a matter of positive difficulty to get to sleep."

" Friday afternoon, six o'clock.

" I REGRET to inform you that Mr. Slug's plaster has proved of no avail. He is in great agony, but has applied several large, additional pieces notwithstanding. How affecting is this extreme devotion to science and pursuit of knowledge under the most trying circumstances !

" We were extremely happy this morning, and the breakfast was one of the most animated description. Nothing unpleasant occurred until noon, with the exception of Doctor Foxey's brown silk umbrella and white hat becoming entangled in the machinery while he was explaining to a knot of ladies the construction of the steam-engine. I fear the gravy soup for lunch was injudicious. We lost a great many passengers almost immediately afterwards."

" Half-past six.

" I AM again in bed. Anything so heart-rending as Mr. Slug's sufferings it has never yet been my lot to witness."

" Seven o'clock.

" A MESSENGER has just come down for a clean pocket-hand-kerchief from Professor Woodensconce's bag, that unfortunate gentleman being quite unable to leave the deck, and imploring constantly to be thrown overboard. From this man I under-stand that Professor Nogo, though in a state of utter exhaustion, clings feebly to the hard biscuit and cold brandy and water, under the impression that they will yet restore him. Such is the triumph of mind over matter.

" Professor Grime is in bed, to all appearance quite well ; but he *will* eat, and it is disagreeable to see him. Has this gentleman no sympathy with the sufferings of his fellow-creatures ? If he has, on what principle can he call for mutton-chops—and smile ? "

" Black Boy and Stomach-ache,
Oldcastle, Saturday noon.

" You will be happy to learn that I have at length arrived here in safety. The town is excessively crowded, and all the private lodgings and hotels are filled with *savans* of both sexes. The tremendous assemblage of intellect that one encounters in every street is in the last degree overwhelming.

"Notwithstanding the throng of people here, I have been fortunate enough to meet with very comfortable accommodation on very reasonable terms, having secured a sofa in the first-floor passage at one guinea per night, which includes permission to take my meals in the bar, on condition that I walk about the streets at all other times, to make room for other gentlemen similarly situated. I have been over the outhouses intended to be devoted to the reception of the various sections, both here and at the Boot-jack and Countenance, and am much delighted with the arrangements. Nothing can exceed the fresh appearance of the saw-dust with which the floors are sprinkled. The forms are of unplaned deal, and the general effect, as you can well imagine, is extremely beautiful."

" Half-past nine.

"THE number and rapidity of the arrivals are quite bewildering. Within the last ten minutes a stage-coach has driven up to the door, filled inside and out with distinguished characters, comprising Mr. Muddlebranes, Mr. Drawley, Professor Muff, Mr. X. Misty, Mr. X. X. Misty, Mr. Purblind, Professor Rummun, The Honourable and Reverend Mr. Long Eers, Professor John Ketch, Sir William Joltered, Doctor Buffer, Mr. Smith (of London), Mr. Brown (of Edinburgh), Sir Hookham Snivey, and Professor Pumpkinskull. The ten last-named gentlemen were wet through, and looked extremely intelligent."

" Sunday, two o'clock, p.m.

"THE Honourable and Reverend Mr. Long Eers, accompanied by Sir William Joltered, walked and drove this morning. They accomplished the former feat in boots, and the latter in a hired fly. This has naturally given rise to much discussion.

"I have just learnt that an interview has taken place at

the Boot-jack and Countenance between Sowster, the active and intelligent beadle of this place, and Professor Pumpkin-skull, who, as your readers are doubtless aware, is an influential member of the council. I forbear to communicate any of the rumours to which this very extraordinary proceeding has given rise until I have seen Sowster, and endeavoured to ascertain the truth from him."

" *Half-past six.*

" I ENGAGED a donkey-chaise shortly after writing the above, and proceeded at a brisk trot in the direction of Sowster's residence, passing through a beautiful expanse of country, with red brick buildings on either side, and stopping in the market-place to observe the spot where Mr. Kwakley's hat was blown off yesterday. It is an uneven piece of paving, but has certainly no appearance which would lead one to suppose that any such event had recently occurred there. From this point I proceeded—passing the gas-works and tallow-melter's—to a lane which had been pointed out to me as the beadle's place of residence; and before I had driven a dozen yards further, I had the good fortune to meet Sowster himself advancing towards me.

"Sowster is a fat man, with a more enlarged development of that peculiar conformation of countenance which is vulgarly termed a double chin than I remember to have ever seen before. He has also a very red nose, which he attributes to a habit of early rising—so red, indeed, that but for this explanation I should have supposed it to proceed from occasional inebriety. He informed me that he did not feel himself at liberty to relate what had passed between himself and Professor Pumpkinskull, but had no objection to state that it was connected with a matter of police regulation, and added with peculiar significance ' Never wos sitch times!'

" You will easily believe that this intelligence gave me considerable surprise, not wholly unmixed with anxiety, and that I lost no time in waiting on Professor Pumpkinskull, and stating the object of my visit. After a few moments' reflection, the Professor, who, I am bound to say, behaved with the utmost politeness, openly avowed (I mark the passage in italics) *that he had requested Sowster to attend on the Monday morning at the Boot-jack and Countenance, to keep off the boys; and that he had further desired that the under-beadle might be stationed, with the same object, at the Black Boy and Stomach-ache!*

"Now I leave this unconstitutional proceeding to your comments and the consideration of your readers. I have yet to learn that a beadle, without the precincts of a church, churchyard, or workhouse, and acting otherwise than under the express orders of churchwardens and overseers in council assembled, to enforce the law against people who come upon the parish, and other offenders, has any lawful authority whatever over the rising youth of this country. I have yet to learn that a beadle can be called out by any civilian to exercise a domination and despotism over the boys of Britain. I have yet to learn that a beadle will be permitted by the commissioners of poor law regulation to wear out the soles and heels of his boots in illegal interference with the liberties of people not proved poor or otherwise criminal. I have yet to learn that a beadle has power to stop up the Queen's highway at his will and pleasure, or that the whole width of the street is not free and open to any man, boy, or woman in existence, up to the very walls of the houses—ay, be they Black Boys and Stomach-aches, or Boot-jacks and Countenances, I care not."

" Nine o'clock.

"I HAVE procured a local artist to make a faithful sketch of the tyrant Sowster, which, as he has acquired this infamous celebrity, you will no doubt wish to have engraved for the purpose of presenting a copy with every copy of your next number. I enclose it. The under-beadle has consented to write his life, but it is to be strictly anonymous.

"The accompanying likeness is of course from the life, and

372

complete in every respect. Even if I had been totally ignorant of the man's real character, and it had been placed before me without remark, I should have shuddered involuntarily. There is an intense malignity of expression in

The Tyrant Sowster.

the features, and a baleful ferocity of purpose in the ruffian's eye, which appals and sickens. His whole air is rampant with cruelty, nor is the stomach less characteristic of his demoniac propensities."

373

REPORT OF THE SECOND MEETING

"THE great day has at length arrived. I have neither eyes, nor ears, nor pens, nor ink, nor paper, for anything but the wonderful proceedings that have astounded my senses. Let me collect my energies and proceed to the account.

" SECTION A.—ZOOLOGY AND BOTANY.

FRONT PARLOUR, BLACK BOY AND STOMACH-ACHE.

President—Sir William Joltered. *Vice-Presidents*—Mr. Muddlebranes and Mr. Drawley.

" MR. X. X. MISTY communicated some remarks on the disappearance of dancing-bears from the streets of London, with observations on the exhibition of monkeys as connected with barrel-organs. The writer had observed, with feelings of the utmost pain and regret, that some years ago a sudden and unaccountable change in the public taste took place with reference to itinerant bears, who, being discountenanced by the populace, gradually fell off one by one from the streets of the metropolis, until not one remained to create a taste for natural history in the breasts of the poor and unin- structed. One bear, indeed,—a brown and ragged animal,— had lingered about the haunts of his former triumphs, with a worn and dejected visage and feeble limbs, and had essayed to wield his quarter-staff for the amusement of the multitude; but hunger, and an utter want of any due recompense for his abilities, had at length driven him from the field, and it was only too probable that he had fallen a sacrifice to the rising taste for grease. He regretted to add that a similar, and no less lamentable, change had taken place with reference to monkeys. These delightful animals had formerly been almost as plentiful as the organs on the tops of which they were accustomed to sit ; the proportion in the year 1829 (it appeared by the parliamentary return) being as one monkey to three organs. Owing, however, to an altered taste in musical instruments, and the substitution, in a great measure,

374

of narrow boxes of music for organs, which left the monkeys nothing to sit upon, this source of public amusement was wholly dried up. Considering it a matter of the deepest importance, in connection with national education, that the people should not lose such opportunities of making themselves acquainted with the manners and customs of two most interesting species of animals, the author submitted that some measures should be immediately taken for the restoration of these pleasing and truly intellectual amusements.

" THE PRESIDENT inquired by what means the honourable member proposed to attain this most desirable end?

"THE AUTHOR submitted that it could be most fully and satisfactorily accomplished, if Her Majesty's Government would cause to be brought over to England, and maintained at the public expense, and for the public amusement, such a number of bears as would enable every quarter of the town to be visited—say at least by three bears a week. No difficulty whatever need be experienced in providing a fitting place for the reception of these animals, as a commodious bear-garden could be erected in the immediate neighbourhood of both Houses of Parliament; obviously the most proper and eligible spot for such an establishment.

" PROFESSOR MULL doubted very much whether any correct ideas of natural history were propagated by the means to which the honourable member had so ably adverted. On the contrary, he believed that they had been the means of diffusing very incorrect and imperfect notions on the subject. He spoke from personal observation and personal experience, when he said that many children of great abilities had been induced to believe, from what they had observed in the streets, at and before the period to which the honourable gentleman had referred, that all monkeys were born in red coats and spangles, and that their hats and feathers also came by nature. He wished to know distinctly whether the honourable gentleman attributed the want of encouragement the bears had met with to the decline of public taste in that respect, or to a want of ability on the part of the bears themselves?

"Mr. X. X. Misty replied, that he could not bring himself to believe but that there must be a great deal of floating talent among the bears and monkeys generally ; which, in the absence of any proper encouragement, was dispersed in other directions.

"Professor Pumpkinskull wished to take that opportunity of calling the attention of the section to a most important and serious point. The author of the treatise just read had alluded to the prevalent taste for bears'-grease as a means of promoting the growth of hair, which undoubtedly was diffused to a very great and (as it appeared to him) very alarming extent. No gentleman attending that section could fail to be aware of the fact that the youth of the present age evinced, by their behaviour in the streets, and at all places of public resort, a considerable lack of that gallantry and gentlemanly feeling which, in more ignorant times, had been thought becoming. He wished to know whether it were possible that a constant outward application of bears'-grease by the young gentlemen about town had imperceptibly infused into those unhappy persons something of the nature and quality of the bear. He shuddered as he threw out the remark ; but if this theory, on inquiry, should prove to be well founded, it would at once explain a great deal of unpleasant eccentricity of behaviour, which, without some such discovery, was wholly unaccountable.

"The President highly complimented the learned gentleman on his most valuable suggestion, which produced the greatest effect upon the assembly ; and remarked that only a week previous he had seen some young gentlemen at a theatre eyeing a box of ladies with a fierce intensity, which nothing but the influence of some brutish appetite could possibly explain. It was dreadful to reflect that our youth were so rapidly verging into a generation of bears.

"After a scene of scientific enthusiasm it was resolved that this important question should be immediately submitted to the consideration of the council.

"THE PRESIDENT wished to know whether any gentleman could inform the section what had become of the dancing-dogs?

"A MEMBER replied, after some hesitation, that on the day after three glee-singers had been committed to prison as criminals by a late most zealous police-magistrate of the metropolis, the dogs had abandoned their professional duties, and dispersed themselves in different quarters of the town to gain a livelihood by less dangerous means. He was given to understand that since that period they had supported themselves by lying in wait for and robbing blind men's poodles.

"MR. FLUMMERY exhibited a twig, claiming to be a veritable branch of that noble tree known to naturalists as the SHAKSPEARE, which has taken root in every land and climate, and gathered under the shade of its broad green boughs the great family of mankind. The learned gentleman remarked that the twig had been undoubtedly called by other names in its time; but that it had been pointed out to him by an old lady in Warwickshire, where the great tree had grown, as a shoot of the genuine SHAKSPEARE, by which name he begged to introduce it to his countrymen.

"THE PRESIDENT wished to know what botanical definition the honourable gentleman could afford of the curiosity.

"MR. FLUMMERY expressed his opinion that it was A DECIDED PLANT.

"SECTION B.—DISPLAY OF MODELS AND MECHANICAL SCIENCE.

LARGE ROOM, BOOT-JACK AND COUNTENANCE.

President—Mr. Mallett. *Vice-Presidents*—Messrs. Leaver and Scroo.

"MR. CRINKLES exhibited a most beautiful and delicate machine, of little larger size than an ordinary snuff-box, manufactured entirely by himself, and composed exclusively of steel, by the aid of which more pockets could be picked in one hour than by the present slow and tedious process in four-and-twenty. The inventor remarked that it had been put into active operation in Fleet Street, the Strand, and other thoroughfares, and had never been once known to fail.

"After some slight delay, occasioned by the various members of the section buttoning their pockets,

"THE PRESIDENT narrowly inspected the invention, and declared that he had never seen a machine of more beautiful or exquisite construction. Would the inventor be good enough to inform the section whether he had taken any and what means for bringing it into general operation?

"MR. CRINKLES stated that, after encountering some preliminary difficulties, he had succeeded in putting himself in communication with Mr. Fogle Hunter, and other gentlemen connected with the swell mob, who had awarded the invention the very highest and most unqualified approbation. He regretted to say, however, that these distinguished practitioners, in common with a gentleman of the name of Gimlet-eyed Tommy, and other members of a secondary grade of the profession whom he was understood to represent, entertained an insuperable objection to its being brought into general use, on the ground that it would have the inevitable effect of almost entirely superseding manual labour, and throwing a great number of highly-deserving persons out of employment.

"THE PRESIDENT hoped that no such fanciful objections would be allowed to stand in the way of such a great public improvement.

"MR. CRINKLES hoped so too; but he feared that if the gentlemen of the swell mob persevered in their objection, nothing could be done.

"PROFESSOR GRIME suggested, that surely, in that case, Her Majesty's Government might be prevailed upon to take it up.

"Mr. Crinkles said, that if the objection were found to be insuperable he should apply to Parliament, which he thought could not fail to recognise the utility of the invention.

"The President observed that, up to this time Parliament had certainly got on very well without it; but, as they did their business on a very large scale, he had no doubt they would gladly adopt the improvement. His only fear was that the machine might be worn out by constant working.

"Mr. Coppernose called the attention of the section to a proposition of great magnitude and interest, illustrated by a vast number of models, and stated with much clearness and perspicuity in a treatise entitled 'Practical Suggestions on the necessity of providing some harmless and wholesome relaxation for the young noblemen of England.' His proposition was, that a space of ground of not less than ten miles in length and four in breadth should be purchased by a new company, to be incorporated by Act of Parliament, and inclosed by a brick wall of not less than twelve feet in height. He proposed that it should be laid out with highway roads, turnpikes, bridges, miniature villages, and every object that could conduce to the comfort and glory of Four-in-hand Clubs, so that they might be fairly presumed to require no drive beyond it. This delightful retreat would be fitted up with most commodious and extensive stables, for the convenience of such of the nobility and gentry as had a taste for ostlering, and with houses of entertainment furnished in the most expensive and handsome style. It would be further provided with whole streets of door-knockers and bell-handles of extra size, so constructed that they could be easily wrenched off at night, and regularly screwed on again, by attendants provided for the purpose, every day. There would also be gas lamps of real glass, which could be broken at a comparatively small expense per dozen, and a broad and handsome foot pavement for gentlemen to drive their cabriolets upon when they were humorously disposed—for the full enjoyment of which feat live pedestrians would be procured from the workhouse at a very small charge per head. The place being inclosed, and carefully screened from the intrusion of the public, there would be no objection to gentlemen laying aside any article of their costume that was considered to interfere with a pleasant frolic, or, indeed, to their walking about without any costume at all, if they liked that better. In short, every facility of enjoyment would be afforded that the most gentlemanly person could possibly desire. But as even these advantages would be incomplete unless there were some means provided of enabling the nobility and gentry to display their prowess when they sallied forth after dinner, and as some inconvenience might be experienced in the event of their being reduced to the necessity of pummelling each other, the inventor had turned his attention to the construction of an entirely new police force, composed exclusively of automaton figures, which, with the assistance of the ingenious Signor Gagliardi, of Windmill-street, in the Haymarket, he had succeeded in making with such nicety, that a policeman, cab-driver, or old woman, made upon the principle of the models exhibited, would walk about until knocked down like any real man; nay, more, if set upon and beaten by six or eight noblemen or gentlemen, after it was down, the figure would utter divers groans, mingled with entreaties for mercy, thus rendering the illusion complete, and the enjoyment perfect. But the invention did not stop even here; for station-houses would be built, containing good beds for noblemen and gentlemen during the night, and in the morning they would repair to a commodious police office, where a pantomimic investigation would take place before the automaton magistrates,—quite equal to life,—who would fine them in so many counters, with which they would be previously provided for the purpose. This office would be furnished with an inclined plane, for the convenience of any nobleman or gentleman who might wish to bring in his horse

Automaton Police Office, and Real Offenders

as a witness; and the prisoners would be at perfect liberty, as they were now, to interrupt the complainants as much as they pleased, and to make any remarks that they thought proper. The charge for these amusements would amount to very little more than they already cost, and the inventor submitted that the public would be much benefited and comforted by the proposed arrangement.

" PROFESSOR NOGO wished to be informed what amount of automaton police force it was proposed to raise in the first instance.

" MR. COPPERNOSE replied, that it was proposed to begin with seven divisions of police of a score each, lettered from A to G inclusive. It was proposed that not more than half this number should be placed on active duty, and that the remainder should be kept on shelves in the police office ready to be called out at a moment's notice.

" THE PRESIDENT, awarding the utmost merit to the ingenious gentleman who had originated the idea, doubted whether the automaton police would quite answer the purpose. He feared that noblemen and gentlemen would perhaps require the excitement of thrashing living subjects.

" MR. COPPERNOSE submitted, that as the usual odds in such cases were ten noblemen or gentlemen to one policeman or cab-driver, it could make very little difference in point of excitement whether the policeman or cab-driver were a man or a block. The great advantage would be, that a policeman's limbs might be all knocked off, and yet he would be in a condition to do duty next day. He might even give his evidence next morning with his head in his hand, and give it equally well.

" PROFESSOR MUFF.—Will you allow me to ask you, sir, of what materials it is intended that the magistrates' heads shall be composed?

" MR. COPPERNOSE.—The magistrates will have wooden heads of course, and they will be made of the toughest and thickest materials that can possibly be obtained.

"Professor Muff.—I am quite satisfied. This is a great invention.

"Professor Nogo.—I see but one objection to it. It appears to me that the magistrates ought to talk.

"Mr. Coppernose no sooner heard this suggestion than he touched a small spring in each of the two models of magistrates which were placed upon the table; one of the figures immediately began to exclaim with great volubility that he was sorry to see gentlemen in such a situation, and the other to express a fear that the policeman was intoxicated.

"The section, as with one accord, declared with a shout of applause that the invention was complete; and the President, much excited, retired with Mr. Coppernose to lay it before the council. On his return,

"Mr. Tickle displayed his newly-invented spectacles, which enabled the wearer to discern, in very bright colours, objects at a great distance, and rendered him wholly blind to those immediately before him. It was, he said, a most valuable and useful invention, based strictly upon the principle of the human eye.

"The President required some information upon this point. He had yet to learn that the human eye was remarkable for the peculiarities of which the honourable gentleman had spoken.

"Mr. Tickle was rather astonished to hear this, when the President could not fail to be aware that a large number of most excellent persons and great statesmen could see, with the naked eye, most marvellous horrors on West India plantations, while they could discern nothing whatever in the interior of Manchester cotton mills. He must know, too, with what quickness of perception most people could discover their neighbour's faults, and how very blind they were to their own. If the President differed from the great majority of men in this respect, his eye was a defective one, and it was to assist his vision that these glasses were made.

382

"MR. BLANK exhibited a model of a fashionable annual, composed of copper-plates, gold leaf, and silk boards, and worked entirely by milk and water.

"MR. PROSEE, after examining the machine, declared it to be so ingeniously composed, that he was wholly unable to discover how it went on at all.

"MR. BLANK.—Nobody can, and that is the beauty of it.

"SECTION C.—ANATOMY AND MEDICINE.

BAR ROOM, BLACK BOY AND STOMACH-ACHE.

President—Dr. Soemup. *Vice-Presidents*—Messrs. Pessell and Mortair.

"DR. GRUMMIDGE stated to the section a most interesting case of monomania, and described the course of treatment he had pursued with perfect success. The patient was a married lady in the middle rank of life, who, having seen another lady at an evening party in a full suit of pearls, was suddenly seized with a desire to possess a similar equipment, although her husband's finances were by no means equal to the necessary outlay. Finding her wish ungratified, she fell sick, and the symptoms soon became so alarming, that he (Dr. Grummidge) was called in. At this period the prominent tokens of the disorder were sullenness, a total indisposition to perform domestic duties, great peevishness, and extreme languor, except when pearls were mentioned, at which times the pulse quickened, the eyes grew brighter, the pupils dilated, and the patient, after various incoherent exclamations, burst into a passion of tears, and exclaimed that nobody cared for her, and that she wished herself dead. Finding that the patient's appetite was affected in the presence of company, he began by ordering a total abstinence from all stimulants, and forbidding any sustenance but weak gruel; he then took twenty ounces of blood, applied a blister under each ear, one upon the chest, and another on the back; having done which, and administered five grains of calomel, he left the patient to her repose. The next day she was somewhat low, but decidedly better, and all appearances of irritation were removed. The next day she improved still further, and on the next again. On the fourth there was some appearance of a return of the old symptoms, which no sooner developed themselves, than he administered another dose of calomel, and left strict orders that, unless a decidedly favourable change occurred within two hours, the patient's head should be immediately shaved to the very last curl. From that moment she began to mend, and, in less than four-and-twenty hours was perfectly restored. She did not now betray the least emotion at the sight or mention of pearls or any other ornaments. She was cheerful and good-humoured, and a most beneficial change had been effected in her whole temperament and condition.

" MR. PIPKIN (M.R.C.S.) read a short but most interesting communication in which he sought to prove the complete belief of Sir William Courtenay, otherwise Thom, recently shot at Canterbury, in the Homœopathic system. The section would bear in mind that one of the Homœopathic doctrines was, that infinitesimal doses of any medicine which would occasion the disease under which the patient laboured, supposing him to be in a healthy state, would cure it. Now, it was a remarkable circumstance—proved in the evidence— that the deceased Thom employed a woman to follow him about all day with a pail of water, assuring her that one drop (a purely homœopathic remedy, the section would observe), placed upon his tongue, after death, would restore him. What was the obvious inference ? That Thom, who was marching and countermarching in osier beds, and other swampy places, was impressed with a presentiment that he should be drowned ; in which case, had his instructions been complied with, he could not fail to have been brought to life again instantly by his own prescription. As it was, if this woman, or any other person, had administered an infinitesimal dose of lead and gunpowder immediately after he fell, he would have recovered forthwith. But unhappily the woman concerned did not possess the power of reasoning by analogy, or carrying out a principle, and thus the unfortunate gentleman had been sacrificed to the ignorance of the peasantry.

" SECTION D.—STATISTICS.

OUT-HOUSE, BLACK BOY AND STOMACH-ACHE.

President—Mr. Slug.   *Vice-Presidents*—Messrs. Noakes and Styles.

" MR. KWAKLEY stated the result of some most ingenious statistical inquiries relative to the difference between the value of the qualification of several members of Parliament as published to the world, and its real nature and amount. After reminding the section that every member of Parliament for a town or borough was supposed to possess a clear freehold estate of three hundred pounds per annum, the honourable gentleman excited great amusement and laughter by stating the exact amount of freehold property possessed by a column of legislators, in which he had included himself. It appeared from this table, that the amount of such income possessed by each was 0 pounds, 0 shillings, and 0 pence, yielding an average of the same. (Great laughter.) It was pretty well known that there were accommodating gentlemen in the habit of furnishing new members with temporary qualifications, to the ownership of which they swore solemnly —of course as a mere matter of form. He argued from these *data* that it was wholly unnecessary for members of Parliament to possess any property at all, especially as when they had none the public could get them so much cheaper.

"SUPPLEMENTARY SECTION, E.—UMBUGOLOGY AND DITCHWATERISICS.

President—Mr. Grub.   *Vice-Presidents*—Messrs. Dull and Dummy.

" A paper was read by the secretary descriptive of a bay pony with one eye, which had been seen by the author standing in a butcher's cart at the corner of Newgate Market. The communication described the author of the paper as having, in the prosecution of a mercantile pursuit, betaken himself one Saturday morning last summer from Somers Town to Cheapside; in the course of which expedition he had beheld the extraordinary appearance above described. The pony had one distinct eye, and it had been pointed out to him by his friend Captain Blunderbore, of the Horse Marines, who assisted the author in his search, that whenever he winked this eye he whisked his tail (possibly to drive the flies off), but that he always winked and whisked at the same time. The animal was lean, spavined, and tottering; and the author proposed to constitute it of the family of *Fitfordogsmeataurious.* It certainly did occur to him that there was no case on record of a pony with one clearly-defined and distinct organ of vision, winking and whisking at the same moment.

"Mr. Q. J. Snuffletoffle had heard of a pony winking his eye, and likewise of a pony whisking his tail, but whether they were two ponies or the same pony he could not undertake positively to say. At all events, he was acquainted with no authenticated instance of a simultaneous winking and whisking, and he really could not but doubt the existence of such a marvellous pony in opposition to all those natural laws by which ponies were governed. Referring, however, to the mere question of his one organ of vision, might he suggest the possibility of this pony having been literally half asleep at the time he was seen, and having closed only one eye.

"The President observed that, whether the pony was half asleep or fast asleep, there could be no doubt that the association was wide awake, and therefore that they had better get the business over, and go to dinner. He had certainly never seen anything analogous to this pony, but he was not prepared to doubt its existence; for he had seen many queerer ponies in his time, though he did not pretend to have seen any more remarkable donkeys than the other gentlemen around him.

"Professor John Ketch was then called upon to exhibit the skull of the late Mr. Greenacre, which he produced from

a blue bag, remarking, on being invited to make any observations that occurred to him, 'that he'd pound it as that 'ere
'spectable section had never seed a more gamerer cove nor
he vos.'

"A most animated discussion upon this interesting relic
ensued; and, some difference of opinion arising respecting the
real character of the deceased gentleman, Mr. Blubb delivered
a lecture upon the cranium before him, clearly showing that
Mr. Greenacre possessed the organ of destructiveness to a
most unusual extent, with a most remarkable development of
the organ of carveativeness. Sir Hookham Snivey was proceeding to combat this opinion, when Professor Ketch suddenly interrupted the proceedings by exclaiming, with great
excitement of manner, ' Walker!'

" THE PRESIDENT begged to call the learned gentleman to
order.

" PROFESSOR KETCH.—' Order be blowed! you've got the
wrong un, I tell you. It ain't no 'ed at all; it's a coker-nut
as my brother-in-law has been a-carvin', to hornament his
new baked tatur-stall wots a-comin' down 'ere vile the
'sociation's in the town. Hand over, vill you?'

" With these words, Professor Ketch hastily repossessed
himself of the cocoa-nut, and drew forth the skull, in mistake
for which he had exhibited it. A most interesting conversation ensued; but as there appeared some doubt ultimately
whether the skull was Mr. Greenacre's, or a hospital patient's,
or a pauper's, or a man's, or a woman's, or a monkey's, no
particular result was obtained."

"I cannot," says our talented correspondent in conclusion,
"I cannot close my account of these gigantic researches and
sublime and noble triumphs without repeating a *bon mot* of
Professor Woodensconce's, which shows how the greatest minds
may occasionally unbend when truth can be presented to
listening ears, clothed in an attractive and playful form. I
was standing by, when, after a week of feasting and feeding,

that learned gentleman, accompanied by the whole body of wonderful men, entered the hall yesterday, where a sumptuous dinner was prepared; where the richest wines sparkled on the board, and fat bucks—propitiatory sacrifices to learning—sent forth their savoury odours. 'Ah!' said Professor Woodensconce, rubbing his hands, 'this is what we meet for; this is what inspires us; this is what keeps us together, and beckons us onward; this is the *spread* of science, and a glorious spread it is.'"

THE PANTOMIME OF LIFE

BEFORE we plunge headlong into this paper, let us at once confess to a fondness for pantomimes—to a gentle sympathy with clowns and pantaloons—to an unqualified admiration of harlequins and columbines—to a chaste delight in every action of their brief existence, varied and many-coloured as those actions are, and inconsistent though they ocasionally be with those rigid and formal rules of propriety which regulate the proceedings of meaner and less comprehensive minds. We revel in pantomimes—not because they dazzle one's eyes with tinsel and gold leaf; not because they present to us, once again, the well-beloved chalked faces, and goggle eyes of our childhood; not even because, like Christmas-day, and Twelfth-night, and Shrove-Tuesday, and one's own birthday, they come to us but once a year ;—our attachment is founded on a graver and a very different reason. A pantomime is to us, a mirror of life; nay, more, we maintain that it is so to audiences generally, although they are not aware of it, and that this very circumstance is the secret cause of their amusement and delight.

Let us take a slight example. The scene is a street: an elderly gentleman, with a large face and strongly marked features, appears. His countenance beams with a sunny smile, and a perpetual dimple is on his broad, red cheek. He is evidently an opulent elderly gentleman, comfortable in circumstances, and well-to-do in the world. He is not unmindful of the adornment of his person, for he is richly, not to say gaudily, dressed; and that he indulges to a reasonable extent in the pleasures of the table may be inferred from the joyous and oily manner in which he rubs his stomach, by way of informing the audience that he is going home to dinner. In the fulness of his heart, in the fancied security of wealth, in the possession and enjoyment of all the good things of life, the elderly gentleman suddenly loses his footing, and stumbles. How the audience roar! He is set upon by a noisy and officious crowd, who buffet and cuff him unmercifully. They scream with delight! Every time the elderly gentleman struggles to get up, his relentless perse-cutors knock him down again. The spectators are convulsed with merriment! And when at last the elderly gentleman does get up, and staggers away, despoiled of hat, wig, and clothing, himself battered to pieces, and his watch and money gone, they are exhausted with laughter, and express their merriment and admiration in rounds of applause.

Is this like life? Change the scene to any real street;— to the Stock Exchange, or the City banker's; the merchant's counting-house, or even the tradesman's shop. See any one of these men fall,—the more suddenly, and the nearer the zenith of his pride and riches, the better. What a wild hallo is raised over his prostrate carcase by the shouting mob; how they whoop and yell as he lies humbled beneath them! Mark how eagerly they set upon him when he is down; and how they mock and deride him as he slinks away. Why, it is the pantomime to the very letter.

Of all the pantomimic *dramatis personæ*, we consider the pantaloon the most worthless and debauched. Inde-pendent of the dislike one naturally feels at seeing a gentle-man of his years engaged in pursuits highly unbecoming his gravity and time of life, we cannot conceal from ourselves the fact that he is a treacherous, worldly-minded old villain, constantly enticing his younger companion, the clown, into acts of fraud or petty larceny, and generally standing aside to watch the result of the enterprise. If it be successful, he never forgets to return for his share of the spoil; but if it turn out a failure, he generally retires with remarkable caution and expedition, and keeps carefully aloof until the affair has blown over. His amorous propensities, too, are eminently disagreeable; and his mode of addressing ladies in the open street at noon-day is downright improper, being usually neither more nor less than a perceptible tickling of the aforesaid ladies in the waist, after committing which, he starts back, manifestly ashamed (as well he may be) of his own indecorum and temerity; continuing, nevertheless, to ogle and beckon to them from a distance in a very unpleasant and immoral manner.

Is there any man who cannot count a dozen pantaloons in his own social circle? Is there any man who has not seen them swarming at the west end of the town on a sunshiny day or a summer's evening, going through the last-named pantomimic feats with as much liquorish energy, and as total an absence of reserve, as if they were on the very stage itself? We can tell upon our fingers a dozen pantaloons of our acquaintance at this moment—capital pantaloons, who have been performing all kinds of strange freaks, to the great amusement of their friends and acquaintance, for years past; and who to this day are making such comical and ineffectual attempts to be young and dissolute, that all beholders are like to die with laughter.

Take that old gentleman who has just emerged from the *Café de l'Europe* in the Haymarket, where he has been dining at the expense of the young man upon town with whom he shakes hands as they part at the door of the tavern. The affected warmth of that shake of the hand, the courteous nod, the obvious recollection of the dinner, the savoury flavour of which still hangs upon his lips, are all characteristics of his great prototype. He hobbles away humming an opera tune, and twirling his cane to and fro, with affected carelessness.

Suddenly he stops—'tis at the milliner's window. He peeps through one of the large panes of glass; and, his view of the ladies within being obstructed by the India shawls, directs his attentions to the young girl with the band-box in her hand, who is gazing in at the window also. See! he draws beside her. He coughs; she turns away from him. He draws near her again; she disregards him. He gleefully chucks her under the chin, and, retreating a few steps, nods and beckons with fantastic grimaces, while the girl bestows a contemptuous and supercilious look upon his wrinkled visage. She turns away with a flounce, and the old gentleman trots after her with a toothless chuckle. The pantaloon to the life!

But the close resemblance which the clowns of the stage bear to those of every-day life is perfectly extraordinary. Some people talk with a sigh of the decline of pantomime, and murmur in low and dismal tones the name of Grimaldi. We mean no disparagement to the worthy and excellent old man when we say that this is downright nonsense. Clowns that beat Grimaldi all to nothing turn up every day, and nobody patronizes them—more's the pity!

"I know who you mean," says some dirty-faced patron of Mr. Osbaldistone's, laying down the Miscellany when he has got thus far, and bestowing upon vacancy a most knowing glance; "you mean C. J. Smith as did Guy Fawkes, and George Barnwell at the Garden." The dirty-faced gentleman has hardly uttered the words, when he is interrupted by a young gentleman in no shirt-collar and a Petersham coat. "No, no," says the young gentleman; "he means Brown, King, and Gibson, at the 'Delphi." Now, with great deference both to the first-named gentleman with the dirty face, and the last-named gentleman in the non-existing shirt-collar, we do *not* mean either the performer who so grotesquely burlesqued the Popish conspirator, or the three unchangeables who have been dancing the same dance under different imposing titles, and doing the same thing under various high-sounding names for some five or six years last past. We have no sooner made this avowal, than the public, who have hitherto been silent witnesses of the dispute, inquire what on earth it is we *do* mean ; and, with becoming respect, we proceed to tell them.

It is very well known to all playgoers and pantomime-seers, that the scenes in which a theatrical clown is at the very height of his glory are those which are described in the play-bills as " Cheesemonger's shop and Crockery warehouse," or " Tailor's shop, and Mrs. Queertable's boarding-house," or places bearing some such title, where the great fun of the thing consists in the hero's taking lodgings which he has not the slightest intention of paying for, or obtaining goods under false pretences, or abstracting the stock-in-trade of the respect-able shopkeeper next door, or robbing warehouse porters as they pass under his window, or, to shorten the catalogue, in his swindling everybody he possibly can, it only remaining to be observed that, the more extensive the swindling is, and the more barefaced the impudence of the swindler, the greater the rapture and ecstasy of the audience. Now it is a most remarkable fact that precisely this sort of thing occurs in real life day after day, and nobody sees the humour of it. Let us illustrate our position by detailing the plot of this portion of the pantomime—not of the theatre, but of life.

The Honourable Captain Fitz-Whisker Fiercy, attended by his livery servant Do'em—a most respectable servant to look at, who has grown grey in the service of the captain's family —views, treats for, and ultimately obtains possession of, the unfurnished house, such a number, such a street. All the tradesmen in the neighbourhood are in agonies of competition for the captain's custom ; the captain is a good-natured, kind-hearted, easy man, and, to avoid being the cause of disap-pointment to any, he most handsomely gives orders to all. Hampers of wine, baskets of provisions, cart-loads of furniture, boxes of jewellery, supplies of luxuries of the costliest descrip-tion, flock to the house of the Honourable Captain Fitz-Whisker Fiercy, where they are received with the utmost readiness by the highly respectable Do'em; while the captain himself struts and swaggers about with that compound air of conscious superiority and general blood-thirstiness which a military captain should always, and does most times, wear, to the admiration and terror of plebeian men. But the tradesmen's backs are no sooner turned, than the captain, with all the eccentricity of a mighty mind, and assisted by the faithful Do'em, whose devoted fidelity is not the least touching part of his character, disposes of everything to great advantage; for, although the articles fetch small sums, still they are sold considerably above cost price, the cost to the captain having been nothing at all. After various manœuvres, the imposture is discovered, Fitz-Fiercy and Do'em are recognized as confederates, and the police office to which they are both taken is thronged with their dupes.

Who can fail to recognize in this, the exact counterpart of the best portion of a theatrical pantomime—Fitz-Whisker Fiercy by the clown; Do'em by the pantaloon; and supernumeraries by the tradesmen? The best of the joke, too, is, that the very coal-merchant who is loudest in his complaints against the person who defrauded him, is the identical man who sat in the centre of the very front row of the pit last night and laughed the most boisterously at this very same thing,—and not so well done either. Talk of Grimaldi, we say again! Did Grimaldi, in his best days, ever do anything in this way equal to Da Costa?

The mention of this latter justly celebrated clown reminds us of his last piece of humour, the fraudulently obtaining certain stamped acceptances from a young gentleman in the army. We had scarcely laid down our pen to contemplate for a few moments this admirable actor's performance of that exquisite practical joke, than a new branch of our subject flashed suddenly upon us. So we take it up again at once.

All people who have been behind the scenes, and most people who have been before them, know, that in the representation of a pantomime, a good many men are sent upon the stage for the express purpose of being cheated, or knocked down, or both. Now, down to a moment ago, we had never been able to understand for what possible purpose a great number of odd, lazy, large-headed men, whom one is in the habit of meeting here, and there, and everywhere, could ever have been created. We see it all, now. They are the supernumeraries in the pantomime of life; the men who have been thrust into it, with no other view than to be constantly tumbling over each other, and running their heads against all sorts of strange things. We sat opposite to one of these men at a supper-table, only last week. Now we think of it, he was exactly like the gentlemen with the pasteboard heads and faces, who do the corresponding business in the theatrical pantomimes; there was the same broad stolid simper—the same dull leaden eye—the same unmeaning, vacant stare; and whatever was said, or whatever was done, he always came in at precisely the wrong place, or jostled against something that he had not the slightest business with. We looked at the man across the table again and again; and could not satisfy ourselves what race of beings to class him with. How very odd that this never occurred to us before!

We will frankly own that we have been much troubled with the harlequin. We see harlequins of so many kinds in the real living pantomime, that we hardly know which to select as the proper fellow of him of the theatres. At one time we were disposed to think that the harlequin was neither more nor less than a young man of family and independent property, who had run away with an opera-dancer, and was fooling his life and his means away in light and trivial amusements. On reflection, however, we remembered that harlequins are occasionally guilty of witty, and even clever acts, and we are rather disposed to acquit our young men of family and independent property, generally speaking, of any such misdemeanours. On a more mature consideration of the subject, we have arrived at the conclusion that the harlequins of life are just ordinary men, to be found in no particular walk or degree, on whom a certain station, or particular conjunction of circumstances, confers the magic wand. And this brings us to a few words on the pantomime of public and political life, which we shall say at once, and then conclude—merely premising in this place that we decline any reference whatever to the columbine, being in no wise satisfied of the nature of her connection with her parti-coloured lover, and not feeling by any means clear that we should be justified in introducing her to the virtuous and respectable ladies who peruse our lucubrations.

We take it that the commencement of a Session of Parliament is neither more nor less than the drawing up of the curtain for a grand comic pantomime, and that his Majesty's most gracious speech on the opening thereof may be not inaptly compared to the clown's opening speech of "Here we are!" "My lords and gentlemen, here we are!" appears, to our mind at least, to be a very good abstract of the point and meaning of the propitiatory address of the ministry. When we remember how frequently this speech is made, immediately after *the change* too, the parallel is quite perfect, and still more singular.

Perhaps the cast of our political pantomime never was richer than at this day. We are particularly strong in clowns. At no former time, we should say, have we had such astonishing tumblers, or performers so ready to go through the whole of their feats for the amusement of an admiring throng. Their extreme readiness to exhibit, indeed, has given rise to some ill-natured reflections; it having been objected that by exhibiting gratuitously through the country when the theatre is closed, they reduce themselves to the level of mountebanks, and thereby tend to degrade the respectability of the profession. Certainly Grimaldi never did this sort of thing; and though Brown, King, and Gibson have gone to the Surrey in vacation time, and Mr. C. J. Smith has ruralised at Sadler's Wells, we find no theatrical precedent for a general tumbling through the country, except in the gentleman, name unknown, who threw summersets on behalf of the late Mr. Richardson, and who is no authority either, because he had never been on the regular boards.

But, laying aside this question, which after all is a mere matter of taste, we may reflect with pride and gratification of heart on the proficiency of our clowns as exhibited in the season. Night after night will they twist and tumble about, till two, three, and four o'clock in the morning; playing the strangest antics, and giving each other the funniest slaps on the face that can possibly be imagined, without evincing the smallest tokens of fatigue. The strange noises, the confusion, the shouting and roaring, amid which all this is done, too, would put to shame the most turbulent sixpenny gallery that ever yelled through a boxing-night.

It is especially curious to behold one of these clowns compelled to go through the most surprising contortions by the irresistible influence of the wand of office, which his leader or harlequin holds above his head. Acted upon by this wonderful charm he will become perfectly motionless, moving neither hand, foot, nor finger, and will even lose the faculty of speech at an instant's notice; or on the other hand, he will become all life and animation if required, pouring forth a torrent of words without sense or meaning, throwing himself into the wildest and most fantastic contortions, and even grovelling on the earth and licking up the dust. These exhibitions are more curious than pleasing; indeed, they are rather disgusting than otherwise, except to the admirers of such things, with whom we confess we have no fellow-feeling.

Strange tricks—very strange tricks—are also performed by the harlequin who holds for the time being the magic wand which we have just mentioned. The mere waving it before a man's eyes will dispossess his brains of all the notions previously stored there, and fill it with an entirely new set of ideas; one gentle tap on the back will alter the colour of a man's coat completely; and there are some expert performers, who, having this wand held first on one side and then on the other, will change from side to side, turning their coats at every evolution, with so much rapidity and dexterity, that the quickest eye can scarcely detect their motions. Occasionally, the genius who confers the wand, wrests it from the hand of the temporary possessor, and consigns it to some new performer; on which occasions all the characters change sides, and then the race and the hard knocks begin anew.

We might have extended this chapter to a much greater length—we might have carried the comparison into the liberal professions—we might have shown, as was in fact our original purpose, that each is in itself a little pantomime with scenes and characters of its own, complete; but, as we fear we have been quite lengthy enough already, we shall leave this chapter just where it is. A gentleman, not altogether unknown as a dramatic poet, wrote thus a year or two ago—

> " All the world's a stage,
> And all the men and women merely players:"

and we, tracking out his footsteps at the scarcely-worth-mentioning little distance of a few millions of leagues behind, venture to add, by way of new reading, that he meant a Pantomime, and that we are all actors in The Pantomime of Life.

SOME PARTICULARS CONCERNING
A LION

WE have a great respect for lions in the abstract. In common with most other people, we have heard and read of many instances of their bravery and generosity. We have duly admired that heroic self-denial and charming philanthropy which prompts them never to eat people except when they are hungry, and we have been deeply impressed with a becoming sense of the politeness they are said to display towards unmarried ladies of a certain state. All natural histories teem with anecdotes illustrative of their excellent qualities; and one old spelling-book in particular recounts a touching instance of an old lion, of high moral dignity and stern principle, who felt it his imperative duty to devour a young man who had contracted a habit of swearing, as a striking example to the rising generation.

All this is extremely pleasant to reflect upon, and, indeed, says a very great deal in favour of lions as a mass. We are bound to state, however, that such individual lions as we have happened to fall in with have not put forth any very striking characteristics, and have not acted up to the chivalrous character assigned them by their chroniclers. We never saw a lion in what is called his natural state, certainly; that is to say, we have never met a lion out walking in a forest, or crouching in his lair under a tropical sun, waiting till his dinner should happen to come by, hot from the baker's. But we have seen some under the influence of captivity, and the pressure of misfortune; and we must say that they appeared to us very apathetic, heavy-headed fellows.

The lion at the Zoological Gardens, for instance. He is all very well; he has an undeniable mane, and looks very fierce; but, Lord bless us! what of that? The lions of the fashionable world look just as ferocious, and are the most harmless creatures breathing. A box-lobby lion or a Regent-street animal will put on a most terrible aspect, and roar fearfully, if you affront him; but he will never bite, and, if you offer to attack him manfully, will fairly turn tail and sneak off. Doubtless these creatures roam about sometimes in herds, and, if they meet any especially meek-looking and peaceably-disposed fellow, will endeavour to frighten him; but the faintest show of a vigorous resistance is sufficient to scare them even then. These are pleasant characteristics, whereas we make it matter of distinct charge against the Zoological lion and his brethren at the fairs, that they are sleepy, dreamy, sluggish quadrupeds.

We do not remember to have ever seen one of them perfectly awake, except at feeding-time. In every respect we uphold the biped lions against their four-footed namesakes, and we boldly challenge controversy upon the subject.

With these opinions it may be easily imagined that our curiosity and interest were very much excited the other day, when a lady of our acquaintance called on us and resolutely declined to accept our refusal of her invitation to an evening party; "for," said she, "I have got a lion coming." We at once retracted our plea of a prior engagement, and became as anxious to go, as we had previously been to stay away.

We went early, and posted ourselves in an eligible part of the drawing-room, from whence we could hope to obtain a full view of the interesting animal. Two or three hours passed, the quadrilles began, the room filled; but no lion appeared. The lady of the house became inconsolable,—for it is one of the peculiar privileges of these lions to make solemn appointments and never keep them,—when all of a sudden there came a tremendous double rap at the street-door, and the master of the house, after gliding out (unobserved as he flattered himself) to peep over the banisters, came into the room, rubbing his hands together with great glee, and cried out in a very important voice, "My dear, Mr. —— (naming the lion) has this moment arrived."

Upon this, all eyes were turned towards the door, and we observed several young ladies, who had been laughing and conversing previously with great gaiety and good humour, grow extremely quiet and sentimental; while some young gentlemen, who had been cutting great figures in the facetious and small-talk way, suddenly sank very obviously in the estimation of the company, and were looked upon with great coldness and indifference. Even the young man who had been ordered from the music shop to play the pianoforte was visibly affected, and struck several false notes in the excess of his excitement.

All this time there was a great talking outside, more than once accompanied by a loud laugh, and a cry of "Oh! capital! excellent!" from which we inferred that the lion was jocose, and that these exclamations were occasioned by the transports of his keeper and our host. Nor were we deceived; for when the lion at last appeared, we overheard his keeper, who was a little prim man, whisper to several gentlemen of his acquaintance, with uplifted hands, and every expression of half-suppressed admiration, that —— (naming the lion again) was in *such* cue to-night!

The lion was a literary one. Of course, there were a vast number of people present who had admired his roarings, and were anxious to be introduced to him; and very pleasant it was to see them brought up for the purpose, and to observe the patient dignity with which he received all their patting and caressing. This brought forcibly to our mind what we had so often witnessed at country fairs, where the other lions are compelled to go through as many forms of courtesy as they chance to be acquainted with, just as often as admiring parties happen to drop in upon them.

While the lion was exhibiting in this way, his keeper was not idle, for he mingled among the crowd, and spread his praises most industriously. To one gentleman he whispered some very choice thing that the noble animal had said in the very act of coming up-stairs, which, of course, rendered the mental effort still more astonishing; to another he murmured a hasty account of a grand dinner that had taken place the day before, where twenty-seven gentlemen had got up all at once to demand an extra cheer for the lion; and to the ladies he made sundry promises of interceding to procure the majestic brute's sign-manual for their albums. Then, there were little private consultations in different corners, relative to the personal appearance and stature of the lion; whether he was shorter than they had expected to see him, or taller, or thinner, or fatter, or younger, or older; whether he was like his portrait, or unlike it; and whether the particular shade of his eyes was black, or blue, or hazel, or green, or yellow, or mixture. At all these consultations the keeper assisted; and, in short, the lion was the sole and single subject of discussion till they sat him down to whist, and then the people relapsed into their old topics of conversation—themselves and each other.

We must confess that we looked forward with no slight impatience to the announcement of supper; for if you wish to see a tame lion under particularly favourable circumstances, feeding-time is the period of all others to pitch upon. We were therefore very much delighted to observe a sensation among the guests, which we well knew how to interpret, and immediately afterwards to behold the lion escorting the lady of the house down-stairs. We offered our arm to an elderly female of our acquaintance, who—dear old soul!—is the very best person that ever lived, to lead down to any meal; for, be the room ever so small, or the party ever so large, she is sure, by some intuitive perception of the eligible, to push and pull herself and conductor close to the best dishes on the table;—we say we offered our arm to this elderly female, and, descending the stairs shortly after the lion, were fortunate enough to obtain a seat nearly opposite him.

Of course the keeper was there already. He had planted himself at precisely that distance from his charge which afforded him a decent pretext for raising his voice, when he addressed him, to so loud a key, as could not fail to attract the attention of the whole company, and immediately began to apply himself seriously to the task of bringing the lion out, and putting him through the whole of his manœuvres. Such flashes of wit as he elicited from the lion! First of all, they began to make puns upon a salt-cellar, and then upon the breast of a fowl, and then upon the trifle; but the best jokes of all were decidedly on the lobster salad, upon which latter subject the lion came out most vigorously, and, in the opinion of the most competent authorities, quite outshone himself. This is a very excellent mode of shining in society, and is founded, we humbly conceive, upon the classic model of the dialogues between Mr. Punch and his friend the proprietor, wherein the latter takes all the up-hill work, and is content to pioneer to the jokes and repartees of Mr. P. himself, who never fails to gain great credit and excite much laughter thereby. Whatever it be founded on, however, we recommend it to all lions, present and to come; for in this instance it succeeded to admiration, and perfectly dazzled the whole body of hearers.

When the salt-cellar, and the fowl's breast, and the trifle, and the lobster salad were all exhausted, and could not afford standing-room for another solitary witticism, the keeper performed that very dangerous feat which is still done with some of the caravan lions, although in one instance it terminated fatally, of putting his head in the animal's mouth, and placing himself entirely at its mercy. Boswell frequently presents a melancholy instance of the lamentable results of this achievement, and other keepers and jackals have been terribly lacerated for their daring. It is due to our lion to state, that he condescended to be trifled with, in the most gentle manner, and finally went home with the showman in a hack cab: perfectly peaceable, but slightly fuddled.

Being in a contemplative mood, we were led to make some reflections upon the character and conduct of this genus of lions as we walked homewards, and we were not long in arriving at the conclusion that our former impression in their favour was very much strengthened and confirmed by what we had recently seen. While the other lions receive company and compliments in a sullen, moody, not to say snarling manner, these appear flattered by the attentions that are paid them; while those conceal themselves to the utmost of their power from the vulgar gaze, these court the popular eye, and, unlike their brethren, whom nothing short of compulsion will move to exertion, are ever ready to display their acquirements to the wondering throng. We have known bears of undoubted ability who, when the expectations of a large audience have been wound up to the utmost pitch, have peremptorily refused to dance; well-taught monkeys, who have unaccountably objected to exhibit on the slack wire; and elephants of unquestioned genius, who have suddenly declined to turn the barrel-organ; but we never once knew or heard of a biped lion, literary or otherwise,—and we state it as a fact which is highly creditable to the whole species,—who, occasion offering, did not seize with avidity on any opportunity which was afforded him, of performing to his heart's content on the first violin.

MR. ROBERT BOLTON,

THE "GENTLEMAN CONNECTED WITH THE PRESS"

In the parlour of the Green Dragon, a public-house in the immediate neighbourhood of Westminster Bridge, everybody talks politics, every evening, the great political authority being Mr. Robert Bolton, an individual who defines himself as " a gentleman connected with the press," which is a definition of peculiar indefiniteness.   Mr. Robert Bolton's regular circle of admirers and listeners are an undertaker, a green-grocer, a hairdresser, a baker, a large stomach surmounted by a man's head, and placed on the top of two particularly short legs, and a thin man in black, name, profession, and pursuit unknown, who always sits in the same position, always displays the same long, vacant face, and never opens his lips, surrounded as he is by most enthusiastic conversation, except to puff forth a volume of tobacco smoke, or give vent to a very snappy, loud, and shrill *hem!*   The conversation some-times turns upon literature, Mr. Bolton being a literary character, and always upon such news of the day as is exclu-sively possessed by that talented individual.   I found myself (of course, accidentally) in the Green Dragon the other evening, and, being somewhat amused by the following conversation, preserved it.

"Can you lend me a ten-pound note till Christmas?" inquired the hairdresser of the stomach.

" Where's your security, Mr. Clip?"

"My stock in trade,—there's enough of it, I'm thinking, Mr. Thicknesse. Some fifty wigs, two poles, half-a-dozen head blocks, and a dead Bruin."

"No, I won't, then," growled out Thicknesse. "I lends nothing on the security of the whigs or the Poles either. As for whigs, they're cheats; as for the Poles, they've got no cash. I never have nothing to do with blockheads, unless I can't awoid it (ironically), and a dead bear's about as much use to me as I could be to a dead bear."

"Well, then," urged the other, "there's a book as belonged to Pope, Byron's Poems, valued at forty pounds, because it's got Pope's identical scratch on the back; what do you think of that for security?"

"Well, to be sure!" cried the ⸝baker. "But how d'ye mean, Mr. Clip?"

"Mean! why, that it's got the *hottergruff* of Pope.

'Steal not this book, for fear of hangman's rope;
For it belongs to Alexander Pope.'

All that's written on the inside of the binding of the book; so, as my son says, we're *bound* to believe it."

"Well, sir," observed the undertaker, deferentially, and in a half-whisper, leaning over the table, and knocking over the hairdresser's grog as he spoke, "that argument's very easy upset."

"Perhaps, sir," said Clip, a little flurried, "you'll pay for the first upset afore you thinks of another."

"Now," said the undertaker, bowing amicably to the hairdresser, "I *think*, I says I *think*—you'll excuse me, Mr. Clip, I *think*, you see, that won't go down with the present company —unfortunately, my master had the honour of making the coffin of that ere Lord's housemaid, not no more nor twenty year ago. Don't think I'm proud on it, gentlemen; others might be; but I hate rank of any sort. I've no more respect for a Lord's footman than I have for any respectable trades-man in this room. I may say no more nor I have for Mr. Clip! (bowing). Therefore, that ere Lord must have been born long after Pope died. And it's a logical interferance to defer, that they neither of them lived at the same time. So what I mean is this here, that Pope never had no book, never seed, felt, never smelt no book (triumphantly) as belonged to that ere Lord. And, gentlemen, when I consider how patiently you have 'eared the ideas what I have expressed, I feel bound, as the best way to reward you for the kindness you have exhibited, to sit down without saying anything more—partickler as I perceive a worthier visitor nor myself is just entered. I am not in the habit of paying compliments, gentlemen; when I do, therefore, I hope I strikes with double force."

"Ah, Mr. Murgatroyd! what's all this about striking with double force?" said the object of the above remark, as he entered. "I never excuse a man's getting into a rage during winter, even when he's seated so close to the fire as you are. It is very injudicious to put yourself into such a perspiration. What is the cause of this extreme physical and mental excitement, sir?"

Such was the very philosophical address of Mr. Robert Bolton, a shorthand-writer, as he termed himself—a bit of equivoque passing current among his fraternity, which must give the uninitiated a vast idea of the establishment of the ministerial organ, while to the initiated it signifies that no one paper can lay claim to the enjoyment of their services. Mr. Bolton was a young man, with a somewhat sickly and very dissipated expression of countenance. His habiliments were composed of an exquisite union of gentility, slovenliness, assumption, simplicity, *newness*, and old age. Half of him was dressed for the winter, the other half for the summer. His hat was of the newest cut, the D'Orsay; his trousers had been white, but the inroads of mud and ink, etc., had given them a piebald appearance; round his throat he wore a very high black cravat, of the most tyrannical stiffness; while his *tout ensemble* was hidden beneath the enormous folds of an old brown poodle-collared great-coat, which was closely buttoned up to the aforesaid cravat. His fingers peeped through the ends of his black kid gloves, and two of the toes of each foot took a similar view of society through the extremities of his high-lows. Sacred to the bare walls of his garret be the mysteries of his interior dress! He was a short, spare man, of a somewhat inferior deportment. Everybody seemed influenced by his entry into the room, and his salutation of each member partook of the patronizing. The hairdresser made way for him between himself and the stomach. A minute afterwards he had taken possession of his pint and pipe. A pause in the conversation took place. Everybody was waiting, anxious for his first observation.

"Horrid murder in Westminster this morning," observed Mr. Bolton.

Everybody changed their positions. All eyes were fixed upon the man of paragraphs.

"A baker murdered his son by boiling him in a copper," said Mr. Bolton.

"Good heavens!" exclaimed everybody, in simultaneous horror.

"Boiled him, gentlemen!" added Mr. Bolton, with the most effective emphasis; "*boiled* him!"

"And the particulars, Mr. B.," inquired the hairdresser, "the particulars?"

Mr. Bolton took a very long draught of porter, and some two or three dozen whiffs of tobacco, doubtless to instil into the commercial capacities of the company the superiority of a gentleman connected with the press, and then said—

"The man was a baker, gentlemen." (Every one looked at the baker present, who stared at Bolton.) "His victim, being his son, also was necessarily the son of a baker. The wretched murderer had a wife, whom he was frequently in the habit, while in an intoxicated state, of kicking, pummelling, flinging mugs at, knocking down, and half-killing while in bed, by inserting in her mouth a considerable portion of a sheet or blanket."

The speaker took another draught, everybody looked at everybody else, and exclaimed, "Horrid!"

"It appears in evidence, gentlemen," continued Mr. Bolton, "that, on the evening of yesterday, Sawyer the baker came home in a reprehensible state of beer. Mrs. S., connubially considerate, carried him in that condition up-stairs into his chamber, and consigned him to their mutual couch. In a minute or two she lay sleeping beside the man whom the morrow's dawn beheld a murderer! (Entire silence informed the reporter that his picture had attained the awful effect he desired.) The son came home about an hour afterwards, opened the door, and went up to bed. Scarcely (gentlemen, conceive his feelings of alarm), scarcely had he taken off his indescribables, when shrieks (to his experienced ear *maternal* shrieks) scared the silence of surrounding night. He put his indescribables on again, and ran down-stairs. He opened the door of the parental bed-chamber. His father was dancing upon his mother. What must have been his feelings! In the agony of the minute he rushed at his male parent as he was about to plunge a knife into the side of his female. The mother shrieked. The father caught the son (who had wrested the knife from the paternal grasp) up in his arms, carried him down-stairs, shoved him into a copper of boiling water among some linen, closed the lid, and jumped upon the top of it, in which position he was found with a ferocious countenance by the mother, who arrived in the melancholy wash-house just as he had so settled himself.

"'Where's my boy?' shrieked the mother.

"'In that copper, boiling,' coolly replied the benign father.

"Struck by the awful intelligence, the mother rushed from the house, and alarmed the neighbourhood. The police entered a minute afterwards. The father, having bolted the wash-house door, had bolted himself. They dragged the lifeless body of the boiled baker from the cauldron, and, with a promptitude commendable in men of their station, they immediately carried it to the station-house. Subsequently, the baker was apprehended while seated on the top of a lamp-post in Parliament Street, lighting his pipe."

The whole horrible ideality of the Mysteries of Udolpho, condensed into the pithy effect of a ten-line paragraph, could not possibly have so affected the narrator's auditory. Silence, the purest and most noble of all kinds of applause, bore ample testimony to the barbarity of the baker, as well as to Bolton's knack of narration; and it was only broken after some minutes had elapsed by interjectional expressions of the intense indignation of every man present. The baker wondered how a British baker could so disgrace himself and the highly honourable calling to which he belonged; and the others indulged in a variety of wonderments connected with the subject; among which not the least wonderment was that which was awakened by the genius and information of Mr. Robert Bolton, who, after a glowing eulogium on himself, and his unspeakable influence with the daily press, was proceeding, with a most solemn countenance, to hear the pros and cons of the Pope autograph question, when I took up my hat, and left.

FAMILIAR EPISTLE FROM A PARENT
TO A CHILD,

AGED TWO YEARS AND TWO MONTHS

My Child,

To recount with what trouble I have brought you up
—with what an anxious eye I have regarded your progress,—
how late and how often I have sat up at night working for
you,—and how many thousand letters I have received from,
and written to your various relations and friends, many of
whom have been of a querulous and irritable turn,—to dwell
on the anxiety and tenderness with which I have (as far as
I possessed the power) inspected and chosen your food; re-
jecting the indigestible and heavy matter which some
injudicious but well-meaning old ladies would have had you
swallow, and retaining only those light and pleasant articles
which I deemed calculated to keep you free from all gross
humours, and to render you an agreeable child, and one who
might be popular with society in general,—to dilate on the
steadiness with which I have prevented your annoying any
company by talking politics—always assuring you that you
would thank me for it yourself some day when you grew
older,—to expatiate, in short, upon my own assiduity as a
parent, is beside my present purpose, though I cannot but
contemplate your fair appearance—your robust health, and
unimpeded circulation (which I take to be the great secret

of your good looks) without the liveliest satisfaction and delight.

It is a trite observation, and one which, young as you are, I have no doubt you have often heard repeated, that we have fallen upon strange times, and live in days of constant shiftings and changes. I had a melancholy instance of this only a week or two since. I was returning from Manchester to London by the Mail Train, when I suddenly fell into another train—a mixed train—of reflection, occasioned by the dejected and disconsolate demeanour of the Post-Office Guard. We were stopping at some station where they take in water, when he dismounted slowly from the little box in which he sits in ghastly mockery of his old condition with pistol and blunderbuss beside him, ready to shoot the first highwayman (or railwayman) who shall attempt to stop the horses, which now travel (when they travel at all) *inside* and in a portable stable invented for the purpose,—he dismounted, I say, slowly and sadly, from his post, and looking mournfully about him as if in dismal recollection of the old roadside public-house—the blazing fire—the glass of foaming ale—the buxom handmaid and admiring hangers-on of tap-room and stable, all honoured by his notice ; and, retiring a little apart, stood leaning against a signal-post, surveying the engine with a look of combined affliction and disgust which no words can describe. His scarlet coat and golden lace were tarnished with ignoble smoke ; flakes of soot had fallen on his bright green shawl—his pride in days of yore—the steam condensed in the tunnel from which we had just emerged, shone upon his hat like rain. His eye betokened that he was thinking of the coachman ; and as it wandered to his own seat and his own fast-fading garb, it was plain to see that he felt his office and himself had alike no business there, and were nothing but an elaborate practical joke.

As we whirled away, I was led insensibly into an anticipation of those days to come, when mail-coach guards shall no longer be judges of horse-flesh—when a mail-coach guard

412

shall never even have seen a horse—when stations shall have superseded stables, and corn shall have given place to coke. " In those dawning times," thought I, " exhibition-rooms shall teem with portraits of Her Majesty's favourite engine, with boilers after Nature by future Landseers. Some Amburgh, yet unborn, shall break wild horses by his magic power; and in the dress of a mail-coach guard exhibit his TRAINED ANIMALS in a mock mail-coach. Then, shall wondering crowds observe how that, with the exception of his whip, it is all his eye; and crowned heads shall see them fed on oats, and stand alone unmoved and undismayed, while courtiers flee affrighted when the coursers neigh ! "

Such, my child, were the reflections from which I was only awakened then, as I am now, by the necessity of attending to matters of present though minor importance. I offer no apology to you for the digression, for it brings me very naturally to the subject of change, which is the very subject of which I desire to treat.

In fact, my child, you have changed hands. Henceforth I resign you to the guardianship and protection of one of my most intimate and valued friends, Mr. Ainsworth, with whom, and with you, my best wishes and warmest feelings will ever remain. I reap no gain or profit by parting from you, nor will any conveyance of your property be required, for, in this respect, you have always been literally " Bentley's " Miscellany, and never mine.

Unlike the driver of the old Manchester mail, I regard this altered state of things with feelings of unmingled pleasure and satisfaction. Unlike the guard of the new Manchester mail, *your* guard is at home in his new place, and has roystering highwaymen and gallant desperadoes ever within call. And if I might compare you, my child, to an engine ; (not a Tory engine, nor a Whig engine, but a brisk and rapid locomotive ;) your friends and patrons to passengers ; and he who now stands towards you *in loco parentis* as the skilful engineer and supervisor of the whole, I would humbly crave leave to postpone the departure of the train on its new and auspicious course for one brief instant, while, with hat in hand, I approach side by side with the friend who travelled with me on the old road, and presume to solicit favour and kindness in behalf of him and his new charge, both for their sakes and that of the old coachman,

Boz.

This book, designed by
William B. Taylor
is a production of
Edito-Service S.A., Geneva

Printed in France